At his mercy – and in his bed!

AT THE
TYCOON'S
COMMAND

Complete your collection with
all three books!

In June: *At the Prince's Pleasure*
In August: *At the Billionaire's Bidding*

BOUGHT AND BEDDED BY THESE PASSIONATE POWERFUL MEN!

AT THE
TYCOON'S
COMMAND

JACQUELINE   KIM   SARAH
BAIRD   **LAWRENCE**   **MORGAN**

*M&B™ and M&B™ with the Rose Device
are trademarks of the publisher.
Harlequin Mills & Boon Limited, Eton House,
18-24 Paradise Road, Richmond, Surrey TW9 1SR*

AT THE TYCOON'S COMMAND
© by Harlequin Books S.A. 2009

Pregnancy of Revenge © Jacqueline Baird 2005
The Carides Pregnancy © Kim Lawrence 2005
Sale or Return Bride © Sarah Morgan 2005

ISBN: 978 0 263 87520 1

024-0709

*Harlequin Mills & Boon policy is to use papers that are
natural, renewable and recyclable products and made from
wood grown in sustainable forests. The logging and
manufacturing processes conform to the legal environmental
regulations of the country of origin.*

*Printed and bound in Spain
by Litografia Rosés S.A., Barcelona*

Pregnancy of Revenge

JACQUELINE BAIRD

Jacqueline Baird began writing as a hobby, when her family objected to the smell of her oil painting, and immediately became hooked on the romantic genre. She loves travelling and worked her way around the world from Europe to the Americas and Australia, returning to marry her teenage sweetheart. She lives in Ponteland, Northumbria, the county of her birth, and has two sons.

CHAPTER ONE

'EXCUSE me, Charlotte.' Ted Smyth, the owner of the prestigious London art gallery, gave the woman at his side a smile. 'But the prospective Italian purchaser of "The Waiting Woman" has just arrived. I must speak to him and get him to sign on the dotted line.'

'Of course.' Charlotte Summerville, Charlie to her friends and daughter of the artist whose works were being exhibited at the gallery, watched Ted vanish into the crowd and heaved a huge sigh of relief.

Alone at last. She glanced longingly at the exit. The bald old man who leered back at her must be the Italian purchaser Ted was chasing, she thought grimly. In fact, the whole event was grim to Charlie. Mingling with the top echelons of the London art world was not her scene, and she wondered how soon she could decently leave. Now would be good, she suddenly decided, and edged through the crowd towards the exit.

Jake d'Amato exited Ted Smyth's office having concluded a deal on a painting he had been determined to obtain from the moment he had discovered it existed. He had arrived in London a few hours ago from Italy, and gone directly to a business meeting. But as he'd checked into his hotel afterwards he had glanced over a stand of leaflets advertising forthcoming events, and the name Robert Summerville had caught his attention. He had unfolded the pamphlet announcing that an exhibition of the late artist's work was to open that evening, and an image of his foster-sister Anna had assaulted his vision. Filled with cold black rage, he had determined to prevent the showing.

A call to his lawyer had informed him that the artist's estate owned the copyright, and legally he could do nothing. Frustrated, he had realised he was too late to stop the portrait going on display, but he had made an immediate call to the gallery owner and reserved the painting.

By the time he had arrived at the gallery he had control of his temper. He knew Summerville had a young daughter, and the executors of his estate were entitled to sell the paintings for her benefit.

But Jake had been surprised to discover from Ted that the same daughter had opened the exhibition. What had really captured his interest was the fact she was not the young girl Anna had described to him as a spoilt little selfish brat, but a shrewd businesswoman. It had been her decision to sell the paintings. Robert Summerville was dead and beyond his reach, but a mature daughter put a very different complexion on the situation.

'So which lady is the artist's daughter?' Jake asked Ted with just the right amount of curiosity in his tone. 'I'd very much like to meet her and offer her my condolences on the sad loss of her father.'

And ask her what she intended doing with the exorbitant amount of money she was going to inherit, if the price of the picture he had just bought was anything to go by, Jake thought cynically. Not that he needed to ask—greed, plain and simple, had to be her motivation. Why else would she expose her late father's lovers to public scrutiny without having the grace to inform them first?

He hated Robert Summerville, although he had never met the man. But at least Summerville had had the decency to keep the paintings a secret. Not so his daughter. Jake could have forgiven a young girl for being influenced by the executors of the estate. In his experience most lawyers would sell their own grandmother if the price was right. But for an adult female to have so little respect for the women involved, and one in particular, Jake found disgusting.

His dark eyes narrowed. He could do nothing about the exposure the painting had already received. But he was going to put the woman down verbally and publicly, so neither she nor the assembled crowd would be left in any doubt as to his low opinion of her.

Charlotte Summerville deserved to be shown up for the avaricious bitch she was.

No trace of his true feelings showed on his hard dark face as he watched Ted look around and then point to a woman at the far side of the room.

'That's Charlotte, the blonde over there in black—standing by the portrait you've just bought, as it happens. Come on, I'll introduce you. I can remove the painting at the same time and have it sent to your home as we agreed.'

Musing on the vagaries of the artistic world, Charlie was totally unaware of the interest she had aroused in one particular male patron of the arts.

In life her father had been a modestly successful landscape artist, and it was only after his death that his private collection of nude portraits had come to light. Suddenly Robert Summerville was famous—or perhaps infamous was a better word, as it was rumoured he had been the lover of all the ladies he had painted.

It was probably true. Because, much as she'd loved her dad, there was no escaping the fact that he had been the most self-absorbed, self-indulgent man she had ever known. Tall, blond and handsome, with enough charm to woo a nun out of her habit, he had lived the life of the bohemian artist to the full. But he had never truly loved any woman.

No—she was being unfair. Her father had loved her, she knew. After her mother had died when she was eleven, her dad had insisted she spend a few weeks' holiday every year with him at his home in France. And he had left her everything he owned.

Charlie had known about one of the nude portraits, but she had discovered the rest when clearing out her dad's studio with Ted. It had come as something of a shock, but no great surprise. That was partly because, on her first visit to her father in France after the death of her mother, she had met Jess, his then lady friend, and liked her. But when Charlie had walked into his studio uninvited one day and found her dad naked with Jess, and saw the portrait he was working on, her dad had reacted with shame and fury. From then on he had always sent his current lover away when Charlie spent time with him. For a man of his morals to be so protective of his daughter was ironic, to say the least.

Ted had taken one look at the portraits and suggested arranging an exhibition. He'd advised Charlie to open it, to add human interest and help the sale of her father's work even more than his sudden death at the age of forty-six had done.

At first Charlie had flatly refused. She did not need the money. She had earned her own living for the past six years, when after the death of her grandfather she had taken over the running of the family hotel in the Lake District that had been their business and her home for all her life. But she knew thousands of people who did need the money.

Eventually she had spoken to Jess and offered to give her the painting she had posed for. Jess had been in favour of the pictures being exhibited, and approved of Charlie's idea to give any money made to charity, and Charlie had finally agreed to Ted's proposal.

At least something good would come out of her father's

death, she thought with a tinge of sadness as she proceeded towards her goal.

Almost at the exit, the last canvas arrested her attention for a moment. The lady portrayed had incredibly long dark hair curving over one shoulder and falling almost to her thigh. But it was the face of the woman that really disturbed her. The artist had captured the love, the need in the dark eyes to a point it was almost painful to see.

Poor fool, Charlotte thought with a rare cynical smile twisting her full lips. How had the woman never realised what a philanderer Robert Summerville had been? Of the thirty paintings in the gallery, ten were nude studies of women. With a wry shake of her head she turned to walk away.

Jake d'Amato's narrowed gaze never wavered from the woman Ted had indicated as he moved through the elegant crowd at Ted's side.

She was about five eight, he judged: shapely with long legs, a simple black wool dress moulding her figure, outlining high, firm breasts and the gentle curve of her hips and thighs. Her hair was ash blonde and swept up in a twist on top of her head. Jake's dark eyes glittered with primitive male appreciation, and surprisingly he found himself drawing in a stunned breath. She wore little make-up and yet she was quite beautiful. She had obviously inherited her father's good looks but in an innocent, understated way.

Then his body tensed, and his dark eyes flared with barely leashed rage. Anna had been right. Charlotte Summerville had refused to meet Anna in life, and in death her disdain for her father's last lover was obvious in the knowing cynical smile that twisted her full lips, followed by a dismissive shake of her head as, with a sexy sway of her hips, she turned away from the portrait. As for innocent—he doubted

a woman with a body like hers even remembered the meaning of the word.

'Charlotte, darling.' Ted's voice rang out loud and clear.
'I have someone here who wants to meet you.'

Charlie stiffened, cursing under her breath. Dwelling on
the past, she had left it too late to escape. Reluctantly she
lifted her head, resigned to wasting yet more time being
polite to some wealthy fat old man who got off on looking
at paintings of nude women. All in pursuit of the great god
Mammon. Bare mammary glands were obviously a great
money-spinner. Her lips curved up in a naughty smile at the
thought.

'Allow me to introduce you to Jake d'Amato. He is a
great admirer of your father's work, and has just bought this
painting.'

Charlie's blue eyes, still lit with humour, met Ted's. 'Yes,
of course.'

Privately she thought the man must be mad or blind. In
her opinion her dad had been a much better landscape
painter than portrait—apart from the last one; that did have
character in the face. But she let nothing show on her face
as, lifting her hand, she raised her eyes to the man at Ted's
side.

There her gaze stuck as though hypnotised by the sheer
physicality of the man. He wasn't the fat old man she had
thought—anything but.

From his bronzed skin taut over high cheekbones to the
straight nose and the firm mouth beneath, and finally to a
hard, square jaw, the man was devastatingly attractive. Tall,
something over six feet, and broad of shoulder, he exuded
an aura of supreme confidence and masculine power that
eclipsed every other man in the room. With his well-
groomed black hair falling casually over his broad brow and
his dark good looks he was clearly of Mediterranean de-

scent. He was the most compellingly attractive man she had
ever seen, and he was smiling down at her.

'Charlotte. I am delighted to meet you, and may I say
how sorry I am at your sad loss?'

Somehow Charlie found her small hand enfolded in a
strong male grasp, and he did not let it go. Not for him the
brief handshake; and the piercing quality of the dark eyes
that held hers was almost frightening in its intensity. She
felt the power of his overwhelming masculinity like a blow
to the heart, and her breath lodged in her throat.

A black brow quirked in amused enquiry as the silence
lengthened and belatedly Charlie managed to respond with
a mouth that had suddenly gone dry. 'Thank you, Mr
d'Amato.'

'Oh, please, call me Jake. I do not want to stand on formality with you.' He lightly squeezed her hand. 'I too have
recently lost a member of my family and I know exactly
how you feel.'

Charlie fervently hoped not, because the warmth of his
hand holding hers was sending an incredible surge of awareness through her whole body. But along with her purely
physical reaction, she could not help being impressed by his
sympathy. Her blood tingled and a curious spiralling excitement sizzled through her that made her even more
tongue-tied, and she simply stared at him.

'But it must be a great consolation to you that your father
has left you such a remarkable body of work.'

Body being the operative word. Charlie had the irreverent
urge to giggle, and she could not prevent her lips parting in
a broad smile.

'Yes, thank you,' she agreed, and tore her sparkling eyes
from his to stare down at their joined hands. For heaven's
sake, get a grip, she chided herself, and strove to control
her erratically beating pulse. Finally she made a tentative

effort to withdraw her hand from his, a responsive quiver lancing through her as he tightened his grip. In that moment she knew she would happily have held onto the man for ever, so fierce was her response to Jake d'Amato.

Jake noted her brilliant smile and it only added to his anger, but he let nothing show on his impressive features. 'It is my pleasure,' he said softly, and, bending his dark head, he pressed a swift kiss on the back of her hand, before finally releasing it. 'It is an honour to meet you. And now, please, you must give me your honest opinion on the painting I have purchased.' Placing a guiding hand at her waist, he turned her back to look at the portrait. 'Lovely, don't you agree?' Jake was determined to make her look at Anna's face—a woman she had insulted in life, but was happy to exploit after death.

The sound of Jake's deep, melodious voice sent another responsive quiver through Charlie, and his hand on her waist and the warmth of his great body seemed to envelop her. For the first time in her life she experienced the bone-melting awareness at the touch of a man, a sensation that overwhelmed her, and she knew with a feminine instinct as old as time that this man could be her destiny.

Charlie frowned. She wasn't given to flights of fantasy and it scared her, plus her intense awareness of him was tempered by the distaste she felt that he had bought the nude. Gathering together the shreds of her control, she said, 'Lovely, yes,' then added dryly, 'if you have a penchant for pictures of naked ladies.'

'You show me a man who does not, Charlotte, and I will show you a liar,' he said teasingly, his heavy lidded eyes sweeping over her beautiful face and lower to linger on the provocative thrust of her breasts. 'Though I must admit, I much prefer the live variety.' The brown eyes darkened, an unmistakable message in their depths, leaving Charlie more flustered than ever.

She could not believe it. Jake d'Amato was flirting with her. She didn't know how to respond so she simply smiled like some idiot teenager. She felt her nipples harden beneath the lace of her bra, and, hopelessly embarrassed, she blushed scarlet and was lost for words yet again.

Jake d'Amato stilled. The sexual attraction visible in her brilliant blue eyes plus the invitation in the tight nipples starkly outlined beneath the fabric of her dress had an unexpected effect on his powerful body. It had been a long time since a woman had so instantly aroused him. That it should be this woman would have shocked him rigid—if he had not been rigid already for a much more basic reason.

He did not like it. He had had every intention of putting her down in public. Revealing her as the selfish, money-grubbing parasite she was, and leaving. But suddenly that scenario no longer held such great appeal. Instead he found himself imagining what her lush lips would taste like—the high, firm breasts in his hands, in his mouth…and the only place he wanted to put her down was naked on a bed under him.

He must be going crazy. The Summerville family were responsible for the untimely death of Anna Lasio, and for the grief of her parents. Embarrassing Charlotte was nothing compared to the turmoil the Summervilles had caused in what was the closest thing to a family Jake possessed. Given that Charlotte Summerville was not the young girl he had been led to believe, but a mature woman who should know better, a much more satisfactory course of action sprang to mind.

He was here on business, with meetings lined up over the next fortnight. For once in his life combining business with pleasure held great appeal. Without conceit, he knew he was a good lover and it would be interesting to slowly seduce the lovely Charlotte until she was desperate to share his bed, as her father had done his foster-sister...

Turning on the charm, he murmured softly, 'Ah, I see I have embarrassed you, Charlotte.' His dark eyes narrowed on her face. 'You think I am some old lecher who spends his day ogling naked women, perhaps?' he prompted, and noted the deepening flush in her pale cheeks with amusement. It was a long time since he had seen a woman blush and Charlotte Summerville did it beautifully. She played the innocent to perfection, even though he was sure she was anything but.

'Let me set your mind at rest, Charlotte. I am a businessman first and foremost, and when I see a good deal I snap it up, whether it be a company or art. The painting is an investment. I do not wish to sound callous, but you, who sanctioned the exhibition, must be well aware work by a dead artist is much more marketable than that by a living one.'

The ease with which he had read her thoughts was scary. But Charlie knew his cynical assessment was correct. 'Yes,' she murmured, finally finding her voice.

'And let me reassure you...' his deep voice thickened as he turned back to the painting '...this is the only nude I want to own. I believe it is your father's best and last.'

Following the line of his gaze, Charlie looked once more at the picture, in which her father had captured the mood of the woman perfectly.

'Yes, she is beautiful,' she agreed again. But, though it might be his best, she knew it wasn't his last. There was a half-finished portrait in her possession of a red-headed woman. Determined to try and match his sophistication, she looked up at Jake. 'But not, I think, his last,' she said archly, and was about to tell him of Robert's last affair in what she hoped was a sophisticated attempt to keep his interest. But her effort was wasted; he wasn't listening. She saw the glazed look in his dark eyes, and reality hit her like a slap in the face. The man was transfixed by the portrait.

But then, he had just paid a hefty amount of money for the picture—why wouldn't he be fascinated? she told herself firmly. What was she thinking of, trying to impress a man she had just met? A man, moreover, who was captivated by the portrait of a luscious brunette. Where did that leave her, a very average blonde? Precisely nowhere, and she castigated herself for being a fool.

Her first assessment had been right before she'd ever seen Jake d'Amato. He was certainly no fat old man. The very opposite—a more striking male would be hard to find. But as for the rest, she had been correct. He was wealthy—it was evident in the supreme confidence he displayed, and in every line of the designer suit right down to the handmade shoes, never mind the fact he had bought the painting. But that aside, she told herself firmly if a little regretfully, he was also the type of guy who got off on looking at pictures of nude women.

Not her sort of man at all. She had been here far too long and it was scrambling her brain. She tightened her grip on her clutch bag and with a swift sidestep put some space between them.

'Well, I wish you joy of your purchase, Mr d'Amato. Nice to meet you, but now I must be leaving.' And, spinning on her heel, she dived headlong into the crowd before she made a bigger fool of herself than she already had.

Safely in the ladies' cloakroom, she studied her reflection in the mirror. Her face was flushed, her blue eyes unusually bright. She could not believe a man who was obviously from the same mould as her father could have such a startling effect on her, and it scared her witless. She had loved her dad, but only a complete idiot would willingly get entangled with a philanderer of the same ilk.

The only reason Charlotte existed was because Robert Summerville, nineteen and studying art, had got her mother pregnant, and her parents had insisted they marry. It was probably the only time in his life Robert had been coerced into anything. When he had graduated two years later he had left wife and daughter with the maternal grandparents in the Lake District and gone to find his 'true artist's soul'. Charlie and her mother hadn't seen him for three years, and only then to obtain the inevitable divorce.

Charlie suddenly thought it was quite possible Jake d'Amato was also a married man, and she had been so over-whelmed by his effect on her she had behaved like a fool. How embarrassing was that? She needed to get back to her own world, and quick. A taxi back to the apartment her friend Dave had lent her, a simple dinner and an early night were what she needed, not swooning over some man. Straightening her shoulders, she walked out of the cloak-room, and hastily left the building.

She stood on the edge of the pavement and glanced up and down the street. Not a taxi in sight. 'Damn it to hell,' she muttered.

'Now is that any way for a lady to talk? Shame on you, Charlotte,' a deep, dark voice drawled mockingly.

Charlie spun around, and found herself only inches away from a large male body. 'Mr d'Amato,' she said coolly, but she could do nothing about the surge of colour in her cheeks.

'Jake,' he corrected. 'Now what seems to be your prob-lem, Charlotta? Maybe I can help.'

The accented way he said her name was enough to give her goose bumps. 'Most people call me Charlie, and I am trying to get a taxi back to my flat.'

'Charlie is no name for a beautiful woman and I refuse to use it,' he declared firmly. 'As for the taxi, that is no problem.' The smile accompanying his words held such devastating charm Charlie could not help smiling back. 'My car is here.' He gestured with one hand to the sleek navy blue saloon parked on double yellow lines about ten yards away. 'I'll take you wherever you want to go.'

'Oh, no, I couldn't possibly—'

'Preferably to dinner, and of course you can.'

Five minutes later she was seated in the passenger seat of a luxury car and Jake was in the driving seat, having ascertained she'd intended to eat alone, and bulldozed her into dining with him at a well-known London restaurant.

'Do you always get your own way?' Charlie asked dryly.

Jake turned slightly, his thigh brushing hers in the process. 'No, not always,' he said seriously, his dark eyes capturing hers. Reaching out, he clasped her small chin between his thumb and finger and tilted her face towards him. 'But when it is something or someone I truly want, I always succeed.'

Charlie swallowed hard and sought a witty comeback, but words failed her as his hands dropped to curve around her shoulders. He made no attempt to pull her into his arms. He didn't need to. His mouth covered hers and he coaxed her lips to part to the gentle invasion of his tongue. The steadily increasing passion of his kiss ignited a slow burning sensation deep down in her belly that was entirely new to her. Suddenly Charlie wanted him with a hunger that shocked even as it thrilled her, and instinctively her hands lifted to his broad shoulders, but she didn't reach them.

'*Dio mio!*' Jake exclaimed shakily, and, grasping her hands, he pulled back and pressed them to her sides. His heavy-lidded dark eyes swept over her dazed face, and lingered on her softly swollen lips.

'You are some woman,' he commented, and for a moment Charlie thought there was anger in the dark eyes that stared down at her. Then he pressed a brief kiss on the tip of her nose and added, 'I promised you dinner, the rest must wait.' He slanted her a wickedly seductive smile, before starting the car and driving off.

Charlie didn't say a word. She could hardly believe what had happened; it was so unlike her. Where had her common sense, the steely nerve she was noted for, gone? Banished into oblivion by one kiss. Her entire body thrummed with a strange excitement and she had never in her wildest dreams believed a man could make her feel so wonderfully, vibrantly alive. But what was even more unbelievable was that Jake seemed to be as captivated by her as she was with him. She had felt it in the pounding of his heart, his shaken reaction when he had ended the kiss.

Suddenly the dinner she had tried to refuse held great appeal.

CHAPTER TWO

IT WAS an exclusive French restaurant and at first glance appeared to be full, but within seconds of them entering the head waiter was at Jake's side, and declaring it was a great pleasure to see him again, and his charming companion. His shrewd eyes flashed an appreciative glance over Charlie as he bowed courteously and led them to a small table set for two in an intimate corner of the room.

She looked around the dining room, her blue eyes widening in awe as she recognised a couple of politicians and a few famous faces from television. 'You must have friends in high places,' she said, grinning across the table at Jake. 'I read an article about this restaurant in a Sunday supplement. But it's even better than I imagined, though I never thought I would ever eat here.' Eyes shining, she leant forward slightly. 'Apparently one has to book months in advance.'

'Obviously not in my case,' Jake said arrogantly as the waiter arrived with the menus.

Disconcerted by his cool reply, Charlotte felt her smile fade as she realised her mistake. He was a big man and every inch the dominant male. Add wealth and sophistication, and it would take a very brave man or a fool to turn him down. As for women—she only had to recall how easily he had overcome her objections to dining with him to know the woman probably wasn't born who could say *no* to him.

She gratefully accepted the menu from the waiter and buried her head in it, telling herself to get a grip. Instead of spouting off like some overenthusiastic teenager, she would

19

show Jake d'Amato she could be as sophisticated as any woman.

'What would you like to eat? I am going to have the hot smoked salmon followed by the steak. How about you? The same?'

She placed the menu on the table and lifted her head. 'No, Jake,' she said coolly, before turning to the waiter and asking him in perfect French what he recommended. A lively debate ensued on the relative merit of the red sea bass or the chef's special stuffed trout. Finally Charlie gave her order for a starter of seasonal spring salad followed by the bass to a now beaming waiter, with a brilliant smile of her own.

'So, Charlotte,' Jake commented mockingly as the waiter departed. 'You are a woman of many talents, it would seem.'

Charlie turned sparkling eyes to the man seated opposite. 'Well, I'm not an idiot.' She smiled, her confidence restored.

'No, but, French aside, you did turn the poor waiter into a drooling idiot.' His eyes flashed with a hint of some dark emotion, then softened perceptibly as his gaze roamed down to the soft curve of her breasts. 'Though I can't say I blame him,' he added huskily.

She felt a flush of heat creep from her stomach to cover her whole body at his sensuous gaze, and she had to take a deep breath before she could respond steadily. 'Thank you for the compliment.'

'My pleasure, I assure you.'

Out of nowhere the thought of Jake at her pleasure deepened Charlie's colour, and she frowned. In the sexual stakes she was not in his league, and she wondered what she was letting herself in for.

Jake reached out to cover her slender hand resting on the table with his own. For some reason the reservation in her eyes bothered him. 'Charlotte, don't look so serious,' he said softly. Entwining his fingers with hers, he lifted her hand and pressed a tiny row of kisses across her knuckles. 'Please, relax and enjoy your meal, and let us see if we can get to know each other a little better. We can become friends—can we not?'

Friends? With every nerve in her body quivering at his casual touch, Charlie doubted she could ever be just *friends* with such a supreme specimen of the male sex as Jake. But it was a start.

'Friends. Yes.' Striving to appear cool, she continued conversationally, 'So, tell me, why the name Jake? It doesn't sound very Italian.'

'My mother was engaged to an engineer in the US Navy. She gave me his Christian name because he died in an accident at sea before she could give me his surname.'

'That is so sad.' Her eyes softened on his. 'Your mother must have been devastated, losing her fiancé like that.'

'Strange,' Jake said with an odd note in his voice. 'Most people respond with embarrassed silence or embarrassed laughter and a quip like, "I always knew you were a bastard." But you are obviously romantic at heart.' The fingers entwined with hers tightened slightly. 'And you are right. My mother was devastated. She never looked at another man to her dying day. Except me, of course, whom she adored,' he added with a soft chuckle, his dark eyes smiling warmly into hers.

'I'm not surprised.' Charlie grinned, relieved her casual query about his name had not embarrassed him. In fact, suddenly the atmosphere between them seemed much more relaxed. Maybe friendship with Jake was not so impossible after all, she thought happily. Though she wasn't sure she agreed that she was a romantic. She had always considered herself the most realistic of women. But then that was before she had met him…

'A compliment. I am flattered.' Jake grinned back.

'I didn't mean you. Well, maybe I did,' she added with a chuckle. 'But really I was referring to your mother. Having committed to getting married, she must have been as distraught at his death as any widow.'

'In my mother's case, yes, but that is very rare.' He leant back in his chair but still retained his grasp on her hand. 'In my experience, plenty of women see an engagement as simply a way of getting money out of a man.'

His cynical attitude appalled her. 'In your experience? You were engaged?'

'I was, once, when I was twenty-three and naive. I bought the ring, gave her money for the wedding, the whole nine yards.'

'And then you left her, I expect.' Charlie pinned on a smile as it struck her again that he might be married, and she hadn't asked—a glaring omission on her part, which she immediately rectified. 'Or else you're married.'

For a moment Jake looked astonished, then he laughed, but the humour didn't reach his eyes. 'How like a woman to blame the man.' His cool dark gaze held hers. 'But you are wrong. My fiancée left me, and spent the money on something else. So, no, I am not married, nor ever likely to be. It is not an institution I believe in.'

Feeling foolish, Charlie realised appearance could be deceptive. She could not imagine any woman turning Jake down, but she had been wrong, and that long-ago rejection must have hurt. Her soft heart went out to him. 'I'm sorry.'

'Don't be. I am not. But enough about me. Tell me how you learned to speak fluent French—and do you speak any other language?'

'No, just French.' She accepted his change of subject.

Obviously it still hurt him to talk about his ex-fiancée, and it made him seem more human somehow. 'I learned French at school, but I became fluent mainly because from the age of eleven I used to spend a few weeks' holiday every year with my father at his home in France. Not so often in recent years, but I did stay with him last year, a little while before he died.'

'Ah, yes, your father. I should have guessed.' He dropped her hand, and a shadow seemed to pass over his face. Charlie wondered what she had said to cause it—or perhaps he was still thinking of his ex-fiancée? Then the wine waiter arrived with a bottle of Cristal champagne and filled two glasses before placing the bottle in the champagne cooler and leaving, and she banished the dark moment to the back of her mind.

'To us and the start of a long friendship,' Jake said, raising his glass, and Charlie reciprocated, her blue eyes shining into his as another waiter arrived with their food.

'So tell me, have you any other family?' Jake asked casually as they both tucked into their first course.

'My mother died when I was eleven, my grandmother when I was seventeen and my grandfather three years later. My father was an orphan, so I'm alone in the world now he's died.'

'With a father like yours, can you be certain of that?' Jake queried sardonically.

'Yes, I'm certain.' She glanced up, surprised by his cynical question, and thought she saw a bitter look in the dark eyes, but she must have been mistaken, as the next moment he grinned.

'Ah, another illusion bites the dust. I should have known the exploits of your father were more fiction than fact— probably circulated to increase the price of his work.'

'Well, I don't know about that,' Charlie murmured, pushing her empty plate away. There was something in the tone of his seemingly jocular comment that struck a discordant note and made her wary. Plus she was not comfortable talking about her father or about money.

'No, of course you wouldn't,' Jake agreed smoothly, and for the rest of the meal he endeavoured to keep the conversation general while trying to discover more about the woman before him. Though he was loath to admit it, Charlotte was beginning to intrigue him more than any woman he had met in a long time.

For Charlie the next hour passed in a hazy bubble of happiness. Jake was a great conversationalist and, without her realising it, she had soon told him where she lived and how, after the death of her grandmother, she had left school to help her grandfather run the small family hotel overlooking Lake Windermere.

'And you inherited the hotel, of course,' Jake prompted when she fell silent for a moment.

'Yes. Yes, I did.' The thought of the family she had lost dulled the sparkle in her eyes for a moment.

'Lucky you,' Jake said. Charlie frowned and she was about to argue there was nothing lucky about losing one's family, when he added, 'But I was very lucky in a way,' and to her surprise proceeded to tell her more of his own past. After the death of his mother when he was eight, he had been placed in an orphanage and got involved with a bad crowd. But miraculously he had been fostered at the age of ten by a man whose pocket he had tried to pick. It had saved him from a life of crime and had been the incentive he had needed to study and become a marine engineer, and owner of his own company. His foster-parents were still alive and he visited them regularly.

Charlie simply beamed at him, and thought how kind. He must have a very caring nature.

Also a very sensual nature, because as they ate the meal and drank the bottle of champagne Jake subtly managed to keep her in a state of simmering sexual tension. A forkful of his food offered to her willingly parted lips, a casual touch of his hand, an intimate smile. By the time they got to the coffee stage Charlie was unaware she had consumed the lion's share of the champagne, and as she spooned sugar into her cup and added cream any resistance to his sophisticated charm was well and truly vanquished.

'I am glad to see you are not one of these women who have to watch their figure all the time,' Jake said, glancing at her coffee cup, then allowing his gaze to glide slowly up over her high firm breasts and to her beautiful if slightly flushed face. A lazy smile curved his sensuous lips as his dark eyes finally met and held Charlie's. 'Though it is well worth watching—quite perfect,' he declared throatily.

She recognised the male appreciation and the suggestion of more on offer in his gleaming dark eyes. She wasn't totally naive; she had experienced sexual chemistry before, but never as potent as this. Her pulse started to thud under her skin, and instinctively she lifted her hand to the hollow at the base of her throat. Her tongue slipped out to lick over her suddenly dry lips and she saw Jake's gaze drop to her mouth, and she heard his sharp intake of breath.

'Let's get out of here,' he commanded suddenly, rising to his feet and dropping a pile of notes on the table. He reached a hand around her upper arm and almost hauled her to her feet, muttering something in Italian under his breath.

'Why the rush?' she queried as he hustled her out of the restaurant, tension in every line of his long body.

'Don't pretend you don't know, Charlotte,' he said, his voice raw and thick with a sensual hunger that made Charlie shiver. Then he dropped her arm and curved his own around her waist in a possessive hold that thrilled and slightly frightened her as he led her to the car.

'Get in,' Jake said, wrenching open the passenger door and guiding Charlotte inside. Walking around the bonnet, he wondered what the hell he was doing. He had nothing but contempt for her type of woman, and yet he found her incredibly desirable. To his unemotional, analytical mind it did not make sense. But right now all his thinking processes seemed to be centred below his waist, and the quicker he got her into bed, the quicker his problem would be solved.

Alone for a moment, Charlie began to wonder what on earth she was doing, but seconds later, when Jake slid into the driving seat and reached for her, she knew.

His hand slid around the back of her head as he covered her mouth with his, his tongue thrusting between her softly parted lips with a hunger that awakened the same fierce need in Charlie.

She slid her hands around his neck, all of a sudden wild with wanting something she had never had. Her fingers tangled in his thick dark hair, and her entire body trembled as one strong hand stroked down her throat and over the proud swell of her breasts. His dark head lifted and her dazed blue eyes meshed with molten black. 'Jake.' She breathed his name.

It had been a very long time since any woman had turned Jake d'Amato on so fast or so fiercely. Hard as a rock and hurting, he felt her tremble, heard the plea in her tone, and he wanted to rip the all-encasing black dress from her body and take her hard and fast. But while his hot-blooded nature was urging him to do just that, the sound of a police siren growing to ear-splitting levels brought him back to his senses.

His dark head jerking up, he saw the police car flash past.

He cursed under his breath in Italian and, thrusting Charlotte back against the seat, he slammed back in his own.

'Damn!' He ran a hand through his dark hair, and glanced at the woman beside him. 'I haven't made out in a car since I was a teenager, and now twice in one evening.' His accusing eyes swept over her beautiful, bemused face, and lingered on her softly swollen mouth, and he almost groaned out loud.

'I never have,' Charlie breathed honestly, slowly surfacing from the whirlpool of passion that had engulfed her.

Jake stared down at her, shocked at her revelation, and he almost believed her. No, it couldn't be true. Her father had been a master seducer. Different gender, but it was obvious she had inherited his talent, as his taut body was painfully confirming. With a less than steady hand he jabbed the key in the ignition and started the car. He was furious with himself, but even more so with the blue-eyed siren who was causing him to act so out of character.

'Where are you staying?' he demanded. If she had told him, he had forgotten—most unlike him. He knew she lived in and owned the Lakeview Hotel, but as for where she was staying in London, he had no idea. Jake breathed in deep. He was a man who prided himself on always being in control, and the knowledge she could shake that control only increased his inner anger still further.

The rasping edge to his deep voice sent a shiver through Charlie, and through her bewilderment she managed to retain enough hold on reality to ask herself what she was doing kissing a relative stranger. She straightened up in the seat, shocked by her own reckless behaviour. 'Dave, a friend of mine, has lent me his flat while I am in London.' She rattled off the address in what she hoped was a cool voice.

'Nice location,' Jake said, his teeth clenching as he changed gear with less than his usual fluency. That left him no longer in any doubt there was a man in her life—a wealthy man, it would seem, if he owned an apartment in that area. It wasn't surprising; it only confirmed what he already suspected. Like father, like daughter. A woman like Charlotte was never going to be without a man for long, and the thought did nothing for his temper.

'But perhaps you would prefer a nightcap at my hotel before I take you home?' His original intention had been to move slowly, hoping to enthral her, the way her father had Anna. But now his only intention was to get her into his bed as soon as humanly possible, and keep her there until the memory of any other man was wiped from her mind. And at the same time cure his own irrational need for a woman whom by nature he should despise.

Colour swept Charlie's face. Was that the equivalent of, 'Your place or mine?' Whichever, she wanted to cry, *Yes!*— and it shook her to feel so vulnerable. She was hopelessly out of her depth and sinking fast. She had never met a man like Jake before.

Charlie had grown up in a home full of adults, and she had to some extent been left to run wild around the mountains and crags of her beloved Lakes. Her hobbies were sailing and rock climbing. She was a member of the local rescue team, and also of the International Rapid Rescue Team. With a good manager to run the hotel on a day-to-day basis, Charlie took care of the accounts and it worked out well. She kept her gear packed at all times at home, and simply postponed the paperwork when she was needed elsewhere.

She had recently returned from a trip to Turkey, where she had helped in an earthquake recovery, and gone straight into the hectic Easter holiday at the hotel. The two weeks she was spending in London were at the suggestion of Dave, her team leader. He thought that with the recent death of her father and running two jobs, she needed a complete change. Time to take an ordinary holiday, instead of being at the beck and call of other people all the time.

Charlie had agreed. She had visited hot spots all over the world, but now she was taking the chance to visit some of the highlights of her own capital city, something she had never done before.

As for men, she knew plenty on a professional level, but they all treated her as one of the boys, which was how she liked it. Glancing at Jake's perfectly chiselled profile, she realised that never in a million years could she think of him as one of the boys. In fact, she had trouble thinking at all around him.

The car came to a smooth stop, and Jake turned slightly in his seat, his black eyes gleaming with intent, capturing hers. 'So what is it to be—a nightcap? This is my hotel.'

She knew what he was offering, and it wasn't just a drink. The air in the close confines of the car positively crackled with sexual tension as he waited for her answer and suddenly Charlie was afraid. She tore her gaze from his and glanced out of the window. It was a very plush hotel, one of the best in the city, and she knew she couldn't do it…not yet.

'I think I have had enough to drink,' she said carefully, 'Thank you all the same.'

His dark eyes narrowed slightly, and she wondered if he was angry. But as she watched he shrugged his broad shoulders. 'Your decision.' Dropping a brief kiss on her brow, he turned and started the car before adding, 'I will pick you up for lunch tomorrow at twelve,' his attention on the road ahead. 'And we can move on from there.'

'Can we indeed?' she shot back. 'It would be nice to be asked instead of told.' But there was no bite to her words; secretly, she was relieved her attack of maidenly modesty had not ruined her chance with him after all. 'I'm here on holiday, following the tourist trail, and I intend to visit the British Museum tomorrow.'

Jake's every masculine instinct had been screaming out at him to persuade her into his bed, but the almost frightened look in her blue eyes had disconcerted him. She might be selfish and money-grubbing in her love affairs—in his experience, most women were—but it didn't necessarily follow she was promiscuous. Jake was very choosy himself. He preferred to pick his lovers with care and his affairs were always as discreet as he could make them, given his high profile in the international business world.

The only reason he was without a lover at the moment was, ironically enough, because of Charlotte's father. His death had created a set of circumstances that had kept Jake at home in Italy and caused him to neglect his last lover, Melissa, a New York model, who had therefore moved on to another wealthy man.

It hadn't surprised him. Melissa had been a high-maintenance lady, he thought cynically as he stopped the car outside the apartment block, and slipped out to open the passenger door.

'Come on, Charlotte, I will see you inside.' He reached for her hand. 'And there I promise to leave you until tomorrow,' he reassured her with a dry smile. 'And before you argue—' he placed a finger over her lips '—we will do both. Lunch and the museum.' Fingers entwined, he walked her to the lift. Again he registered the wariness in her incredible eyes, and grinned. Little did she know she was in no more danger from him tonight. He drew the line at making love to her in a bed she had shared with another man. 'Until tomorrow.' He kissed her brow and left.

CHAPTER THREE

JAKE D'AMATO prowled around the enormous hotel suite. He was too frustrated to sleep, and it was all the fault of a particular blue-eyed blonde. Not quite all, he allowed—the painting of Anna played heavily on his mind as well.

It had taken all of his considerable powers of self-control to stand in that damned gallery and stare at the portrait, which, as the purchaser, had been expected of him. Anna was the nearest thing he had ever had to a sister and it had seemed almost incestuous to see her exposed in such a way.

As for the title, 'The Waiting Woman'—how apt, he thought grimly. She had waited and hoped for two years for Robert Summerville to marry her. A deep, dark frown marred his austere face as the memories flooded back. Jake had been twelve when Anna was born, and to his foster-parents her birth had seemed like a miracle. Jake had adored the new baby, and had watched her grow into a delightful little girl by the time he had left his foster home at eighteen.

He should have kept a closer eye on her. But after university he had been totally involved in his work as an engineer and building his own business. He had not had much time to visit his foster-family, mainly birthdays and holidays, but when he had Anna had always seemed fine. And as the Lasios had never appeared to have any worries about her, neither had Jake.

When Anna had turned twenty-one, Jake, then the head of the vast d'Amato International corporation, had thrown a lavish party on board his yacht for her birthday. Anna had seemed to be a happy, well-adjusted young woman, full of

31

enthusiasm for her fledgling career as a graphic artist. Satisfied she was okay, Jake had carried on his own very busy life and respected that, as an adult, Anna was entitled to do the same.

But not any more.

Rage and regret welled up inside him. How could she have had an affair with, and posed naked for, a man who was old enough to be her father? How could she have driven when hopelessly drunk and killed herself? How could she have let a man do that to her?

There was no answer, and the burden of his own guilt had weighed heavily on his mind since Anna's death. He had lived with Anna from the moment she was born until she was six and with hindsight he knew he should have done much more to protect her.

He had known about her relationship with Summerville. She had told him over one of their infrequent lunches in Nice two years ago. At that time she had still been working and living in an apartment Jake had bought for her, and although Jake had never heard of the man, he had not queried her choice, because she had so obviously been happy, and confident it was only a matter of time before they married.

But now, remembering how appalled he had been when Anna had turned up at his home in Genoa five months ago, he bitterly regretted not investigating Summerville as soon as he'd heard the name.

Looking a shadow of her former self, Anna had cried on his shoulder and told him the whole sorry story of the affair. How she had given up her job and had been living with the man for over a year, but Robert had sent her away three months before he'd died, all because of his daughter.

He had explained she was his only child and had been spoilt by her mother. She was a bit insecure and very possessive of him, and flatly refused to meet Anna. He didn't want to upset his daughter, so Anna had to leave while she was in residence. But he had assured Anna it would only be for a few weeks. In other words, to quote Anna, 'Robert's daughter was a selfish little spoilt brat.' Anna had not even heard of his death in time to attend the funeral. For himself, after hearing the tale, if the man had not been dead already, Jake would have quite happily killed him.

Anna's tragic death a few weeks after their last meeting had gutted him, and it didn't help that the man who in Jake's mind was indirectly responsible was already six feet under and out of his reach. As for Anna's parents, they were crippled with grief.

Jake had spent the past three months simply being there for his foster-parents, his work for once taking second place.

This was his first trip abroad since her death, and catching sight of that catalogue in Reception had ignited his fury all over again. But at least he now knew the painting was safely on its way to his home in Italy. He was still angry he had been unable to prevent its showing, but, as he intended to destroy the painting, with a bit of luck Anna's parents need never know it had ever existed. It was the least he could do for them.

Jake considered himself a modern, sophisticated man of the world. He enjoyed women and was rarely without a lover. Over the years he had had several affairs, and at least two of the women, as models, had been displayed naked on countless magazine covers. It hadn't bothered him at all. Yet he saw nothing paradoxical in his reaction to the public exposure of Anna.

But what he did see after meeting the lovely Charlotte was a way to get revenge on the family that had brought about her death…and thoroughly enjoy doing so.

Spinning on his heel, he headed for the bathroom, and a

cold shower. His last for some time, he reckoned, a predatory smile curving his firm mouth.

Charlie took one last look at her reflection in the mirrored
door of the wardrobe. Slim-fitting grey trousers traced her
long legs, and with them she had teamed a soft pink cashmere sweater. A heavy chain belt that fastened with a large
clasp was slung low around her hips. A grey hide purse and
matching loafers completed her outfit. Comfortably casual,
she told herself, but in reality she hadn't much choice: the
only dress she had with her was the one she'd worn last
night and the rest of her holiday clothes consisted of trousers
and casual tops. She tweaked a stray tendril of hair behind
her ear, and wondered again if she should pin it up. As it
was it fell in loose curls to her shoulders. No, you look
good, girl, she decided with a broad grin.

Last night, tossing and turning in bed, unable to sleep for
thinking about Jake, replaying in her mind his every kiss
and touch, her body aching for him, she had reached a mo-
mentous decision. Given the chance, she was going to pursue her relationship with Jake. He had said they could at
least be friends, but innate honesty forced her to admit that
she wanted much more from him. She had only known him
for a few hours but he had tilted her world. She had no
experience of love, but this intense physical desire for Jake,
this flood of feeling that consumed all her senses, had to be
love or something very like it.

In her work with International Rapid Rescue she had witnessed death and destruction on a huge scale. If the job had
taught her anything, it was that life was precious but could
be snuffed out in an instant by an act of nature. She was a
twenty-six-year-old virgin, probably because all her life she
had been a tomboy and the few men she knew considered
her more of a buddy than a woman. She was not totally

inexperienced—she had kissed men, but had thought the experience vastly overrated. But all that had changed last night when she had met Jake.

This holiday, the first she had taken in years, was supposed to be a complete change, a chance to rethink her hectic lifestyle. She was her own woman; she could do whatever she wanted, and what she wanted was Jake. She knew deep down on some elemental level that Jake could be her soul mate.

The voice of the doorman boomed over the intercom telling her a Mr d'Amato had arrived and should he send him up? She dashed to answer it. 'No need, I'll be right down.'

Her legs were shaking as she rode the lift to the ground floor and when the doors opened Charlie drew in a deep, calming breath, stepped out, and froze to the spot, her blue eyes fixed on the spectacular male animal leaning against the reception desk.

In a business suit Jake had looked stunning, but today he took her breath away. He was wearing black jeans that lovingly clung to long legs and taut, masculine thighs. A black button-down shirt, left open at the neck, revealed the strong column of his throat, and a black leather jacket fitting casually across broad shoulders completed the picture.

Telling her foolish heart to stop bounding, she wondered what it was about Italian men that enabled them to wear clothes with such casual elegance. She could not tear her fascinated gaze away. She saw his proud head lift as though scenting the air like some great jungle beast suddenly aware of his prey, and, straightening up, he turned towards her.

'Charlotta-a...at last.' He lingered over her name like a caress, his hooded dark eyes sweeping over her in blatant masculine appraisal as in a few lithe strides he covered the space between them. 'You look exquisite.' Before she could draw breath, a large male hand curved around her hips, another up her back to tangle in the loose fall of her hair.

The swift, exquisitely gentle brush of Jake's lips against her own turned her legs to jelly, and when he teased her lips apart, the arousing sweep of his tongue in the moist interior of her mouth suddenly filled her body with a molten heat.

Charlie had thought the kisses they had shared in the car last night mind-blowing. But now, held in intimate contact with every hard inch of his big powerful frame, she was shocked by the force of his obvious arousal and secretly thrilled she could do that to him. Weak at the knees with wanting, she pressed unconsciously closer into his taut strength, and felt his great chest heave.

'I promised you lunch,' Jake rasped against her mouth and lifted his head.

Charlie stared up. 'What?' she murmured, flicking the tip of her tongue along her bottom lip, an invitation in her sapphire gaze she didn't realise was there.

'Lunch.' Jake stepped back, his hands resting on her shoulders to keep her steady. 'Before we really give the doorman something to talk about.'

Realising where she was and that she was staring at him far too hungrily, she dipped her head, a tide of red scorching her cheeks. 'Yes, of course,' she mumbled.

'A lady who can still blush. I like it,' Jake drawled, keeping an arm around her shoulder as he walked her out of the building.

'No car?' Charlie queried as his arm fell from her shoulders and he took her hand in his and began strolling along the pavement.

Jake looked at her, amused indulgence in his gaze. 'Your wish is my command,' he said smoothly. 'You wanted to do the tourist bit, and visit the museum. Most tourists pound the pavement. No?' He shrugged his elegant shoulders. 'Plus I want to share everything with you, starting with a bottle of wine with lunch.'

He looked so attractive, and so unlike any tourist she had ever seen, Charlie burst out laughing. 'I might have known you would have an ulterior motive. It's not me but the wine that motivates you.'

'You wouldn't believe my motives if I told you,' Jake responded dryly and spun her into his arms to kiss her with an urgency that left her dazed and breathless—so dazed she did not see the cynicism in his dark eyes. And for Charlie the kiss set the pattern for the rest of the day.

Jake kept his word and they shared a bottle of wine over lunch at the restaurant in the central courtyard of the British Museum. After lingering over coffee and cognac they eventually got around to touring the various exhibits.

It was seven in the evening when they walked back to his hotel.

The warmth of his arm felt so right around her waist, and when he stopped and asked, 'What's it to be, Charlotte? Dinner with me here or do you want to walk on to your apartment?' they both knew what he was really asking. The whole day had been leading to this point.

Charlie raised her face to him and saw her own need reflected in the gleaming depths of his dark eyes. The force of emotion flooding through her kept her speechless for a moment.

'We can call it a day,' Jake heard himself say in a sudden surprising attack of conscience. Amazingly, he had enjoyed Charlotte's company. In different circumstances he knew he would have dated her anyway—and he would still have been determined to get her into his bed.

He reached out and ran a long finger over her smooth cheek, and down her throat, his finger resting on the rapidly pounding pulse in her neck. She wanted him, he knew it, but she was still hesitating. Real or acting he did not know, but he knew enough about women to realise they all craved permanency in a relationship. Obviously Charlotte was no different. She was here on holiday and seemed determined to follow the tourist trail—and his quick brain had the answer.

He smiled, an intimate curl of his firm lips. 'Whatever you decide. I am staying in London for a couple of weeks on business.' He slowly raked her body with his gaze, registering the burgeoning peaks of her breasts beneath her sweater before he let his eyes meet hers. 'And after the great time we have had today...' He paused, his hand softly caressing her throat. 'Work permitting, I would love to explore the tourist trail with you, Charlotte.'

The only trail he was really interested in exploring was every curve of her delectable body, every hill and hidden valley, until he sated himself in her. But he wasn't crazy enough to tell her so. Though if he did not have her soon, he very well might, and that *really* worried him.

In the early hours of the morning Charlie had decided to pursue her relationship with Jake and see where it led, and all day she had fallen deeper and deeper under his spell. Now, with the impact of Jake's deep eyes burning down into hers, and his huskily voiced desire to see her again echoing in her head, she knew it was the moment of truth. He had told her last night he would never marry, so either she had to accept what he was offering, an affair for a couple of weeks, or walk away. With blinding clarity she realised she did not have a choice. She could no longer deny her basic sexual instinct, an instinct she had only just discovered she possessed, an instinct she knew deep down inside she would only ever feel with Jake.

Charlie drew in a slow steadying breath. 'I've done enough walking for one day.'

'Me too.' Reaching for her hand once more, he linked his long fingers through hers and led her into the hotel.

On one level Charlie couldn't believe what she was doing as Jake ushered her into the lift and the metal doors closed on them. But on another purely sensual level the feelings were so immense she could not deny them, however much she tried. She stole a surreptitious glance at him through the thick veil of her lashes. He was so ruggedly attractive, so overtly masculine, simply looking at him made her heart beat faster. It wasn't just his looks, though; she had seen men with more classically beautiful features. It was some unfathomable intense connection she could hardly believe was real. But every atom in her body was telling her it was.

'This is it,' Jake said, dropping her hand and splaying his palm across the small of her back, his powerful body tense as he urged her out of the lift to a door directly opposite. A quick flash of the card key and she was in his suite. He fought the instinct to simply sweep her off her feet and into the bedroom. Instead he shrugged off his jacket as he headed for the bar.

'What would you like to drink?' he asked, turning back to look at her, and stiffened. Damn it, but she was gorgeous, and the way she filled that pink sweater had been causing him agony all day.

Standing where he had left her Charlie glanced around the elegant room. It was as luxurious as she had expected. But Jake's behaviour was not what she had imagined. She had thought he would sweep her into his arms, and make mad, passionate love to her. How naive was that? she castigated herself. Jake was a sophisticated man of the world, a man of discernment; of course he would never behave so crassly, she thought. But she was wrong again.

'I'll—' She was going to ask for a glass of juice, but she never got the chance.

'To hell with a drink,' he growled and in a couple of lithe strides he reached her and hauled her hard against his chest. His expert mouth swooped down to capture hers, a soft moan escaped her, and, taking full advantage, his tongue slipped between her parted lips with devastating effect.

Charlie did not know what hit her. Before his kisses had excited her, but had ended abruptly and left her aching for more. This time Jake showed no such restraint. His tongue swirled around hers, igniting a passion that was red hot. His arms were tight around her, pressing her against his aroused body, telling her without words how much he wanted her. Her slender hands lifted to his broad chest, a finger catching on his shirt button.

She felt his smile as he murmured against her lips, 'Go ahead, take it off for me.' His dark eyes gleamed down into hers, an invitation explicit in the black depths.

Feverish colour flooded Charlie's face, and she was stunned to realise he actually thought she was experienced enough to undress him without a qualm. Her body burned and her finger flexed against his chest. Dared she? Yes— this was what she wanted. She freed one button, and her stomach somersaulted as her fingers scraped the hot skin beneath.

'Don't stop now, *cara*,' Jake husked, his hands sliding caressingly up and down her back. 'Or perhaps you prefer I undress you first?' His sensuous mouth swooped down to taste hers again, and went lower to nuzzle the elegant curve of her neck, and Charlie stifled a frustrated groan when he broke the connection.

'Patience, *cara*,' he teased, a knowing smile curving his firm mouth. 'First let me get rid of this damn belt.' One strong hand slid around her waist. 'It could do a man a serious injury,' he added, his fingers deftly unfastening the buckle, and the offending item fell to the floor. 'Now tell me what you want, and I promise I will oblige.'

What she wanted was Jake, and her fingers, with a dexterity she did not know she possessed, swiftly unbuttoned his shirt. Then she stopped, her blue eyes widening to their fullest extent at the sight of a wedge of broad tanned chest, and the dusting of soft black curls that accentuated his powerful pectoral muscles. She swayed against him, her hands tentatively splaying on his naked chest. She could feel the heat through her palms, and her awed gaze lifted to his. 'You are beautiful,' she murmured softly.

'I think that is my line,' Jake mocked, but his eyes glinted with a hint of masculine satisfaction and something more. His dark head bent and his lips brushed across hers as he gathered her hard against him, and kissed her long and deep. So deep that when he suddenly eased her away from the heat of his great body, she was breathless, her legs felt like rubber and she could hardly stand.

But she didn't need to.

CHAPTER FOUR

'THIS is not the place,' Jake said and swept Charlie up in his arms. 'And we have too many clothes on,' he added with a teasing grin as he strode into the bedroom and lowered her down against him onto her own feet, before stepping back, kicking off his shoes and shrugging out of his shirt.

The partial view of his broad chest had not prepared her for the awesome beauty of his naked torso. Mesmerised, she simply stared. His shoulders were wide, his chest broad and tapering down to a lean waist, his skin gleaming like burnished gold in stark contrast to the mass of black curling hair arrowing down his strong body. His long arms were hard and muscular and had their own dusting of hair. His hands...his hands were unfastening his trousers. Charlie gasped, her heart skipping a beat.

'Something wrong, *mia bella Charlotta*?' His hands settled on her waist and Charlie was glad of the support, shaken by the intensity of her own desire for him.

'No,' she murmured. 'Never more right.' She strove to match his sophistication but her voice shook ever so slightly.

'But you still have too many clothes on, *cara*.' A slow, sensuous smile curved his wide mouth, his eyes gleaming beneath black curling lashes. 'Let me help you,' he suggested throatily as his fingers caught the edge of her sweater and he eased it up from her hips.

Hypnotised by the intensity of his dark gaze, like a puppet on a string, Charlie raised her arms and he slipped the sweater over her head. His hands stroked down her naked back, and her bra went the same way as the sweater.

'Magnificent,' Jake husked as his hands swept round and up to cup her high, firm breasts.

Charlie sucked in a feverish breath, her breasts suddenly heavy, the small nipples swelling and tightening into pin-points of pleasure. She had never imagined she could stand brazenly half naked before a man and, lifting her eyes, she felt her cheeks flood with colour at his intent masculine scrutiny.

'You have nothing to blush about, *cara*.' His smouldering gaze met hers, his voice fracturing a little. 'You have perfect breasts, and I can't wait to see the rest of you.'

'Nor me you,' she mumbled inanely, and she got her wish.

Jake lowered his hands from her breasts, but not before rubbing her tight, swollen nipples with skilful fingers as he kissed her again with erotic thoroughness before pulling back from her and calmly stripping off.

Faced by a totally naked Jake, she could not stop staring. He was all hard muscle, and sleek golden skin, from his broad chest down to his taut, flat stomach, and lean hips. A ribbon of paler skin circled the top of his powerful thighs. So he didn't sunbathe nude, she thought, and it was her last sensible thought.

Eyes widening, her face burning along with every other inch of her body, for the first time in her life she was con-fronted by a magnificently virile aroused male and she could not tear her gaze away.

'You're lagging behind,' Jake said with a husky chuckle. As she hastily lifted her head her entranced blue eyes con-nected with sensuous black and she couldn't say a word. 'Here, let me help you,' he added and skimmed her trousers and briefs down her hips with a deftness that spelt of years of practice. He gathered her up in his arms and laid her on the bed.

'Unbelievable,' Jake murmured, staring down at the silky softness of her creamy skin, and the rosy-tipped peaks of her lush breasts. For a second embarrassment overcame Charlie and she lifted her hands to cover herself from his scorching gaze.

'No, don't,' Jake growled. Sitting down beside her, he took her hands and pressed them onto the bed, one each side of her head. His dark gaze swept her. Her body was curvaceous yet toned to perfection with firm, beautifully shaped breasts, a narrow waist, flaring hips and fabulous long legs. 'You are absolutely stunning,' he said throatily, his gaze roaming back up over her incredible body and lingering on tight rosy nipples before lifting to her face. 'And so very sexy.' And he covered her mouth with his own.

The feel of his long hard body against hers, and the magic of his firm, sensuous mouth, his tongue tangling with hers, the taste of him… Charlie lost her every last inhibition. She tried to pull her hands free. 'Please, I want to touch you,' she said with a naive honesty.

'Feel free.' Jake grinned and let go of her hands, his heavy-lidded eyes gleaming into hers. 'I certainly intend to touch every part of you, my sweet Charlotte, in every way.' Dipping his head, he trailed kisses down her throat, sucking on the tiny pulse racing beneath her silken skin, before moving lower and licking and nipping the rosy nipples with his teeth and tongue, while his hand stroked down the curve of her waist and traced her inner thigh.

Charlie buried her hands in the thick dark hair of his head, her spine arching up to him, and she groaned out loud at the exquisite sensations lancing from her breast to the apex of her thighs. He kissed and caressed a sensuous path from her breasts to her navel, and traced the line of her hip and thigh right down to the soles of her feet with a hungry, erotic thoroughness that made her wriggle and squirm in feverish delight, before returning to her mouth and kissing her with a driving, possessive passion that she met and matched with helpless abandon.

She wrapped her arms tight around him, on fire for him. Her hands swept over the wide muscular shoulders, traced the indentation of his spine, and splayed over the strong shoulder blades. She pressed up into him and, with an eroticism she had never dreamt she was capable of, rubbed her achingly sensitised breasts against the hard wall of his chest, glorying in the excitement the friction aroused.

It was as if some other female had taken over, a sexy, liberated female, and she nuzzled into the hard curve of his shoulder, and moaned as his fingers toyed with her breast once more. When the hand on her thigh slipped ever closer to the centre of her femininity, she shivered in delicious anticipation. She was damp and hot and aching for him and her legs moved apart instinctively. Her head burrowed lower, looking for a taut male nipple, one hand sliding over his lean hips searching for something else.

Jake's hand tangled in her hair and urged her head up. 'Not so fast, *cara*.' He laughed softly, his face inches from hers. 'I want to make this good for you, to make it last.'

With passion-dazed eyes she looked into his face, the smouldering black eyes, the dishevelled hair that she was responsible for, and the wickedly sinful mouth smiling down. It was the smile that goaded her even as her insides were melting like hot treacle. Daringly her slender fingers inched around his hip and touched the long velvet shaft, and she heard him groan. 'Why wait?' she prompted breathlessly, her sapphire eyes widening to blaze with a need and knowledge as old as Eve. 'We can always do it again.'

Jake was not made of stone, though at that moment he

was as hard as any rock. He caught her hand and lifted it up to his chest, though it nearly killed him to do so. *Dio*, but she was a temptress, and she was right. Once would never be enough with this woman, he knew, and he took her teasing mouth with a savage hunger he could barely control.

Charlie fought to drag air into her starving lungs as he broke the kiss, his head swooping down, his tongue flicking over her aching breasts once more, even as his long fingers eased through the golden curls at the junction of her thighs, and expertly stroked the moist feminine heart of her. She wrapped her arms around him and clung, her hips rising from the bed, as with torturous strokes he teased and probed her tight, silken depths until she was sure she could stand no more. Her body was white hot and wound up so tight she felt she would shatter into a million pieces with sensual excitement.

Jake lifted his head, his eyes molten pools of black jet, his bronzed skin flushed along his high cheekbones. 'You want me.'

'I'm crazy for you,' she groaned. He rose over her, and she was unaware he reached for something from the bedside table as the subtle stroke of his lean fingers took her to the edge again.

'Yes,' Jake rasped and in one smooth motion he grasped her hips, and lifted her.

She felt the hard length of him touch her, stroke her once, twice. Her whole body shuddered, and she drew in an audible breath as with one powerful move he entered her.

Jake stilled as a gasp of protest escaped her. He was a big man to accommodate, he knew, and she was so tight that the thought crossed his mind it must have been some time since she had indulged. He pulled back ever so slightly, and eased into her slow and deep, and felt her silken muscles clench around him.

The sudden slight pain had caught Charlie by surprise, but was instantly forgotten as Jake stroked deeper, and in that moment she lost it completely. She cried out loud, 'Oh, yes, Jake, yes,' at the incredible sensations convulsing her slender body with a fierce pleasure that shattered all her innocent illusions, and left her shuddering in ecstasy. So this was…it. But the thought never fully formed, as Jake plunged harder and faster in a wild, primitive rhythm that drove her higher and higher.

Charlie clung to him in a fever of need, oblivious to the fact her nails were digging into his flesh. She felt as if he were lifting her out of herself to a realm where nothing existed but his hot, hard body filling her, possessing her. And she was totally unaware of the breathless plea for more escaping her as he captured the erotic sound with his mouth. She felt his great body shudder violently, and she cried out his name as wave after wave of explosive sensations swept her into an ecstatic oblivion.

Slowly Charlie opened her eyes. Jake was collapsed on top of her, his eyes closed. But even so she smiled mistily up at him. So that was it, the little death she had read about, and it was all, and much, much more than she could have ever imagined.

Their bodies were damp with perspiration, their hearts thundering in the aftermath of passion, and a deep sense of peace washed over her. Jake was the man she was born for, she thought dreamily.

'*Grazie*, Charlotte,' Jake murmured close to her ear, burying his face in the silken, fragrant mass of her hair for a moment. 'That was fantastic.' He smoothed the tumbled hair from her brow. 'I was right, you are some woman.' He eased his heavy body from hers, and from the bed.

'Don't go,' Charlie murmured, reaching out a hand to him.

'Don't worry, I am not going far.' Jake stood, unashamedly naked, looking down at her. 'I am only going to the bathroom to dispense with this and replenish supplies. Unless you would like to do it for me,' he suggested teasingly.

Sprawled on the bed totally naked, she looked dazedly up into his grinning face, registering the black hair flopping over his brow, the smouldering eyes, and the wickedly masculine mouth. He was utterly gorgeous and he was hers. Her eyes roamed leisurely down the naked length of him and only then did the import of his words sink in.

'No, I don't think so,' she squeaked. Of course he had used protection—it was nothing to be embarrassed about, in fact she should be grateful, but it did not stop her blushing scarlet and dragging the sheet up over her naked body.

Jake let out a bark of laughter. 'You're incredible—sex on legs and verbal with it, and yet you blush like a schoolgirl.' He shook his dark head. 'That is some trick.' And he headed for the bathroom.

Charlie didn't know whether to be flattered because he thought she was incredible and sexy, or affronted because he thought her blushing was a trick. If only, she thought ruefully. Blushing was the bane of her life. Perhaps now she was truly a woman the blushing would cease, and that led her to another thought. How come Jake hadn't realised he was her first lover? Not that it mattered; she was quite flattered that he seemed to think she was experienced. She had a sneaking suspicion that if he had known the truth he would not have touched her, and it crossed her mind to wonder how old he was. Mid thirties, she guessed, with a great body. A body she now knew in every intimate detail. A reminiscent smile curved her soft mouth that quickly changed into a triumphant grin. At last she was truly a woman—Jake's woman, she thought, a sense of euphoria sweeping through her. The sheet forgotten, she punched her arms up in the air. 'Yes, yes, yes!'

Jake strode back into the bedroom, a towelling robe tied loosely around his waist, and stopped. With her blonde hair cascading down her back, natural he now knew, and her beautiful face devoid of make-up, she was punching the air like some crazed cheerleader when her team scored a goal.

She was the most naturally sexy woman he had ever known, and he was a long way from finished with her yet. But she looked about sixteen, and he found himself grinning. 'Is that yes for me?' he asked with a chuckle, which quickly turned into a shout of laughter as her startled blue eyes swung towards him, and she dived back beneath the covers.

'No. Yes. I mean, maybe,' Charlie babbled, appalled he had caught her acting like an idiot instead of the sophisticated lady she wanted to appear.

'Well, make your mind up, *cara*,' Jake prompted. 'I'm hungry.' It wasn't food he had in mind. With her beautiful hair spread across the pillow, and her face scarlet with embarrassment, he had the oddest urge to protect her—and, as the instant stirring in his groin reminded him, every which way.

The thought disturbed him and his heavy brows drew together in a frown. His initial intention had been simply to get Charlotte into bed and then dismiss her. But it hadn't worked out quite like that. With her exquisite body shuddering beneath him, her silken sheath so hot, so tight, the restraint he had imposed upon himself had deserted him completely. A captive to his own desire, he had taken her with a driven power he was helpless to control, and when she had convulsed around him, sobbing his name, he had gone with her, something that rarely happened to him.

Even now he was itching to slip back into bed beside her and start all over again. No wonder Anna had been so besotted with Robert Summerville. If the man had been anything like the natural-born sensualist his daughter was, it was not surprising Anna had become addicted to the man.

Remembering Anna and the way Charlotte had hurt her by refusing to meet her stopped Jake in his tracks. The Charlotte he had spent the day with and just made love to didn't seem to be a selfish bitch, but then experience had taught him women were great deceivers.

'I'll go and order dinner. Join me when you're ready,' Jake said bluntly, and, spinning on his heel, he left the room.

Charlie stared at his back, shocked by his abrupt departure. She had behaved like an overgrown schoolgirl. No wonder Jake had opted for food. Still, the night was young, she thought, a secret smile curving her swollen lips, and Jake was her lover. She stretched in preparation of rising from the bed. A shower, food, and Jake again…sounded good. Rolling out of bed, she collected her clothes and headed for the bathroom.

It was a splendid bathroom, all veined white marble and mirrors, with a huge glass-fronted shower stall. Reaching into the stall, she turned on the taps. With the water running at a comfortable temperature, she rifled among the luxurious toiletries provided and found aromatherapy soap. A touch of pampering was just what she needed, Charlie told herself, and stepped under the soothing spray, a deep sigh of satisfaction escaping her.

So this was love. She sighed, let her head fall back and closed her eyes, and began slowly lathering her arms, shoulders, and her firm breasts. She stroked the tender skin, and revived the memory of Jake touching her there—everywhere—and the incredible power of his passion, and she almost groaned.

Jake tipped the bellboy, and strode back into the bedroom. The bed was empty, and inexplicably his stomach knotted painfully, and his eyes darkened angrily. She was gone. Then he heard the sound of running water, and common sense prevailed. Of course she was in the shower.

For a moment there he hadn't been thinking straight, but now he was. Silently he entered the *en suite*, and for a moment was disorientated, his body tensing at the sight of Charlotte's silhouette reflected several times over in the mirrored walls. Then he saw her behind the glass screen. Her head was thrown back, her hair falling wet and sleek down her back, and her hands were running over her breasts, her body. He had never seen anything more erotic in his life, but it was the look of sensual pleasure on her beautiful face that aroused him with gut-wrenching speed.

Charlie didn't hear the bathroom door open. The first intimation she had she was not alone was when a husky voice declared from behind her, 'Allow me.'

Her eyes flew open and she spun around, her feet slipping on the tiled floor, and only Jake's arm around her waist saved her from falling. 'What are you doing?' she exclaimed. He was naked, the water flattening his black hair into a sleek cap, and his dark eyes burnt with sensual promise.

'Just what you were doing, my sweet Charlotte.' Somehow he had the soap in his hand and was rubbing it against her breasts. 'Washing you.' He dropped the soap and his hand began to lather the soft bubbles over her swelling breasts. 'Now, isn't that better?' Jake growled.

'Oh, yes,' Charlie sighed. Her body was hot, and it had nothing to do with the water, and everything to do with a naked Jake pressing her back against the cubicle wall, his hands administering a leisurely soaping to her quivering body. Her breasts felt heavy and swollen, and the straining peaks tautened into hard points of aching need. 'Don't stop.'

With a throaty laugh Jake bent his head, and took her softly parted lips with a leashed hunger that quickly deepened into a hard, possessive kiss. 'I am not going to,' he rasped, and, with all pretence of washing gone, he lifted her bodily and placed her legs around his lean waist.

'No, I'll fall,' she squealed, and grabbed for his head, linking her arms around his neck. But she didn't fall as his strong hands cupped her hips and in one smooth thrust he filled her. Her eyes closed and her head fell back as her legs locked around him, his swift possession engulfing her quivering body in a wave of crazy excitement.

Jake growled low in his throat. Passion riding him, he drove hard and fast, and cried out her name as he climaxed with embarrassing speed. Her body shuddered in convulsive ecstasy around him, draining him to the core.

Gently he steadied her on her feet, his hands almost spanning her slender waist. She was looking up at him, her gorgeous blue eyes dilated with shock. 'I shouldn't have done that,' he murmured.

'In the shower,' Charlie breathed incredulously. 'I didn't know you could,' she added, dazed but happy.

'Apparently around you, anywhere will do,' Jake remarked, realising she was nowhere near as experienced as he had thought if she had never shared a shower with a man. Suddenly he wondered just how much she had shared with other men as he recalled her pained gasp the first time they had sex. The uneasy feeling he might have just made a huge mistake made his hands tighten involuntarily around her waist, and he surveyed her with a frown. Her incredible blue eyes were sparkling cheekily up at him, and she had the sexiest body he had ever seen. No, it wasn't possible.

He shook his dark head, dismissing the notion. 'Actually, I came to tell you dinner had arrived, but I got distracted.'

'You and me both,' Charlie quipped, and reached up to press a kiss on his jaw. 'But now get out and let me get dried and dressed.' The fact that Jake could be overcome with passion for her made her proud, and fed her confidence in herself as a woman.

But her confidence took a severe nosedive ten minutes later when she padded barefoot back into the sitting room of the suite. Jake was fully dressed in a white shirt and dark blue pleated trousers, and somehow she felt at a disadvantage wearing the same sweater and trousers she had worn all day. He was seated on one of the two sofas with the dinner trolley set between them and he did not acknowledge her at all. It was only when she sat down on the sofa opposite him that he deigned to glance at her.

'This is probably not so hot now,' he said, but he might have been talking to a stranger. 'If you don't mind waiting, I can order something else before you leave.'

Leave. Her heart sank. But she told herself not to be so foolish. Think of the embarrassment if she did stay all night and had to walk through the hotel in the morning. Everyone would know what she had been doing. No, Jake was simply being a gentleman. But then she saw his dark eyes, which held no warmth or tenderness, none of the passion they had recently shared, only a cool reserve.

She shivered. 'This will do fine.' She gestured to the trolley, and wondered why she should suddenly feel such a chill. 'I'm not very hungry.'

'Good, but you must eat something.' He lifted the covers and portioned some kind of meat casserole and vegetables onto a plate and handed it to her. His mouth smiled but his eyes did not. 'Enjoy.'

Feeling worse by the minute, Charlie took the plate and

stared down at it, sure it would choke her. But she forced herself to eat, her mind searching for a reason for his cool behaviour. Perhaps he was just naturally subdued after making love, she tried to tell herself, but without much conviction as she recalled how several times over dinner last night he had behaved in much the same way, a certain remoteness in his dark gaze effectively masking his expression.

'You're very quiet,' she offered.

'I'm eating,' Jake said with a sardonic arch of an ebony brow in her direction, and she watched as he dug into the casserole with apparent enjoyment.

Turning back to her own plate, she swallowed a few more mouthfuls. But it tasted like sawdust in her mouth, and she placed it back on the trolley. It must be her fault Jake was so reserved, but what had she done wrong? Perhaps Jake had seen through her attempt to be sophisticated and was disappointed at her performance in bed. She had read men put great store on a woman's abilities in bed, and Jake was no boy; he must have slept with a lot of women.

'How old are you?' she blurted, and bit her lip wishing she could take the question back. But at least it got his full attention.

'Thirty-eight. Probably old enough to be your father.' His voice held a sharp edge of contempt that she could not fail to recognise.

Suddenly everything became clear and her heart lifted. Jake, her sophisticated, powerful Jake, was feeling guilty about the age difference between them. Impulsively she jumped to her feet and sat on the sofa beside him, resting her hand on his thigh, determined to reassure him. 'Not unless you started before you were a teenager,' she said, glancing up at his superb profile. 'I'm twenty-six, hardly a girl.'

Jake turned his head and looked down at the small hand

on his thigh and then up into her smiling face. 'You think there is nothing wrong in an older man taking a much younger woman for a lover?' he asked with such bitterness in his voice that she was shocked.

'Not if he...' She was going to say *loves her*, but stopped. 'Not if he really wants her and the feeling is mutual. No,' she said carefully, not confident enough to imply Jake loved her. But she did want to convince him his age didn't matter.

'You honestly believe that.'

'Yes, of course,' she said firmly.

'Probably only because you had to put up with a father who had quite a few young lovers. Does it never occur to you other people may not share your views?' he queried with a cynical drawl.

'No, not really. And as for my father, he was a law unto himself, and I never had to put up with his lovers. I only ever met one,' Charlie said honestly. 'But we're not talking about him, but you.' She found it incredible to believe a man as stunning as Jake should feel vulnerable about his age and yet it endeared him to her all the more.

'Are we?' Jake said with a sardonic arch of an eyebrow. Charlotte had just confirmed what Anna had told him. *She never had to put up with her father's lovers.* She was the selfish bitch after all. But as he looked down into her earnest sapphire eyes, and with her hand on his thigh, somehow confronting her with what he knew didn't seem important. Instead he imagined her slender hand gliding up his thigh. Fighting down the sudden jerk of excitement in his groin, he backtracked swiftly. 'If you say so.'

The veiled statement confused her. 'Well, why else would you mention the age difference?'

Jake flung her a dazzling smile and put his arm around her shoulders. 'No reason at all, Charlotte, *cara*. You're right, what is twelve years between friends?' But, looking into his dark eyes, she had the uneasy feeling he was not telling the truth, but simply placating her. Then he tilted her chin with one finger and brushed his lips lightly against hers.

Charlie exhaled a relieved sigh at the touch of his mouth and eagerly parted her lips and Jake took full advantage, probing the moist depths with a leisurely expertise that squashed all her irrational doubts about him.

'If I don't get you out of here soon,' Jake groaned against her ear, 'I'll take you on the sofa.'

CHAPTER FIVE

THE image Jake conjured up in Charlie's head was explicitly erotic, and sent her pulse rate rocketing. Heat curled in her belly and her slender fingers involuntarily flexed and stroked up his muscular thigh.

Dark eyes flaring, Jake drew in a harsh breath and leapt to his feet, his square jaw set at a determined angle. 'It is time I sent you home.'

Blinded by lust, he had already taken her in the shower without thought of the consequences, and, looking into her sultry blue eyes, he had very nearly slid into her hot little body yet again. A warning voice in his head told him he had to regain control of his suddenly overactive libido around Charlotte or he was in danger of making another mistake. 'I'll call you a cab,' he said curtly, and surprised himself by trying to soften the abrupt dismissal with the lame excuse, 'I have to work tomorrow.'

Charlie slumped back against the sofa and looked up at him with wide, puzzled eyes. A moment ago he had been looking at her as if he could eat her alive, but now his eyes were shuttered, and she could sense the disapproval in the firm set of his jaw. What was it he had said, something about working? 'But tomorrow is Sunday,' she murmured inanely.

A black brow elevated. 'So?'

The heat in her stomach turned into a cold knot of humiliation as it slowly dawned on her she had overstayed her welcome and he was trying to give her a polite brush-off. Rising to her feet, she avoided looking at him. 'I'll just be a minute. I need my shoes and bag from the bedroom, then I'll leave you in peace.'

As she attempted to walk past him Jake closed a strong brown hand around her wrist and prevented her from moving away. He saw the hurt she could not hide in her expressive eyes and he knew exactly what she was thinking.

'Peace is not something I will ever associate with you, *cara*,' he said with a rueful shake of his dark head. Wanting her was a weakness. He had every reason to dislike her, but she turned him on like no other woman he had ever known, and he'd wanted her from the minute he had set eyes on her. He still wanted her and only a fool turned down what she was offering. He was no fool, though he had been acting like one for the past half-hour, torn between conscience and chemistry. Chemistry won as Jake curved her own wrist around her back and drew her close to him again. 'Your effect on me is quite the opposite, and I like the way you make me feel.'

'You really do?' Charlie queried uncertainly, a tide of red sweeping up over her pale face as her body responded with quivering eagerness to the powerful strength of his embrace. She was hopelessly confused. She couldn't understand why he blew hot and cold. She couldn't understand men, full stop! she thought helplessly.

With a husky chuckle Jake bent his dark head. 'If you need me to confirm it after the past few hours, then I obviously have not fulfilled your expectations.' And he took her shocked open mouth with his in a display of erotic expertise that left her in no doubt of his desire for her.

'This is madness,' Jake groaned a moment later, lifting his head to look down at her with stormy black eyes. 'But you are a fire in my blood and I can't resist you.'

Charlie should have been flattered by his comment, but there was something suspiciously like resentment in his dark gaze that sounded warning bells in her head. He was a gorgeous virile male, streets ahead of her in experience and sophistication, and yet he said it was madness. Perhaps it was! She had fallen headlong in love with him, but what did she really know about him? Other than that he was a fabulous lover and they had come together with what some, herself included, would say was unseemly haste, since meeting two days ago!

'Maybe I should leave,' she said stiffly. 'It's late.'

After he had admitted he was burning for her, not a confession he usually made, Jake was disconcerted by her sudden about-face. Dark colour flared over his high cheekbones, and he drew in a ragged breath and relaxed his hold on her. Having spent years calling the shots with the women in his life, he found it a salutary experience to have Charlotte do the same to him. His heavy-lidded eyes half closed as he stepped back and glanced at his wrist-watch. 'You're right, it's after one—there's no point waiting for a cab. I'll drive you home.'

Charlie thought she had offended him, so the relief she felt was immense when he drew up outside the apartment block with a squeal of brakes and turned to her. 'Thank you for a wonderful day, Charlotte, and an even better evening. Give me your number and I will call you tomorrow. Something so good should not be ignored.' He grinned.

Quickly she withdrew a business card and pen from her purse, and wrote Dave's number on the back. She also took out her door key.

'Home and here,' she murmured as Jake took the card from her fingers, and slid out of the car to walk around the bonnet and open the passenger door.

'Come on, Charlotte.' He held out his hand and, relieved, she took it and walked up the steps to the entrance foyer.

She swiped the card through the slot, and the glass doors

slid open. 'Good evening, Miss Summerville,' the security guard on the reception desk called out. Charlie returned the greeting, and then glanced back at Jake, reluctant to part from him but not sure how to proceed. Stupid, she knew, when not long ago she had been in bed with the man, but she couldn't help it. Before Jake she had imagined love to be some perfect life-enhancing dream; the insecurity she now felt had not been part of it.

Sensing her dilemma, Jake cupped her face in his hands, and brushed his lips to hers. 'Goodnight.' He felt her tremble and smiled. 'I'll call.' And he left.

His smile and gentle kiss lingered on her lips like a benediction and when she reached her apartment she fell into bed and slept like the proverbial log.

Charlie yawned and stretched, then groaned. She ached in places she never knew she had. *Jake.* She murmured his name, and images of the previous day ran like a video recording through her mind. A deep, shuddering sigh escaped her and even the fine cotton cover felt too warm on her overheated flesh.

She glanced at the bedside clock, and looked again. Ten o'clock! She had overslept big time. Jake might have already called, and, leaping off the bed, she dashed into the shower. She dressed with feverish haste in her favourite blue jeans and a white cotton shirt, and swept her hair up in a pony-tail. She looked at herself in the mirror as she rubbed a light moisturiser into her face and paused, noting the sparkle in her eyes, the flush of excitement along her delicate cheekbones, and marvelled at the difference having a man in her life had made. Her total transformation from a brisk, efficient young woman to the hungry, sensuous creature that smiled back at her took some getting used to. Still smiling, she walked into the tiny kitchen and pressed the call retrieve button on the wall-mounted telephone. Her smile faded as the automated voice informed her, 'No messages.'

She switched on the coffee percolator and consoled herself with the fact Jake had said he was going to work. Then she discovered she had no milk. She disliked black coffee, but she managed to drink one cup, and ate an apple, the only food in the place. She really should do some shopping, but she was too afraid to leave the apartment in case she missed Jake's call.

She washed her cup before strolling back into the living area. It took her all of ten minutes to tidy it up, then, ascending the stairs to the galleried sleeping area, she made the bed. For the next two hours she paced the apartment, one minute elated, sure he would call, and the next moment in despair, convinced he wouldn't.

Finally by midday she realised she was behaving like a besotted idiot. She needed milk, and, grabbing her bag and keys, she took the lift to the ground floor. The doorman told her where the nearest convenience store was and she stepped out into the spring sunshine, telling herself if Jake did call he would probably leave his number and she could call him back, no problem.

The store was a lot further than the doorman had made it sound, and it was an hour later when Charlie, a carrier bag in one hand, her head bent in gloom, trudged back into her apartment building.

'*Buon giorno, cara.*' The deep, melodious voice was music to her ears, and her head shot up. 'I see the wanderer has returned.'

Jake was waiting in the foyer. He strolled towards her and stared down at her from his great height, a slow smile curving across his handsome face. 'Charlotte.'

As he said her name Charlie's heart beat a frenzied tattoo in her chest and she blushed, as the memory of last night seemed all too real. He was here, inches away from her; she could reach out and touch him.

'Let me help you with that.' He took the carrier from her hand, and smiled wryly when he saw the expression on her face. His dark head bent and he brushed his lips lightly against her cheek. 'I called to see if you would like to have lunch with me.' His deep accented drawl and the promise in the dark eyes that met hers made her ache for so much more.

'Jake. You're here.' She finally found her voice. 'I thought you were going to ring.'

He straightened up, and the eyes that held hers were suddenly dark and unfathomable. 'I hope I have not called at an inconvenient moment, interrupted anything.'

'No, not at all,' she hastened to reassure him, her eyes sliding lovingly over him, taking in the casual cream trousers and the open-necked, slightly darker polo shirt that revealed the perfect musculature of his chest. She swallowed hard and said, 'Come on up. I only have to put the milk in the fridge and then I'm yours.'

'You're sure about that?' Jake demanded. 'If you're involved with someone else, say so now, Charlotte.'

She shook her head. 'Of course not.' She could sense the sudden tension in him, and wondered at its cause. 'Whatever gave you that idea?'

'Maybe because you are staying in another man's apartment.'

She laughed in relief. 'Oh, Dave is just a very old friend.'

'Then I trust he stays that way, and I can assume I am your current lover exclusively. I do not believe in sharing, and, I trust, neither do you,' he drawled with silken emphasis. 'Or did I get that wrong?'

'No—yes.' He was staring down at her with dark, almost

angry eyes and Charlie was hopelessly confused. 'I mean, of course you are.'

My God! Jake actually sounded jealous, she realised, although he had no reason to be. She was about to tell him so, and explain Dave was her boss at International Rapid Rescue, but she didn't get the chance.

'Good.' Looping an arm around her waist, he ushered her into the lift. 'Third floor, correct?'

Mildly affronted by his abrupt manner, she asked, 'I thought you had to work today?' She was not a complete pushover, even if she had given Jake that impression.

'A certain lady left me wide awake and aching, so I worked for what was left of the night.'

She smiled up at him, feeling the tension in the arm that held her leaving him. 'Gosh, unable to sleep? That's funny, I slept like a log.' Her stomach twisted in knots at the thought of Jake aching for her.

'Witch,' he chuckled, and at that moment they reached her floor.

Inexplicably, Charlie felt nervous showing Jake into the apartment. Taking the carrier from his hand, she said, 'Make yourself at home while I put this away,' and dashed for the kitchen before she did something foolish like grabbing him. She didn't want to appear too desperate.

Jake's dark gaze roamed around what was a basic studio apartment. The place was tiny, and it was obviously used for one thing only: the bed.

A tiny living area contained a sofa that faced a television and music centre, and in between a sheepskin rug covered most of the wood floor. An open staircase led up to a gallery that held a large bed and nothing much else except a door that obviously had to lead to the bathroom. The space beneath the stairs housed a desk and computer and a row of bookcases, and that was it.

It confirmed all his worst suspicions: this was a love nest, or a bachelor pad at best. He cursed the crazy impulse that had made him come looking for Charlotte. It was not like him at all. But after a sleepless night, when visions of her exquisite body had tormented him, and he had sat for a few hours at the computer but had not been able to even occupy his mind with work, his curiosity had got the better of him—and, if he was honest, so had his libido. And he had determined to see her again. Big mistake.

He strode across to the window and the view did nothing to improve his mood: the back of a warehouse. Then he noticed the silver photo frame on the window-sill. He picked it up, his dark eyes narrowing on the picture it contained. A tall, burly, fair-haired man, with a slim dark woman at his side and three children kneeling at their feet. Surely Charlotte's last lover could not be a married man?

'That's Dave and his family.' He turned his head at the sound of her voice. She was standing in the kitchen doorway smiling at him.

Jake remained standing by the window, uneasiness clutching at his gut. His hooded dark eyes raked over Charlotte's slender figure and beaming face. She looked totally unashamed, innocent almost, and yet she was using another man's apartment. A married man at that.

'Very nice.' Jake placed the frame back on the table. 'And this apartment is very cosy, but hardly a family home?' he prompted.

'No. Dave has a house in Dorset and only uses this flat when he is in London on business.'

Jake stiffened. She was as good as admitting a married man had been her lover, and it disgusted him. 'Convenient,' Jake said cynically, subjecting her to a hard, steady appraisal. 'For you.'

His relationship with Charlotte had started out straightforwardly enough, as an act of revenge. After last night he should have left it at that.

Charlotte was moving towards him, her incredible eyes wide and guileless as she flashed him a brilliant smile. 'For everyone. Lisa, his wife, loved the place; she said it was a perfect bolt-hole for the pair of them when the children got too much.' She continued walking towards him. 'Come September Joe, the eldest son, is moving in when he starts at university.'

'You know the whole family?' Jake queried, his suspicion of this Dave as the man in her life fading a little.

'Have done almost all my life.' Charlotte stopped beside him and picked up the picture. 'They've been regulars at the hotel for almost twenty years or so. This is an old photo from when the children were young—they're all teenagers now.' An abstracted smile curved her full lips. 'Lisa was a great friend of my mother's, and after her death Lisa and Dave were great to me, a bit like an honorary aunt and uncle. I stayed quite a few times at their home in Dorset.'

Jake draped a casual arm around her shoulder, took the picture from her unresisting fingers and placed it back on the table, his relief intense. She glanced up at him, and looked a little sad, but she was entitled to be. She was like him, alone in the world, and it worried him. As the elusive Dave no longer worried him. He did what he had ached to do from the moment he had seen her again.

Charlie saw his darkening gaze and just had time to be surprised by the oddest flash of relief in his eyes as he bent towards her and gathered her close and took her softly parted lips in a deep, open-mouthed kiss that inflamed all her senses. Her hand reached for his broad shoulders, and her slender fingers threaded up through the sleek black hair as his tongue pursued a subtle exploration of her mouth. He released her lips and she groaned as his tongue found the delicate coils of her ear. His fingers were deftly moving to the buttons of her shirt, releasing them. She had dressed in haste and was braless and his hand took full advantage, pushing aside the soft cotton and cupping her naked breast. Her body leapt in immediate response, a low groan of pleasure escaping her.

'No,' Jake rasped, lifting his head. He saw the desire in her smoky blue eyes, and forced himself to ignore it as he deftly refastened her blouse and hugged her tight. She deserved better than a quick lay. 'Not here, *cara*. I came to take you to lunch.'

'I'm not that hungry.'

'But I am, and the restaurant at my hotel provides very good food.' He eased her away from him, his dark gaze roaming over her lovely face, and lingering on her lips, and his good intentions were shot to hell. 'And excellent room service,' he added huskily.

'Suddenly, I'm starving. And I would love to join you for lunch.' She beamed back at him.

The openness of her smile, the undisguised sensuality in her brilliant eyes, sent a thrill of anticipation running through Jake's veins, and another course of action occurred to him. 'In that case, while I am on a winning streak—you did say you were on holiday, so how about you pack your bags and take advantage of all the amenities of a first-rate hotel suite, including me, for the next couple of weeks, instead of this tiny apartment?'

'Move in with you?' Charlie was shocked, and still reeling from his assault on her senses. She wanted to, but felt she had to demur. 'But we only met two days ago, we hardly know each other.'

'All the more reason. It will give you time to get to know me. And don't worry, I can truthfully declare I am a financially viable, clean-living, totally unattached male. It is a two-bedroom suite and if you prefer you can have your own room.'

'I don't know,' she murmured. A voice of caution in her head was reminding her Jake wasn't offering her happy ever after. He had told her he would never marry. But her feelings for him overpowered every other consideration.

'Yes, you do,' he said confidently. 'The sexual chemistry between us is electric. We both want the same thing, and badly.' Lifting his hand, he brushed his fingers along the edge of her jaw, and Charlie instinctively moved her head like a cat seeking the stroking fingers. 'And you know it,' he said with a throaty chuckle.

She looked up at him, a brief smile curling her mouth, and said softly, 'Your hotel sounds a lot of fun, Jake. I'll go and pack.'

Jake watched the sway of her pert bottom as she walked up the stairs. His body hardened yet again, and he was tempted to follow her. But instead he lowered himself down on the sofa. He felt strange. He had just asked Charlotte to stay with him for two weeks, something he never did with the women in his life. A weekend, yes, maybe, but longer— never. He shook his head. Two impulsive actions in one day; not like him at all.

Ten minutes later Charlie skipped down the stairs, a holdall in her hand. 'Right, I'm ready.'

'That's it?' Jake rose to his feet, his dark eyes narrowing on the single bag she carried. 'I thought you told me you were on holiday for two weeks.'

'I am, but I always travel light.'

'Amazing.'

'Not really,' Charlie said seriously. 'It's just a question of knowing what you need and packing carefully.'

'If you say so,' Jake agreed and, taking her bag and with

his other hand in the small of her back, he urged her out of the apartment.

Following Jake into the hotel, Charlie had a moment of panic. She wished her mother or Lisa were still alive so she had someone to talk to—another female to give her advice about the overwhelming emotions she was experiencing and the action she was about to take.

She glanced around the massive foyer, and the people milling around. The clientele were elegantly dressed, and she was terribly conscious of the simplicity of her own attire. Why, oh, why hadn't she changed, or at least done something about her hair instead of leaving it in a childish pony-tail? She glanced at Jake. He had everything: a great body, stunning looks, he oozed sex appeal, and he wore his casual clothes with an elegance that few men could aspire to.

Sensing her disquiet, Jake closed a comforting hand around her arm. 'Not having second thoughts?'

'No. But I look like something the cat dragged in, compared to everyone here. I stand out like a sore thumb.'

A smile touched his mouth. 'You stand out because you are the most beautiful woman here,' he drawled. 'But if you feel uncomfortable there is an easy remedy.'

Before Charlie realised his intention he had led her across the foyer and into a designer boutique. He spoke to the assistant and informed her, 'This is Miss Summerville. I would like you to provide her with anything she needs.' He produced a diamond credit card from his pocket and placed it on the counter before glancing down at Charlie, a cynical edge to his smile. 'Problem solved. Now take your pick, but don't be long. I'm hungry.'

Blue eyes flashing flames, Charlie said through clenched teeth, 'No, thank you.' If they had been alone she would have hit him. He might be comfortable throwing his money around dressing his lady friends, but Charlie had never felt so mortified in her life. Scarlet-faced, she marched out of the shop.

Jake's arm snaked around her waist. 'I appreciate your haste to get me alone, but you were a little rude walking out on that rather charming lady,' he said mockingly as he led her into the lift.

As soon as the doors closed Charlie spun out of his hold. 'Get you alone!' she exclaimed. 'Are you crazy? I walked out because I have never been so embarrassed in my life. I am perfectly capable of buying my own clothes, and paying my own bill.'

One dark brow arched in astonishment. 'Paying the bill? Forget it! You are my guest—and as for embarrassed, *cara*, why? Women expect the man in their bed to buy them gifts and pay the bills. It is nothing to be embarrassed about. I'm not,' he said with a shrug of his broad shoulders.

Charlie stared at him incredulously. 'Then all I can say is you must have bedded some pretty awful women if you believe that claptrap.' She almost laughed at the look of outrage on his handsome face.

'None that were as outspoken as you, that's for sure,' he shot back. 'Next you will be trying to tell me you have never shared a holiday, or even lived with a man and allowed him to pay the bills.'

Charlie opened her mouth to yell, and stopped. His assumption about her lifestyle was partially her fault; she had tried to be more sophisticated than she really was. She glanced briefly up at him through the thick veil of her lashes. His features were impassive, relaxed, and yet she was aware of a tightly leashed primitive passion just below the surface that made her pulse race and her heart begin its familiar pounding. There was nowhere she wanted to be more than in his arms, and in his bed, and she knew if there was any chance at all of extending their relationship longer than a couple of weeks, it had to be with honesty and trust. Something Jake appeared to have very little faith in.

'No, actually, I have not,' she said quietly, raising her eyes to his and adding, 'This is a first for me.'

Her eyes must have given her away as he muttered something thickly in Italian, and reached for her. The doors slid open and he swore, and walked her across the hall and into his suite with unseemly haste.

'You are an incredible woman. You never cease to surprise me,' Jake husked, and he captured her mouth with his own in a deeply passionate kiss.

She could feel the heavy thud of his heart beneath the palms of her hands resting against his chest… Both his arms were around her, pressing her against him, and she felt his body hardening, merging with hers. She trembled as his lips feathered brief, tormenting kisses against her temples and down to the vulnerable curve of her neck.

'*Dio*, I want you,' Jake murmured against her ear, and, sweeping her up in his arms, he carried her into the bedroom.

They spent the rest of Sunday in bed, and all night. By the time Charlie surfaced on Monday morning she was a different woman. No woman ever had a more ardent lover, she was sure, and she had told Jake so, over and over again, fascinated by his big, hard-muscled body as he taught her with skill and eroticism how responsive her own could be.

She stretched languorously on the bed, and watched Jake, who had ten minutes earlier deserted her for the shower, stroll back into the bedroom wearing only a towel slung low on his hips. He had a magnificent body, all golden skin and rippling muscle, and after last night Charlie was no longer too shy to look.

She followed his progress around the room, saw him

withdraw a smart grey suit and white shirt from the wardrobe, and smiled at the intimacy of seeing him dress. First the white boxers, then the white shirt and elegant hip-hugging trousers. 'Going somewhere?' she asked, dragging herself up on an elbow and shaking back the tumbled mass of her ash blonde hair from her face. 'That doesn't look the kind of garb for sightseeing.'

Jake turned from the chest of drawers, a rueful smile on his handsome face and a pair of black socks in his hand, and crossed to sit down on the bed beside her. 'I have a meeting this morning. I did warn you, *cara*, I am here on business.' He smiled wryly when he saw the pout of her love-swollen lips, and, lifting his hand, he ran his fingers through her hair. 'And, no, I am not going to kiss you, otherwise I will never make my meeting.'

His deep, dark eyes gleamed down into hers as he added softly, 'After the last eighteen hours maybe you could use a rest—or to do your own tourist thing today. But I want you back here by six. I'll be waiting.' He pressed a brief kiss on the tip of her nose, before bending down to slip on his socks. A moment later he had donned his shoes, jacket and tie, and turned back to look at her.

'You're amazingly quiet, Charlotte.'

'I was just wondering if I should unpack my clothes in the other bedroom,' she teased. She was too happy to be angry with him and anyway he had said originally it would depend on his business obligations, but she wasn't letting him slope off totally scot-free.

'Ah, I might have lied about that,' Jake returned smoothly, his dark eyes lit with amusement smiling down into hers. 'The second bedroom was converted into an office for the duration of my stay, so unless you want to sleep on the desk...' He paused. 'Then again, a desk has distinct possibilities,' he suggested, a wicked gleam in his dark eyes.

Charlie picked up a pillow and threw it at him. 'Shame on you,' she cried and burst out laughing at the bemused expression on his striking face.

'I'll get you for that later.' Placing the pillow on the foot of the bed, he added, 'And that is a promise, so feel afraid, woman.' He sent her a quick blinding smile that took her breath away. Then he was striding out of the room, with the wave of a hand and a, *'Ciao, cara.'*

Charlie didn't go sightseeing; instead she hit the shops, and blew her clothes allowance for the next year because she wanted to look good for Jake. When she returned slightly after six, he was waiting.

'Typical woman: late and couldn't resist shopping,' he said mockingly as she walked in with a handful of carriers.

'But not from the hotel's overpriced boutique, and paid for by me,' she mocked back.

Without a single word of warning strong hands curved under her arms and hauled her hard against a taut male body, a dark head descended and she was kissed senseless. The carriers fell unnoticed to the ground as she linked her arms around his neck. A few hours later they called room service.

And so it continued for the next few days. Pressure of business meant Jake never accompanied her during the day as she roamed around London, visiting all the places of interest that appealed to her, but she didn't mind because she knew she would see him later. But the nights in the privacy of the suite were the best. He had only to look at her in a certain way, and her whole body heated in instant response.

CHAPTER SIX

FRIDAY showed all the signs of being a beautiful spring day, and as she sat dressed in only a bathrobe Charlie wondered what her chances were of getting Jake to share it with her. She looked across the table at him, noting the magnificent broad shoulders clad in a perfectly tailored dark jacket, the white shirt enhancing the bronzed skin of his almost indecently attractive face. She could look at him for ever. He had finished his breakfast and was filling his cup with coffee for the third time. That was something else she had noted about him: he always drank three cups of coffee.

'You drink too much coffee, Jake,' she declared, her eyes sparkling as she held his faintly brooding gaze. 'And you work too hard. If you're not at a meeting you're on the phone or attached to that computer. You need to relax more. Spend the day with me?'

'If I relaxed any more with you, *cara*, I would be in danger of having a heart attack,' he mocked gently, his dark gaze sliding down to where the soft swell of her breasts was exposed by the lapels of her robe, and back to her face.

'I didn't mean that.' Charlie blushed and Jake laughed. 'For your information,' she said firmly, 'I'm going to Kew Gardens to meander around the tropical plants and pretend I'm on a tropical island somewhere.'

'Now, that I can envisage: you on a paradise island wearing only a grass skirt,' he said. 'We'll do that for real when I have time. But, unfortunately, I can't join you today. I do have a huge corporation to run, and thousands of people who depend on me for their livelihood.'

'Very laudable.' His casual remark suggesting they had a future had made her heart sing. 'But you should remember the old adage: "all work and no play makes Jack a dull boy",' she teased with a smile that faded as she saw his dark brows draw together in a frown.

'I was just joking,' she said.

Jake was not amused, mainly because he knew there was some truth in her words. His gaze focused on her features, noting the sudden faint wariness in her eyes, and he felt bad. She gave him everything in bed and out; her enthusiasm for her ridiculous sightseeing tours, and the pleasure she took in explaining them to him, amused him, and he gave little back.

'I know you were, *cara*,' Jake hastened to reassure her. Charlotte had surprised him this last week. He could count on one hand the women he had actually allowed to share his life for more than a weekend. He preferred to wine, dine, and make love to the woman in his life and return to his own bed to sleep.

Charlotte was the exception, probably because she was the least demanding woman he had ever met. She was nothing like the greedy, selfish bitch he had first believed her to be. He hadn't spent a penny on her, and guiltily he realised he had never actually taken her out all week.

He wasn't the type of man who explained his actions, but Charlotte deserved some explanation. 'Before I met you, I had spent the past three months confined to my home in Italy, because my foster-parents were in poor health and needed my constant support. This trip to London is the first of many overdue visits, and in the next few months I must visit America and the Pacific Rim countries, so if I have appeared a little preoccupied with work, that's why. But all that is about to change.'

Charlie almost gasped out loud at the warmth of the smile

he bestowed upon her as, rising to his feet, he crossed to where she sat and turned her around in her chair, and, bending slightly, tipped her chin up with one long finger.

'Be back from your jungle adventure early. We have tickets for the theatre tonight and the curtain rises at seven-thirty.' He lied: he had not got tickets, but he would. 'And tomorrow I am completely at your disposal. You can take me where you want.' Straightening up, he added, 'Though I do have a property to check out in the morning. Perhaps we can combine the two.'

His information about his parents, work and the difficulties he'd had in the past few months was a first, and Charlie was delighted. At last Jake was beginning to confide in her. Hugging him around his hips, she tilted back her head, her blue eyes dancing. 'Careful or you might spoil me,' she chided him, and Jake laughed.

'And you be careful where you hug a man.' He took her hands from around his hips and shot her a mocking glance. 'You could give him the wrong idea.'

She was late. It was almost seven, and she was so looking forward to the theatre. Dashing out of the lift, she opened the door to their suite and stopped.

'Where the hell have you been? We're due at the theatre in thirty minutes.' Jake was standing in the middle of the room, immaculate in a dark evening suit, but with a face like thunder.

'I know, I know,' she wailed. 'But the tube was delayed and I got stuck in the rush hour.'

'The tube? You travelled on the tube? Are you crazy?'

'Not so you would notice, I hope.' She moved towards him and opened her shoulder-bag at the same time. 'It's okay, I'll be ready in fifteen minutes.'

'It is not okay.' She was made aware of the tension in

his tall, commanding figure as he grasped her arm. 'The tube is dangerous for a woman on her own. Have you no sense?' Jake demanded, studying her in angry challenge.

'Oh, Jake, come down from your rarefied planet. It's perfectly safe. I've been using it all week, and no one has leapt on me yet.'

'You…all week!' Hooded eyes, glinting strangely, clashed with blue. 'No more tubes, Charlotte. There will be a car and driver at your disposal from now on. It will be a great deal more convenient and, whatever you say, I am not having you exposed to any danger, however slight.'

'Gosh, I never knew you cared,' she remarked with a grin, and saw the shutters fall across his dark eyes as his hand fell from her arm.

'I care for any person in my charge,' he said stiltedly. 'Hurry and dress. We will be late.'

Delving in her shoulder-bag, she lifted out a box. 'Here, this is for you. I got it in the gift shop at Kew Gardens. When I saw it I thought of you.' She placed it in his hand, and caught his look of astonishment as she turned and headed for the bedroom.

Jake looked at the box in his hand as if it were about to explode. Slowly he opened the box. He withdrew the glass globe, and blinked at the beauty of the delicate exotic flower within. He could not remember the last time anyone had given him a gift for no apparent reason, let alone such an exquisitely simple gift, and he was totally humbled.

A quick shower and Charlie was back in the bedroom in a matter of minutes. Slipping on white lace briefs, she withdrew from the wardrobe the dress she had bought on Monday. It had looked glamorous in the shop, pale pink with a bustier bodice and short straight skirt, but now it looked a little too daring to her mind, and she wondered if Jake would like it. She slipped it over her head anyway.

Wondering about Jake had become a full-time occupation, and she now wondered if he liked her present as she sat down at the dressing-table and began to apply a light moisturiser to her face.

It was a black orchid petrified in glass as a paperweight, and now she realised why it reminded her of Jake. He was dark and beautiful, like the orchid, and like it, his true feelings were buried deep in a protective layer. But in his case the glass was probably bulletproof. When she had teased him earlier about caring, the familiar shuttered expression had appeared. But was that so surprising, she mused, given his early life? He had lost his mother young, and been on his own for two years, and that must have affected him. And later, when he had thought he had found love, his fiancée had walked out on him. No wonder he had concentrated all his attention on building up a business empire, and put his feelings in cold storage.

A slow, sensual smile curved her warm mouth. Well, perhaps not that cold. Her mind was made up. She loved Jake and it was up to her to chip away at the glass until she prised the loving, caring man she knew he could be free.

Standing up, she ran a comb through her hair—there wasn't time for anything else—and, smoothing the skirt down over her waist and hips, she picked up her shawl and purse and turned towards the door.

Jake was standing where she had left him in the middle of the room, turning the paperweight over and over in his hand. He swung around, his hooded eyes gleaming with a brightness that looked almost like tears.

'You like it.' She smiled, and Jake's reaction was peculiar.

He placed the paperweight on the table and walked slowly towards her. He placed his hands on her shoulders and said in a low voice husky with emotion, 'Thank you for the gift,

Charlotte. I will treasure it always.' Very gently he pulled her against his hard body, and lowered his head to hers.

The kiss was like no other kiss they had shared. It was soft and unbearably tender and went on and on. She lifted her free hand to curve around the nape of his neck, but his head lifted and he released her with a small sigh.

'I promised you the theatre and we will be late,' he offered by way of explanation. Taking her pashmina from her hands, he wrapped it around her shoulders. 'You look beautiful, absolutely stunning.' His dark eyes gleamed with amusement and something more sensual. 'But that is one dangerous gown and you are one dangerous lady. And I am not letting you out of my sight.'

They were too late to catch the first act, but were allowed to enter the auditorium for the second act. At the intermission Jake ordered her a glass of champagne. Leaning against the bar, dark eyes gleaming enigmatically down at her, he said, 'So, what do you think of it so far?'

'Honestly?' She quirked an elegant brow at him. 'It would not have made a blind bit of difference if we had seen the first act. The play is totally incomprehensible. And as for the poor young boy with the bandy legs who keeps appearing in what I suppose is a loincloth, but looks like a nappy—what on earth was his mother thinking of putting him on the stage? He could be traumatised for life.'

Jake threw back his head and laughed out loud. 'Brutally honest,' he said. 'But *I* couldn't have put it better myself. Let's get out of here and find somewhere to eat.'

The following day Charlie left Jake sleeping for a change. She showered and dressed carefully in more new additions to her wardrobe. Natural linen trousers with a matching tooled leather belt hung low on her hips, a figure-hugging camisole almost met the trousers, and a loosely tailored jacket completed the outfit. She left the jacket off, and ordered room service. When the waiter arrived she took the trolley from him and wheeled it into the bedroom.

Sprawled flat on his back across the bed, naked except for the sheet that just about covered his thighs, Jake was a tempting sight, and for a long moment she feasted her eyes on him. Black hair dishevelled and with an early morning shadow darkening his jaw, he looked like a pirate. All he needed was a gold earring, Charlie thought dreamily.

'Are you going to give me that coffee some time today?' One dark eye opened and Charlie nearly jumped out of her skin.

'You're awake.' She pushed the trolley nearer the bed. 'I thought you might like breakfast in bed.'

Jake hauled himself up on one elbow, his dark, sensuous gaze skimming over her face. 'I would if you were going to join me,' he offered lazily.

'No way. Much as I love you, you promised me the day out,' she shot back. 'And I'm holding you to it.'

His eyes darkened and then became hidden beneath the sweep of his lashes, and she realised what she had just said. But she refused to be embarrassed. It was the truth and Jake could accept it, ignore it, or tell her to get lost. She was tired of trying to play by his rules and she wasn't hiding how she felt any more.

'Then pour me a coffee, and I'll be yours in no time at all.' Obviously he was going to ignore her declaration of love, but at least he had not told her to get lost, which was some consolation. She handed him a cup of coffee and left.

Two hours later, Charlie stood on the balcony of a penthouse apartment situated on the bank of the River Thames, and looked around her, absorbing the stunning view of the city spread out before her. She was a country girl at heart but she could certainly get used to this. Her lips twitched

in the beginnings of a smile as she turned to go back inside.
Fat chance.

She walked across to where Jake was leaning over a table,
studying a blueprint. 'Are you really going to buy this apartment?' she asked.

'Actually, I was thinking more of the whole building.'
Jake cast her a sidelong glance and straightened to his full
height. 'It's an excellent long-term investment. But as it
happens, this apartment is available, and it might be useful
to have a permanent base in London.' He lifted an enquiring
brow. 'What do you think?'

'I love it.' She felt flattered he had asked her opinion.
'But then, I'm not in your league when it comes to business.'

'It wasn't business I was thinking of.' Reaching an arm
around her waist, he pulled her to him. 'But from a woman's
point of view, would you rather spend time with a man
here?' His eyes glinted when he saw her blush. 'Or in a
hotel?'

'If it was the man I loved, it wouldn't matter,' Charlie
responded honestly, her sapphire eyes holding his.

They stared mutely at one another for a long moment,
and Jake was the first to break the contact. His arm fell from
her waist and he took a step back to lean against the table.
'A typical romantic response. You must know very little
about your own sex if you believe that.' She was struck by
the sudden cold glitter in his dark eyes. 'Take it from me,
most women will run a mile if the man in their life doesn't
support them in the manner to which they would like to be
accustomed.'

'That is a sweeping generalisation,' she said. 'And I don't
believe it for a minute.'

'Try telling that to my ex-fiancée. She took off like lightning when she realised I wasn't as wealthy as she had thought.'

'That must have hurt,' Charlie murmured.

'No.' Jake took in a controlled breath. 'Her leaving did not hurt at all, and how in the hell did we get onto this subject?' He shook his head and wrapped a strong, lean hand around Charlie's wrist, which he twisted around her back, pulling her in close to his great body. His other hand came up and touched her smooth cheek. 'What is it about you that makes me tell you things I don't mean to?'

'My fatal charm,' she replied cheekily. She had learnt more about Jake over the last few days and understood a lot better now why he appeared so hard-headed and controlled.

'You could be right at that,' Jake husked, his dark head bending. Her lips involuntarily parted for his kiss, but instead he whispered in her ear, 'You can prove it later.' He dropped his fingers from her cheek to rest on her hip, his dark eyes laughing down at her. 'As it happens, I already bought this place yesterday. Come on, the rest of the day is for you.'

They spent it at London Zoo and Charlie, with her arm linked through Jake's, for the first time felt as if they were a normal couple. They laughed at the monkeys, and she shivered at the snakes while Jake held her close. They ate sandwiches outside the café in the zoo, and when Charlie fell in love with a soft cuddly panda in the gift shop, Jake bought the toy for her. Much later they dined on scampi and chips sitting outside a pub on the river. Jake was convinced that whatever was in the popular English dish had never been in the sea, and they were still light-heartedly arguing on the merits of Italian versus English food when they returned to the hotel. Finally Charlie threw her hands up and admitted that Italian cuisine won hands down, and

Jake took advantage of her position to whip her top over her head…

Sometimes Charlie had to pinch herself to believe he was real, and she told him so early on the Friday of the second week.

Jake laughed lazily, and told her to feel him and make sure. She did, all over. And he called her a natural-born sensualist, and made wild, passionate love to her, until she thought she would lose her mind with the excitement of his powerful body driving her to the edge of sense and beyond.

Exhausted, they lay sprawled together on the bed. She said in a breathless voice, 'Now I know why I love you. And I'm totally convinced you're real.' She spread her fingers through the damp hair on his chest, feeling the rapid pounding of his heart beneath her palm. She heard him chuckle and she pulled gently on the short, curling body hair.

'Find me funny, do you?' she teased. But the telephone rang on the bedside table before he could respond. She watched as he lifted the receiver, and said something in Italian. She felt his body tense, and heard the change of tone in his rich deep voice, even though she could not understand what he was saying.

Ending the call, Jake sprang off the bed, and glanced down at her. 'That was my office in Italy. I have to leave immediately.' Without another word, he headed for the bathroom.

Stunned, she stared at his broad back as he disappeared into the bathroom. She loved Jake and he was leaving. It had to happen eventually, she knew, but blindly she had pushed the knowledge to the back of her mind, not wanting to face reality. Now she had no choice.

Well, what had she expected, for heaven's sake? she asked herself. Jake had a huge corporation to run, and her manager was expecting her back on Sunday. So Jake had to leave a day earlier than planned. It was no big deal. She would see him again.

Jake strolled back into the room. 'Okay.' He tossed her a brief glance, and proceeded to dress with the same brisk efficiency he did everything.

Charlie had watched him countless times before, but somehow this morning she couldn't. She was too afraid of betraying her misery at his imminent departure. Jumping off the bed, she crossed to the walk-in wardrobe, selected navy trousers and a blue ribbed sweater, then collected fresh underwear and stepped into the bathroom.

Standing in the shower, she told herself not to overreact. If the last two weeks had proved anything, it was that they were great together. She loved him and she felt it in her bones that Jake cared about her. They were both mature adults with busy careers; it was natural they would be apart sometimes.

As she walked into the lounge ten minutes later she was still telling herself she had nothing to worry about.

Jake was standing by the table, leafing through some papers in a briefcase, the expression on his face one of intense concentration. The suitcases by his side told her he had already packed. He was dressed in a dark pinstriped business suit, white shirt and grey silk tie, and he looked every inch the hard-headed tycoon. But she knew the other Jake, the passionate tender lover, and a sob caught in her throat at the thought of him leaving.

She must have made some sound because his dark head lifted and she walked across to him. 'You're already packed.'

'Yes.' Jake placed a brief, somewhat distracted kiss on her cheek. 'I'm sorry I have to leave so quickly, but my presence is required in Italy.'

'I know. But it's a shame we are going to lose our last day together.' She couldn't prevent the slight tremble of her lips.

Jake placed a finger over her mouth. 'There will be other days, Charlotte. I'll call you tonight. Stay here and enjoy your last day.'

Her pleasure at his promise to call her was dented by his suggestion she stay on at the hotel. To be here alone held no appeal. 'No, I wouldn't feel comfortable staying here without you. I'll go home.'

'Whatever you want,' he said gruffly. Suddenly a conscience that had never troubled Jake before where women were concerned reared its head. He was the 'love them and leave them' type, the women suitably rewarded of course, but Charlotte was different. Sure, he had lusted after her, but his original intention had been less than honourable and he prided himself on being an honourable man.

He couldn't just walk away from her. So he did something he never did: he wrote a number on the back of a business card. 'This is my home number in Genoa. If you need me, call me. And now I really must go—the jet is waiting.'

Charlie watched him snap shut his briefcase, blinking back the tears.

'Already?' The tremble in her voice gave her away.

'Afraid so.' The bellboy arrived to take the suitcases and Jake brushed a brief kiss against her trembling lips and left.

Dr Jones had been Charlie's GP all her life. He dined at the hotel restaurant regularly, and quite often Charlie joined him: he was more friend than doctor. But looking at him now, she was horrified.

'You're sure?' she asked for the third time.

'Yes, Charlie dear. From the date you have given me, you are almost seven weeks pregnant.'

'But we used protection,' she murmured, shaking her head in disbelief.

'Obviously not enough,' Dr Jones said dryly. 'But it isn't the end of the world. You're pregnant, not ill; you're a very fit young woman, Charlie, and I know you will have a beautiful, healthy baby. So I'm sure you have nothing to worry about. Go home and tell the lucky man.'

Easier said than done, Charlie thought, staring blindly at the pile of invoices on the desk in front of her three days later.

'It's no good sitting daydreaming, Charlie.'

At the sound of her manager Jeff's voice, her head lifted. 'I am not dreaming,' she snapped. 'I'm trying to work.'

'If you say so.' Jeff stopped by the desk and looked down at her, compassion in his grey eyes. 'You should tell the father. He has a right to know. It's not like you to shirk your responsibilities.'

Jeff had known Charlie since she was twelve, when he had been hired by her grandfather to manage the hotel. She had been a bright, lively child, a joy to all who knew her, and he hated to see her so miserable.

'This baby is my responsibility, and what I would like to know is, how the hell did all the staff find out I was pregnant the same day it was confirmed?' Charlie demanded, running a hand distractedly through her blonde hair.

'Maybe because you came back from your holiday, glowing like a woman in love, you mentioned Jake d'Amato just once or twice and bought a ''Teach Yourself Italian'' book. So when you started dashing off to be sick every day, it was a bit of a give-away. Plus everyone knew you had a doctor's appointment,' Jeff said with a chuckle. 'They all care about you, and most of them guessed you were pregnant long before you realised what was up.'

'Thanks! Thanks very much! So not only does everyone in the hotel know I'm pregnant, they think I'm a pregnant idiot for not recognising the signs.' Charlie groaned. 'What am I going to do?'

'I've told you. Ring the man, and do it now. I have to go and fill in on the desk. Amy was supposed to be on Reception but she has an optician's appointment. I'll catch you later. Do it,' Jeff reiterated, walking out the door.

The trouble was, Charlie thought forlornly, she already had called Jake's home near Genoa three times since the doctor had confirmed her pregnancy, hoping to get a message to him, but she had only managed to speak to some woman called Marta, whose English was as bad as Charlie's Italian.

In the five weeks since she had last seen Jake, her tentative belief that he might love her as she loved him had taken a severe jolt. He'd rung to make sure she'd arrived back home safely, and then nothing for a week. Then he'd called to tell her he was going to America and would get in touch when he got back. She had heard nothing since, but had lived on hope and consoled herself with the fact she knew he was in America.

But yesterday, leafing through a magazine one of the departing guests had left behind, she had seen a double-page spread of a prestigious charity dinner in New York, and staring out from one picture was Jake d'Amato with a stunning brunette at his side. According to the item accompanying the picture, Jake's companion was Melissa, a model and long-time 'friend' of Jake, better known for her string of wealthy lovers than her modelling career.

Charlie hadn't tried to call Jake again. Face it, she told herself sadly, she had been taken for a fool. While she had fallen in love, to Jake she had been nothing more than a passing fancy. She blinked back the tears that moistened her eyes. She was not going to cry. She had done enough of that in the past few weeks and she had to stop.

She should have known a man like Jake d'Amato was far too sophisticated to be attracted by a naive virgin for long. Remembering the last day when they had parted, she knew she had felt him withdrawing from her. He had been cool and his kiss goodbye had been little more than a peck. In fact, when Charlie thought about it now, the only thing that was surprising was that he had bothered to call her at all!

Anger and pain bubbled up inside her. In every other area of her life she was super-efficient. She could run a hotel, climb a rock-face, or search for the dead and dying in any catastrophe around the world. She was compassionate by nature and slow to anger. Yet in the male-female stakes she was an absolute novice.

Morosely, she concluded falling in love was heaven and hell. In her case mostly hell: the butterflies in the stomach, the hunger, the need for one man and the constant doubt as to whether Jake felt the same. Well, it was all going to change. She had been acting like a lovesick fool long enough.

Angrily she brushed her hand across her eyes and, shoving back the chair, she stood up, squaring her slender shoulders. No man was going to take her for a mug and get away with it, she vowed. In fact... Impulsively she grabbed the telephone and pressed out a number she knew by heart. She heard the *'Pronto,'* through a red mist of anger, and burst into speech. She didn't care if Marta only understood one word in ten. Charlie was going to have her say.

'Tell that no-good bastard you call a boss, I am pregnant and he is going to be a father. *Charlotte incinta, Jake papà—capisco?*' She sarcastically inserted the few Italian words she knew, regardless of grammar, and slammed the phone down.

Whether they made sense or Marta understood, Charlie didn't care. It had made her feel a hell of a lot better. Plus, she thought as she left her office, she could tell Jeff quite honestly she had done the right thing and told the father, and get him off her back.

'I could cover Amy's shift for you, Jeff,' she offered, stopping at the reception desk. With the hotel booked solid for the summer, the staff were at full stretch, and Charlie was adept at filling in when the need arose.

'No, I'm fine. Why don't you take the day off? You've hardly been out of the place in weeks. The sun is shining and Dave and his brood are going sailing for the day. Chef is preparing a picnic. I'll tell him to add a few of your favourites and you can join them. It will do you the world of good.'

Jeff was right. She had hung around the hotel day and night like an idiot waiting for the phone to ring, hoping Jake would call. Well, not any more. She had another human being to worry about now.

'You're right as usual, Jeff,' she admitted with a wry self-mocking smile. 'I have been behaving like an idiot.'

'You, an idiot? Never.' A laughing voice floated over her shoulder. Charlie spun around and smiled at the big, burly grey-haired man grinning down at her. Dave had obviously just left the dining room, with his brood: Joe, eighteen, James, sixteen, and Mary, two years behind. 'You are a pearl among women, and if you would help me control this lot for the day, I'll even put it in writing,' he teased.

A day sailing was a far better prospect than moping around the hotel another minute. 'Yes, okay, Dave.' The fresh air and the company of good friends was just what she needed to help her banish the depressing thoughts about Jake. 'I'll go and change and meet you at the jetty in twenty minutes.'

'Come on, Charlie,' the boys yelled. 'The water's great, it's not like you to be the last in.'

Wearing a black bikini and stretched out on a towel placed on the fore deck of the sailing boat, Charlie was feeling surprisingly content. She grinned and waved a lazy hand. 'No, I've eaten far too much, maybe later.'

They had sailed to the southern end of the lake, and dropped anchor at a favourite little cove to have their picnic. The three teenagers all had healthy appetites, and Charlie had been no slouch.

'Very wise.' Dave flopped down beside her. 'You have to be careful in your condition.'

'Oh, God!' Charlie groaned. 'Not you as well. You only arrived yesterday, for heaven's sake. Surely the bush telegraph isn't that fast?'

'Afraid so. Jeff told me over a couple of beers last night. He thought I should know as your team leader and more importantly as your friend, Charlotte.' Charlie knew she was in for a lecture when Dave used her full name. 'You know of course you're off the International Rapid Rescue now, but finding a replacement of your calibre is not my main worry. You are, Charlie. I've known you since the first time Lisa and I came here on holiday almost twenty years ago, and you are as dear to me as my family. And Lisa would say the same if she was still alive,' he said seriously.

She had known she would have to give up the team, but it was the sentiment Dave had expressed that made Charlie blink the sudden moisture from her eyes. Lisa and Dave had visited the hotel with their expanding family for almost as long as she could remember. And she knew how hard Lisa's death from breast cancer last year had hit Dave and the children. 'Thank you for that,' she murmured.

'Yes, well, the thing is, I can't help feeling responsible for the condition you're in. If—'

'You are certainly not responsible. I think I'd know if I had slept with you,' she cut in with a cheeky grin, trying to lighten the atmosphere.

'Forget the jokes, Charlotte, this is serious. If I had never said you needed a change of scene and offered you the use of the studio, maybe you'd never have met the man who has been careless enough to make you pregnant. But that aside, the important question is, do you love each other?'

There was no point in denying the truth. Dave knew her far too well and would see through a lie in a second. 'I love Jake, but I doubt he loves me,' she said flatly.

'According to Jeff, the man is some kind of industrial tycoon who lives abroad. But you do keep in touch with him? Whether he loves you or not, you have to tell him you're pregnant. It is natural for you to have doubts in your condition, but you will probably be pleasantly surprised. Trust me, I know my own sex. Any man would be ecstatic to have a woman like you for his wife and the mother of his children.'

'Yes, sure,' she agreed dryly. At that point three very wet teenagers flopped on the deck and ended the adult conversation, much to Charlie's relief, for the rest of the afternoon.

It was late, almost six, when they finally tied the boat up at its mooring. The teenagers yelled, 'Race you to the hotel!' and set off at a run.

'Ah, to be thirty years younger,' Dave groaned.

Charlie flashed him a grin and raced off after the others. The day on the water had done her the world of good, but she was tired and finally had to stop and catch her breath. She looked up at the hotel with the backdrop of the woods embracing it. The grey stone walls gleamed in the evening sun, the immaculate garden stretched down to where she stood with the lake behind her, and she thought she had never seen the old place look more beautiful.

A bittersweet smile curved her soft lips. She was almost home. She placed her hand over her still flat stomach in a tender gesture of reassurance to her unborn child. 'Whatever else happens in life, you and I will always have a home here,' she said with a deep sigh of contentment.

The day out had cleared her head. She was expecting Jake d'Amato's baby, and already she loved them both. But she knew better than most there were no guarantees in life. She had lost all her family, and she had seen through her work generations of families destroyed, even whole towns. She was pregnant, and she now had the chance to build her own little family. Charlie knew with absolute certainty that she had the ability and the strength of will to give her child a good life. As for Jake, she loved him and probably always would, but whether they got together was no longer the main issue. Her baby was her first concern, now and always.

'Age catching up with you too?' Dave quipped as he reached her, and placed a guiding hand around her waist. 'Come on, I'll help you up the hill.'

Charlie laughed. 'Shouldn't that be the other way around, old man?'

The Lakeview Hotel was a beautiful old building, in a magnificent setting and not at all what Jake had expected. It had to be over a hundred years old, and constructed in stone with an elegant terrace along the front. The interior was Victorian in style with stone-mullioned windows, and mahogany-panelled walls, the wood mellowed with the patina of years. He doubted if the place had changed much since it was built, and, glancing at the key rack while waiting for the receptionist, he noted there were only twenty letting rooms. Hardly a big enough hotel to make much of a profit. Not surprising Charlotte was eager to contact him, he thought cynically.

He had begun to believe in the two weeks they had spent together she was not the greedy, selfish bitch he had first thought. But now he realised she was cleverer than most. She had been aiming for the jackpot, a meal ticket for life. Impatiently he drummed his fingers on the desk. Where the hell was the receptionist?

A tall thin man finally appeared. 'Can I help you, sir?'

'Yes, I want to see the owner. Charlotte Summerville,' Jake snapped. He wasn't used to waiting.

'Your name, sir?'

'Jake d'Amato. She knows who I am,' he said impatiently.

'I am the manager—perhaps I can help?'

Jake looked at him and caught a look of amusement in the pale eyes. 'No, you damn well can't. I want to see Charlotte.' He was furious and he was taking no insolence from any man. 'Tell her I'm here.'

'That might be difficult, sir, as she has gone sailing for the day. We are expecting her about six.' Jake glanced at his watch. He would have to cool his heels for over an hour. 'If you would care to wait, I'll have the waitress serve you tea.'

There was no point in arguing—it wasn't the manager he was mad at. Taking a seat in the lounge, he suffered the attentions of a stony-faced waitress. He drank tea, which he loathed, and got the distinct impression from the cold looks slanted his way by the members of staff who passed by that they actively disliked the guests. Or perhaps it was just him in particular. Well, he had had enough. Slapping the paper he had been trying to read down on the table, Jake rose to his feet and strode towards the double doors leading to the garden and beyond.

Three teenagers were running towards him, laughing and shouting, and he quickly stepped up onto the terrace that fronted the hotel. Where the hell was Charlotte? he wondered, gazing out over the glorious gardens to the lake beyond, and then he saw her.

Clad in the briefest of white shorts and a cropped top, she looked incredibly beautiful. Her long blonde hair, glinting with platinum streaks in the evening sun, tumbled around her shoulders and her long legs moved with lithe grace as she ran towards him.

A brilliant smile of pure masculine satisfaction cut across Jake's strong face. She still adored him. He forgot he was furious. Five long weeks he had been without her—he must have been mad to wait so long. But not any more and a charge of testosterone fired up his body with incredible excitement. Then she stopped.

In the next second Jake realised he could swing from euphoria to a fury that threatened to explode as the truth hit him like a blow to the solar plexus. She was not running towards him, she had not even seen him, and she was not alone. From his vantage point, with his grip white-knuckled on the terrace balustrade, he watched Charlotte laugh happily up into the face of the older man who had stopped beside her, and, with an ease born of long practice, slipped an arm around her bare waist.

Jake jerked his proud head back, and drew in a sharp lungful of air. No man touched his woman, not ever. Outraged and furious beyond belief he vaulted over the balustrade and strode towards her.

Charlie, in blissful ignorance of the impending confrontation, was happily regaling Dave with details of her trip around Kew Gardens when Dave interrupted her, his arm falling from her.

'Don't look now, but a very large, very dark and very angry man has just leapt off the terrace and is heading our way.'

Charlie's head spun to the front. Jake! It was Jake in the flesh, and a quivering excitement lanced through her, quickly followed by a shiver of something very like fear. She could feel the anger, the fury sizzling from him at twenty paces.

'Charlotta. At last,' he drawled, his black molten gaze capturing hers as he closed the distance between them, hauled her into his arms, and crushed her against his broad chest. 'I came at your call, *cara*.' His deep accented voice resounded in her ear, and for a split second she remained frozen. Then she trembled helplessly, the familiar wild excitement rushing through her veins as he angled his head and took her slightly parted lips, probing straight between them with a savage, possessive passion that left her breathless and weak at the knees when he finally ended the kiss.

Heavy-lidded black eyes gleamed steadily down at her flushed face and slightly swollen mouth. 'You missed me...yes?' he prompted.

Charlie nodded her head. Jake was here, and he still wanted her.

'Good. Then perhaps you would care to introduce me to your companion.' He recognised the man from the photograph, but Jake had a point to make.

'My companion?' Charlie was not thinking straight; in fact she was having trouble thinking at all. She lifted puzzled eyes to his face, and was taken aback to discover he was looking coolly over her head. Only then did she remember Dave. She turned brick-red and tried to ease out of Jake's hold, but he was having none of it. Instead he simply spun her around, one strong arm curved across her bare waist trapping her back against his chest.

His free hand he offered towards Dave, his blatantly possessive masculine stance saying clearer than words that she was his woman. 'Jake d'Amato, and you are?'

Cool and calm, Dave took the extended hand. 'Dave Watts. A very old friend of the family and a kind of honorary dad to Charlie since the death of her parents.'

'Really. I trust not of the sugar variety.'

'Definitely not,' Dave said bluntly. 'But I can see why you would be worried. She is very sweet.'

Charlie was shocked at Jake's outrageous comment and she felt the sudden tension in his body. Twisting her head, she glanced up at him. His dark eyes were narrowed with piercing intensity on Dave, and, twisting back, she saw Dave was equally intense. They resembled nothing so much as two great predatory beasts meeting head to head before fighting to the death.

Then it struck her. Jake's passionate kiss had been arrogant macho posturing at the sight of Dave. Jake didn't love her, but his massive ego would not allow him to entertain the thought she might have another man. Simmering with resentment, she watched in silence as the two men eyeballed each other. Then suddenly Dave laughed out loud.

'You'll do.' He slapped Jake on the back as if they had been friends for years. 'But hurt her and you'll have me to reckon with. And now I better go and chase up the boys, before they cause any damage. See you later, Charlie.' And he walked away.

She'd been unwilling to cause a scene in front of Dave, but Charlie had no such qualms when he left. 'Let go of me, you big jerk,' she snapped and twisted violently in Jake's hold.

'Certainly.' Jake spun her around to face him. 'But first,

tell me, where is Dave's wife? He seems overly protective of you as a happily married man,' he demanded, all hard male arrogance.

'Lisa died last year,' Charlie said flatly. 'And before you insinuate Dave is my lover, let me tell you not all men have the morals of a sewer rat.'

'Implying I have?' Jake drawled. He was an astute judge of character, and he knew his own sex well. The arm Dave had had around Charlotte's waist had not been avuncular, and given half a chance Dave would take it. But not any more. Jake had made that plain. As for Charlotte…his intense dark eyes swept over her beautiful face. She looked the picture of innocence, but then she always had looked innocent. It was the first thing he had noticed about her at the art gallery before he had seen her cynical smile and dismissive shake of her head when viewing the painting and dismissed it as play-acting. But then she had also felt innocent, he recalled, as the first time they had made love flashed in his mind. Her startled gasp, her incredible hot, tight body was not a good image to remember when he was already rigid with desire, and, dropping his arm from her waist, he stepped back. He adjusted his suit jacket and stuck his hands into the pocket of his tailored trousers, his fingers curling into fists.

The jury was still out on Charlotte. The fury that had engulfed him when Marta had passed on Charlotte's message this morning and fuelled his immediate flight to England was still simmering.

'If the cap fits,' Charlie sneered, lifting stormy blue eyes to his, and was even more incensed. Jake was so suave, so in control. He was immaculately clad in a tailored slate-grey business suit, and he should have looked incongruous in the casual setting, but he didn't. He looked magnificent, swaying back on his heels waiting…and watching.

The silence lengthened, and the tension. Biting her lips, she reined in her temper. 'What are you doing here, Jake?'

She was no fool. His passionate embrace on arriving had been nothing more than his high-handed way of manipulating her feelings in front of Dave. But no matter how hurt and suspicious she was, she still wanted Jake. She had ached and cried over him for five painful weeks, in a roller-coaster ride of emotions, ecstatic when he called and plagued with doubt when he didn't. Ashamed of her weakness, she tilted her chin. 'Apart from insulting my friend, that is.'

Jake studied her with fixed attention, his dark eyes gleaming below thick black lashes. He wondered if she had any idea how desirable she looked, her lovely face flushed with anger and her chin tilted at a defiant angle. 'I don't wish to argue with you over your friend.'

'I bet you don't,' Charlie mocked, the picture in the magazine still fresh in her mind. Jake was a two-timing snake. 'Enjoy yourself in New York, did you? I hear you met up with your *old friend* Melissa,' she snarled and watched as his black brows drew together in a frown.

'You saw the magazine article,' he said, with a smug smile dawning that made her want to knock it off his face.

'Dinner good, was it? Or was the smile on your face for the afters you were anticipating?'

'Very good, and it was for a very good cause,' Jake said silkily. Charlotte was jealous and, much as he was tempted to play her along, there were more important matters at stake here. 'Melissa *is* an old friend, and, yes, before you ask, we were lovers, but it was over months before I met you. She left me for another wealthy man who, as it happens, was her date at the dinner—not I.'

'She left you!' Charlie exclaimed. Furious with the man, she still found it incredible that any woman would willingly dump Jake d'Amato.

He shrugged. 'It was no big deal. A mutual parting of the ways.' Charlie was inclined to believe him, because she knew from personal experience Jake was a workaholic and she doubted any woman was a big deal to him, including herself. 'But enough about my past love life. It is the present I am here to talk about, and preferably not in public view.'

Only then was Charlie aware there were a few guests strolling around the garden. She went from outraged anger to mortification in one second flat.

'Unless of course you would like everyone in the hotel to know you are pregnant. After all, you had no hesitation in telling my housekeeper before me. That is why you called me, isn't it?' he demanded curtly.

Fiery colour burned her cheeks. Her Italian must have been better than she thought. Jake knew she was pregnant. As if that were not bad enough, so did almost everyone in the hotel, and she had a horrible suspicion that if Jake ever discovered he was the last to find out, he was not going to be delighted.

'I—I—uh, yes. And it seems like a good idea to talk in private,' she said, her huge eyes studiously avoiding his. 'If you'll follow me, my home is around the back. Over there, the west wing, actually.'

CHAPTER SEVEN

CHARLIE heaved a sigh of relief when they finally reached the safety of her sitting room without encountering anyone. 'Would you like a drink? Tea or coffee?' She headed for the kitchen, and turned. 'Or something stronger,' she suggested politely. Jake was standing in the middle of the room, big, dark and threatening.

'No, thank you. I've had a stomach full of your English tea.' By the grim glance he gave her, he'd had enough of her as well.

Charlie ran clammy hands down her shorts, hovering in the kitchen doorway, uncertain what to do next. Her shock and delight at his arrival had quickly changed to fury and finally embarrassment. She should never have made that phone call. 'I—I take it you got my message,' she said, swallowing nervously, her heart beating like a drum in her chest.

'Yes.' His dark eyes didn't leave her face as he moved to stop a few inches in front of her. 'Interesting, Charlotte: your knowledge of Italian has improved enough to tell my housekeeper you are pregnant, and I am going to be a papa. Not something I appreciated,' he said through gritted teeth. 'Nor having to disturb my pilot on a Sunday and fly halfway across Europe to discover the truth.'

She had never seen him so angry. It was in every line of his big taut body, intimidating in its intensity. 'You could have just phoned,' Charlie murmured when he continued to stand and stare grimly at her, and she lowered her eyes, unable to meet the hard censure in his.

The call had been foolish, she knew, but then she had been hurting badly. She had told him she loved him, laid her heart on the line in the hope he cared, and yet he had not called her for a month—and to see a picture of him in a magazine with another woman… She had flipped. Her hunger for him was an ever-present ache; the longing to see his rare brilliant smile, to hear his voice, to touch him, haunted her dreams.

'No, I could not,' he said. 'A phone call wouldn't do for me. I want to be looking into your eyes when you tell me I am going to be a father.' His dark eyes narrowed to angry slits, and he caught her chin with a thumb and finger and forced her to look at him. 'Are you pregnant, Charlotte?'

'Yes, I am,' she said bluntly. She was thrilled and excited at the prospect, but also frightened, and she wanted nothing more than for Jake to take her in his arms and tell her it would be all right. But by the look on his face she doubted he would.

'And just when did you fall pregnant?' he demanded roughly.

'Seven weeks ago.' She still had not got over the shock that she had got pregnant the first or second time she had made love. 'How unlucky is that?' Charlie didn't realise she had spoken her thought out loud until his hand fell abruptly from her chin and he stepped back and looked at her as if she were contaminated. She saw the humourless smile that twisted his firm lips and flinched at the venom in it.

'Unlucky?' His dark eyes held tightly leashed rage. 'For me, maybe, but damned convenient for you. Amazingly, it is exactly how long we have known each other.'

Jake was madder than hell. It was so obvious: she had put him squarely in the frame as the father…but was he? No woman had enraged and inflamed him as comprehensively as Charlotte. He had tried to put her out of his mind, but his body would not let him, a galling admission to make, but not one he intended to act on. His dark eyes raked assessingly over her. The tiny white shorts hugged her hips like a second skin, and her stomach still appeared flat, but perhaps her breasts were a little fuller... No! He didn't want to go there. Yes, he did. But he had no intention of being conned by a blue-eyed little gold digger, however desirable, his hard eyes sweeping back up to her lovely face.

'Isn't it rather early to have a pregnancy confirmed?' he queried with biting cynicism. 'Unless the woman in question is eager to get pregnant.'

'Not if you are as sick as a chip every day for three weeks,' she flashed, looking up at him, and stopped. 'You don't believe me,' she said slowly. She could see it in his eyes, in the cynical curl of his lips. She shook her head, and, turning away from him, she crossed to the sofa and collapsed onto it, folding her arms around her waist, suddenly cold. It had never occurred to her Jake wouldn't believe her.

'I never said that,' he pointed out, following her.

'You didn't need to,' she flared back at him. She could see the anger in every tense line of his body, hear it in every word he spoke. The Jake she loved, the Jake she thought she knew, was not this furious stranger towering over her.

'Can you blame me? You would not be the first woman to try and trap a wealthy husband with a mythical pregnancy. I want proof.'

A wealthy...proof... Charlie heaved in a shuddering breath. She was slow to anger, but this arrogant man standing before her had succeeded in doing just that. Jake had arrived at her home unannounced, insulted her and her friend, and then had the colossal nerve to suggest she was lying and was only after his money.

Fury made her leap up from the sofa and stand glaring at

him. 'Call yourself a man?' she derided, her eyes flashing blue flame. 'You sleep with me for a fortnight and then string me along with a couple of calls, ignore me for a month, and then you come charging over here in your private jet, full of self-righteous rage. Terrified I might cost you *money*,' she said with enough scorn to make him clench his fists at his sides to control his anger. 'Demanding proof I'm pregnant.' Shaking with rage, she shoved him in the chest with the flat of her hand, and his mouth tightened to a thin line, but he let her. 'What do you suggest?' she demanded hysterically. 'I slash my belly open to show you? Is that it, is that what you really want—a convenient termination? Is that cheap enough for you?'

Jake's cool façade cracked wide open and he paled like a man in shock. 'No. *Dio*, no.' His strong hands reached out to grasp her shaking shoulders and he pulled her to him, his face only inches from her own. 'Don't say that, Charlotte, don't even think it.' His black eyes, wide with horror, were fixed on hers, his fingers biting into her flesh.

Shocked out of her near hysterics by the force of his reaction, she snapped, 'Don't worry, I have every intention of keeping my child. And let go of me, you're hurting me.'

Jake drew in a deep, audible breath. 'I didn't realise.' His hands gentled on her shoulders, but he did not let her go.

Which was just as well because Charlie suddenly felt weak. 'What a disaster,' she murmured. Her hormones were all over the place, and the emotional turmoil of the past few weeks was finally getting to her. And discovering the father of her child thought she was after his money didn't help. The only positive was Jake had made it very clear he didn't want her to terminate the pregnancy.

'It does not have to be a disaster,' Jake said. 'I will marry you.'

Her head jerked up. 'Marry—? If that was a proposal it

lacked something in the offering,' she said bluntly. 'I am having this baby, and, I can assure you, living as I do, I am in an ideal position to bring up my own child.' She was being perverse, she knew. Jake was offering her everything she had ever dreamed of, and half an hour ago she would have jumped at the chance, but now she was no longer so sure. She had never heard him so angry or so insulting.

Jake stiffened, his hands dropping from her shoulders, and suddenly he was back to his cool, arrogant best, all trace of emotion gone, more like the Jake she knew so well. 'Don't be ridiculous. There is nothing ideal about bringing up a child without a father. Believe me, I know. So we will get married as soon as it can be arranged.'

He was right, she knew. So why was she so reluctant? Because she wanted it all: she wanted Jake to love her, as she loved him. Was she being unreasonable?

'You know it makes sense,' he prompted. His dark eyes meshed with hers, and something in the glittering depths made her heart twist. 'What I said before about being trapped into marriage, I didn't mean it—not with you, never with you. But I was shocked and mad at the way I heard the news, and reacted badly.'

'Very,' she said dryly, but she could understand. Telling his housekeeper had been a bit over the top.

'The two weeks we were together were the happiest I have spent in my life,' he said, and Charlie felt a glimmer of hope ignite in her heart. 'We are good together.' He lifted a finger and trailed it gently down her cheek. 'You know we are, better than good. Marry me. You know you want to.' His hand slipped down to curve her waist and his hand on her naked flesh sent a shiver down her spine.

Jake was the only man in the world for her and, with his eyes still locked to hers, the warmth in them unmistakable, she wondered why she was arguing with him. He was offering her everything she ever wanted. If only he could say the word *love*.

Then he broke the eye contact and his hand moved to rest on her flat stomach, a slow smile curving his wide mouth. 'I take it the child is mine. Not that it matters.'

Fury swept through her again and she batted his hand away. 'Yes, it damn well is!' She glared at him, her eyes wild with outrage. 'You are the only man I was ever dumb enough to sleep with in my life, and look where that got me!' she snarled, mortally offended he even needed to ask.

She felt him tense and saw a gleam of incredible emotion in his dark eyes before long lashes lowered, masking his expression. 'All the more reason why you should marry me,' he argued. 'You find me irresistible among men.' A sudden rare brilliant smile illuminated his extraordinarily handsome features. 'You love me.'

'Sex, that's all it was,' Charlie shot back. 'You conceited jerk, that's all I was…' She stopped, as the last of his insulting question registered. *Not that it matters.* He had said—Jake was prepared to marry her unconditionally. He must love her even if he could not say the words.

'No,' Jake denied. 'It was never just sex with you and me.'

An image flashed before him of Charlotte naked in the shower their first night together, her legs wrapped around his waist, her eyes wide and incredulous as he had surged into her sleek, silken body without a thought of protection. And earlier, when he'd registered the tightness of her incredible body, her startled gasp, and concluded it must have been a while since she had been with a man. Now he knew the truth: she had been a virgin, and his mouth twisted in a grimace of self-recrimination. He had treated her abominably. It wasn't surprising she was reluctant to marry him.

His heavy-lidded eyes swept over her lovely face and her

scantily clad body. He was only a hand's reach away; he could feel her body heat, scent her unique fragrance, and the rigid control he had managed to maintain over his rampant libido finally snapped.

Charlie flinched as he closed the distance between them and rested a strong, lean hand on her shoulder. 'Charlotta,' he said. 'Please marry me.'

Her head told her to wait, step away. But her heart kept her still, the soft *please* echoing in her head. She felt the tremor in the hand that rested on her shoulder. He was so close that she could see the tell-tale darkening of his gorgeous eyes. And ultimately she said, 'Yes,' because she loved him and could not say no.

'*Dio grazia.*' Jake drew her into his arms, his mouth finding hers with unerring accuracy.

For Charlie it was like coming home, her body melting into his. Five long weeks of abstinence were echoed in the hunger of his mouth, the hot, unbridled passion that swept away all her doubts in a flood of excitement. She felt the hardness of his body against hers, and squirmed ecstatically against him. Jake was back and she wanted his hands on her breasts, her thighs, everywhere. She was starving for his touch, the taste of him, and she wrapped her arms around his neck, her fingers burrowing through the thick dark hair of his head, holding him to her.

He groaned against her mouth. '*Dio*, Charlotte, I have missed you, missed this.' His hands lifted and cupped her breasts, his fingers skimming over the cotton that covered her swelling flesh, and she moaned as his fingers plucked the sensitised peaks and a quick stab of arousal lanced from her nipples to her loins.

'Oh, Jake, I've missed you too, so much,' she sighed ecstatically as he nipped her bottom lip between his teeth, and kissed her again with a deep, hungry passion until she was mindless and shaking in his arms. 'I love you so much, love what you do to me,' she moaned, almost incoherently—but not quite.

'I know.' Jake smiled against her mouth. It was one of the things he adored about her, she was such a vocal lover, and slowly he slid his hand down her body. His long fingers curled beneath the hem of her shorts and he cupped her between her thighs, and she moaned his name again.

'Charlie, I need the keys to the safe...'

Jake's hand shot from between her thighs to grip her around the waist and hold her tight against him as he let fly with a string of Italian curses that would have made the devil blush.

'Oops! Not the best of timing, but I am glad to see you've kissed and made up.' Her manager's voice finally got through to Charlie's love-hazed mind.

'Jeff!' she squeaked, pushing against Jake's chest, her face the colour of a beetroot. 'Have you never heard of knocking?' She tried to squirm out of Jake's hold, dying inside with embarrassment.

'My sentiments exactly,' Jake said sardonically, looking at the other man over the top of Charlotte's head.

'Sorry.' Jeff grinned, looking not in the least sorry. 'So, Charlie, does this mean I can tell the staff wedding bells are on the cards, and finally put them out of their misery?' he queried, tongue in cheek.

Jake stilled, his brows drawing together in a puzzled frown, and then he suddenly grinned. 'Ah, now I understand the staff's attitude,' he said dryly.

'What attitude?' Charlie demanded. 'Was someone rude to you?'

'Not exactly, but let me guess. They all know you're pregnant, and they all know my name.'

'Well, I might have mentioned you in passing.' She had the grace to blush.

Jake laughed out loud, his arm tightening around her shoulders. 'As you appear to have been doing all the talking so far, at least allow me to make this announcement. As the man concerned, it is only fair,' he added mockingly.

Charlie stayed dumb.

'Jeff, isn't it? I believe we met earlier. As you have seen for yourself, Charlotte and I can't keep our hands off each other, and so, yes, we are getting married, just as soon as it can be arranged. Feel free to tell everyone. If you don't, I'm sure Charlotte will.'

'Certainly, Mr d'Amato.' Jeff laughed. 'Obviously you know our Charlie well. I'll just get the keys and leave.'

'So, Charlotte, it is done. We are to marry—no going back.' He drew her into his arms again.

'I won't change my mind.' Never one to duck a challenge, she asked bluntly, 'Is it because I'm pregnant? Or do you really love me?'

'Yes, *cara*. I adore you.' And he kissed her.

They were married two weeks later in an outdoor ceremony in the grounds of the hotel. The wedding breakfast was over and the speeches done, and Charlie, with Jake's arm around her shoulder, was still in shock from the speed of it all.

'One more and that's it.' Diego Fortuna, Jake's best man, was a famous fashion photographer.

'I feel as though I should strike a pose or something,' Charlie murmured, slightly intimidated.

'The *something* being, let's get out of here. I want you to myself. And I don't want to waste any more of our wedding day, or more importantly wedding night, chatting to your friends—nice as they are,' Jake added, his dark eyes roaming over the exquisite vision in ivory silk at his side.

His wife. He congratulated himself on having made the right decision. He had discovered, on being introduced to quite a few of her male friends, that she was a member of the local mountain rescue team. Not only was she beautiful, and very beddable and carrying his child, she was also brave, though the climbing would have to stop, he decided. He didn't believe in love, but he had no trouble accepting Charlotte's declarations of love. Life didn't get any better than this.

'You have a one-track mind.' Charlie chuckled, her blue eyes laughing up at him.

'Do you blame me? It has been seven weeks.'

'No, I can't wait either,' she said honestly. She had never felt more loved, more cherished in her life than when the registrar had said, 'You may kiss the bride,' and Jake had taken her in his arms, and kissed her with a tenderness that had brought tears to her eyes. But now she wanted more.

The day he had proposed had turned into a party at the hotel, and by accident or design Jeff and Dave had turned it into a stag night for Jake. Pressure of business had forced Jake to leave early the next morning. Even so, he had with Jeff and Dave's assistance organised everything long distance. The only thing Charlie had done was shop for her trousseau. She had bought lacy underwear and a few totally impractical flimsy nightgowns. She had limited herself to one cocktail dress with the prospect of a bulging tummy in mind, and, ever practical, for her wedding outfit she had chosen an exquisitely made designer suit.

A sophisticated column of ivory silk, the dress was strapless and revealed a hint of cleavage before skimming her still slender figure to end just on her knees. Apart from a posy of rosebuds, her only other adornment was a choker of pearls around her throat. Jake had flown in last night and given them to her over dinner at the hotel, but they had not spent the night together. Amy, the receptionist, had made sure of that, saying it was unlucky, and sharing Charlie's room herself, much to Jake's chagrin.

Diego, the best man, had arrived this morning, and Charlie had met him for a few moments before the ceremony. He and Jake had been room-mates at college and were old friends, and he was almost as handsome as Jake.

'Right, that's it,' Diego cried. 'I need a drink.'

Charlie flung her posy into the crowd, and Amy, her bridesmaid, caught it amid much laughter. A few moments later Amy stepped forward and handed Charlie her suit jacket and her purse. 'Enjoy your honeymoon and have a wonderful life.'

'Thanks.' Charlie grinned.

'Thanks,' Jake echoed. 'Pressure of work means the honeymoon is on hold for the moment, unfortunately, but the wedding night isn't. Though we won't even have that if the damn car doesn't show up. I need to have a word with Dave,' he muttered darkly. Pressing a swift kiss on Charlie's smiling lips, he added, 'Wait here, I'm going to find out what's happened.'

Charlie watched her new husband stroll purposefully towards the hapless Dave. If she knew Dave, he had probably hijacked the car and covered it with bottles and cans and cheesy comments. She heaved a sigh of pure delight. This was the happiest day of her life.

'Big sigh for a new bride,' Diego said, reappearing with a glass of champagne in his hand.

'A sigh of pure happiness,' Charlie answered, slanting Diego a brilliant smile before her gaze sought out her husband. He looked so devastatingly handsome in a tailored silver-grey three-piece suit and she watched as he gesticulated wildly with one hand towards the drive. He was so very Latin, and she loved him.

'Changing your name from Summerville to d'Amato obviously suits you,' Diego said and drained the champagne.

'Yes, it does,' Charlie murmured, not paying much attention. All her thoughts were with Jake and the night ahead.

'Are you any relation to the artist Robert Summerville?' Diego asked.

'Yes, he was my father. In fact he was responsible for my meeting Jake,' she offered, remembering the first time she had seen Jake in the art gallery.

'Ah! Now I see,' Diego exclaimed. 'You have known Jake for much longer than I thought. I did wonder when he said he was getting married in two weeks. He is not the type to act in haste. But you must have known Anna when she lived with your father. You met Jake through her—or at her funeral, perhaps?' He shook his dark head. 'Her death so soon after your father's demise was such a tragedy.'

Charlie's brow furrowed as the full import of Diego's words sank in. Suddenly the nude painting Jake had bought when she met him loomed large in her mind. With it came the conviction she now had a name for her father's ex-lover—Anna—and if Diego was to be believed, she had been a close personal friend of Jake. But why hadn't Jake said anything?

Feeling a sudden chill that had nothing to do with the sunny weather, she slipped on the short jacket that matched her dress. 'You mean Anna with the beautiful long dark hair, almost to her thighs?' she queried softly, describing the woman in the portrait.

'That's her. So you did know her. It was a sad business all around, no? But what am I thinking of?' Diego grinned. 'Forgive me. Today is not a day for recalling past losses. Life is for celebrating.' He drained his brandy glass. 'Jake is a very lucky guy to have found you. I wish I had seen you first,' he added with a teasing, slightly inebriated glint in his eyes.

'You're a charmer.' Charlie smiled, but with difficulty. Diego had aroused a suspicion in her mind. There was a mystery here she did not understand. But he was right: this was not a day for recalling the past, but for looking forward to the future. Jake loved her, Jake had married her, and nothing was going to spoil her day.

'I was always the charmer,' Diego asserted, sliding an arm around her waist. 'And Jake was always the worker. But he did have his moments. Mostly with engines, rather than women,' he added drolly. 'Though he did once take a girl out on a powerboat he built, and it sank. Needless to say, she never spoke to him again.'

Twenty feet away Dave listened to Jake's tirade before slapping him on the back. 'Relax, Jake, the car will be here in five minutes. I understand you intend keeping our lovely Charlie in Italy? I hope you realise you're a very lucky man. She's an all-or-nothing kind of woman, so you'd better take very good care of her. We're all going to miss her at International Rapid Rescue. But I've told Charlie we'll be looking forward to seeing her back after she has the baby.'

'You…what?' Jake's black brows arched in amazement, and in the next few minutes he discovered he did not know his wife at all. That Charlotte would willingly risk her life in search and rescue all over the world appalled him. His head reared back, his eyes searching for her across the heads of the guests, and narrowed angrily when he saw she was talking to Diego, and the devil had his arm around her.

'Forget about Charlotte ever working again, Dave. I have other plans for her,' he threw over his shoulder as he made a beeline for her.

'What is this, a mutual admiration society? Get your arm off my wife, Diego.'

'Spoilsport.' Charlie grinned. 'Diego was just telling me about your college exploits.'

'Was he indeed?' Jake put his own arm around Charlotte, drawing her close into his side. He said something in rapid-fire Italian to Diego, who responded equally quickly, then turned a grin of pure devilment on Charlie.

'I am sorry you have to leave so soon, Charlotte. I feel I was just getting to know you, but I understand Jake's haste.' Taking a card from his pocket, he gave it to Charlie. 'This is my number. If you ever get tired of this jealous bozo, give me a call.'

'*Basta*, Diego, and stop trying to pick up my wife on our wedding day,' Jake growled.

'As if I would.' Diego winked at Charlie. 'Though I have tried with the lovely Amy—unfortunately she's already taken. But I now have my eye on a rather attractive barmaid.' Waving his empty glass, he said, 'Wish me luck,' and headed for the bar.

'Diego is fun. I like him.'

Moving her supple body in front of him, Jake looked down into her luminous sapphire eyes. 'Not too much, I trust; you're my wife now.' With his free hand he cradled the back of her head and kissed her passionately.

A scarlet-faced Charlie heard the cheers of the guests, and Dave's yell that the wedding car had arrived, in something of a daze. Jake took an exaggerated bow, and she had to laugh as he swung her into his arms and carried her to the waiting vehicle.

'Oh, my God!' she squealed. She had been right about the cans, bottles and slightly dubious graffiti scrolled all over the white limousine. But Jake, not in the least fazed, lowered her into the back seat and quickly followed her.

'Now I see why the car was delayed.' He chuckled and with a single finger he outlined her softly parted lips. 'But you, my darling wife, are worth any wait. You're so beautiful, you make me ache.' And his mouth took hers in a kiss of such wondrous promise and passion she knew that whatever the future held for them she would always love Jake—her husband.

CHAPTER EIGHT

A LIMOUSINE met them at Genoa airport and, tucked under Jake's arm, Charlie gazed out of the window as the car cruised along a winding road by the sea and into the hills, stopping at a massive pair of iron gates, complete with gatehouse. A security guard opened the gates and the car sped up a mile-long drive to what to Charlie looked like a mansion.

Jake helped her out of the car and she looked up in awe. The house was magnificent. Of surprisingly modern design, it was mostly constructed in glass and steel. It was situated a few miles from Genoa, with the Dolomites as a backdrop, and a spectacular view of the Mediterranean to the front.

'Your new home, Signora d'Amato. Do you like it?'

'It's spectacular.' Laughing, Jake swept her up in his arms and carried her through the massive double doors. 'Oh, my God, a glass staircase! It's fantastic,' Charlie exclaimed, and then she realised a reception committee of two were waiting in the enormous hall.

Lowering her to her feet, Jake introduced her to Marta, a pretty, dark-haired lady, and Charlie blushed as she shook her hand, remembering her crazy call. Then she was introduced to an adorable little boy, Marta's son Aldo, and to Charlie's delight he spoke to her in good schoolboy English. Marta's husband Tomas joined them: he was the chauffeur, and a bottle of champagne was produced and a toast drunk. Then Tomas and his family departed to their cottage in the grounds with smiles and grins, and Jake closed and locked the door behind them.

Charlie looked around. The furniture was an eclectic mix of traditional and modern but it was the paintings that caught her attention. She recognised a Matisse and two Monets.

'At last we are alone.' Jake swept her up in his arms and carried her up the stairs. Her shoes fell off and she tightened her grip around his neck with a startled, 'Oh!'

'One less item to remove.' Jake gave her a wicked grin and they both burst out laughing as he walked into the master bedroom.

With less than his usual grace, he stumbled over her suitcases already deposited in the bedroom. 'Don't you dare drop me,' Charlie commanded, still laughing.

'Never,' Jake responded with an abashed grin. Their eyes met and the laughter stopped.

Slowly he lowered her to her feet, and her eyes widened fractionally as he touched a gentle finger to her lips and traced the upper outline, and then the lower curve. Incredibly she suddenly felt nervous. She had slept with Jake countless times, but this time was different.

Jake's eyes didn't leave hers as he stepped back and shrugged off his jacket and tie. Then, with slow, deliberate movements, he removed the rest of his clothes until he was standing before her, tall and broad-shouldered with bronzed skin sheathing hard-backed muscle and sinew and wearing only white silk briefs that did little to hide his arousal. Warm colour tinged her cheeks, and for a long moment she simply stared, the sexual tension simmering between them.

'No need to be nervous, Charlotte,' Jake said, accurately reading her mind, and closed the distance between them. 'Have I told you today you look beautiful, *cara*?' he asked softly as he lowered his head down to hers.

Warmth flooded her body and became a pulsing heat as

he slid her jacket from her shoulders, and a moan sounded in her throat at the touch of his mouth on her own.

His hands skimmed her breasts, and down her thighs, and in one fluid movement the raw silk dress slid down to pool at her feet leaving her naked except for delicate white lace French panties.

Jake stepped back, the better to appreciate her lush shapely body tantalisingly enhanced by the pearl choker and the seductively cut lace panties. Her breasts were fuller, her stomach where his child lay still flat.

'I feel as if I have waited a lifetime to see you like this.'

It was incomprehensible, but Charlie, who had the confidence to do anything, was suddenly plagued by self-doubt as Jake's dark, obsessive gaze roamed intently over her. He was so perfect, tall and golden, and she wanted to be perfect for him, but she was pregnant and it was over seven weeks since they had been together. Her breasts were fuller, not so firm, and Jake was used to perfection: his house, his art. Her eyes flicked past him in a brief panicky movement and she saw the picture on the wall behind him. It was a Gauguin, an island woman with long black hair, and it reminded her of another painting and Diego's comment about Anna.

Jake's hands reached for her and settled on her waist.

'Who was Anna?' She murmured the thought even as her eyes were drawn back to meet smouldering black and the uninhibited desire, the raw hunger she saw there ignited a fire deep in her belly.

But as she swayed towards him his head reared back, his fingers digging into her waist almost to the point of pain in a knee-jerk reaction to her question. 'Where the hell did that come from?' he ground out harshly.

'It was nothing,' she said quickly. 'I caught sight of the

painting on the wall and it reminded me of the painting you bought and something Diego said today.'

Jake's face hardened, but his hands eased slightly on her waist. 'Diego has a big mouth. Whatever he said, forget it, and drop the subject.'

If the command had not been so curtly delivered Charlie might have done so, but his strange attitude made her all the more determined to get to the bottom of the mystery.

Before she could lose her nerve she said, 'Diego thought you and I might have met earlier, because she was my father's lover and also a friend of yours. He actually thought Anna might have introduced us.' Drawing in a shaky breath, she asked the question she had wanted to avoid. 'Was she an ex-lover of yours?'

'*Dio*, no.' Jake was angry, ridiculously angry, and he had no right to be. Her question was ill-timed, but perfectly valid. Unfortunately, the subject of Anna aroused conflicting emotions inside him: the loyalty he owed to the Lasios, the guilt he could not quite dismiss, and the frustration he felt that his wife of a few hours was looking at him with puzzled rather than passion-filled eyes.

Flattening her hands on his shoulders, she tilted back her head. 'Then why won't you tell me who she was?'

'You know who she was,' he said with a harsh laugh that was no laugh at all. 'She was the lover of your lecherous father, and over twenty years his junior. Now let's forget her, and concentrate on us.' He pulled her hard against him. 'This is our wedding night, and arguing with you was not what I had in mind.'

He was being evasive, but he was also right. A few seconds of feminine insecurity and she had ruined the mood. Why hadn't she kept her mouth shut? Because she was curious about the mysterious Anna of the portrait. She sighed, answering her own question.

'I'd like to think that was a sigh for me, for sex,' Jake said dryly. 'But I rather think it is frustration of another sort: your insatiable curiosity about a certain painting.'

He had read her mind and she flushed a little, but there was no point in denying it.

He shrugged his broad shoulders, his austerely handsome face suddenly devoid of all expression. 'You want the truth? Why not? According to all the marriage pundits, it's the way to go for a good marriage and so far ours appears to be going nowhere fast.' His voice was sardonic. 'Anna was my foster-sister, and I loved her. I was there when she was born, I watched her grow into a beautiful young woman, and I saw her destroyed by your father. She imagined herself in love with him and for two years she thought he was going to marry her.'

Charlie paled as the full import of his words sank in. The relief she had felt that Anna had never been Jake's lover vanished as she realised the truth was much worse. An ex-lover could be forgotten, but a sister never.

When she had met Jake he'd told her the painting was the only one he wanted. Not surprising if, as Diego had said, Anna had died recently. She remembered the look in the girl's eyes. And she remembered the glazed look in Jake's when he'd looked at it. How he must have hated to see her exposed like that...

A host of moments with Jake spun in the whirlpool of her mind, and began to assume a different meaning. Their first night together. She recalled his coldness after they had made love, his questioning her as to what she thought about an older man taking a young woman as a lover. Naively she had thought he was referring to the twelve-year gap between them. Now she realised he must have been thinking of her father.

She caught her breath in shock. 'My God! You hated my father.' She stared at him in horror. 'I'm right, aren't I?'

'I never met him, but, yes, I hated him.' Jake slid a lean hand around her waist. 'But don't let it bother you.' His voice was almost mocking. 'The man is dead, as is Anna. And you are my wife.' His other hand stroked down her throat and deftly unfastened the choker so it fell unheeded to the floor before trailing lower to cup her breast, a thumb testing the hardening peak. 'And we have wasted enough time already.'

'No.' She tried to deny him, but her treacherous flesh was already craving more. 'Let go of me,' she said jaggedly in an atmosphere suddenly raw with sexual tension. 'We need to talk.'

'What you need is very evident.' His dark eyes slanted down to her naked breast, where the rigid tip was a real give-away, then back to her face. His mouth touched hers, very lightly. 'And it certainly isn't talk. It is me, *cara*.'

The arrogance of his comment and the truth of it mortified her and inflamed her temper at one and the same time. He admitted he hated her father and in the next breath expected her to fall into his arms. His conceit was monumental, and, twisting out of his hold, she took a hasty step back and crossed her arms defensively over her aching breasts.

She was an intelligent woman, and with hindsight suddenly a lot of little things he had said made sense. While she had been driven by an all-consuming desire, even love, for Jake straight into his bed, she was now forced to question what had been his real motivation. The day they had gone to the museum, he had joked about his motivation, and the answer, she saw now, had been enigmatic.

Closing her eyes for a moment, she slowly fought to achieve a semblance of self-control, then, opening them again, she flicked a glance at his hard, handsome face.

'No, Jake, what I need from you is the truth,' she said, proud of her ability to control the tremor in her voice, even though inside she was shaking like a leaf. 'Why did you ask Ted to introduce you to me at the gallery? Surely if you hated my father so much I must have been the last person you would want to know?' Her mouth was dry as she waited for his response.

'I was curious to see what kind of daughter a man who had so little respect for women had produced. But what does it matter now?' He shrugged. 'We are married and have the future to look forward to.'

She saw the familiar shuttered look in his eyes that protected his deepest thoughts, and knew he was not telling her the whole truth. But she was achingly aware of how much she loved him. Her wedding night was fast turning into a nightmare, not what she wanted at all. Jake was right, none of it mattered any more, and she unfolded her arms and took a tentative step towards him.

'I am sorry about your sister, Jake.' She swallowed hard. The words were inadequate, she knew. 'No one knows better than me what a womanising rogue my father was. And if Anna loved him it must have been terrible for her when he died. I know how I felt, and I know the hurt you must have felt when Anna died. What can I say?'

Slowly his eyes drifted over her—assessing eyes that did not betray a flicker of warmth. Not the reaction she had expected for her sympathy. 'Nothing, nothing at all,' he finally drawled. His arm once more slipped around her waist, and with his free hand he tilted her head back. 'It has already been said.' And the sizzling scorn in the black eyes that clashed with hers sent a shiver of fear snaking down her spine. 'Your father sent Anna away and we both know why. So you can drop the mock sympathy.' His mouth twisted in a hard, humourless smile. 'You refused to meet her.'

For a split second Charlie was convinced she had heard wrong. But his dark eyes held contempt and the immobility of his hard features told her she had not.

'I refused to meet her?' she parroted. When she had visited her dad for a couple of weeks three months before his death, he had told her he was between lovers. Not that she'd believed him; it had been his standard response for years in his misguided attempt to protect Charlie from his women. But Jake had a different view. Why, she had no idea.

'Anna told me everything. Your father sent her away because his *bitch of a daughter* insisted upon it. Apparently the girl was arriving for a holiday and she was so selfish she refused to share her father with his lover. Brave of you to admit it, I suppose,' Jake allowed dryly.

'I can't believe what you're saying!' Charlie shook her head free of his controlling fingers, her mind sifting the information Jake had given her with lightning speed. The full horror of what he implied chilled her to the bone, the conclusion unmistakable. The relationship between her father and Anna was immaterial. Jake, her lover, her husband, thought she was a selfish bitch.

'No,' she murmured, briefly closing her eyes, Jake could not possibly believe that of her. She opened them again; her stunned gaze met his. 'I loved my father, but—' She was going to explain it was her father who never allowed her to meet his lovers, not the other way around.

'But, as they say, the rest is history,' Jake cut in mockingly. 'Your father died—if he hadn't I would have destroyed him myself—and Anna crashed her car into a tree a few months later and followed him to the grave. But on the upside you made a lot of money, so it's not all doom and gloom. Now forget it. The past is past. It is the present that concerns me.'

The past shapes the future. Charlie had read that somewhere, and Jake's throwaway comments that he would have destroyed her father given the chance, and about the money he thought she'd made by his death, made her sick to her stomach. But she had to hear the truth from his mouth, however much it hurt. She had been blinded by love for far too long.

She tried to pull free of him, but he tightened his arm around her waist and she refused to demean herself by struggling. 'Given you thought I was not just a selfish bitch, but greedy as well...' her voice was flat and toneless, and she wondered how it was possible for her skin to burn at the contact with his while an icy chill built up inside her '...tell me again why you asked Ted to introduce us. The truth, this time.'

The muscles in his jaw tightened for an instant, and then his chiselled features relaxed, and his dark eyes gleamed with a hint of self-deprecatory humour as they meshed with hers. 'Truthfully? Because Anna had given me the impression Summerville's daughter was a child. When Ted told me you were a businesswoman who had sanctioned the exhibition, I wanted to meet you. What I could forgive in a child, I could not forgive in an adult, and I admit revenge did cross my mind. Poetic justice, if you like. But to be honest, I took one look at you and wanted you, *cara*. Still do.'

Revenge was such an ugly word, and such an ugly emotion, and at first Charlie did not want to believe what she was hearing. But as it sank in she was horrified at his colossal confidence, his despicable arrogance—that he would assume she was such a pushover that she would accept such an explanation and continue as though nothing had happened. She swallowed hard. 'Why did you ask me to marry you?' She had to know the worst.

'You are carrying my child, Charlotte.' His free hand slipped to her stomach and rested there.

Tears of anger and pain stung her eyes, and she fought them back, achingly aware of his strong, near-naked body touching her own from chest to thigh, but also finally aware—on her wedding night, of all nights—that Jake didn't love her, never had, and probably never would.

She wanted to scream and yell her pain to the world as her heart shattered into a million pieces. But she didn't. Instead the chill inside her grew until a blessed numbness froze the pain and she said, in a voice that seemed to come from a long way off, 'And to think when you proposed, I asked you if you loved me, and you lied and said yes.'

'As I remember you asked if I was marrying you because you were pregnant or because I loved you, and I answered yes, I adored you.' His unreadable eyes swept her carefully controlled features, a smile as insincere as any she had seen curving his beautiful mouth. 'How you interpreted my response was up to you.'

'A question of semantics,' she mocked hollowly, and dragged her gaze from his. The revelations this evening had cut her to the bone. But she could not betray her weakness. She had to be strong, not just for herself but also for her child. With a proud tilt of her head she looked at him coldly, her voice displaying no trace of emotion as she said, 'Be honest, Jake, you don't love me. All I ever was to you was a body to enjoy while you fed your sick need for revenge, but unfortunately I got pregnant.'

'You're wrong. I no longer have any need for revenge, and as for enjoying your body...' His dark eyes gleamed with sardonic humour. 'So far I am not having much luck, but that is about to change.'

His dark head bent and she saw it in his eyes, felt it in the tightening grip of his hands, and she knew he was going to kiss her. Belatedly Charlie lifted her own hands and shoved against his chest. 'No.' She struggled frantically, her hands curling into fists, and she punched him on the chest—anywhere she could reach. 'No, no!' she cried.

His mouth silenced hers and the possessive passion of his kiss and the sudden heated response that arced through her completely shamed her. Charlie tore her mouth from his and struck out wildly, but with his superior height and strength he simply swept her up in his arms, and deposited her surprisingly gently on the bed.

Lashing out with her feet, Charlie scrambled up into a sitting position. 'Don't you touch me, don't you dare,' she yelled. 'And you can take your damn ring!' she cried, twisting desperately at the wedding band on her finger.

Rage tore through Jake and, leaning over her, he grasped her hands in one of his before she could remove the ring from her finger. 'Leave it, Charlotte!' he roared. And as he saw the hurt and fury in her eyes he froze.

What the hell was he doing? Drawing a deep, shuddering breath, he let go of her hands and straightened up. He could not argue with her. She was upset, and she was pregnant.

Frustration riding him, he stared down at her, his eyes raking over her body: the high, full breasts, the narrow waist and the gentle rounded curves of her hips; the transparent scrap of lace she was wearing doing little to hide the shadow of her femininity… No, he could not go there. Abruptly he raised his eyes to her face. She was looking at him as if he had developed two horns and a tail, and it was his own damned fault. Whichever marriage expert had recommended absolute truth needed their head read. If he had not been so out of his mind with sexual hunger for Charlotte, he might have had the sense to keep his mouth shut.

But he wouldn't be in this unenviable position if someone else had kept his mouth shut, he thought bitterly, silently cursing Diego for mentioning Anna and ruining his wedding night. He had burned the damned painting weeks ago. He didn't care about revenge; he didn't care about anything except Charlotte, he realised with shock. His stunned gaze roved over her flushed face, he saw the defiance in her gorgeous eyes, and felt a sharp pang of regret for the loss of her unfeigned adoration. And a frustrated fury he could barely control.

'The only thing I want to leave is you.' Charlotte slotted the words into the lengthening silence. Jake took a step closer. His dark eyes narrowed to angry slits, and she drew in a stunned, slightly unsteady breath.

'You are not going anywhere.' His face was a taut mask of rigidly controlled rage. 'But I will leave.' For one heart-stopping moment she thought he meant for good. 'We will talk about this in the morning.' Dipping down, he retrieved something from the floor and flung it at her. 'When hopefully you remember why you wore that today, and grow up.' And spinning on his heel, he left, slamming the door behind him.

The sound echoed in the sudden silence of the room as Charlie fingered the crumpled wedding dress he had thrown at her, the events of the evening racing through her tormented mind. This was her wedding night. How had it gone so terribly wrong? Because she had finally chipped through Jake's—her husband's—monumental control and discovered the truth, and it was not the love she had hoped and dreamed of.

White-knuckled, she gripped the gown and began to shiver. Acting on autopilot, she slipped off the bed. She found her suitcase and withdrew a blue satin nightgown, then shoved her wedding dress inside and shut the case. She slid the blue satin over her head. It wasn't very warm, but then she had not bought it with warmth in mind. She blinked and blinked again as she walked back to the bed, and lay back down, pulling the sheet up over her shaking body. Then, and only then, she buried her head in a pillow and surrendered to the agony and despair that tore at her very soul. Finally when there were no more tears left, only dry racking sobs, and her stomach ached with the pain, she realised she had to stop—if not for herself, for the sake of the baby.

She didn't know what she was going to do. All she did know was the happy, laughing bride of a few hours ago was no more. Jake had seen to that. 'Damn Jake—damn him to hell,' she muttered under her breath as hurt and anger rose to the fore. Who the hell did he think he was? What right had he to sit in judgement of her or her father's morals when he had the morals of an alley cat by all accounts?

Charlie tossed restlessly on the bed. She had to be strong. Already she was coming to terms with the revelations this evening had brought, and given time she would work out the best plan of action. She was an independent woman, or had been before she had met Jake and let love cloud her judgement—but no more, and no more tears. She rubbed her eyes with the sheet. And if Jake thought she was going to sit around playing the grateful little wife and mother, Jake was in for a rude awakening.

With his name lingering on her lips she fell into an exhausted sleep, unaware that her husband had returned and was staring down at her. He saw the tears that leaked from under her pale lids as she slept, and sorrow dampened his eyes as he quietly turned and left.

CHAPTER NINE

'GOOD, you're awake.'

Charlie shot up in bed, her gaze winging to the door, her eyes widening in shock as Jake, barefoot and wearing a maroon silk robe, entered the room. In his hands was a tray set with breakfast with a vase containing a single red rose as a centrepiece. 'Not quite the conventional honeymoon breakfast of champagne, due to your condition. But I have made you tea and scrambled eggs on toast.' He smiled, approaching the bed.

Jake looked so pleased with himself, Charlie had to fight back a reciprocal smile and consequently she said more harshly than she intended, 'You needn't have bothered.'

'Hostilities resumed, I see,' Jake mocked, his eyes darkening, a muscle tightening in his jaw as he placed the tray down on the bedside table.

For a fleeting moment she regretted ignoring what was obviously an olive branch from Jake, but only for a moment. The hurt had gone too deep for Charlie to forgive or forget. 'I'm pregnant, not an invalid. I could have made my own breakfast.'

'You don't need to; that's Marta's job. But I gave her the day off for some reason that escapes me now,' he said sardonically. He filled a cup with tea and handed it to her and, careful to avoid touching his hand, she took it.

'Thank you,' she murmured, slanting a glance at his handsome face.

A cynical light gleamed in the dark eyes that met hers. '*Prego.* Eat, enjoy, and we will talk.'

'I don't see we have much to talk about. You said it all last night.' She drank the tea, and replaced the cup on the tray. She didn't want to talk; she didn't want to look at him. Charlie felt as though a veil had been torn from her eyes last night and for the first time since she had met Jake she had seen him in his true colours. He was a ruthless, hard-hearted bastard who hit back at anyone who crossed him, as he perceived her father had—and her as well.

'Last night I said too damn much.' Jake snorted disgustedly. 'But the past is dead and buried with your father and Anna. Surely you can see that?' he asked seriously. 'We were married yesterday. Forget last night and let us start again.' Sitting down on the side of the bed, he covered her hand where it lay on the coverlet with his much larger one.

The sensual warmth of his touch triggered an immediate response in Charlie that filled her with dismay and a rising anger. Hastily she jerked her hand away, and, taking a deep calming breath, she raised her head. Blue eyes clashed with black and for a moment she was stunned by the tenderness in Jake's expression—but then, he was a great deceiver, she reminded herself.

'You might find it convenient to forget last night, but I never will. I must have been stark raving mad to marry you. You are a devious, rotten liar.' She had behaved like the world's biggest fool, and it hurt, it hurt like hell to know she had fallen so completely for Jake while he had a totally different agenda. But no way was she compounding her folly by continuing with this sham. 'And I want out of this fiasco of a marriage.' The smile left his handsome face and if she hadn't known him better she would have thought he was in pain, but then his dark brown eyes narrowed to angry slits and the air between them was suddenly electric with tension.

'Don't be ridiculous, Charlotte. I—'

She cut him off sharply. 'I'm not being ridiculous, just stating a fact. I want out.'

Nobody called Jake a liar and got away with it, not even Charlotte. 'Never. You are my wife,' he sliced back, his gaze roaming over her beautiful but mutinous face and lower to where the creamy mounds of her breast were temptingly revealed by the slip of blue satin that passed as a nightgown. Jake's control was stretched to the limit. He felt bad about throwing the dress at her last night, but it had been either that or throwing himself on her. He had had such high hopes this morning when he had made breakfast that she would put the unpleasantness of last night behind her and act like a reasonable adult. But if anything she was more determined to defy him than ever, while he was getting more frustrated by the second, as the ache in his groin reminded him. 'You will stay in my home,' he commanded in a dangerously quiet voice. 'And in my bed. Understand?'

Charlie shivered, her flesh chilled at the deadly certainty with which he voiced his intentions. But she refused to be cowed. She had been a doormat for far too long.

'In your dreams. I'm out of here tomorrow.'

'No.' He shook his head.

Succinct and clearly unmovable. She realised it had not been the most sensible time to tell him when she was still in bed. He was staring at her, his chiselled features as hard as stone while a savage, sensual smile played around his mouth. She tore her gaze from his, but a strong hand cupped her chin and turned her back to face him. Her pulse beat a frantic rhythm through her whole body at his touch, and she was horrified at her own weakness.

'I am not staying here with you. Not now.'

His smile was softly derisive. 'You have no choice in the matter. The security around here is superb. You don't leave without my say-so.'

'You can't force me to stay here. You wouldn't dare,' Charlie flung back at him, but she saw the implacable gleam in his dark eyes and knew he would dare anything to get what he wanted.

'I won't have to. I know you, Charlotte. You want the best for our child and you know that is both parents living together in harmony.' Sliding his hand around the nape of her neck, he urged her head forward, and brushed his lips against her cheek. 'I also know you are too proud to return to England and admit failure,' he added and, dipping his head, captured her mouth in a deeply provocative kiss.

In direct opposition to her will, a slow fire began to course though her veins, bringing every nerve in her body to tingling life. The seductive pressure of his mouth and her own heated response was totally humiliating and yet when he broke the kiss she felt bereft. Then she noticed where his gaze had fixed and, grasping the sheet, she raised it up over her chest, suddenly aware of the brevity of the nightgown she had donned unthinkingly last night.

The dark eyes narrowed knowingly on her flushed face. 'It is allowable, Charlotte,' he mocked. 'You're my wife, the soon-to-be mother of my child. Concentrate on that and we will get along fine.'

Charlie saw the arrogance, the supreme masculine confidence in his gaze and her eyes closed against the pain she felt deep inside. She wanted to cry, but her pride would not let her, and pride was all she had left. She opened her eyes. 'Given that according to you I am trapped in this place, it would seem I don't have much of a choice,' she said scathingly. 'What do you intend to do, lock me up?'

Jake's expression changed to one of frustrated fury. '*Dio*, no! But the way you are behaving could drive a man to it,' he snarled. 'Damn it to hell, Charlotte. How do you expect me to react when you declare you want to end our marriage before it has even begun? Over a damned painting—and not a very good one at that!' he added with biting sarcasm.

'A painting you lied to me about the night we met,' she said bitterly. 'You said you wanted it for an investment, dead artist and all that. I believed you because you looked that hard-headed. But I should have guessed you had a deeper purpose, when I saw the mesmerised way you looked at it. I should have left.'

Jake stared at her, and remained silent for what seemed an age. His voice when he finally spoke was menacingly soft. 'Not much of a lie. For any other purchaser it could be the truth. As for being mesmerised—I blanked it out because it felt incestuous to see it. I only looked at it because it was expected of me, as I had just bought the damn thing. I bought it to destroy it before Anna's parents discovered its existence. They have suffered enough pain losing their daughter, without the added pain of seeing her naked body displayed to the world. And you, Charlotte, might have thought of that before you blithely exposed your father's private collection to the public without having the decency to ask those concerned, simply to make money.'

Charlie found it difficult to swallow the lump that rose in her throat at his reason for buying the painting. It had been a noble gesture to prevent the people he cared about being hurt. But his last comment had confirmed yet again what she already knew: he did see her as a selfish, greedy bitch. Not a good basis for marriage.

Suddenly her pain gave way to angry resentment. She could explain the money was for charity, but the arrogant swine did not deserve to know. Jake was so damned sure of himself—so confident he was right about everything. Not two minutes ago he had been telling her he knew her well. What a joke! 'You assume I am a money-grubber, but you don't really know me at all,' she said bitterly. He could think what the hell he liked for all she cared.

Jake shook his head in disgust at himself. His image of Charlotte as a calculating woman who had been lucky enough to inherit a business and exploited her father's inheritance had mellowed in the two weeks they had spent together. Being brutally honest, he would probably have seen the art exhibition as a wise business decision, if it hadn't contained the picture of Anna. And Charlotte's refusal of a designer wardrobe and her delight in a soft toy, plus Dave's revelation about her rescue work, had blasted any doubts he had had into oblivion.

'Maybe I don't, but I want to. Which is why we need to talk,' he said quietly, his long, lean fingers tightening the belt of his robe around his waist. Watching him, Charlie had the oddest notion he was nervous. Glancing at his face, her blue eyes met guarded black, and, intrigued, she bit back the denial that hovered on her lips.

'My fault, if you could call it that, was in not revealing the intimate details of people I cared about when we met. And let's be honest, you are as guilty of concealing aspects of your life as I. It took a wedding guest to tell me you were in the mountain rescue team, and Dave's revelation that you worked for him with the International Rapid Rescue Team was a hell of a shock.'

'The subject never came up,' Charlie said defensively, watching him with wary eyes, not sure where he was leading.

'Perhaps we have both been less than open with each other, Charlotte. But as of now it has to stop—along, I might add, with any notion in that crazy head of yours that you will ever risk your life and limb with a rescue team of any kind again.' His eyes were narrowed intently on her face as he paused for a moment. 'We owe it to our unborn child to try and make this marriage a success, and with that in mind the first rule is we forget about the past, and move on from here. We have a lot going for us. We are great in bed together—you can't deny the chemistry is there—and I am a wealthy man. I can provide you with everything you need. Neither you nor our child will ever want for anything. What more could a wife want?' he demanded, and had the bare-faced nerve to smile at her.

Love, she thought, but could not say it, as her throat ached with the effort to hold back the tears that threatened for her lost dreams. 'Nothing, you're right,' she agreed, not believing him for a second. His concept of marriage horrified her. It was nothing more than a business deal: he paid the money and got the wife and child. But what were her options?

She couldn't think and the pressure of trying to retain her composure instead of bawling her eyes out stopped her from arguing with him. She lifted a hand and rubbed her temple in an attempt to ease the dull throbbing there.

'Here, let me do that.' Jake reached out and cupped her head in his hands.

For a moment Charlie stiffened, but only for a moment as his thumbs gently massaged her temples, soothing and unthreatening. Charlie's eyelids drifted shut in helpless response to the incredible sensitivity of his touch. The pressure in her temple eased and she breathed in deeply and sighed.

'Better?' Jake asked.

'Much,' she murmured, slowly opening her eyes. His face was only inches from her own, and the hands that had been holding her head dropped to her shoulders as his wide, sensual mouth closed over hers. Taking advantage of her open-mouthed surprise, he slid his tongue between her parted lips.

She raised her hands to push him away, but they met with

the hard, hot wall of his chest and lingered as he deepened the kiss with a skilful, persuasive expertise. Her passionate response was humiliating but undeniable, and when his mouth moved from her lips to suck the sensitive hollow at the base of her throat, a low moan escaped her.

'I want you,' Jake rasped. His dark eyes, black with barely controlled desire, seared into hers as his hands on her shoulders eased her back against the pillows, his body following her down. 'You're mine, Charlotte. Forget the rest and let our marriage start here.'

The intensity of his gaze thrilled even as it threatened her, and she willed herself not to respond, but it was hopeless. The husky sound of his voice alone seduced her even as his sensual mouth claimed hers once more. His teeth nipped at her lower lip, and then soothed with a lick of his tongue, before probing the soft inner tissue of her mouth.

A low moan escaped her as he broke the kiss and reared up over her. Shrugging off his robe, Jake grasped the straps of blue satin at her shoulders and stripped the nightgown from her. His hot dark eyes studied her naked body with hungry pleasure. 'You are so beautiful.' His gaze lingered on her full breasts before lifting to her flushed face.

Charlie felt her whole body blush, heat racing through her. Her eyes skated helplessly over his handsome face, noting the sensuous curve to his full lips, and on down to the broad expanse of his muscular chest, the curling black body hair, down past his navel, and back to his face. She was totally mesmerised by the sheer masculine perfection of him, as she had always been.

Jake lifted one long finger and, with a feather-light touch, traced the curve of her cheek, her lips, her throat, and lower to her breast. 'Exquisite,' he said huskily. 'I want to taste you.'

His dark head lowered, his firm lips following the trail

his finger had taken, lingering on her lips, more tempting than demanding, and then lower, to draw the aching peak of her breast into the heat of his mouth.

Her slender body arched involuntarily to the source of its pleasure, even as his fingers slid tantalisingly between her thighs. The musky male scent of him, his exquisite touch, had ignited a fire inside her only his full possession could douse.

'*Dio*, I need you, Charlotte,' he groaned, his sensuous mouth claiming hers once more. She felt it in the hunger of his kiss, and the pressure of his fiercely aroused flesh against her thigh. The fact he had said *need* rather than *want* somehow inflamed her senses to fever pitch. Her fingers tangled in the silken hair of his head as he broke the kiss to trail a tongue of flame down her throat and lave the rigid peaks of her breast with tongue and teeth. And all the while his hands continued to caress her quivering flesh.

'You want me, Charlotte.' His dark head lifted from her breast, his glittering gaze seeking hers. 'And, *Dio*, I want you. I always have,' he groaned.

He was right. There was no point in denial. She loved him and her body ached for his, while he only lusted after hers, she knew. But she no longer cared as, driven by an unstoppable passion, she pressed her mouth to his throat. She bit his satin-smooth skin, felt his body tighten, and exulted in his husky groan. Her hands roamed feverishly over his powerful muscled body. She caressed and teased with mouth and teeth, using all the skills he had taught her, and he returned the favour. Pacing her pleasure with his own, he led her with a skilful, erotic ease to the very brink of ecstasy over and over again, until she almost wept from the sheer wonder of it.

He raised himself away from her, his night-black eyes molten with desire burning down into hers as he lifted her hips and surged into her, and the cry that rose in her throat was stilled as his mouth closed over hers.

She felt the quivering tension in his great frame as he thrust deeper and faster, her body instinctively picking up his rhythm. Her fingers dug into his bronzed skin and she was conscious only of Jake and the incredible joy of his possession, until the pleasure was almost too exquisite to bear. The fusion of their two bodies was mystical in its intensity, and she bit her lip to stop from screaming his name even as her body convulsed in a shattering climax that met and absorbed Jake's pulsating release.

His head fell to her shoulder, his harsh groan of masculine satisfaction echoing in her ears. She felt the heavy pounding of his heart against her own, their sweat-slicked bodies still shuddering in the aftershock of passion. She let her hands rove possessively over his damp skin, knowing that Jake had proved once again on a physical level they were in perfect accord.

Had it ever been that profound before? she thought dazedly. Her own aggression had sparked a fierce reaction in Jake, raw in its intensity, but with a phenomenal control he had excited her almost to the edge of oblivion and the final incredible climax had been the deepest, most potent fulfilment of all.

Maybe their marriage could work after all...

'Now you are truly my wife, *mia amore*,' Jake said huskily, burying his face in her mass of hair. But his last words struck a jarring note in her mind.

'Don't call me that,' Charlotte said sharply.

'Why not? You are my wife.' Jake raised his head, his dark eyes smiling lazily down at her. 'I seem to remember we got married yesterday.'

She saw the amusement in his gaze and the sense of betrayal came flooding back. 'As if I could forget.' She turned her head away. It was not the *wife* she was objecting to, but the *mia amore—my love*. But she had no intention of telling him so. That he should use the term of endearment now, when he never had before, was like a knife to the heart. Their lovemaking had been so perfect, but remembering what he had revealed earlier made her want to weep.

She was not his love, never had been, and never would be. She meant no more to Jake than any of the other women who had shared his bed. Less! Because he had as good as admitted he thought she was a greedy bitch, and he had only taken her out to get revenge.

'Charlotte.' He lifted up on one elbow, and looked down at her, his dark eyes gleaming with gentle amusement. 'I know what is the matter. You never ate your breakfast.' He reached out and smoothed the tangled mass of blonde hair from her brow in a gentle gesture. 'My fault again. In your condition you need food at regular intervals.'

'And who made you a doctor?' Charlie sniped back, his tenderness more than she could bear right now. But his reaction stunned her.

'Oh, hell!' He glanced at his watch, the only thing he was wearing, and leapt off the bed. 'I have a meeting later this morning, but first you and I have an appointment with a doctor in exactly forty-five minutes. It won't take me ten minutes to get ready next door, and I'll make you a sandwich—you can eat it in the car, because allowing for travelling time, you only have thirty minutes to get ready.'

'You have some nerve!' He was standing there, unashamedly naked, ordering her around, and Charlie was incensed. 'I am not going anywhere with you.' Her blue eyes blazed defiance. 'Just because we had sex, it does not mean you can tell me what to do.'

'We did not *just* have sex, and we do not have time to

argue yet again. And you are going to the doctor if I have to carry you there.'

A naked man should not be able to look arrogant and threatening, but somehow Jake managed it, Charlie thought helplessly. 'What on earth for? I'm fine,' she asked, curbing her temper.

Jake gave her a hard look, and lashed out, 'What do you think? To confirm the state of your pregnancy, of course. After all, that is why I married you.' He knew he was speaking in a moment of anger, but he had thought everything was back on track between them. Now, looking at Charlotte, he doubted it. 'You have twenty-five minutes,' he flung over his shoulder as he left the room.

He could not have spelt out more clearly why he had married her if he had carved it in stone. And with that knowledge Charlie's heart turned to ice in her breast.

Twenty minutes later, wearing a blue and white patterned chiffon slip dress that effectively skimmed the slight thickening of her waistline and ended just above her knee, teamed with kitten-heeled white pumps and a matching purse, she descended the glass staircase into the hall, where Jake was waiting.

'A punctual woman.' Jake walked towards her and stopped at her side. 'And a very attractive one,' he complimented, subjecting her to a blatant masculine appraisal that made her tummy knot with tension. She hoped it was tension and nothing more primitive.

'If I have to see your doctor, can we go?' she said edgily.

'Sure. Take this.' He handed her a baguette stuffed full of meat and wrapped in cling film. Then a strong hand spread across her back and ushered her out into the brilliant morning sun.

A black limousine was waiting, and a man she had never

seen before was holding open the rear door. Jake said something in rapid-fire Italian and the driver responded, and gave Charlie a long assessing look.

'Charlotte, *cara*, this is Marco.' Jake made the introduction, and Charlie politely shook the man's hand—a hand that was the size of a gorilla's. 'He will take care of you when Tomas is not available.'

'I am perfectly capable of taking care of myself. I don't need a minder.' She shot Jake a fulminating glance.

'Humour me, hmm?' His hand at her waist urged her into the rear seat of the car and he slid in beside her. 'And eat.'

At least it gave her something to do instead of having to talk to Jake, and surprisingly the sandwich was quite good.

The consultant gynaecologist, Dr Bruno, whom Jake took her to see was a small, friendly old man with twinkling eyes. He spoke fluent English and Charlie liked him on sight. He told her he had known Jake for years, from the time his son Paulo and Jake were at school together. Jake was the godfather to Paulo's son and daughter, his much-loved only grandchildren.

But she did not like him quite so much when the examination was over and Jake proceeded to question him on her and the baby's state of health, and he answered in a great deal of detail Charlie could have done without.

'Will you shut up?' Charlie hissed in exasperation and embarrassment as the older man turned to his desk to extract some booklets on pregnancy. 'It has nothing to do with you.'

'The child has everything to do with me,' Jake commented with a sardonic lift of an ebony brow, and continued his conversation with Dr Bruno in Italian, which did nothing for Charlie's temper. At least before she'd known what they were saying, but now she had no idea.

She heaved a sigh of relief when she finally stepped onto

the pavement again, but her relief was short-lived as Jake caught her hand and led her towards the limousine waiting by the kerb.

'I know you have a meeting, so I think I'll have a look around the town, do some shopping,' she said lightly, banking on the fact Jake would not argue with her on the busy pavement. She pulled her hand free.

A muscular arm wrapped around her shoulders and Jake, his strong face taut, studied her with dark serious eyes. 'My home is not your prison, Charlotte, and I don't believe you will leave. Dave was right—you are an all-or-nothing kind of woman, and with you and I it cannot be nothing, as we will always have our child between us. So I am banking on the *all* when you get over the argument we had last night. Go shopping if you like.' His dark head bent and he brushed his lips against her hair. 'Marco will take you—and before you object, it's to make sure you don't get lost. This is a big city and you don't know your way around.'

'That sounds like a jailer to me,' she said stiffly, but in her heart she knew Jake was right.

Scornful dark eyes skimmed over her mutinous face. 'I thought we had reached an understanding this morning, but obviously I was wrong. Think what you like, you will anyway. But Marco stays.' Turning, he walked down the street.

Charlie inwardly cringed at the scorn in his expression. It was painful to have to admit, but she no longer wanted to leave Jake. Knowing he had only married her because she was pregnant did not stop her loving him and she watched his departing figure with a mixture of anger and sorrow in her suddenly moist eyes.

She didn't go shopping. She went back to the house—whether she would one day think of it as home, she didn't know.

CHAPTER TEN

CHARLIE ate a breakfast of fruit and cereal in the kitchen with young Aldo and grinned at his excellent attempts to speak English. When he left for school her smile vanished. It was a sad reflection on her marriage that her best friend and the person she spent most time with was an eight-year-old boy. He finished school at one and after lunch they had taken to exploring the extensive grounds together. He had shown her his favourite place, a cave set in the cliffs at the rear of the house, and she had told him about the fun she had rock climbing at her home in England.

Restless and on edge, Charlie rose to her feet, and with a thank you to Marta she carried her cup of tea outside to the small patio tucked away around the back of the kitchen. A pergola shaded the area, the crimson bougainvillaea trailing over it giving Charlie the sense of privacy she needed, and she let the sweet morning air work its magic on her troubled mind.

A week…she had been married a week today, but her wedding day seemed a lifetime away. The woman who had stood in the gardens of the Lakeview Hotel convinced it was the happiest day of her life was no more. A cynical smile twisted her lush lips. Love's young dream was just that—a dream. It had taken Jake to show her the truth.

She never saw him during the day, and dinner was pretty much a silent affair, or a battleground. Jake tried to make conversation but she replied with icy politeness, or with a bitter sarcasm that was totally alien to her usual sunny nature, until, finally exasperated with her, he retired to his study to work, and she retired to bed.

They shared a bed, but she was beginning to think it was for appearance's sake only, to prevent gossip among the staff. Once or twice she had awakened in the night to find his arm around her, but they had never made love since the morning after their disastrous wedding night. It was painful to have to admit, but she missed the intimacy.

She could see no clear end to the emotional mess she had made of her life unless she learnt to accept her marriage on Jake's terms. Probably thousands of couples lived in a loveless marriage for the sake of the children quite successfully. Would it be so bad?

Sighing, Charlie drained her cup of tea. It couldn't be any worse than what she had now, and it was her own fault. She could not forget the anger and hurt she felt, and it showed. Then there was her unborn child to think about—but worrying wasn't going to help either of them, and with another sigh she replaced the cup on the table and leant back in her chair. The silence had a therapeutic effect on her, and slowly she felt herself begin to relax, but that feeling did not last for long. A shadow fell across her face and she looked up to see Jake's tall frame leaning against a timber pillar of the pergola.

She was shocked. He came to bed late and was always gone when she woke up in the morning. But today was different—Jake was different, the cool control of the past week no longer evident. Instead his mouth was tight and she felt the vibration of his underlying anger across the space between them.

'Shouldn't you be out making millions?' she said sarcastically. 'Instead of disturbing my peace and quiet.'

'I'm flattered I disturb you, Charlotte, but don't worry, I am not stopping. I have no desire to spend any more time than I have to with a sulky, immature girl.' Then, surprisingly, in an uncontrolled gesture he ran a frustrated hand through his thick dark hair. 'What the hell is the matter with you?' he demanded harshly. 'This constant sniping that passes as conversation from you has to stop. Can't you lighten up occasionally, or don't you have a sense of humour any more?'

'My sense of humour is still intact, thank you.' Anger was her only defence, but her words lacked their usual force. 'But after discovering on my wedding night that my husband did not love me but married me out of a desire for revenge and the child I am carrying, it is hardly surprising humour deserts me around you.'

'Love,' he sneered. '*Dio*, you are great at throwing that word around like a talisman, but it seems a pretty poor emotion to me that can't forget the slightest misdeed. Not even a deed—a wayward thought is enough,' he added bitterly. 'Give me honour and respect any day.'

Taken aback by his outburst, Charlie tried to defend herself. 'At least I believe in love.'

'You probably have to cling to the illusion with a father like yours, who had no honour or respect for women, marriage or anything else,' he said scathingly.

She went pale as his harsh words sliced into her and she linked her hands together on the table to stop them shaking as she recognised there was some truth in what Jake said. With the exception of herself, her father had respected no one, not even himself. He had drunk, smoked and drugged himself to death by the age of forty-six. She drew in a long shuddering breath, finally forced to accept that her dad had loved her in his own way, and that way had included ignoring her for the first eleven years of her life and, if Jake was to be believed, lying about her to his lady friends. Not the perfect love she dreamed of, and maybe that was her problem—she had expected too much.

Jake bent over and grasped her chin so she was forced to look at him. 'You have told me countless times you love me, but what you really felt for me, *cara mia*, for the first time in your life, was a lust for sex.' His other hand curved around her breast. 'And you still do.'

'No.' Her voice faltered to a halt and her mouth ran dry. His dark, handsome face was so close she could feel the warmth of his breath on her skin, and she looked away quickly, but not fast enough to stop her stomach curling tightly, and her breast hardening beneath his hand.

Jake's wide mouth curved in a cynical smile and he straightened up. 'Who's lying now, Charlotte?' She went from white to red, and he laughed. 'Still blushing.'

'Oh, shut up.' Her frustration boiled over and she lifted her glass to throw it at him. He grasped her hand.

'That is more like the exuberant girl I first met.' He grinned. 'Instead of the sulky silent shrew of the past week.' Dragging her to her feet, he added quietly, 'We could have a good life together, all three of us.' He slanted a glance at her stomach. 'With a bit of goodwill on both sides.'

She opened her mouth to say, *Never*, and closed it again.

'Wise woman,' Jake murmured gruffly, and pulled her against his hard body. She saw her own need reflected in his dark eyes and relaxed as his mouth closed over hers in a kiss that was achingly tender. A whole week without the taste of his lips on hers was in her response, and when he finally released her she was left swaying and breathless.

'Your hair is a mess,' Jake commented as he brushed a lock of hair back behind her ear. 'But don't worry, we are dining out tonight, and my PA, Sophia, is waiting to meet you in the house. She has kindly offered to take you to town to shop, get your hair done, whatever you women do.'

Slipping his hand in his pocket, he held out a wad of money and a credit card in her name. 'Take this.'

'I don't need your money.'

'I know, and I will never forgive myself for once suggesting otherwise. So take it to save my soul.'

'That's a bit extreme,' Charlie said with a chuckle and took the money.

'There now, that didn't hurt.' Raising one hand, he lightly tapped her cheek. 'You have finally found your smile again, Charlotte. There is hope for us yet.' Grasping her hand, he led her back through the kitchen and into the hall.

Charlie took one look at the small elegant brunette waiting in the hall and felt terrible again. The woman was immaculately clad in what was obviously a designer suit, and Charlie felt like a scruff in comparison in a simple yellow sundress. It didn't help that Jake smiled at the other woman and said something in Italian whereupon they both laughed, and then turned to look at her, still grinning.

'Charlotte, *cara*, this is Sophia, my right-hand woman, and I could not do without her.' Smiling down at the beautiful woman, he added, 'Sophia: my wife, Charlotte.'

Reluctantly Charlie moved forward and took the small hand the other woman held out to her. She said rather stiffly, 'How do you do?' and wondered just exactly how much Sophia did do for Jake. Did it include sharing his bed? But as the woman smiled at her Charlie was struck by the warmth and kindness in her eyes.

'I have to go,' Jake said. 'Tomas will drive, and Marco will accompany you to carry your purchases so you will be safe in Sophia's hands, Charlotte.'

'Safe or secured?' Charlie shot back automatically, and felt even worse as she watched a tide of dark colour flood up Jake's face as he moved towards her, and curved a hand around her neck. He was right: she was turning into a shrew.

'Both,' he murmured, his dark head swooping to capture her mouth in a deeply possessive kiss. Only when he felt her quivering response did he trail his lips to her throat, nuzzling her neck. 'Don't you dare try to make our private battle public ever again, or you will live to regret it,' he whispered in her ear before straightening up and smiling down at her. The humour did not reach his eyes. 'Let Sophia show you around, listen to her advice and try to enjoy yourself—hmm?' Swinging on his heel, he slammed out of the house.

'Phew.' Sophia wiped her brow with the back of her hand. 'Talk about sparks flying, and I thought my husband and I were bad.' She grinned up at Charlie. 'But you shouldn't be too hard on Jake. He is bound to be a bit over-protective with the woman he loves. Now let's hit the shops.'

Charlie replaced the receiver, a bittersweet smile on her face. Talking to Jeff had restored her spirits a little. It was good to know the hotel was running smoothly and was waiting for her when and if she returned. Even though it did mean lying to Jeff that her marriage was running just as smoothly. But all that was about to change, she hoped.

While bathing and dressing for dinner she had come to a decision: she was going to give their marriage a chance. She knew it was partially the result of Jake's passionate kisses this morning, but more than that—his derisory comment about a love that would not forgive the slightest misdeed or even thought had hit home.

Jake was late. He had told her to be ready by seven, and she had been waiting for over ten minutes already. She was nervous, and she strolled into the family sitting room—a misnomer if ever there was one, she thought wryly, glancing around the elegant lounge. Perfectly presented but soulless was a more accurate description, much like her marriage, and it was up to her to do something about it.

'Your trip was a success?' Jake leant back against the doorjamb, and noted the slight thrust of her chin, the cool expressive features as she faced him. He suppressed a faint smile at the sleek, upswept hairstyle that ended with a purposely contrived bunch of wild curls on the top of her head. Very elegant, very chic: the many facets of his lovely wife were a source of constant fascination to him, though he would never admit it. One minute, playing with young Aldo in shorts and shirt, she looked like a teenager. He knew because every night he had studied the security videos of them exploring the grounds. Then in the evening, cool and reserved opposite him at the dinner table, or, best of all, curled up in his bed, her beautiful face relaxed and innocent in sleep. He could watch her for hours, had done…

His loins stirred and he shifted away from the door willing his wayward libido under control. No, now was not the time. Tonight he was hosting a dinner party in an exclusive country restaurant that had been hired privately for the evening. He had instructed Sophia to arrange the party a couple of days before his wedding. At the time he had thought it was a great idea, a second reception to introduce Charlotte to all his friends. He had hoped it would be a wonderful surprise for her; now he only hoped they got through the night without her obvious antagonism showing.

'If you call being trussed up like a dog's dinner a success, then yes,' Charlie said wryly. The dress was a brilliant blue, which matched her eyes, and had a scooped neck with very short sleeves whose sole function was to hold up the princess-line bodice because the back was virtually non-existent to her waist. Sophia had assured her that her tummy didn't show and the dress, which ended above her knee, was the height of fashion. She had also approved the three-inch stiletto-heeled sandals that accentuated the length of her legs.

'You are no dog, Charlotte.' Jake grinned, his dark eyes gleaming with male appreciation. 'Sophia has done a good job. You look exquisite, the epitome of sophisticated young woman. Now prove you can act like one. Bring me a whisky on the rocks, upstairs—I'm going to get changed.'

She was about to refuse, but as she studied his handsome face with its dark eyes set beneath hooded lids and the almost permanent tightness that seemed to have taken control of his chiselled mouth she realised he looked tired. 'Okay.'

Charlie poured the amber liquid over ice cubes, and, lifting the crystal glass, she rotated it in her hand, her mind prey to conflicting thoughts. Ordered to serve her master, or a much-needed pick-me-up for a hard-working husband? For the first time since her wedding night, she allowed compassion to cut through her fierce pride, and slowly made her way upstairs.

She walked into the bedroom, looked around, and was about to put the drink down as Jake walked in from the *en suite*.

She stifled a gasp and all she could do was look at him. Black hair sleeked back from his forehead accentuated his handsome features. His superbly muscled body was naked except for a precariously slung white towel around his lean hips shielding his essential masculinity.

Hastily she lifted her eyes but it was difficult to meet his gaze as she moved towards him. 'Your drink as ordered.' She held out the glass with a hand that shook slightly.

'You have surprised me,' Jake said with a husky chuckle, and took the glass from her outstretched hand. 'Thank you. I need this.'

'My pleasure.' She forced herself to look up, to meet his eyes before she fled. But the searching intensity of his dark gaze kept her motionless. Since this morning something had changed between them—Jake had changed. The air in the room was suddenly heavy with sexual tension. Charlie drew in a quivering breath. She could feel the swell of her breasts beneath the fabric of her gown, and hastily she tore her gaze from his.

Noting her reaction, Jake quirked his lips in the briefest of grins, immensely satisfied that she was not as immune to him as she tried to pretend. And though it was chauvinistic to admit as much, he was privately delighted that Charlotte's experience of men was limited to him, and he intended it to stay that way. With that thought in mind, Jake broke the vow he had made to himself, and allowed a wicked, sensual grin to break the handsome contours of his face. 'And it will be your pleasure later, *cara*.'

Charlie blushed scarlet and fled, sure she could hear his throaty laughter as she closed the door behind her.

Back in the family room, she eyed the drinks cabinet in something like desperation. Never had she felt more like a drink in her life, but with her pregnancy it wasn't an option. Dear heaven! This acting the happy wife was a lot more nerve-racking than she had bargained for. A couple of kisses this morning and a teasing smile this evening, and she was in danger of melting at his feet in a puddle and reverting to the stupid girl who had gazed at him in dumb adoration before she had found out what a ruthless devil he could be. That was not what she wanted at all, but an equal relationship built on mutual respect and trust.

'You dashed off before I could give you this.' Jake's deep drawl had her spinning around to face him.

Charlie's eyes flicked over his broad frame, taking in the dark dinner suit, the white silk shirt and black bow tie, and she struggled to control the sudden racing of her heart as he approached her.

Where is your pride, girl? she admonished herself with a defiant tilt of her head, but her blue eyes collided with gleaming black, and she made no protests as he stopped and one strong hand circled her throat.

'Exquisite though you are, the dress lacks something,' he declared softly, a finger and thumb sliding down to caress the delicate hollows at the edge of her neck, igniting a sensual heat in the pit of her stomach.

'Bare is beautiful, but I thought something to reflect your sparkle, Charlotte.' With his free hand he withdrew a handful of jewels from his pocket.

'I don't need—' she began stiffly.

'Quiet, *cara*. Indulge me, because I do need.' Deftly he fastened a magnificent sapphire and diamond pendant around her neck.

Charlie gasped and lifted her hand to touch the jewels but Jake caught it and slipped a matching bracelet on her wrist. 'I don't want…'

'You do want,' Jake drawled with dry mockery. 'But you don't want to admit as much.' And before she could grasp his meaning, he had lifted her hand and slipped an equally fabulous diamond and sapphire ring on the third finger of her left hand to rest snugly against her wedding band.

'There, that is better.' He cupped her shoulders, his dark eyes roving over her with obvious satisfaction. 'No one this evening will be in any doubt you are my much-adored wife.' He drew her against him to press a swift kiss on the tip of her nose. 'Come, we must leave now or our guests will think we have deserted them.'

Free from the mesmerising effect of his dark eyes, Charlie's first thought was to remove the jewellery.

'Don't even think about it,' Jake commanded, reading her mind.

'If you think you can buy me, forget it. I am not for sale,' Charlie snapped back.

'I realised that some time ago,' Jake said with a wry smile and, clasping her hand in his, he linked his long fingers through hers. Together they left the house and got into the waiting car.

'What did you mean, meet our guests?' She belatedly remembered his other comment, when Jake slid into the back seat of the limousine beside her. 'I thought we were going out for dinner.'

'And so we are.' As the car sped through the evening traffic towards Portofino Jake explained it was by way of being a wedding reception for his friends and business acquaintances who had not been able to make the original service in England.

The thought of being on display before all his friends filled her with trepidation and she didn't offer a word for the rest of the drive to the restaurant. But she was intensely aware of Jake at her side. She had been in a state of nervous tension all day, and his thigh brushing lightly against hers was not helping at all.

Charlie heaved a sigh of relief when the car stopped and she slid from the seat the moment the chauffeur opened the door. But her relief was short-lived as Jake took her arm and led her up the massive stone steps of an elegant old building that belonged to another era, and into a marble entrance hall.

It was almost eight when they entered the dining room, and Charlie's eyes widened in shock as a trio of musicians stationed on a raised dais in one corner of the room immediately struck up with 'Here Comes the Bride', followed by an almighty cheer from all the assembled guests.

Blushing furiously, she was grateful of Jake's supporting arm as he introduced her to the elderly couple that stepped forward to meet them. They were his foster-parents, Mr and Mrs Lasio, and, seeing them hug Jake and then smile at her, she was struck by the underlying sadness in their eyes. It made her realise that Jake's reaction to the death of their daughter was not that extreme after all. And when they wished her a long and happy marriage with obvious sincerity, she felt incredibly guilty on her father's behalf.

'Don't worry. They don't know,' Jake murmured, accurately reading her thoughts, and, taking her arm, he led her to another group. The next half-hour was a blur of names and faces to Charlie as Jake introduced her to the hundred people that were his close friends and business colleagues.

She met Paulo Bruno, the doctor's son, and his wife Stephanie, and they did register with Charlie because within seconds of meeting them they were congratulating her on her marriage and her pregnancy.

Charlie coloured to the roots of her hair, and spared Jake a quick angry glance. She caught the faint gleam of amusement in his dark eyes, and realised he didn't give a damn who knew she was pregnant.

'This is Italy, *cara*,' he stated with a shrug of his broad shoulders. 'The prospect of a child is something to be celebrated at the earliest opportunity, not something to hide.' His dark eyes slid down to the barely perceptible swell of her tummy beneath the cleverly constructed slight A-line shape of her gown. 'But you do it well,' he added mockingly.

'You're impossible. And I need the bathroom,' she hissed, but not softly enough.

'I'll show you the way,' Stephanie offered. 'I can remember when I was in your condition and running to the loo all the time. It was hell.' Everyone laughed.

Having completed her ablutions, Charlie smiled at Stephanie. 'I suppose we have to rejoin the fray.'

'Yes, unless you want Jake hammering on the door looking for you. I have never seen him in love before and it is amazing.' She gripped Charlie's hand. 'I'm so happy for you both, and especially for your baby. Jake will make a great father,' she said as they left the bathroom. 'And you don't want to believe all the stories you hear about the women he has supposedly known. Paulo told me they are vastly exaggerated—not that he has led the life of a monk, but Jake is a very moral man, old-fashioned in some ways. So you have nothing to worry about. He will make a marvellous husband and father.'

If Stephanie had sought to reassure Charlie, her information about all the women he was rumoured to have known had the opposite effect. Her determination to give their marriage a chance took a wobble—but face it, she told herself, she didn't have much of a choice.

'Charlotta, I thought you had got lost.' Jake's husky accented drawl, and the arm that curved around her waist, were a welcome relief from Stephanie's unwanted confidences, and her troubled thoughts. 'Dinner is about to be served,' he added and she made no demur as he led her back into the dining room.

The women were all elegantly dressed in the latest designer fashions, and Charlie said a private prayer of thanks to Sophia for guiding her in what to wear. As for the jewels, Jake had been right about that: she would have looked positively bare in this company where the diamonds on display had to equal a king's ransom—and not only on the women, she noted with an amused smile as Jake introduced her to a Signor Dotello. The diamond stud in the man's ear was the size of a gull's egg. His dress shirt was open almost to his waist and an enormous chain circled his neck, but that was not all: a massive diamond crucifix glittered against his deeply tanned chest.

'I believe that is what is called bling,' she murmured to Jake as the man left to take his place at one of the ten circular tables arranged around the periphery of the room, to leave space for dancing in the centre.

'Correct,' he said with a husky laugh. 'Dotello is a New York gems dealer and likes to show his wares.'

'Along with half his chest.'

'Not that you should not have noticed,' Jake declared possessively as he led her to the top table and saw her seated before joining her.

Jake deftly reacquainted her with their table companions. His foster-parents were next to him and then Sophia and her husband Gianni, followed by Paulo and his wife Stephanie who smiled at Charlie like an old friend.

The food was superb and the champagne and conversation flowed freely through half a dozen courses, except for the last couple at the table: Diego and a stunning Russian model called Lenka, who could not speak a word of any language but her own.

'Lenka is a typical Diego type,' Jake murmured to Charlie in a soft aside as Stephanie, having finished her sweet, tried to engage the model in conversation. 'Diego likes his women to be models, mobile and mute.'

'And of course you don't?' Charlie mocked with an elegant lift of a finely arched brow, remembering Melissa. Her blue eyes dimmed and she speared a solitary morsel of gateau left on her plate and popped it into her mouth.

'I have dated several, I can't deny it.' Jake settled back in his chair and regarded her with dark intent eyes. 'But my preference is for a beautiful English blonde, with a penchant for climbing, but not of the social variety, and maybe just a little bit too much mouth.' Leaning forward, he lifted a finger. 'Speaking of your delectable mouth, you have a crumb.' The pad of his index finger stroked the corner of her mouth and lingered.

'Come on, you two, less of the canoodling and lead the dancing,' Diego called with a laugh.

'Shall we?' Jake suggested smoothly as the band struck up the wedding waltz, and, rising to his feet, he took her hand and led her onto the dance floor.

With all his friends watching she could not disagree, but it struck her forcibly how little she really knew of Jake as he slid an arm around her, his hand splaying firmly across the centre of her back as he moved her in close to him. 'Do you realise I have never danced with you? I don't know if I can.'

'Trust me,' Jake murmured, grinning down at her. 'For a woman who moves like you in my bed, dancing is a given.' And he was right.

CHAPTER ELEVEN

THEY danced, Jake stroking his hand gently up Charlie's bare back, while the other caught her hand and held it tight to his chest. They circled the floor once to the applause of the crowd, and then other couples joined them.

'Thank God. I hate being the centre of attention,' Charlie murmured, tilting back her head to glance up at him.

'I thank God for you,' Jake murmured, his dark gaze intent on her upturned face.

Charlie's lips parted. The compliment was so unlike Jake she had trouble believing him, but there was something so convincing in his tone she couldn't help herself. Their eyes met and desire sharp as a rapier lanced between them. He raised her hand to his shoulder and left it there, to slide his own down to curve over her hip and urge her closer, one long leg edging between hers. She felt him stir against her and the familiar heat flowed through her.

Dear heaven, he felt so good, and though she knew he did not love her there was a sensual part of her that ached for his strength, the heat and power of his possession. She sank against the hard, lean length of him, her fingers instinctively linking behind his neck, her head resting on his shoulder as she gave herself up to the slow music and the sheer joy of being in his arms.

They were cocooned in a world of their own, and there was only the brush of thigh on thigh, hand on skin, the sensual stimulation of two bodies in perfect harmony as they moved to the slow, dreamy music.

Then the tempo changed to a loud disco beat.

Jake stopped, but held her close, his dark head dipping to hers. 'How long do you think before we can decently leave our own party?' he husked, his breath a warm caress against her cheek.

Mistily, Charlie glanced up at him, her blue eyes meshing with gleaming brown as he added with wry, self-deprecatory humour, 'Or, in my case, indecently.' The increased pressure of his hand on her bottom told her exactly what he meant.

She made no response; she simply gave him a slow sensual smile.

'That's it,' Jake growled. 'We're leaving.'

'We can't, the guests will be disappointed,' she murmured, not very convincingly, and saw his dark eyes flare and take on a devilish gleam.

'Not necessarily.' He grinned. 'Follow me.'

Five minutes later, after Jake had spoken to his foster-parents and a few of the guests, she found herself once more in the back of the limousine with Jake's arm draped around her shoulders.

'What on earth did you say to everyone to make them look at me so sympathetically?'

'I told them you felt faint and needed to lie down.'

'You what?' Charlie should have been furious, but instead her lips twitched in the beginnings of a smile. 'You liar.'

'Not exactly. *I* need to lie down.' His deep dark drawl fractured and his long fingers curved her neck. He tilted her head and his smouldering black eyes blazed down into hers. 'Quite desperately...with you.' His thumb stroked her nape, and then his mouth was brushing her lips slowly—oh, so slowly.

Her eyes fluttered shut, and his lie was suddenly the truth. She did feel faint. Faint with the myriad sensations flowing through her body, faint with love... Her mouth opened beneath his and a tiny moan sounded in her throat as the kiss deepened into a hungry, devouring force. He moved close, his hand raking up through her hair, sending the carefully contrived style into chaos as he angled her head. Her upper body was tight against him. The thought of resistance didn't enter her head, and when his hand slipped under the bodice of her dress, his fingers finding and teasing the pebble-like nipple, she shuddered, heat flowing through her like a river of fire. She wanted him, ached for him…

'*Dio!* What is it with you and cars?' Jake rasped, his dark head lifting, his hand slipping from her breast, his arms enfolding her to hug her tight. 'We have arrived, *cara*.' And it was only then Charlie realised the car had stopped.

In minutes they were naked on the bed, though Charlie had no clear memory of how they got there, and Jake was beside her, his dark eyes like molten jet sliding over her.

Her hair was loose, and he ran a hand through it, spreading the golden strands across the pillow in an almost reverent gesture before his head lowered and he took her mouth in a deep, open-mouthed kiss that went on and on.

For Charlie it was like coming home. She looped her arms around his shoulders, her fingers stroking through the silky hair of his head, and moaned her delight as she felt the caress of his hand on her breast. Heat flooded her veins, filling her body with sensual excitement as she arched against the teasing torment of his clever fingers. And she groaned out loud as he broke the kiss to dip his head and take the swollen peaks into his mouth, suckling first one and then the other. Her inner muscles clenched with need, desire lancing through her, making her hot and wet with arousal, and so very ready for him. Hungrily her hands roamed over him. He was all power and heat, and she gloried in the perfection of his body, and shuddered as he stroked and caressed her, kissing the slight swell of her stomach, and murmuring husky words of adoration to their unborn child. Then with tongue and hands he resumed his sensual quest, finding every sensitive pulse, tasting every intimate part of her, until she was a shaking, whimpering creature, lost to everything but the erotic pleasure he gave her.

Suddenly he reared back, and she stared in mute fascination at his arousal, a magnificent potent force between his thighs, wild with wanting. Then his hands gripped and lifted her and he was there where she ached for him to be, easing into her slowly, inch by perfect inch, his sensuous probing electrifying her until every nerve in her body was screaming for release.

She wound her arms around his neck, her head falling back, as with a powerful surge he slid in to the hilt. He repeated the movement, increasing the pace, his mouth finding her breast once more. She clawed at his back and sought his skin with her teeth, wanton in her need, and she cried out as her inner muscles spasmed around him in an explosion of pleasure.

Jake gave a deep, primitive growl and increased the pace and with one final thrust that seemed to touch her very womb his body shuddered in violent release. He fell back on the bed, taking her with him, and she lay sprawled on top of him, her body quivering and her head buried in the curve of his throat.

Jake's arms wrapped around her and he stroked her trembling body, gently, softly, until she sighed and lay still in his arms.

Tenderly he rolled her onto her back on the bed and leaned over her. '*Dio*, I needed you so much, *amore mia*,' he husked, bestowing a kiss upon her brow while his hand lazily traced the line of her shoulder and lower to cup her breast as if testing the weight, and then gently traced the swell of her stomach.

He needed her. It was music to her ears, and this time she did not object to the *amore mia* as a deep sense of peace flooded through her. After what they had just shared, she could let herself believe he meant it.

But she was rudely disillusioned a moment later as his hand was abruptly withdrawn and he stared down, his hooded lids lowering to shield his expression. 'But I should not have done it.'

'Leave the party, you mean?' she said softly, a smile playing around her mouth as she lazily lifted her hand to his square jaw. 'I'm sure no one will mind.' Her fingers caressed his slightly roughened chin. 'I know I don't.' She raised languorous blue eyes to his, and for a moment she saw some deep emotion in his dark gaze.

'Maybe not. But that isn't what I meant.' He placed a hand on her stomach. 'I couldn't bear it if I hurt our baby.'

'There's no fear of that. They are tough little beggars.'

'And you would know? You have had one before?' he mocked gently.

'No, but then neither have you,' she mocked back, tracing the line of his high cheekbone and up to his temple, the pad of her finger resting on the tiny pulse that beat there.

'I almost did once,' Jake murmured.

Her eyes widened on his and the anguish she saw in the swirling black depths had her hand falling from his face in shock. 'But…you…how?' she stammered. She felt the sudden tension in his long body pressed against hers, and heard it in his deep voice as he began to speak.

'I was young and careless, and five months into a not-really-serious relationship when my girlfriend told me she was pregnant. Naturally I offered to marry her. I bought her the engagement ring she wanted, and gave her the money she demanded to arrange the wedding, but when she realised I ploughed most of my money into building up my business and was not as wealthy as she thought, my fiancée spent the money on a holiday and an abortion instead of the wedding.'

'Oh, my God. That is appalling,' Charlie exclaimed, her hands involuntarily stroking his chest in a gesture of comfort. She could feel his pain as if it were her own, hear it in his voice.

'What is truly appalling,' Jake rasped, 'is the knowledge I paid to kill my own child.'

'No, you can't believe that. It wasn't your fault,' she told him. His hand pressed lightly on her stomach, but his mouth hardened as she watched.

'We are all responsible for our own actions, Charlotte, and the effect they have on those around us. She was my fiancée, not for any great love I felt for her, but out of necessity, and I should have known better than to trust her. But I learnt from it. I have never made the mistake of trusting a woman again.'

Her heart ached for him. He was such a proud man—what it must have done to him to know the woman in his life could betray him so abominably... With her new-found knowledge, she realised why he had so little trust in her sex. After what had happened to him, he had a right to be cynical. 'But not every woman is like your ex-fiancée, and you can't possibly want to live your life without trust,' she said softly.

Jake rolled onto his back. 'I've managed perfectly okay so far,' he said, pulling her into the curve of his arm. 'Forget about what I said. You have the damnable ability to make me reveal more than is good for either of us.'

Charlie leant up on one elbow. He looked so self-contained and devastatingly attractive that she felt anger mounting inside her. 'How can you say that, when it was that attitude that had you ranting and raving at me about money and proof when you discovered I was pregnant?' She paused as it hit her forcibly: Jake's insistence on marriage had not been solely about her baby, but the one he had lost. She remembered the expression on his face when she had wildly threatened to slit her belly open, convinced he wanted her to have a termination. How wrong had she been!

'That was why you insisted on marrying me. You had lost one child and were going to make sure it didn't happen again.'

'Charlotte,' he said tersely and the familiar shuttered look was back in his dark eyes. 'Does it matter why? We are married and I will support and protect you and our child.'

'The same way you protect yourself,' she said more scathingly than she intended. 'Blanking out anyone who tries to get close to you with a wall of ice around your true feelings. That's no way to live.'

He rose abruptly, and his narrowed glance held hers as he methodically picked up his robe and slipped it on. 'It sure as hell beats having to listen to your psychobabble in the middle of the night. I have to leave for Japan in the morning and I need to get some sleep. The bed next door will do me just fine.' And he turned on his heel and left.

She shivered, cold with the kind of heart-rending chill that came with rejection, and as she watched his back moisture filled her eyes. The euphoria she had felt in his arms was replaced by a growing certainty that Jake would never let himself see her as anything but the mother of his child, and a convenient lay when his overactive libido got the better of him.

Charlie brushed the tears from her cheeks, disgusted with herself for being such a fool as to love a man who didn't know the meaning of the word, and didn't want to. How many times was she going to let him use her, only to be slapped in the face with rejection afterwards? She deserved better than that.

Face it, she told herself. Knowing the reasons why Jake kept such a close control on his feelings or lack of them, and why he was so cynical about her sex, had done her no good at all. Because Jake was perfectly happy the way he was. He wasn't prepared to listen and had walked away.

Feeling listless, Charlotte refused young Aldo's requests to play with him after lunch, and decided to take a siesta instead. She hadn't slept or eaten much since Jake's departure five days ago. He had called her every day but the conversations had been short and stilted and yesterday she had put the phone down on him. She could not be bothered to talk to him as a polite little wife. She had reached her limit. And she wasn't sure she cared any more.

She felt as if she were living in a deep fog, where there were no longer any clear lines to follow, any certainty or purpose in her life, except for the baby she carried. She had been a woman of action, but she now seemed incapable of taking any, and she didn't like the woman she had become. Not bothering to remove her shorts and top, Charlie flopped down on the bed and closed her eyes, hoping that in sleep she could forget her troubles.

The sun was low in the sky when she awakened and, rising off the bed, she straightened her T-shirt and slipped her feet into white canvas loafers. She was thirsty and, running a hand through her dishevelled hair, she headed for the kitchen. A glass of juice would be good.

She filled a glass, drained it thirstily, and replaced the glass on the bench. Idly she looked around and wondered where everyone was. She strolled out onto the patio, and heard the sound of voices raised in what sounded like argument and the plaintive cry of some animal in distress. Walking around to the rear of the house, she glanced between the clutter of outbuildings to the rock garden and cliff beyond that provided a natural security barrier to the outside world, and her mouth fell open in shock.

Marta was at the entrance to Aldo's cave and crying her eyes out. Tomas was trying to comfort her, and Marco was speaking on a cell phone. The other security man from the gatehouse was surveying the cliff face.

Charlie heard the cry again before she reached the others, and as she lifted her head her heart turned over with shock. It wasn't an animal, but Aldo.

A couple of feet from the cave was a deep narrow fissure in the rock that widened out some twenty feet up and reached almost to the top of the cliff. Aldo had somehow managed to climb to where the gap widened and a narrow ledge protruded slightly. A colourful kite was visible on the ledge, no doubt Aldo's reason for the dangerous escapade. Unfortunately, with his small hands gripping the slight over-hang and unable to haul himself up, he appeared to be stuck.

Tomas was struggling to climb up the fissure, but he was too large. Swiftly assessing the situation, Charlie did not hesitate. All three of the men were far too large to navigate the narrow chimney, and hastily she explained to Marco, who spoke the best English, what she was going to do. He tried to argue that the rescue team were on their way. But one glance at the perilous position of Aldo told Charlie they might be too late and she said as much, adding as reassurance, 'I am an expert rock climber and I free climb for fun. Trust me.'

And seconds later she began to climb. Looking up, she cried words of encouragement to Aldo. She had no doubt she could reach him—she had to. But she had grave doubts that she could get him back down safely. Her expert eye quickly concluded the ledge was her best hope. With luck she could lift him onto it and wait for the rescue service.

She quickly realised how Aldo had managed to get so far.

The first fifteen feet were quite simple, providing a choice of finger and toe-holds. But she was a good deal larger than him and as she grazed her thigh, her knees and her back she cursed the fact she was wearing shorts and canvas shoes. As she got higher and the fissure widened again, she felt the sweat break out over her whole body as she struggled to find finger holds.

She paused for breath and thought of her unborn child, praying her exertions would not cause any harm. With one hand she sought the next hold, a tiny gap. It was big enough for Aldo's small fingers but she had to grasp it with her fingertips. Her knuckles white with the strain, she hauled herself up a little further. She chanced a brief glance down and they were all staring up at her, degrees of fear on their faces. She forced a confident smile to her lips for Marta's benefit, and then searched for the next hold, vaguely registering the sound of a racing car and sirens in the distance.

Her chest heaving, she looked up at Aldo. 'Keep still, stay still, Aldo. *Fermaressere,*' she called softly and hoped it was the right word—she didn't want him any more frightened than he already was. Taking a deep, ragged breath, her heart pounding fit to burst, she made one final effort. Legs and arms aching, she struggled on until she was alongside him.

'Charlie.' He stared at her, his dark eyes terrified and his little face streaked with tears.

'Don't move, it's all right. I'm here.' Using all the skill of years of training, she found toe-holds either side of him, her own body covering his, and with her superior height and reach she curved one arm over the ledge, her long fingers searching to find the safest grip.

This was the difficult part, Charlie knew. She could simply hang there and wait for the rescue service—but if he panicked and let go, would her body take the weight? She doubted that would work, because any sudden movement on Aldo's part would probably dislodge her. The alternative was to tighten her grip on the ledge with one hand and hope to push him up and onto the ledge taking his weight at her own time.

Quietly she spoke to him, telling him to be brave, to stay calm and do exactly as she said, and prayed he understood.

Jake swore violently as he gunned the Ferrari through the wide-open security gates. What the hell was the point of paying for security if they left the damn gates wide open? Someone would pay for this, he thought savagely as he stopped the car with a spin of wheels outside the house. He didn't actually know what he was doing back in Italy when he had meetings lined up in Japan. But ever since yesterday, when Charlotte had quietly put the phone down on him, he had had an irrational need to see her again. Charlotte was feisty and sometimes furious, but never apathetic. Something was definitely wrong. He had ordered the jet and flown straight back to Italy, and now as he marched up the steps he was sure of it.

The great double doors were wide open. *Dio! Please, no, Charlotte,* he prayed as he stormed through the house calling her name. Run away, kidnapped or worse—he didn't know; he just knew he had to have her back.

Pain squeezed his chest. How could he have been so stupid? He, Jake d'Amato, head of an international company and renowned for his business acumen, his ability to make the right decisions, his rapier-like intelligence, hadn't been able to protect his wife of barely two weeks.

Entering the kitchen, he saw the open exit door, and walked back outside and around to the back of the house. He saw Marco and the security guard staring at the cliff through a red haze of rage and strode purposefully towards them.

'What the hell do you think you are doing?' he roared at Marco, and froze when they pointed to the cliff, with a gesture of silence.

As if in slow motion he glanced up and the sight that met his eyes made the blood freeze in his veins. Charlotte, his Charlotte, was suspended halfway up the cliff. He dashed to the base of the cliff, scrabbled for a handhold, anything. But strong hands hauled him back telling him it was useless—he was too big and too late, the signora was almost there, and he had to be quiet.

Wild-eyed he looked at them and back at Charlotte. He opened his mouth to yell he would kill her for being so stupid, and closed it again as it struck him like a knife in the gut that she was in grave danger of doing that for herself.

'No. *Dio,* no,' he groaned and watched, his heart in his throat, as her lithe body moved closer to the young boy. He saw her straddle him and her fingers grip the ledge. He saw her hesitate and then her toes sought a firmer hold and in that moment he guessed what she was going to do. He wanted to scream and yell at her not to be so foolish, and, God help him, he didn't care if Aldo made it; all he cared about was Charlotte.

He didn't hear the sirens; he was deaf and blind to everything in the world except Charlotte. For the first time in his adult life he was utterly powerless. Neither his strength nor his wealth could do anything about the tableau unfolding before his eyes. He saw her slender figure tauten and the breath stopped in his lungs as she let go with one hand and reached an arm around the young boy's waist. Ashenfaced, he watched. He felt the strain, the agony she must be feeling with every cell in his body, and he saw her with superhuman strength haul them both onto the ledge.

But it wasn't over yet. Suddenly he was aware of the police cars and the specialist fire appliance, the men all around him, and furiously he berated everyone in sight for their tardiness while scarcely taking his eyes off the ledge.

When it was decided the fire crane was the safest option, he demanded to be the one to go up in the cradle.

'No, sir,' the fire chief told him. 'Only an experienced operative is allowed—'

Jake didn't wait to hear the rest, and moved impetuously forward. A bunch of officers grabbed him. He lashed out wildly and managed to throw them off, but he was too late. The cradle with a fireman on board was winging skyward.

Cold terror gripped him, and he stood frozen to the spot as the rescue cradle was inched higher and higher.

Charlotte lay back on the hard rock fighting to breathe, her arm firmly around Aldo. She felt him squirm and cry. 'No, don't move,' she rasped, and tucked him gingerly into the curve of her shoulder, closed her eyes, and said a quiet prayer of thanks.

When she opened them she gave a sigh of relief. A metal cradle with a man on board was gingerly edging towards the ledge. Aldo moved and she tightened her hold on him.

'But I want my kite,' Aldo objected. 'The string broke,' he said with the simplicity of youth and she had to smile at the irony of it as the kite did a graceful dive off the ledge.

Still smiling, she commanded the man in the cradle, 'Take Aldo first,' slipping into the role of rescuer as she had done countless times before, and easing the little boy up into the officer's waiting arms. Then with Aldo clinging safely to the officer's leg, Charlie was hoisted on board.

The descent to the ground was accomplished in seconds, and as the cradle locked back onto the appliance a mighty cheer went up—'Brava Charlotta,' and much in the same vein she did not understand as she stepped back onto firm ground.

The first person she saw was Jake dressed in his usual garb of elegant suit, but with his tie loosened, and she thought she was hallucinating. 'Jake! What are you doing here?' And she smiled, more from relief at the successful completion of the rescue than any great desire to see her husband.

Fury roared through Jake. She was wearing shorts and a skimpy top, her hair was falling around her shoulders, her arms were scratched and her knee was bleeding, and she was smiling. She was actually smiling as if she had been for a damned walk in the park, and she had calmly asked him what he was doing here. He was damn near dying with fright for her and she… 'Shut up, Charlotte, just shut up!' he growled and took her in his arms and held her close to his chest, a great shudder coursing through him.

Shocked, Charlie looked at him. She had been trained to remain cool in a crisis, but obviously Jake was not. His eyes were cold and angry, exactly as they had been the last time she had seen him. No change there, then. His arms tightened in a deathlike grip around her and she yelped and pushed back. 'Please, you're hurting me. I think I've scraped my back.'

'Scraped your back?' Jake's arms eased slightly, and he stared down at her, his black eyes leaping with violence. 'My God, woman, you're lucky you didn't break your neck! Are you stark staring mad?' His anger washed over her in ever-rising waves. 'What possessed you? You're pregnant, for God's sake. Have you got a death wish or something?'

'Or something,' Charlie snapped back. 'Common human decency, something you know nothing about.' He could not have made it plainer it was only the baby he was worried about.

Jake reeled as if he had been struck, all the anger draining out of him. His passionate, beautiful Charlotte was looking at him with contempt in her magnificent blue eyes, and he deserved it. He had been yelling at her like a madman when what he should be doing was comforting her—loving her. Finally he recognised what in his arrogance and conceit he had tried to deny. He loved Charlotte. He opened his mouth to tell her so, but the moment was lost as chaos reigned.

Marta swept Aldo into her arms, crying her eyes out, and berating him at the same time, then, grabbing Charlie's hand, she kissed it and thanked her over and over again.

Charlie murmured something appropriate, embarrassed by all the fuss. Police and firemen crowded around her with congratulations coming from all sides, and all the time Jake was at her back, his hand resting lightly on her waist, his dark presence towering over her.

All the people, the heat, the noise were making her head spin. A camera flashed right in her face and Jake dived past her to grip the hapless photographer and tear the camera from his hands.

Charlie's legs wobbled and for the first time in her life she fainted.

CHAPTER TWELVE

SLOWLY Charlie opened her eyes, and realised she was lying on the bed in the master bedroom. Jake was leaning over her, his handsome face grey and drawn, his eyes burning like black coals beneath hooded lids.

'You're awake, thank God. How do you feel? Where does it hurt?' he demanded in a voice that was not quite steady, and grasped her hand as if his life depended on it. 'Are you all right?'

'Oh, please,' she sighed, trying to sit up, but Jake gently pushed her back down. 'I'm fine.' And surprisingly, she realised she was.

The fog that seemed to have numbed her brain for the past few days was gone. Climbing the cliff, doing what she knew she was good at, while taking all her energy and skill had paradoxically restored her strength—her belief in herself. She didn't need Jake's concern—she didn't need him—and she glanced up at him, for once unmoved. 'How is Aldo? Is he all right?'

'Aldo is fine, hardly a mark on him, and confined to his room for life if I had my way. It is you I am worried about.'

'No need, I'm okay, but what are you doing here?'

'I could ask you the same question,' Jake said curtly. 'Unconscious in bed and why? Because you decided to scale a cliff to rescue that little devil instead of waiting for the emergency services.' A muscle jerked at the side of his mouth. 'Dio—when I saw you climbing up alongside Aldo...' He shook his head in disbelief. 'If I live to be a hundred I will never forget that image. I nearly went out of

171

my mind. I was sure you were going to fall in a crumpled heap at my feet.'

'You wish,' she mocked, and pulled her hand from his. His concern was too little and too late, as far as she was concerned.

'This is not a game, not something to joke about,' he grated, the tension in every line of his body evident as he added, 'You are my wife, you are carrying my child, and you could have killed the pair of you.'

She would never do anything to harm her child, and she had been as careful as she could. But it wasn't in her nature when any child's life was threatened to stand by and do nothing when she knew she could help. That Jake could think otherwise showed exactly how little he knew her. She might have told him so, but Marta appeared with Dr Bruno and a nurse in tow, and Charlie was grateful for the interruption. She didn't want to see Jake, didn't want to argue with him.

She did her best to ignore Jake's brooding presence as Dr Bruno conducted a thorough examination and pronounced the baby fine, and allowed the nurse to treat her cuts and bruises. Then they congratulated her on her act of heroism, and, horrified, she learned she had appeared on the television news.

'But how?' she asked, sitting up in bed. 'I saw you grab the man's camera.' She addressed her comment to Jake but avoided looking at him directly.

'The police cars have video cameras, as does the fire service; they film all their rescues,' Jake informed her, scowling. 'You are now the lead story on the local news station. And given you're a very beautiful and wealthy woman and you climbed a cliff to rescue a young boy, you will probably be splattered all over the national news, if not international.'

Charlie went pale. 'Oh, my God.'

'In fact, they'll probably dig up your life history, and the house will be besieged by paparazzi—'

'Now, Jake,' Dr Bruno cut in. 'Don't upset your wife; she has had enough for one day. But she is a remarkably fit young woman and the baby is fine, so you have nothing to worry about.'

'Are you sure about that?' Jake queried. 'I think she should be in hospital. She might have hidden injuries. What about a full body scan?'

Charlie looked at him as if he had taken leave of his senses, but the intense expression on his handsome face told her he was serious.

'I am the doctor here, Jake, and I can assure you Charlotte is fine.'

'But she was unconscious,' Jake said. 'Surely she must stay in hospital one night at least.'

'*She* is the cat's mother,' Charlie said in exasperation, sick of the two men talking about her as if she weren't there. 'And I was not unconscious. I fainted. And I fainted because I had little breakfast and no lunch, and after all that exercise I'm starving.' She almost laughed out loud at the stunned expression on Jake's face.

'There you are.' Dr Bruno chuckled. 'When a patient wants food there is not much wrong. Get Marta to feed her. As for you, Charlotte, eat and rest and no more climbing, until after the baby is born.' Turning to Jake, he added, 'As for you, Jake, do try and take better care of your wife. I don't understand you young men of today. In my day a new husband would never have dreamt of leaving his wife alone such a short time after the wedding.'

Jake didn't say a word. He couldn't, because nothing occurred to him but the gut-wrenching knowledge that he had nearly lost her. Dr Bruno was right; he should have taken better care of her. He looked at Charlotte, and her beauty and the shining spirit in her blue eyes shamed him. And all he had done since she had come down the cliff was yell or scowl at her. How could she possibly know it was because he had been terrified at the thought of losing her—still was…?

When Marta bustled in and told him to keep out of the way, she would look after Charlotte, he let her. After the arrogant way he had behaved over the past few weeks he no longer felt he had the right to object. It would be amazing if Charlotte even spoke to him again, and as for loving him, as she had declared frequently in the past—no chance.

Bathed, changed and tucked up in bed, Charlie had eaten a plate of delicious home-made lasagne and a huge wedge of chocolate gateau. Replete and tired, she refused Marta's offer of cheese.

'No, Marta, truly I don't want anything else, only to sleep,' she said gently. 'You go and look after Aldo. I'm fine.' She suffered Marta's thanks for about the thousandth time before Marta finally left.

She lay back against the pillows. It had been a traumatic day, but it had helped her clarify her thoughts on her marriage. She was going back home to England, whether Jake liked it or not, and when she saw him she would tell him so. But not tonight. She was tired. She let her eyelids droop, and was floating on the hazy edge of sleep when she heard the door close.

It was Jake, but he looked like something the cat had dragged in. His black hair was wildly dishevelled, as though he had been running his fingers through it. He had shed his jacket and tie and his shirt was open to the last button. His handsome face tightly drawn, he walked across to her and sat down on the side of the bed.

'What do you want? I was trying to sleep.' His dark

brooding gaze roamed slowly over her, lingering on the gauze bandage on her arm, his mouth tightening. It was a warm summer night and she was only wearing a slip of a nightdress. The cover was draped around her middle, and Charlie gathered the sheet closer about her, feeling absurdly nervous as the silence lengthened.

'Aren't you supposed to be in Japan?' She raised her chin, determined not to let him intimidate her ever again.

'Yes, but my wife hung up on me, and, hard as it may be for you to believe, I was worried about you.' He reached for her hand and grasped it in his. She tried to pull free, but he tightened his grip. 'No, please, hear me out.' There was a look of determination in his eyes, but also an uncertainty about him she had never seen before. 'I did a lot of thinking on the flight over here, and I realised, in the short time we have been together, I have not been totally honest with you because I have not been honest with myself.'

Charlie was pretty certain she knew what he was going to say next and didn't give him the chance. 'You have no need to explain. I know,' she said woodenly. 'Our marriage was a mistake, and we both know it. It was always the baby you wanted and not me. And don't bother denying it.'

'It was never—' Jake began, but she lifted her hand to silence him.

'No, let me finish. I thought for a little while I could live with a marriage solely for the child, but I realised I can't. I'm going back to England.'

'Charlotte, I am—' She cut him off again.

'But don't worry, Jake, I won't deprive you of your child. We are both mature adults, I'm sure we can come to some amicable access agreement.'

'Amicable agreement?' His dark eyes flared, all trace of uncertainty gone. 'I don't want an amicable agreement!' he growled, once more his arrogant, demanding self. 'What

I want is you, and I am trying to tell you I love you, damn it!'

'Oh, yes?' Charlie sneered, not believing him for a moment.

Jake's eyes bored into hers, dark and unfathomable, and a tiny muscle clenched at the edge of his jaw as he attempted to remain in control. 'I do love you, Charlotte. I think I have from the moment I saw you, but I told myself I didn't believe in love.'

'But now you do. How convenient, when I have just told you I am going home.' She tried for sarcasm but her voice wobbled ever so slightly. He sounded so sincere.

'No, love is not convenient, Charlotte. I have learned that much over the weeks we have been together. It is an ache, a hunger, a need that is all consuming. I tried to tell myself you were no different from all the other women I had known. In my heart I knew you were, but I refused to face it,' he said, leaning closer and gently stroking a strand of hair back from her face.

'When I spoke to you yesterday you sounded different, detached, and when you hung up on me—for the first time in my life, I was afraid. I ordered the jet and came straight back, but even then I was not ready to admit I loved you, because I did not fully understand what loving you meant.' He squeezed her hand so tight Charlie almost cried out. 'And then I saw the open gates, the empty house, and the horror scenarios that ran through my mind terrified me. I thought you had gone or been kidnapped, killed, and it was the worst moment of my life, but two minutes later I realised it wasn't when I lifted my eyes and saw you climbing that cliff.'

He was pale, Charlie noticed, but otherwise seemed to be maintaining a tight control. She sensed he was genuinely concerned—but then why wouldn't he be? She was carrying his child. 'You were probably relieved I wasn't kidnapped.' She shrugged, dismissing his fear. 'Think of the money I saved you,' she added nastily.

Jake stared at her, his eyes violent with some inner emotion of such magnitude that it took him a few seconds to successfully mask his expression. 'You think that badly of me?' His voice was bleak and his strong face clenched taut. 'Then you can leave when you like. There is nothing more to be said.' He turned to walk away.

Charlie suddenly saw red. He was doing it again, blanking her out. But this time they hadn't made love, but worse— he had said he loved her.

'Yes, there damn well is!' she shouted. 'You thought that badly of *me*, remember? A selfish greedy bitch selling her father's paintings for gain. Not so nice when the shoe is on the other foot, is it?' she snarled.

He spun around, his eyes hard as polished jet. 'I never said that, you did.'

'But you thought it,' she lashed back, and he did not attempt to contradict her. 'Well, let me tell you, Mr High and Mighty, all the money from my dad's art is going to the earthquake relief fund. With the agreement of Jess, the only one of his models I met. And as for *selfishly* refusing to meet your sister, that was my father's idea. I caught him once with Jess and, like most womanising men, I believe— and you should know,' she snapped, her blue eyes flashing fire, 'he was incredibly strict when it came to his own daughter. He didn't want me to meet his women, and whatever tales he told Anna had absolutely nothing to do with me. In fact, you're just like him, over-protective of your sister, and you'll be just as bad with your own child. So you know what? I'm glad I'm leaving. You're nothing but a workaholic, money-mad megalomaniac. And I hate you.'

Charlie swayed back against the pillows as reaction at the

day's events and regrets for what could have been hit her badly. She placed a protective hand on her stomach and blinked back the tears that threatened.

For several seconds Jake stared back at her in shock. He felt about two inches tall. He could not deny he had once thought her capable of greed and selfishness and hadn't cared. At the beginning he had been content to have a willing Charlotte in his bed. She was right; he was everything she said he was, and more. He was a coward too, because he had never had the nerve to tell her how he really felt until she had almost killed herself. He was useless at this love thing, he thought, momentarily defeated. Then he saw her protective gesture and the tears she was trying so valiantly to hide, and he almost fell apart. But not quite. Instead he did the one thing he knew he was good at. He strode forward and sat down on the bed.

'You still here?' Charlie tried for sarcasm, but her voice wobbled.

'I am not going anywhere,' Jake said, and just snatched her into his arms.

'No? Well, I am.' She was leaving him, but somehow, held close in his arms, Charlie was suddenly too exhausted to fight him.

'No, you are not,' Jake muttered, and claimed her mouth with a gentle, possessive pressure. 'I am everything you say I am, but I love you, Charlotte.' His hand cupped her chin and she was unable to move. 'I am not very good at this, because I have never loved anyone before.' His mouth moved as soft as thistledown to her eyes, and briefly brushed her lids. 'But I can't bear to see you cry, I can't bear to see you hurt. I can't bear to see you in danger,' he told her forcibly. '*Dio!* I love you so much I can't, I won't, let you go.'

She could only look at him. There could be no doubt he

meant every word. It was there in the depth of his dark eyes, the husky determination in his voice, his touch as he brushed away a stray tear from her cheek, and carefully tucked an errant strand of hair behind her ear.

Hope and joy ignited inside her and heat washed through her veins, washing away her fears. Her blue eyes widened in wonder on his.

'I love everything about you,' he murmured softly. 'Though no woman has ever confused and frustrated me so utterly as you have.' His lips curved in a wry smile. 'Nor hurt me as much.'

'Hurt you?' Charlie asked. 'I didn't think that was possible.' But she saw the vulnerability in his dark gaze and was shocked.

'Oh, it is, I assure you,' he said, and then pushed her back against the pillows, his hard body pinning her down, and claimed her mouth with all the fierce passion of his arrogant nature. And she sighed against his lips, and pressed closer.

Jake lifted his head. 'I wanted you so much, Charlotte, but on our wedding day—' His eyes darkened but, as if compelled to talk, he carried on. '*Dio*, I listened to Dave telling me what you did, and felt ashamed I had not known. I glanced across and saw you so brave and so beautiful and thought I was the luckiest man on earth.

'And on our wedding night I needed you, ached for you so badly. I could not believe it when you mentioned Anna and the painting. And if Diego had been there I would have flattened him on the spot for putting the idea in your mind. I had long since given up any idea of revenge—it was a spur-of-the-moment, stupid idea in the first place. And I wanted nothing to spoil our night though even then I could not admit why.'

Charlie's lips parted in a soft, tremulous smile. 'Diego's

revelation gave me a bit of a shock,' she murmured, lifting a hand to weave it through his soft black hair, and saw the expression on the face only inches from hers become slightly hooded.

'Not as shocked as I was when you mentioned the portrait in the bedroom, at the very moment I held you in my arms and kissed you. You have no idea how much it hurt me to see the doubt, the lack of trust in your eyes. I was furious and I lashed out at you.'

'You said you married me only for the baby,' Charlotte reminded him, but the hope in her heart was growing.

'I lied. I didn't marry you because you were pregnant. I didn't marry you for any other reason than I had to because I needed you and only you,' Jake said quietly, and brushed his finger across her cheek and round the contours of her lips. 'The baby is a marvellous bonus. But I was angry with you because it was my own guilt I could not face. Not only thinking badly of you but, if I am honest, because of Anna. You were wrong earlier when you said I was like your father and would be fiercely protective of any child. I never protected my child who was aborted, and I never protected Anna the way a real brother should. I never paid her enough attention—a lunch occasionally, and that was it. I had no right to be angry with you or your father. Anna was a grown woman and made her own mistakes. But I never learnt from mine. I never protected you, my wife, as Dr Bruno so succinctly pointed out.' To see her proud, indomitable husband so chastened, so vulnerable was a shock to Charlie.

'But if you will just give me a second chance, Charlotte, I swear I will protect you and our child with my life. You are the love I never thought existed,' he said huskily. 'And I want you so much.' He groaned, his eyes darkening as his gaze flickered over where the sheet had slipped and exposed the soft curve of her breasts barely covered by her satin nightgown, and then he fastened his mouth on hers in a kiss that was so piercingly sweet it melted her bones.

'You are so exquisite I can't think straight, let alone talk sensibly about anything, but, please, just say you will stay,' Jake pleaded. 'You said you loved me once, let me try to persuade you to love me again.' With a smothered groan he began kissing her again, until she started to tremble with emotion.

'Jake…' she murmured, her hand splaying across his broad chest, feeling the heat of his satin-smooth skin, the tickle of body hair on her palms. But still she pushed him away, and it was the hardest thing she had ever done. 'Please, I need to know,' she faltered. 'I need to know you truly mean this. The very first time we made love,' she said in a rush as Jake tensed, his dark gaze fixed warily on her face as though expecting some knockout blow, 'you turned your back on me and walked away in anger. Why? Was it something I did or didn't do?' She had to know she wasn't opening herself up to get left again afterwards.

'Oh, *cara*.' He paused to take a brief, hard kiss that left her breathless. 'That wasn't your fault, it was mine. You made me angrier than I could ever remember being before. I felt quite savage simply looking at you, because I had just made love to you and I wanted you again so badly. I could not understand the totally overwhelming sensations I felt just kissing you. And to be brutally honest I was still reeling from the shock of discovering the portrait of Anna. I'd only learned of its existence a few hours before I met you, and I felt terribly guilty. I could not understand myself. I had to walk away or reveal my desperation for you, and I was not prepared to do that.'

'You wanted me that badly.' Charlie was thrilled.

'Oh, yes, and I still do, always will,' he said huskily.

But she wasn't totally convinced. 'If that's true, then why

after our wedding day, when we finally made love, did you never touch me again? I hardly saw you. You never came to bed until the early hours and when you did you made a jolly good job of ignoring me,' Charlie protested, his coolness still looming large in her mind. 'Then when we did make love after the party, you stormed off in anger again.'

'That bothered you, hmm?' And his smile had a hint of passion intermingled with a touch of humour. 'You wanted me to make love to you.'

'No—well, yes.' She was sure he was laughing at her.

'Ah, Charlott-a-a. You really will have to learn my language.' He kissed her again, his tongue curling and probing her mouth, and she felt the breath catch in her throat when he lifted his head and smiled down at her, his dark eyes gleaming with love and emotion.

'It was all Dr Bruno's fault. He told me when you had your examination that the first few months were the most crucial of your pregnancy and it was better to refrain from sex. But after a week of abstinence I could not resist and once again I was angry with myself—not with you—for being so weak-willed. And when I told you about the abortion, and saw the compassion in your eyes, and heard your soft voice telling me I had to trust, I so wanted to lose myself in you. I had to leave. How could I endanger our child after what I had just told you?'

'Oh, Jake, that is an archaic idea,' Charlie said. 'Even I know that.'

'I wish you had told me. It would have saved me a lot of sleepless nights, and cold showers.' He hugged her to him, his breath warm against her cheek. 'Every night I would sit in the study and watch the security videos just to see you relaxed and playing with Aldo, and when I finally dared to slip into bed beside you I used to watch you sleep for hours. I knew then I loved you, but I was still fighting it. But today when you stepped out of that cradle with Aldo, and I yelled at you, I knew I could hide it no longer. I had so nearly lost you and life would not be worth living without you in my world. But then everyone mobbed you and I never got the chance.'

His confession was music to her ears. She looked at him and the love was there for her to see. She doubted anyone had ever seen him so vulnerable or ever would again. He was laying his heart on the line for her, and it moved her overwhelmingly. Wrapping her arms around him, she murmured, 'You have now, and I believe you. I have to because I love you, have done since the day we met.'

'At last.' Jake sighed and she saw the awe, the brilliant gleam of triumph in his smouldering dark eyes, as his head bent. 'You're mine—now, and for all eternity.' And his mouth captured hers in a deeply possessive kiss.

Charlie felt heat spreading through her as his mouth slid to her throat and the soft curve of her breast. Jake raised his head and looked at her, his eyes dark and questioning. She smiled and her arms lifted to tighten around his neck, her body arching beneath him. And with a fraught groan his control went and he showed her just how much she meant to him.

Later he held her possessively against his hard body, and studied her beautiful face, the sultry blue eyes, and her light golden skin on which the aftermath of loving had left a golden glow. 'Are you sure you're all right, Charlotte?'

'For a brilliant, intelligent man you really are a bit of a worrier,' Charlotte teased. 'Frightened because I climbed a few rocks—and as for believing Dr Bruno! For heaven's sake, the man himself is archaic.'

'Oh, Charlotte, you are priceless,' Jake said with a deep throaty laugh.

'You didn't always think that,' Charlotte said soberly.

When she thought of how close she had come to leaving him, losing him…

'Forgive me, Charlotte, for every arrogant assumption, every harsh word,' he said softly. 'And I swear I will spend the rest of my life making it up to you and loving you.'

EPILOGUE

NINE months later Charlie peeped out at the beach from behind the corner of the villa. They had arrived on the Caribbean island last night. It was owned by a friend of Jake's who rented out his fabulous villa to a few selected guests. Absolute privacy guaranteed.

A mischievous smile curved her lush mouth as she spotted Jake wearing a pair of old shorts and stretched out on a lounger, a long arm reaching over the side to rock the carefully shaded cradle where their daughter of three months, Samantha, slept. She was the apple of her father's eye. Jake was totally besotted with her. Once a cynic about women, he was devoted to the brown-eyed cherub.

Charlotte took a last surreptitious look around and strolled down the beach. Some sixth sense must have warned Jake because his dark head turned and he leapt to his feet, the look on his face priceless as she sashayed towards him.

'Give me your opinion.' She gave him a twirl, the grass skirt that hung low on her hips rustling as she moved, and a strategically draped garland of flowers around her neck protecting her modesty. Lifting her head, she met Jake's dark, stunned gaze. 'Is it me?'

Jake reached for her bare shoulders, and placed a possessive, hungry kiss on her smiling lips. 'Definitely you. Stunning and beautiful and better than I could ever have imagined,' he said huskily, and folded her in his arms and held her firmly against his chest. 'As is my deep abiding love for you, and the perfect daughter you have given me.' He kissed her again.

'From a day in Kew Gardens to a real paradise island.' Charlotte smiled. 'I never thought we would make it, but we have. All three of us,' she murmured, her blue eyes brilliant with happiness and love.

The Carides
Pregnancy

KIM LAWRENCE

Kim Lawrence lives on a farm in rural Anglesey. She runs two miles daily and finds this an excellent opportunity to unwind and seek inspiration for her writing! It also helps her keep up with her husband, two active sons, and the various stray animals which have adopted them. Always a fanatical consumer of fiction, she is now equally enthusiastic about writing. She loves a happy ending!

CHAPTER ONE

CARL STONE'S control over his financial empire was total, whereas the weather in the Home Counties, for the moment, remained outside his dominion.

It was the day of his only daughter's wedding, and the Met Office had predicted an early snowfall across the country. The ominous clouds overhead suggested that promise would almost definitely be fulfilled.

Sure enough, as a sprinkling of early guests began to arrive, making their way through the tight security cordon around the Cathedral, the first thick white flakes began to fall.

A few snowflakes, however, were not about to dampen the spirits of these guests. Most would have happily struggled through a total white-out, weighed down by their understated—in some cases overstated—elegance, their designer hats, fur coats, and jewels, to attend what was extravagantly being billed as the society wedding of the year!

Only one person appeared not to appreciate his good fortune at being there. The tall, lean figure stood a little apart, with one hand thrust negligently into his trouser pocket, his broad back set against the gnarled trunk of an ancient yew. He was apparently oblivious to the biting cold wind, and the snow that had begun to dust his dark hair and the shoulders of his well-cut morning suit.

If the expression on his dark, startlingly handsome face suggested anything it was intense boredom. This sombreness of expression was lightened occasionally when he responded in kind to a greeting from a friend or family member as they passed by.

One impressionable young lady, gasping as she witnessed such a moment, was heard to declare fervently that she would happily sell her soul to be on the receiving end of that smile. Her more literally-minded sister retorted bluntly that she would like to be on the receiving end of more than his smile!

'Jocasta... India... Behave, girls.' Herding her sulky daughters ahead of her, their mother—a long way from indifferent herself to the attributes of the tall, enigmatic figure with the fallen angel features and the dangerous sexy aura—gave a slightly wistful glance in his direction before following her offspring inside the splendid Gothic edifice.

If others present had been unaware of his identity, his colouring would have immediately placed him on the groom's guest list. *Typically Greek*, they would have said, observing his jet-black hair, warm olive skin, and a profile that could have come straight from an ancient Greek statue. But those better acquainted could have told them that this man wasn't *typically* anything!

The question of identity didn't arise, however, because of course there was hardly a soul amongst the socially prominent guests who wasn't aware of his identity. Any number, if asked, could probably list his star sign, his shoe size, and hazard an educated guess at his bank balance.

Christos Carides, head of the Carides Empire, was actually as instantly recognisable to his fellow guests as was their host, and according to some sources he was even more disgustingly rich! And, it went without saying, *much* better looking.

Despite outward appearances Christos *was* feeling the cold, having spent the last month enjoying warm Australian sunshine, he was keenly aware of the chill in the air. A chill that was very nearly as bone-biting as the one between him and his cousin—the groom.

A spasm of contempt briefly distorted the perfect contours of his sensually moulded lips as his thoughts touched on the subject of his cousin Alex.

At that moment a shortish, cherubic-faced and fair-haired young man emerged from the side of the building. He gave a relieved sigh as he immediately spotted the person he was looking for. Breathless, his jacket flapping open to reveal a striped silk waistcoat, the harassed best man belted along the path, narrowly avoiding several collisions with startled-looking guests.

'I'm Peter,' he blurted out as he skidded to halt in front of the tall, commanding figure of the Greek financier.

'Yes, I remember. You're Carl's godson, aren't you...?'

Peter nodded. 'I'm the best man after...' He stopped, looking uncomfortable.

Christos helped him out. 'After I refused.'

'Yeah, well, you don't know how glad I am to see you.'

'Always glad to make someone happy,' Christos observed drily. 'Can I help you?' he prompted, when the younger man didn't respond.

'You've got to come with me!'

In response to this dramatic statement Christos flexed his shoulders and levered himself with effortless elegance from the tree trunk. 'I have...?' he murmured politely.

The sardonic inflection and the cold light in the dark, deepset eyes that rested on his face caused the breathless younger man's hopeful smile to gutter and fade. This was not a promising start.

'He's asking for you. Please...Mr C-Carides,' he stuttered. 'I don't know what to do. He's a total mess, and if Uncle Carl sees him like this there'll be hell to pay,' he predicted gloomily. 'He drank enough to sink a battleship last night. He really isn't himself.'

Christos did not display surprise—because he *wasn't* surprised. He would have been more surprised if his cousin *hadn't* fallen off the wagon. At times of stress—and presumably marrying the heiress of one of the richest men in Britain came under that title—his cousin always reached for a crutch.

'I think you'll find, Peter, when you have known Alex a little longer, that he *is* being himself.'

He would learn, as people generally did, that underneath the charm Alex possessed in abundance his cousin was essentially weak and, like many insecure men, inclined to be spiteful and manipulative when thwarted.

The younger man looked a little nonplussed by the languid response. 'I don't think you understand. He can hardly stand up and he keeps...' He paused and glanced over his shoulder. '*Crying...*'

It was clear to Christos that in the young Englishman's eyes these masculine tears were the most embarrassing feature of this situation. 'And this should concern me because...?' he enquired, in his deep, accented drawl.

The younger man's expression betrayed his shock and revulsion at this casual response. 'You're not going to help?'

The reply, when it came, was unambiguous. 'No.'

Under normal circumstances the younger man would not have dared speak his mind to the likes of Christos Carides, but the realisation that he was going to have to sort out the mess himself made him recklessly outspoken.

'When Alex said you were a cold, callous bastard I gave you the benefit of the doubt!'

Christos smiled, revealing even white teeth and zero warmth. 'Your mistake, I think,' he observed mildly. 'If you want my advice, for what it's worth, I'd shove his head in a bucket of ice water, fill another with black coffee and force-feed it to him.

'Don't worry too much,' he added. 'He has the consti-
tution of a hospital superbug. Now, if you'll excuse me,
I'm waiting for someone.' With a slight inclination of his
dark head he dismissed the younger man.

The stressed best man retreated a few feet, then turned
back, his resentment roughening his young voice as he
yelled back, 'Uncle Carl is right. You and the rest of
Carides family may think you're a cut above everyone else,
but when it comes down to it you're no better than a
damned pirate. No morals, no scruples and no manners.'

Peter saw that, rather than being offended by the insulting tirade, Christos was grinning, in that instant looking
every inch a swashbuckling buccaneer—one, furthermore,
likely to cut his throat on a whim!

'Is that a direct quote?'

Peter was not a physical young man, but the mockery
gleaming in the Greek's dark eyes filled with him with an
uncharacteristic desire to resort to physical violence. Not
that he did, of course. He was angry, not insane! This was
no sedentary businessman he was talking to. Christos
Carides was only in his early thirties, and besides, he had
to be six five if he was an inch—and he definitely worked
out!

Cooling down slightly, Peter became belatedly aware
that people were staring. And, being much less comfortable
with this attention than his adversary, the young man gritted
his teeth and stalked off with as much dignity as he could
muster.

He would have been comforted to know that there was
someone close by who would have applauded his reading
of the Carides character—and added a few choice obser-
vations of her own!

Becca Summer, mingling with guests, was approaching the
security cordon. At that moment her throat was so dry with

nerves she probably couldn't have strung two words together, and if she had she wouldn't have been able to hear
what she said above the heavy thud of her pounding heart.
Six weeks earlier she hadn't been similarly hindered.

Six weeks earlier she had been uncharacteristically vocal!

'People like these Carides,' she had declared, snarling
the name contemptuously. 'They make me sick! They think
that just because they have money and power they can do
anything they want.' She'd looked at her sister, Erica, and
swallowed past the emotional lump in her throat. 'Regardless of who they hurt.'

'You know, Becca, there's not much point being mad,'
Erica had pointed out defeatedly.

'You mean don't get mad, get even?' The old cliché had
never made more sense to her than it had at that moment.

'Get even?' Erica had exclaimed with a laugh. 'Are you
serious? We're talking about the Carides.'

'So you think that people like the Carides imagine they
can do anything they want?' Becca had retorted.

'I *know* they can, Becca.'

The bleak retort had made Becca's eyes fill. She'd struggled to hold back the tears and declared fiercely, 'One day
I'll teach them that they can't walk all over people and get
away with it! You see if I don't.'

It had been said in the heat of the moment, and deep
down she probably hadn't really believed that such an opportunity would arise—but here she was, about to do her
small part in balancing the scales of justice.

And she was already regretting it big-time!

Becca caught a passer-by staring at her head and quickly
pulled off the knitted cloche—not the sort of head gear that
people wore to posh weddings—crammed over her tangled
titian hair. Pulling a not quite steady hand through her Pre-

Raphaelite curls, she shook her hair back, letting it fan over the dark material of her coat.

Don't give up the day job, Becca. Undercover work is definitely not for you, she told herself, repressing a worried grin.

Part of the problem was that she was not just scared out of her mind, she was exhausted. Hardly surprising, considering that the previous evening she had jumped in her ancient Beetle and driven through the night, halfway across the country, to get here.

Adrenaline and outrage—and seeing the newspaper article concerning the 'society wedding of the year' had given her a double dose of both—could, she discovered, take a protective big sister a long way.

Cars, on the other hand, needed petrol—which was why she had had to walk five miles along a lonely road to the nearest service station at three in the morning. A terrifying experience. And then, just to add to her misery, it had started to snow.

Snow in early November—how unlucky was that?

She had a blister on her right heel to bear witness to her trek, and a suspicion that spontaneity wasn't all it was cracked up to be. After this was over it would be a relief to go back to her normal sensible, cautious, consequence-considering self!

Reckless just wasn't *her*. It wasn't in her nature to throw caution to the wind. In fact, her inability to be spontaneous had been one of the reasons Roger had cited for the failure of their relationship.

Her family and friends had been suitably supportive when the announcement—the very week following their break-up—of Roger's engagement to a bubbly blonde had appeared in the local paper. Becca, uneasily aware that as the dumped fiancée she ought to be feeling more traumatised, had received their sympathy with a degree of guilt.

After a few weeks the role of pathetic victim had begun to get wearing.

When she had said as much to her sister, Erica had said, 'Don't worry—in a few weeks' time they will have a new juicy scandal to talk about.'

Neither of them had suspected at the time that it would be Erica who supplied the scandal!

Erica had told her family about her unplanned pregnancy the same day the ambulance had been called, its sirens ringing, to the neat Edwardian semi where Becca and Erica had grown up

But it had been too late to save the baby.

Later, back home, with the promise that—all being well—their youngest daughter could be discharged the next day, the Summers family had sat down in the sitting room, staring mutely at one another.

Recognising her elderly parents were still in shock—her father was ten years older than her mother, and Elspeth Summer had been forty-five when her younger daughter had been born—Becca had done the only thing she'd been able to think of: she'd made tea.

'She's only eighteen,' her mother had been saying when she'd come back in, carrying the tray.

'Well, maybe this was for the best.'

'For the best…? For the best! How can you even suggest that losing a baby is for the best!' Elspeth had demanded, rounding furiously on her startled husband.

'Dad didn't mean it that way,' Becca had soothed. 'Did you, Dad.'

'No, of course not,' her father had said, looking intensely grateful for the intervention.

'I was just thinking that, knowing our Erica, it would have been you and Becca who ended up looking after the baby,' he'd observed, with an affectionate watery smile.

His wife had given him a reassuring smile back and said

huskily, 'I know you didn't mean it, love.' She'd reached across and clasped his hand. 'I'm just thinking if we'd been stricter with her...'

And that had been the start of a predictable orgy of self-recrimination. Recrimination! Their kind, loving parents were the very last people in the world who had anything to reproach themselves over. Going over that conversation in her head made Becca ashamed that she had almost turned back when she saw the scale of this wedding she intended to crash and disrupt. Her soft lips thinned. She just hoped that plenty of people had their video cameras handy!

Head up, she pinned on a confident smile and, picking up a corsage that someone had dropped on the floor she tucked it at a jaunty angle into her buttonhole. She intended to see to it that the society wedding of the decade *didn't* go without a hitch.

CHAPTER TWO

CHRISTOS watched the irate best man vanish around the side of the building and suppressed a twinge of guilt. For a second he was tempted to follow him, but instead he blew on his fingers to revive the circulation. It struck him as faintly ludicrous that even after all that had happened his first instinct was to bail his cousin out.

What Alex needed was not someone to hold his hand and wipe his nose—he needed to take responsibility for his own actions. Christos's attempt the previous year to instil a sense of responsibility into the younger man had failed spectacularly.

When he had spelt out the new rules to his cousin, the younger man had laughed.

'This is a wind-up. You're bluffing.'

Christos had shaken his head. 'Turn up at the office more than once every six months, and when you're there do more than drink coffee and chat up female staff.'

'I delegate,' Alex had protested.

'No. *I* delegate; you sponge. Work, cousin—or the very healthy cheque that's credited to your bank account every month won't be there.'

Christos hadn't been bluffing.

There were a number of family members who had called him a heartless monster for refusing to be swayed from his decision—though naturally not to his face. Interestingly, there had been an equal number who had said, About time too!

But Alex's response to the challenge had not been what

14

he'd hoped. In fact it had been something he could not have predicted.

Christos had never decided if Alex had *wanted* him to find out, but there was no similar ambiguity when it came to his ex-fiancée's intentions. Melina had known Christos was coming to her flat that evening, to return the keys and pick up the laptop he'd left there.

'Don't be silly—there's no reason we can't be civilised. We have history,' Melina had said when he'd rung to say he would send someone round with the keys. 'You come, darling, and we can have a drink to the good times.'

The look of spiteful triumph in her eyes when he had walked in and found her and Alex naked on the floor, amidst a pile of discarded clothes and several empty wine bottles, had removed any lingering guilt Christos felt about ending their short-lived farcical engagement the previous week.

Mild disgust and contempt were *not* the responses a man was meant to have when he found the woman he had briefly contemplated spending the rest of his life with making love to another man!

He'd felt no desire to take violent retribution, no desire to wipe the supercilious smirk off his cousin's face—just a compelling urge to walk away from the sordid and tasteless spectacle.

And that was what he had done. He had slung the keys on the table and left. His only regret being that he had ever been insane enough to think *all right* and *workable* were thoughts a man should have as prerequisites for marriage.

Before Christos succumbed to frostbite, or to the austerity of his own grim reflections, his great-aunt, whom he had been delegated to escort, arrived. Christos heard her before he saw her. Her bony frame was swamped by several layers of motley fur, and her grey hair was crammed into an ancient shapeless hat, but her voice was not similarly fettered. It was loud and penetrating.

'It is not civilised. I shouldn't be surprised if this British weather kills me!' she was telling a fellow guest.

'I should be very surprised.'

A smile illuminated the lined, leathery face as Theodosia Carides identified the tall figure who had materialised at her side.

'So you did come,' she grunted, offering her rose-scented withered cheek for her great-nephew's respectful salute.

'Seeing you, Aunt Theodosia, makes the effort worth while.'

'Don't try your charm on me,' the old lady recommended, repressing a pleased grin as she accepted the arm her tall handsome nephew offered. 'I'm immune.'

The still-upright septuagenarian, who did not even reach his shoulder, did not see the need to lower her voice as her favourite nephew escorted her into the hushed, vaulted interior of the Cathedral.

'I thought you were in Australia, Christos?'

'I was.' Christos saw Melina, looking as stunning as ever, seated a few feet away. They nodded in a civilised manner to one another.

'Did Alex really ask you to be best man?'

'Yes, he did.'

'And you said no?'

Christos's expression didn't alter as he inclined his dark head in agreement—which, considering the mental picture of his ex, naked astride the groom, which was at that moment flickering across his retina, was no mean achievement.

'I expect you had your reasons…?'

Christos did not satisfy her curiosity. 'Can I take that for you, Aunt?' he asked, indicating the large portmanteau his elderly relative clutched.

'I am not an invalid.' Despite this sharp assertion, she

paused to catch her breath. 'I suppose you know that Andrea is saying your refusal is just another symptom of your deep-seated jealousy?'

Christos's dark brows lifted. 'Jealousy?'

The old lady nodded. 'According to her, you've always been jealous of her precious Alex.' No longer able to conceal her amusement, she gave a loud cackle of mirth and shared the joke. '*Apparently* you never lose any opportunity to belittle him and make him look foolish. Though from what I've seen he doesn't need much help—and so I told his mother. Andrea always was a very silly woman.'

'I must remember to avoid Aunt Andrea.'

'As if you care what she thinks. As if you care what *anyone* thinks.' Her expression suggested she approved of this attitude.

Christos gave one his most charming smiles. 'I care what you think, Aunt Theodosia,' he promised slickly.

The old lady dismissed the comment with a derisive snort. 'Does nobody but me care about tradition any more?' she wondered out loud. 'Nobody would even know this was a Carides wedding,' she continued, in the same disapproving bellow. 'Nobody has yet explained to me why they're not having a proper Orthodox ceremony.'

'Don't look at me, Aunt Theodosia. This wedding has nothing to do with me.' He was only here because his mother had got distressed and played the duty card. *'They'll think you don't like your cousin.'*

'I don't.'

In the event his honesty had not won him any points with his mother. She had bitterly enquired over the phone if he derived some form of malicious pleasure out of tormenting her.

'If he gets a little loud around you it's because you make him feel inadequate,' Mia Carides had explained.

On the other side of the world, Christos had given a wry

grin. *Inadequate* was one of the things a man might be excused for feeling if he found the woman he was to have married having sex with another man. Only he had never really been in love with Melina.

In truth, it had come as something of a surprise to Christos to hear the news of his own engagement!

When Melina had pulled her father to one side and whispered in his ear, Christos had had no inkling of the secret she was sharing. Not until two minutes later, when their host had called for hush and shared the news with the rest of the three hundred or so close friends who were there to celebrate the thirty years of married bliss he and his wife had enjoyed.

'I am happy to announce that my daughter and our dear friend Christos Carides are to be married.'

Christos had had no desire to humiliate the rather drunk Melina, with whom he had enjoyed a casual on-off relationship for several years, so he had smiled through the inevitable congratulations and gone home with the firm intention of ending the engagement the next day.

That had been his first mistake!

His next had been not to agree when a very shame-faced and repentant Melina had turned up the next morning, promising to set the record straight immediately. Her remorse had appeared totally genuine, and she'd obviously been mortified—so much so that he had heard himself saying, 'Why bother? We could give it a trial run.'

'Do you really think so, Christos?'

'Why not? We get on well enough, and it's not as though either of us is waiting for love at first sight.'

Contemplating life without love did not overly concern Christos. A person could not miss what they had never had. And perhaps, as Melina had claimed in one of their many arguments, he was incapable of the emotion?

'What do you mean, *nothing to do with you?* You're

head of the family, aren't you?' Aunt Theodosia demanded shrilly.

With a rueful smile Christos refocused his attention on the demanding little lady at his elbow. When jet lag eventually kicked in he was going to sleep for a week. 'A title with few benefits.'

His dry observation drew a crowing little laugh from the old lady, but she added severely, 'Don't whine, Christos. You have been blessed with brains, looks and health—not to mention a gift for making large amounts of money without breaking a sweat.'

The unsympathetic recommendation brought a smile to Christos's dark, expressive eyes. 'Sorry, Aunt,' he said, bowing his dark head meekly.

'This girl of Alex's has got a face like a horse,' she observed regretfully.

'Sally is a very nice girl,' Christos responded, a quiver in his deep voice.

It was at that moment he saw her.

He stopped dead, and didn't hear what Theodosia was saying—or, for that matter, anything else. She was framed in the doorway, her hair as she entered the Gothic candlelit Cathedral an incredible burnished beacon.

For a few seconds things got *seriously* surreal. But there was in all probability some perfectly prosaic reason for the rest of the world receding, leaving him with the impression that he and the redhead were the only two people in the place.

Christos, his jaw clenched, blinked hard, and the hum of conversation gradually filtered back into his consciousness. Jet lag, he concluded, loosening the constricting tie around his neck a little as he narrowed his gaze on the bright head of the slim, simply dressed woman.

He had never seen her before. Not that this made her exceptional. There were any number of people attending the wedding that he had never laid eyes on before. But, unlike this late arrival, those strangers had no connection with the prickle on the back of his neck. The groove between his dark, strongly delineated black brows deepened as he lifted a hand to the affected area.

With a first-class degree in pure maths, and the owner of a mind that was widely held to be brilliantly analytical and logical, he saw nothing contradictory in trusting his instincts. And there was absolutely no doubt in his mind that the slender redhead represented trouble of a major variety.

Perhaps the danger she represented appealed to him? Could that alone account for his suddenly out-of-control libido? He didn't have a clue, and he was not in a mood to analyse his motivation, he just knew he was going to make sure—even at the risk of major disappointment—of meeting her.

At some level he recognised that even the recent months of self-enforced abstinence didn't totally explain away the compulsion that made him unable to take his eyes off her for fear she would vanish.

Vanish? With that hair? Not likely. His eyes moved hungrily over the mass of rich auburn curls that fell down her shapely narrow back. It was *extremely* unlikely that she would be swallowed up in the crowd, even though that was clearly her desire. A circumstance that he would investigate at a later date, when other more urgent needs, like hearing her voice, were satisfied.

Christos met many attractive, interesting women during the course of his average day, but none that had ever immobilised him with lust. But now… He trained his eyes on the redhead, who was still trying hard to blend in, and drew a deep breath. This was a temptation he had no intention of resisting.

'I don't *dislike* horses, and from what I've seen the girl has got excellent child-bearing hips.'

A thoughtful expression settled on Theodosia's lined face as she imperiously reclaimed her nephew's attention with this outrageous observation and a sharp tug on his jacket.

'Is she pregnant, I wonder? It would explain the unseemly haste. What do you think, Christos?'

With an air of resignation, and still conscious in the periphery of his vision of the redhead, he guided the outspoken old lady into her seat. 'I think I should mind my own business.'

'Not that there's anything *wrong* with a pregnant bride.'

'That is very broad-minded of you, Aunt Theodosia.'

'I'm not a prude, boy.'

Christos's thickly lashed eyes narrowed in affection. 'You do surprise me.'

'And virgins are all well and good,' she observed generously.

The redhead, he noticed, was in danger of disappearing behind a stone column. He had established, to his satisfaction, that she definitely wasn't with anyone, but she was too far away for him to tell if she wore any rings.

'I'm not aware that I know any.' In his opinion it was more important to be the last man in a woman's life, not the first, if that woman was the one you intended to spend the rest of your life with.

Theodosia chose to ignore her nephew's satiric insert beyond tapping him sharply across the knuckles with her cane. 'I hardly think you're in any position to criticise. Greek men can be so hypocritical,' she observed tartly. 'You're no saint yourself, young man. At least,' she continued, 'when you get a girl pregnant *before* you put the ring on her finger you know she's fertile.'

'That's very pragmatic of you.' He cupped the old lady's elbow as she lowered herself slowly into the pew. 'But I'm not sure,' he added in a soft aside, 'that the bride's father shares your viewpoint. Or that the modern female would enjoy being likened to a brood mare.'

Just at that moment his mother, looking flushed and breathless, appeared at his shoulder. 'Christos—I need you.' Under her breath, Mia Carides said with a fixed smile, *'Don't encourage her.'*

'What do you need me for, Mother?' Christos asked, wondering if the glorious redhead's hair was as soft and silky as it looked. A man could dream of falling asleep wrapped in that hair…

'There's a problem with security,' Mia improvised smoothly. 'Such a nuisance. I'm sorry, Aunt Theodosia, you'll have to excuse us.'

Her son responded to the urgent look with a languid smile which made his mother's diplomatic expression wobble for an instant as she clenched her teeth. Her son, as she knew, could be very vexing when he chose.

'Aunt Theodosia and I were just discussing the blushing bride, Mother.'

'I know—I heard you. So did half the guests,' Mia observed, waving graciously and bestowing a serene smile on the bride's indignant parents.

Undeterred, Aunt Theodosia continued, 'This family *needs* more babies. What is wrong with you young people nowadays? When are *you* going to have some babies, Christos?'

Christos bent and pressed his lips in a courtly gesture to the frail, age-spotted old hand. 'When I find someone with as much spunk as you.' *Or, failing that, red hair.* He blinked, wondering where that thought had come from.

The old lady tried to hide her pleased smile. 'If you do,' she predicted, 'it might well be the making of you. That other girl—what was her name?'

'Melina.'

'That was it. I didn't like her. She smiled too much.'

Across the aisle, Melina wasn't smiling at all. In fact she was looking daggers at a girl with red hair, who Christos had barely taken his eyes from.

CHAPTER THREE

'WHY do you encourage her, Christos?' his mother reproached him as she walked down the aisle.

While he lent an attentive ear to his mother, Christos continued to watch the troublesome redhead as she sat down, concealing all but the top of her fiery head from his view.

'Carl looked furious,' Mia added in a hushed tone. 'Especially as Sally *is* pregnant.'

The column was situated so that in addition to the top of her head he could see her neat feet, and as she crossed one leg over the other her ankle-length coat fell back to reveal a pair of worn denim jeans.

'What's the problem with security, Mother?'

'There isn't a problem,' Mia admitted, blissfully unaware that she didn't have her son's total attention. 'I just had to get you away from Aunt Theodosia before you made her say something else outrageous.'

Christos wondered if kissing the unknown redhead, fitting his mouth to hers and parting her moist pink lips, would be considered outrageous. If not, his fertile and over-active imagination was capable of conjuring several alternatives that almost certainly were!

Aware that he was breathing too fast, Christos made a conscious effort to slow his rapid, laboured respirations—not an easy thing to do when your head was filled with imaginings about the taste and touch of a woman.

'I doubt if anyone has ever *made* Theodosia do or say anything.'

'Your voice sounds strange, Christos,' his mother said,

reaching up and touching a cool maternal hand to his brow.
'And you're hot,' she said, shaking her head. 'I do hope
you're not coming down with something. I have never considered air travel healthy.'

'Well, if I die of something airborne you will have the
satisfaction of knowing it was at your instigation I flew
halfway around the world to be here.'

'You,' his mother retorted tartly, 'are as bad as
Theodosia.'

'Thank you. I just hope I can grow old as disgracefully
as she has.'

His mother cast him a reproachful look, before pausing
to be charming to someone important.

'You know, Mother, I think you're wrong about the security problem.'

Mia's eyes widened in alarm. 'There *is* a problem?
What?'

'Nothing I can't handle,' Christos said, his eyes fixed on
the top of that burnished head.

He began to work his way to the rear of the church. On
auto-pilot, he returned the nods and smiles he received, all
the time never losing sight of the redhead.

As she pulled the collar of her ankle-length coat up
around her neck, to frame her face, the breath snagged in
his throat. He had never seen her face before, yet somehow
he felt as though he had known it all his life.

A man could only go on blaming jet lag for so long.
Then he had to take responsibility himself.

A babe in arms chose that moment to cry, its whimper
of complaint magnified by the building's impressive acous-
tics. By reflex her eyes—like every eye in the place—momentarily turned towards the ear-splitting sound.

He stood with his tall shoulders braced against a stone
pillar and pondered the mild electric shock that had passed
through his body as those eyes, the deepest and most shock-

ing shade of blue he had ever encountered, had connected with his. He doubted the moment had been shared. He had the impression she hadn't even registered his presence.

The irony of being ignored was not lost on a man who was used to women pulling every trick in the book to capture his attention.

As he watched, the beautiful stranger raised a hand to her throat under the heavy overcoat, and he saw her chest lift as she exhaled and, biting her lower lip, began to stare straight ahead, an expression of rigid control and ferocious focus on her softly formed fine-boned features.

He studied the strangely familiar face at his leisure. She had the pale, lightly freckled complexion of a natural redhead. Her small nose, in profile, was gently tilted at the tip, and though her wide mouth was drawn taut by the tension that held her entire body rigid, he imagined that under normal circumstances it would be soft.

He got hot as he began to think thoughts inappropriate for the inside of a cathedral. The thoughts concerned that mouth. He not been a victim of such mindless lust since his hormones went crazy in his teens—maybe not even then.

As the place began to fill up he took the seat directly behind the redhead, positioning himself so that he could see her profile. She remained unaware of his scrutiny.

By the time Becca had finally entered the Cathedral the light-headed sensation she had been suffering for the past hour had been joined by a constant low-pitched buzz in her ears. She'd had to thrust her hands into her pockets to hide the fact they were trembling.

Worrying that she might fall into a dead faint at any moment and ruin everything had made it hard for her to maintain the confident air she had adopted, working on the

theory that if she *looked* as if she belonged it might delay
the inevitable moment of discovery.

She suspected all her symptoms had a lot to do with her
caffeine tolerance. The fourth cup of coffee she had drunk
at the motorway services to keep her alert had been a mistake. Her trembling knees had made sitting down sometime
soon a priority.

She'd been looking for a likely place to wait for her
moment when she'd seen one of the uniformly handsome
young men who were smoothly directing guests to their
seats bearing down on her, all charm and slick efficiency.
She'd frozen and looked wildly from left to right. Then,
taking a deep breath and pinning on a painfully bright
smile, she'd begun to wave at some invisible person in the
crowd, before walking purposefully in that direction.

What am I doing?

As she had slowed to let an elderly lady in an incredibly
large hat pass, the full enormity of what she was about to
do had hit her. It had been like running full-tilt into a brick
wall. The fact was that deep down, until that moment,
Becca hadn't expected to get this far.

Well, what were the odds? You just *didn't* walk uninvited into the big society wedding joining the only daughter
of one of Britain's highest profile entrepreneurs to a scion
of the fabulously wealthy Carides family.

The knot of anger lodged behind her breastbone had
swelled as she'd thought of the family who imagined that
money gave them the right to trample over the feelings of
ordinary people. A person who had gone through life not
hating anyone, Becca was now finding it surprisingly easy
to hate anyone who carried the name of Carides.

Head down, avoiding eye contact she'd given a relieved
sigh as she'd spotted an unoccupied pew, but as she'd taken
her seat she'd realised why the spot had been avoided. A
large stone pillar effectively blocked the view of the altar.

Becca didn't mind. She wasn't here for people to see her. They just needed to hear what she had to say.

Just cause... Her wide-spaced blue eyes grew uncharacteristically hard now, as she thought about the 'just cause' that had brought her here. To seduce, impregnate and then dump an impressionable teenage girl was despicable enough—but to do it when you were engaged to another woman...! Well, that made Alex Carides a different class of slimy rat entirely.

An expectant hush fell as the first bars of the 'Wedding March' issued from the organ. Becca stiffened and drew in air through her flared nostrils. On her lap, her fingers twisted. She took a deep breath and told herself, *You can do this.*

But can I?

An image of her sister's pale tragic face as Becca had driven her back from the hospital flashed into her head. It was enough to stiffen her resolve.

She had actually cleared her throat in preparation when the hand she had been expecting all afternoon finally fell on her shoulder.

CHAPTER FOUR

'I REALLY don't think that would be a good idea, do you?'

Good idea? Becca reflected, as the quivering tension left her body in a debilitating rush. That had never had any thing to do with this.

This had always been about standing up, if only in a small way, for Erica and for every other woman who had fallen for that slimy creep's lies. His future wife needed to know what sort of low-life she was getting married to, and the world needed to know what sort of man Alex Carides actually was.

Who am I kidding? This is about revenge—plain and simple!

The deep, interestingly accented voice, complete with sexy rasp, seemed very close to her ear as he added softly, 'I don't think you want to do this.'

Which, in conjunction with the heavy hand on her shoulder, translated as *I'll carry you kicking and screaming from the building if you try.* Becca decided to retreat with a little dignity intact.

Chin up, and looking straight ahead, Becca responded to the pressure of those fingers on her shoulder and smoothly rose from her seat, moving up the aisle and walking with little fuss through the metal-studded oak door just to her right which she hadn't even noticed was there.

Christos was conscious of a slow-burning anger that had started to smoulder the moment he had realised what she intended to do. God knows what 'just cause' she had intended to produce, but there was only one logical conclusion to draw. The woman who was going to feature strongly in his fantasies for the foreseeable future was one of Alex's cast-offs.

A cynical sneer twisted his mouth as he considered the opposite sex's inability to see beyond his cousin's winning smile and slick good looks.

The redhead had appalling taste—but she smelt very good! His eyes widened slightly as he recognised that he was angrier now than he had been when he had caught Melina with Alex.

If this wasn't jet lag he had a serious problem!

Her captor led Becca into a small ante-room. As the heavy door closed it effectively sealed them off from the sounds of the service beyond. At that moment reaction started to set in—in a big way. Her knees began to shake, closely followed by the rest of her.

'He's really not worth it, you know.'

'I know he's not…' As she spoke Becca turned her head, inhaled audibly, and added an unthinking and breathy, *'Goodness!'*

Which, under the circumstances—the circumstances being that she was inches away from the most sinfully gorgeous man she had ever seen—was quite restrained. If you were going to be caught, she reflected, you might as well be caught by someone breathtaking. And my goodness, she thought, still slightly stunned by the dark vision of brooding male perfection, he was gorgeous—and then some!

It was perhaps fortunate that the shaky hand she had lifted to her mouth stopped her saying something unconsidered.

Christos watched the colour rush to her cheeks and then fade quite dramatically away, leaving her marble-pale.

'I think you could do with some fresh air.' In his opinion that was the very least she looked as if she could do with.

Becca started, and realised that she had been staring at this stranger. Goodness knew how long she had been the

prisoner of those hypnotic dark eyes and her own fascination.

She nodded awkwardly.

Her shoulders slumped as she followed the tall man with
the longest eyelashes she had ever seen outside. Another
minute—that was all she'd needed. She could have wept
with sheer frustration. It was so unfair. Why was it that
men like Alex Carides never paid the price?

Shame flooded through her. A great sister I am!

Outside, Becca sank down onto a conveniently situated
bench that had been fashioned from a tree trunk. She was
in no mood to appreciate its aesthetic properties as she bent
forward and buried her face in her hands.

'Later, when you've had a chance to think calmly about
this, you'll realise I've done you a favour.'

Becca's head jerked up. 'A *favour*?' she echoed bellig-
erently. 'Look, I know you were only doing your job—
though if you were any sort of security I wouldn't have got
as far as I did,' she felt impelled to point out. 'But don't
act as if your motives were altruistic.'

The tall, dark and gorgeous stranger looked startled for
a moment, then gave a lop-sided sort of smile that made
her undiscriminating tummy muscles quiver appreciatively.

'I was tempted to let you do it,' he admitted.

Tears of frustration sprang to her eyes. 'I wanted…
wanted…'

'Calm down.'

He really was the most beautiful man she had ever
seen—or even imagined! She ran the tip of her tongue
across the outline of her dry lips and fixed him with a
resentful glare. 'You could have looked the other way.'

'But then,' he observed, 'I'd have lost my job.'

Becca gave a distracted sigh. 'I suppose you would,' she
agreed.

'Did you *really* want to stand up and make a fool of yourself like that?'

'This isn't about wanting, it's about…' She stopped and took a shuddering deep breath as she struggled to regain control. After a few moments her darkened eyes lifted to the face of the man beside her. 'Tell me, do you think it's right that he gets away with ruining someone's life?'

'I think you should consider it a narrow escape,' Christos observed drily.

Becca frowned at the platitude. 'What would you know about it?'

'I know quite a lot about Alex Carides.'

Which might, she mused, explain his expression of contempt.

'How can you work for a man like that?' The thought of being around such a creep made her skin crawl. The thought of being around any Carides full-stop made her skin crawl.

'A man has to eat.'

She flickered him an apologetic smile. 'Sorry—I didn't mean to moralise. Goodness, I'm the last person to do that.'

Her self-deprecating remark wiped all expression from his face.

Confused, Becca watched his dark, cynical gaze drop, and wondered at the almost tangible waves of tension emanating from him. 'Are you pregnant?'

Becca blinked, confused by the speed with which his manner had transformed from sympathy to frozen condemnation. As she read the distaste in his face twin circles of angry colour appeared on the apples of her pale cheeks.

'You think that I—' She bit back her hasty rejoinder. She didn't owe a total stranger any explanation—though knowing that he believed she had slept with a Carides made it hard for her to hold her tongue. 'Your boss makes a habit of getting women pregnant, does he?' she countered.

'Then there *is* a baby?' he said, looking sterner than ever.

'Not any more.'

'A termination?' he said bleakly.

Becca's voice grew husky with emotion as she corrected him. 'A miscarriage.'

The security guard drew a deep breath and, framing her face in his hands said urgently. 'What is your name?'

The peculiarity of his manner stood out as very strange in a day that had possibly been the strangest in her life.

'Your name?' he repeated.

'Becca.'

'Don't move, Becca. I'll be back.'

He didn't have the faintest idea if she had registered what he'd said. It was hard to tell from the glazed expression in her eyes if she was taking in anything much at all. He didn't like to leave her, but the strength of his feelings meant he had to act on them.

His timing was perfect. The main participants, along with the photographer, were emerging from the vestry, their symbolic signatures having been duly witnessed. They all stopped when they saw him.

Without responding to the varied greetings directed at him, Christos grabbed his cousin by the shoulders and pulled him away from his bride.

'What's wrong?'

Christos smiled, and his cousin looked alarmed. 'This is for Becca!' he said, and landed a sharp but controlled jab on the younger man's nose.

The groom yelled and clutched at his nose, blood oozing between his fingers. 'Who the hell is Becca?' he screamed indignantly. So Christos punched him again, and Alex went down.

She had moved. Cursing softly under his breath, Christos ran down a side path and saw her almost immediately.

'I told you to stay put.'

Becca looked at the long brown fingers curled around her upper arm. Until he touched her she had been feeling a lot better. Now her sensitive stomach was quivering violently. 'What do you think you're doing?' she said.

Considering the advice she had dished out on the subject to her sister, she couldn't go down the road of reacting to arbitrary and dangerous sexual attraction without being a total hypocrite!

'More to the point, what are *you* doing?' he queried suspiciously.

'Is that any of your business?' she countered frostily. 'And, thank you, but I can find my own way.' Her eyes slid to the hand on her arm, but he didn't react. 'I don't need an escort.'

'The head of security might have other ideas,' he retorted drily.

'That's not you?' Her frowning regard travelled the length of his tall lean person. No reason, of course, that he had to be the boss. He wasn't wearing a badge or anything. But he didn't act like a man who was used to obeying orders.

On the other hand it was easy to picture him issuing them, and having people fall over themselves to obey. An accusing frown settled on her upturned face.

'You act as if you are.' No matter how hard she tried, she couldn't she see him slotting into any hierarchy of command. This man didn't look like a team player to her.

'I'm new to the game,' he admitted glibly.

'Which probably explains why you're taking your duties too zealously,' she muttered. 'I've not committed a crime or anything. You've got no right to restrain me against my will. In fact,' she added, *'That—'* her nod indicated the hand on her arm '—is probably assault. Actually, I don't think there's any *probably* about it.'

He smiled, and Becca lowered her eyes as she experienced a spasm of sexual awareness that made her knees quiver. *What is it with me? You'd think I'd never seen an attractive man before!*

'Perhaps we should let the police decide?'

The silky suggestion brought her horrified gaze back to his face. 'You're joking?'

He shrugged and looked infuriatingly enigmatic.

Becca couldn't stop the quiver of doubt entering her voice as she added, 'I've told you, I've not committed a crime or anything.'

'You don't think so?'

He made no attempt to prevent her as she pulled her arm free of his grasp and folded it across her heaving chest, glaring up at him defiantly.

'I don't think. I know.'

Despite her confident assertion Becca couldn't prevent a shade of worry entering her voice as she reviewed her gate-crashing.

'Unless this is a question of one law for the rich and another for the rest of us.'

His dark eyes narrowed on her scornful face. 'You have a problem with people being wealthy?'

She lifted a hand to her aching head. 'No, I have a problem with spoilt parasites like the Carides.'

Aware of an expression in her captor's dark eyes that made her uneasy, she bit her lip to cut short this flow of bitter confidences.

'It's a little late to be discreet.'

'I really don't want to debate this with you. I just want—' She broke off and winced as the bells overhead broke into a triumphal peal. Face pale and composed, she lifted her eyes to his face. 'I just want to go home.'

'An excellent plan,' he said, falling into step beside her. Becca tilted her face and studied the hard angles and intriguing hollows of his dark, lean and exasperatingly sexy features. 'What,' she demanded, expelling a gusty sigh, 'do you think you're doing now?'

'Making sure you go home.

'Are you going to escort me all the way to Yorkshire?'

'I'm going to stick to you until I'm sure you can't double back and wreak the destructive vengeance your soul craves.' His eyes locked with hers. 'I take it that *is* what this is about?'

'I suppose you're going to tell me revenge wouldn't make me feel better?'

'No, I wouldn't say that,' Christos responded, thinking of the groom with his bloody nose.

There were times in life when a man had to stop being cerebral and get physical—though he imagined there were a few people inside who might disagree with him at that moment. It would be a long time before he was forgiven for ruining the wedding. But it would be interesting to hear how they explained away the groom's face...

Becca pursed her lips and looked at him with mute dislike. She saw he was smiling. 'You have my word that I won't crash the reception or spoil the wedding photos.'

'Your word...' he mused, dragging a brown hand through his dark collar-length hair. 'You do see my problem there?'

Becca planted her hands on her slim hips and inhaled wrathfully. 'Are you calling me a liar?'

'Not as such. But,' he qualified, 'I do think you're not thinking straight right now.'

'Don't patronise me.' She gritted her teeth as she reflected on his comment. 'Not a liar, but mentally unbalanced. Gosh,' she observed bitterly, 'I feel better already.'

He met her angry eyes and released a low, husky laugh. Becca regarded him with growing frustration, but could see that it might be hard to remain angry with a man who possessed a laugh that warm and attractive. Fortunately she wasn't going to be within laughing distance long enough for it to become a real problem!

'Go ahead—enjoy the joke.' She gave a bleak wintry smile. 'I can see your point. What's a ruined life…? So long,' she added on a bitter quaver, 'as it isn't *your* life!'

'I know it feels like it to you now, but your life isn't ruined.'

She looked different, but she obviously wasn't. She was like any number of women who were willing to overlook the fact that his cousin was a total bastard.

Becca's electric blue eyes narrowed. She had never had the sort of fiery temper that was meant to accompany auburn hair, but his confident assertion had made her see red. As she swallowed hard, trying to contain her feelings, an image of her sister's shadowed eyes flashed into her head.

'What would you know about it?'

Jaw taut, she allowed her hostile eyes to linger on his lean face. Actually, it wasn't a conscious decision. The truth was that once she started looking she found it disturbingly hard to stop.

'You have to put this behind you.' *And I have to stop talking in platitudes.*

'I'd settle for putting *you* behind me. A long way behind me,' she muttered.

'Not going to happen,' he said, planting a hand lightly on her shoulder and directing her to the other side of an ancient gnarled yew tree that grew beside the six-feet-high wall. 'There's a side gate.'

There was. It was covered in ivy and easy to miss if you didn't know it was there. On the other side of the gate, Becca found herself in a narrow cobbled side street with expensive-looking cars parked down one side.

The dark-suited figure patrolling up and down with a walkie-talkie in his pocket spotted her immediately. He advanced, his intention clearly to intercept her—until he saw the man beside her. He nodded in a manner that could only be described as deferential, and walked on to meet them.

As the two men began to speak, Becca, staring straight ahead, walked past them. The narrow lane led to the main road, where people were waiting behind barriers for a glimpse of the bride. She had not quite lost herself in the crowd when she heard a distinctive footfall beside her.

'Look!' she snapped, swinging back. 'I'm not going to crash the reception, or scream abuse at the bride, so will you just back off?' *No, I'm going to sneak back home with my tail between my legs and tell my little sister I did nothing!* 'This has all been a massive waste of time and energy,' she admitted, her shoulders slumping with weary defeat.

'Well, most women in your situation would have contented themselves with a kiss-and-tell story in the tabloids. Though that lucrative option *is* still open to you,' he admitted.

When she didn't respond to this blatant provocation he tried another tack.

'Have you considered what would have happened if you had stood up and done your piece—dramatically stalled the wedding?'

Becca, about to walk away, swung back and blinked in owl-like confusion up at his face. 'What do you mean?'

'We are talking *stalled*, not *stopped*. The wedding would have gone ahead,' he elaborated brutally.

Becca shrugged. 'She's welcome to him.'

'Yes, every time I look at you I feel great waves of indifference.' In his experience a woman didn't travel halfway across the country because she was indifferent.

Stung by his blatant sarcasm, Becca had opened her mouth to deliver a biting retort when involuntarily her eyes dropped over the length of his lean, striking person. *Indifference*, she reflected, aware of the telling leap in her pulse-rate, would not be the most predictable response this man normally excited in the opposite sex.

'Or maybe this isn't about revenge?' he suggested softly.

His comment diverted Becca from the direction her own troubled thoughts had taken. The awful part was, he was right. She hadn't thought this thing through. And now he had forced her to do so she could see that she had almost set into motion a chain of events that would have ended up with the tabloid press camped on her sister's doorstep!

'I don't know what you mean,' she said, feeling sick when she thought of how close she'd come to making things ten times worse for Erica.

'Maybe you thought he'd take one look at you and realise that he'd made a terrible mistake—that you were the one he wanted all along.' As he watched her shake her head in angry denial he experienced a rush of anger. 'It wouldn't have happened,' he informed her harshly. *Because I wouldn't have let it happen.*

Becca took a startled step back when, without warning, he reached across and ran a long finger down the curve of her cheek. After making a moment's startled contact with his dark, strangely compelling gaze she swept her lashes down against her cheek and stayed that way until she had taken several deep, restorative breaths.

'You sound very sure,' she said, feeling normal again bar the strong urge to reach up and press her own fingers to the tingling area on her cheek.

Christos was drawn by the intense china blue of her wide eyes. It occurred to him that being forced to compare this face with that of his prospective bride might have caused even his avaricious cousin to experience a stab of regret.

A muscle in his lean cheek clenched. 'Look, maybe you *were* special.'

To Becca his shrug suggested he had lost interest in the subject. 'Are you trying to make me feel better?' she joked, her eyes hostile as she sketched a grim smile. 'Because I have to tell you you're not very good at it.'

Her observation made his lips quiver slightly. 'You're certainly not Alex's usual type.'

'Really? What do they have that I don't?'

Other than no personality? Christos thought as he grimly ticked off the attributes that normally attracted his cousin on his fingers. 'His usual types are young, low-maintenance blondes, with long legs, a lot of ambition, and virtually no talent for anything but wearing and buying clothes and spending his money.'

This cynical analysis made her eyes flash angrily. 'It sounds like you know the boss pretty well.' *And don't like him much,* she thought, but didn't add.

'Boss?'

Becca looked his curling lip and couldn't help but think he must be awfully good at what he did for any employer to put up with his disdainful manner.

'Well, isn't that what he is?' she challenged. 'Or does it hurt your macho pride to admit you're a lackey, like the rest of us?'

'And who are you in servitude to?'

'I'm a primary schoolteacher.'

'I never had a teacher that looked like you.'

There was an insolent sexual quality to his appraisal that ought to have repelled her. Instead she felt a shiver of excitement slide down her spine.

'Actually,' he added, before she could respond, 'Christos Carides is the head of the company which paid for the wedding security today.'

Becca shrugged. The technicality changed nothing as far as she was concerned. 'He's a Carides.'

His dark brows lifted. 'So you tar everyone of that name with the same brush? Is that fair?'

'Don't lecture me on fairness,' she snapped back, tired of being the voice of impartial reason.

'Are you always this forthright?'

'Say what you mean—you think I'm mouthy?'

The retort drew a reluctant grin from Christos. 'You know, Alex is even more of a fool than I thought he was.'

'If that is meant to be a compliment, save it.' It was not good to start wondering how someone who looked like a sleek predator would kiss. 'I have no taste for insincerity.' *Or beautiful but predatory men,* she reminded herself.

His expression hardened. 'That sounds an odd thing for someone who has been Alex's lover to say. Insincerity is his speciality.'

The inflection in his deep voice as he said *lover* sent an odd, disturbing surge through Becca's body. 'Do you always bad-mouth your employers?'

'I thought you put no value on insincerity?'

'I do put value on good manners, however.'

'Now,' he said, 'you *do* sound like a teacher. I can see you in the classroom.' Not strictly the truth. Christos was seeing her in the bedroom!

The classroom was somewhere she really wished she had never left, Becca reflected. Perhaps she just didn't have the right genes for revenge and retribution? She had certainly made a total mess of this!

CHAPTER FIVE

To BECCA'S horror she felt her lip quiver as her eyes filled with weak tears. 'Damn, damn, *damn*!' she cursed under her breath, as she caught her wobbling lip between her teeth and sniffed.

'Come on,' he urged, taking her arm and pulling her into the doorway of a shop.

The edge of rough concern in his deep voice was tinged with impatience, and one or the other—she wasn't sure which—made Becca's eyes weakly fill all over again.

'I'm not coming anywhere with you,' she contended huskily. 'I'm going back home.' The thought of home did nothing to stem the flow of tears. 'I wish,' she added, burying her nose in a tissue, 'that I'd never left!' Before she lifted her head the hand he had extended towards her had fallen back to his side.

'Compose yourself—people are staring.'

This stern comment drew a strangled laugh from Becca. 'Of course they're staring.' Her watery gaze slid up and down the long, lean, masculine length of him and she started to laugh again.

He shook his head and looked at her as though she was demented.

She spelt it out. 'They're not staring at *me*.'

As she spoke a girl with a very short skirt and very high heels almost dislocated her neck doing a double-take. She caught Becca's eye and blushed.

'With you beside me they wouldn't be staring at me if I were stark naked.'

'Is this something you are planning to do?'

42

People probably always stared at him. Maybe after a lifetime of being beautiful and head-turningly sexy he didn't notice. Then again, maybe he lapped it up.

The latter possibility seemed the more likely to Becca, who had noticed that good-looking men were almost always vain.

As she looked at him it occurred to Becca that she had been a bit tough on her sister—accusing her, in the privacy of her own thoughts, at least, of being a bit of a push-over and not seeing through a love-rat. But maybe it wasn't just the glamour and slick lines Erica had fallen for. Maybe Alex also moved like a panther and oozed pheremones from every pore?

If a man who looked like this one set out to seduce her, what female would be able to resist? How many women had ever said I'm washing my hair *when he suggested jumping into bed?*

Her colour slightly heightened, Becca removed her eyes from the sensual outline of his mobile lips.

'About the only way you could be *more* conspicuous is if *you* were naked.' Then, because she didn't want him to run away with the idea that she'd been imagining him naked, she added accusingly, 'Are you Greek?'

He tipped his dark head fractionally in affirmation and looked faintly amused.

'I should have known.' Of course people like the Carides probably never left home without their own personal army.

'You don't have much of an accent.' He did have a very attractive voice, though. Seductive enough too.

'I was partly educated in America, where I have relatives.'

'That's where you learnt to be a security guard?'

'Operative,' he inserted gravely. 'We in the trade prefer the term *operative*.'

'Look, by all means defend your perimeter, or whatever—I don't care—but will you go away and leave me alone? You're going to look pretty silly if you're out here stalking me and someone's back there nicking the presents.'

'That situation is covered,' he assured her casually. 'And I can't risk you crashing the party on my watch.'

'For heaven's sake, I've already told you I'm not going to.'

'When was the last time you ate?'

Becca ignored him and fished around in her pockets for her car keys.

'I hope you're not considering driving in your condition? You are clearly not capable.'

Becca, whose thoughts had been moving along the same lines, grew defensive at the note of criticism in his tone. 'There's nothing wrong with my *condition*!' she snapped shrilly as she wiped the dampness from her cheeks. 'My condition has not a damned thing to do with you.'

Listen to the woman, said a voice in the part of his brain still functioning.

He watched as she lifted a hand to her head.

'You have a headache?'

'Headache' hardly covered the sick throbbing behind her eyes. 'No,' Becca lied, dropping her chin.

Christos surveyed the lines of strain around her soft mouth and wished he'd hit his cousin some more. *'Why...?'*

The anger in his voice brought her head up. 'Why what?'

'I suppose you think that you love him?' *They always thought that.*

Becca stared at him, then lifted her chin. 'I hate him!' she whispered.

'They say hate is closely related to love.'

'Then *they* are as stupid as you.' She delved again into her pockets, and this time produced a bunch of keys, which she jangled angrily at him. 'I've every intention of driving.'

Her brow furrowed in concentration. 'When I've remembered where I left my car.'

Above her, she heard him sigh deeply in exasperation. 'Hand them over.'

Becca looked at the long brown fingers extended towards her and blinked. 'What...?'

'Hand the keys over.'

'You make it sound as though I'm drunk and incapable!' she protested indignantly.

'You're definitely incapable.'

Why am I standing here like a spineless idiot, listening to him? 'I'm going to walk away, and there's not a thing you can do to stop me.'

'When did you last sleep or eat?'

She looked at him blankly.

'We'll buy some sandwiches on the way to pick up my car.'

'*Your* car?'

He levelled a look of impatience at her. 'Do you intend to wander around the city on foot all day, looking for your car, or do you want help?'

When he put it like that... 'All right,' she said ungraciously, then added, 'I really don't know why you're doing this.'

'That makes two of us,' he responded cryptically.

Becca looked around the luxuriously upholstered leather interior of the car with a suspicious frown. 'This is a Jaguar.'

'Call it a perk of the job,' he suggested, slinging his beautifully tailored jacket carelessly into the back seat. His tie, which he had unfastened from around his throat, rapidly joined it. After he had unfastened the top button of a pristine white shirt to reveal a discreet section of smooth brown flesh he turned the ignition.

'Some perk,' Becca muttered, pressing a hand to her wayward stomach as she concentrated on *not* noticing the shadow of body hair on his chest visible through the fine fabric of his shirt. She had noticed that the uncomfortably visceral effect this man's brand of sexuality had on her had got worse since she'd got into the car.

Which rather begged the question, *Why the hell did I get in?*

He turned his head and looked directly into her eyes and smiled. It was a sinfully sexy smile. Becca vocalised her growing irritation.

'I don't know what I'm doing here with you.'

'You can thank me later.'

'After we've found my car?'

'It's probably been clamped and towed by now,' he predicted. 'You really don't have the faintest idea where you parked?'

Becca flushed. He made it sound as though she made a habit of losing her car. 'I'd been driving all night and I ran out of petrol, and—' She stopped, her expression brightening.

'I bought a parking ticket from one of those pay-and-display things. The stub will be in my—' She looked around for her bag and her face dropped. 'Oh, no!'

'What's wrong now?' This woman, Christos decided, was a walking disaster area.

'I've left my handbag back in the Cathedral. At least,' she qualified, frowning as she mentally tried, without much success, to retrace her steps, 'I *think* I have.'

'My goodness, you really are a great loss to covert operations, aren't you?'

Becca wasn't listening. 'Everything is in it. My wallet...*everything*. Just when I thought this day could not get any worse.' She heaved a sigh. 'I have to go back.'

'Do you really think that is such a good idea?'

She turned her head to glare resentfully at him. 'You make it sound as though I have a choice in the matter. Even if I find my car, I can't get back home without money.' Her lips quivered.

Christos glanced across and saw her blink back the well of tears that made her extraordinary eyes shimmer. 'I can let you have some money,' he said, without analysing the impulse that made him want to help her.

The careless offer made her stiffen. 'You think I'd take money from a total stranger?'

One dark brow angled as his eyes swept across her indignant face. He wondered, not for the first time, how his cousin had got involved with this woman. 'You're assuming that there are strings attached to my offer?'

'No!' The groove between her brows deepened and suspicion formed in her eyes as she wrapped her arms around herself in an unconsciously protective gesture. 'Are there?'

'That is a nasty and suspicious mind you have there. You can treat it as a loan, if that makes you feel better.'

'I won't treat it as anything because—' she began, and then with a gasp broke off and yelled, 'That's my car!'

He briefly removed his eyes from the heavy flow of traffic. 'Which?'

'The blue Beetle.'

'Good grief!'

She bristled at the implied criticism. 'Meaning…?'

'Meaning they don't make them like that any more,' he inserted smoothly. 'Fasten your seat belt,' he added sharply as she began to fumble with the clasp.

Becca ignored him. 'Stop the car!' she countered.

He ignored her in return and she let out a loud wail as she saw her blue Beetle vanish from view. Hands clenched in her lap, she glared at his remote profile. 'Why didn't you stop? Didn't you hear what I said?'

'It would have been hard not to. You have a very penetrating voice. I could not slam my foot on the brakes without causing an accident.'

Her lips tightened. 'Back up, then!'

'This is a one-way street,' he informed her, without responding to her imperious instruction.

'Stop there!' she cried, indicating the empty inside lane.

'That is a bus lane. I'll get arrested.'

Becca cast him a look of extreme dislike and received an insolent half-smile in response. 'And I suppose you've never broken a rule in your life?'

She gave a derisive snort when he didn't respond. One look at him, she thought, and you could see he had been bending rules all his life.

'It wouldn't surprise me if you've got a criminal record a mile long!' she contended crankily. 'Just let me out here and I'll walk back.'

'It is snowing.'

'I'm aware that it is snowing.'

'If I stop the car are you so sure you can locate your car again?'

'Of course I can locate my car.'

'Well, so far you've not displayed even the most rudimentary sense of direction. If you will try to control your impatience I'll get you back to your car. Also,' he added, sliding her a sideways glance, 'throwing yourself from a moving car is not going to help.'

'I'm neither stupid or suicidal,' she snapped.

'Fine—but humour me, will you? Take your hand off the door handle.'

Becca, who hadn't known she was holding it, did as he requested.

'Good girl.'

'Don't patronise me!' she flared.

'Are you always so aggressive? It is hardly feminine,' he observed disapprovingly, just before he drew his vehicle off the road and reversed into a space that Becca wouldn't have dared attempt. 'Now we will go and retrieve your car.'

Becca flung open the door. 'I don't need your assistance.' The fact that she turned and almost lost her balance on a patch of lethal black ice did not lend weight to her contention. She waited for a sarcastic comment, but it didn't come. So, chin up, she strode off.

'You're going in the wrong direction.'

The drawled comment caused Becca to close her eyes. She took two more steps before, with a sigh, she swung back and saw him standing there, his arms folded across his chest, watching her.

'Fine—you lead the way, then,' she returned grudgingly. And, as much as she longed to get back home, part of her hoped he would get lost.

He didn't.

Apparently he was one of those people who possessed an unerring sense of direction—and, not once displaying any uncertainty, moderating his long-legged stride to allow her to keep up with him, he led her back to her parked car.

Becca gave a sigh of relief when she saw it, and ran past him, repressing an urge to hug the rusty old heap. While she was inserting her key in the lock he walked around the car.

'This thing actually goes?'

'Of course it goes,' she retorted with dignity. He lifted a sceptical brow and she added awkwardly, 'Well, thanks for your help.' Frustratingly, he failed to recognise this obvious cue for him to leave.

'You are proposing to drive back home with no money?'

Becca frowned. 'I've told you…'

'Pride is all well and good.' And this woman obviously had too much of it for practical purposes. 'But how do you think you're going to get back to Yorkshire with no money?'

Becca spirits slipped another notch but stubbornly she lifted her chin and glared at him with loathing. 'How do you know I come from Yorkshire?'

'You told me. Service stations are not going to accept an IOU for petrol.'

Becca, unable to deny the accuracy of his statement, looked at the wad of notes folded in his outstretched fingers. Eyes narrowed, she turned her face up to his. 'I've told you, I can't take money from a total stranger.'

Christos gave an exasperated snort and said something incomprehensible in his native tongue.

'I don't understand a thing you're saying.' *But it sounded good when he said it. He really did have the sexiest voice she had ever heard.*

'Roughly translated, I suggested the obvious solution would seem to be for me *not* to be a stranger.'

'Where I come from people who move into the village are called outsiders even when they've lived there for twenty years—' She broke off, her eyes widening as he took her face between his big hands.

At some level she knew that she should have stepped back. There was nothing to stop her—nothing except the strange compulsion exerted by his dark gaze that overrode her natural predisposition to caution.

'What do you think you're doing?' she demanded, desperately trying to sound frosty and in control. In reality her heart was thudding fast and heavy, and she had rarely felt *less* in control in her life.

The question was echoed in Christos's head, but he ignored it. Her skin was so soft. Fascination gleamed in his dark eyes as his thumb explored the smooth contours of her flushed cheek.

Her eyes flew open as he fitted his lips to hers. *How had she known they would be a perfect fit?* Then, as his sensual mouth moved against hers, Becca's lips parted and she

groaned with helpless pleasure into his mouth. She lost all
sense of self-awareness as he skilfully plundered the warm
recesses.

It was only when he'd stopped kissing her, and she was
trying to breathe again that Becca realised her fingers were
laced into his dark hair. Swallowing and biting her lips, she
untangled her fingers, muttering, 'Sorry…' over and over,
like a total moron.

She was shaken to the core by her response; significant
areas of her overheated body still throbbed with the after-
effects.

Deliberately not looking at his face but directing her stare
straight ahead backfired spectacularly—straight ahead was
his chest.

And his chest set in motion a train of thought that began
with recalling how incredible it had felt to be held against
his lean hard body. It ended with her going weak with sheer
longing as she remembered the intimate pressure of his
erection grinding into her belly through the layers of clothing that separated them.

'Right, so now we are no longer strangers.'

Her dazed eyes lifted at this throaty observation. 'We're
not…?' Personally she had never felt stranger in her life.

'At least where I come from we're not.'

It was some comfort that he looked slightly less assured
than normal.

He took her wrist and unfurled her fingers. 'So now you
can take this in good conscience.'

Becca looked blankly at the money he'd pushed into her
hand, then back at him as her cheeks began to burn in
shame.

'I'll return it,' she said, taking one last look at his lean,
dark face through the sweep of her lashes.

She took the money—not because she was concerned
about how she was going to get home, but because it was

easier to take it and run than examine what had just happened.

She flung the money on the front seat and belted herself into the Beetle. Crunching the gears atrociously, she drove away without a backward glance. It wasn't until she had gone a mile that she realised she had no idea what his name was or where she should return the money to.

CHAPTER SIX

THE snow got steadily thicker. Becca had spent a couple of worrying miles wondering if it would be better to stop when the decision was taken out of her hands. The engine cut out and, despite repeated attempts, she failed to revive it.

What to do now? Sit tight, or walk for help?

That decision too was almost immediately taken out of her hands when her door was flung open and the tall dark stranger snapped.

'Come on.'

'What are you doing here?' she gasped.

'Saving you. But you can say thank you later.'

Becca's thought were racing. 'Were you following me?'

He poked his snow-covered head inside, clenched his teeth and grinned—and things inside Becca clenched too as mindless desire clutched low in her belly.

'No, I just happened to be passing.' He rolled his eyes and clicked the catch on her seat belt. 'Of course I was following you!' he yelled, his voice very loud in the confined space. 'Now, come on—before my car gets snowed in too.'

Stepping out into the snow, she felt the wind steal her breath for a moment. He grabbed her hand and yelled above the wind. 'Come on!' He drew her towards the Jaguar that he had pulled up just behind her Beetle.

Sitting in the warmth and comfort of his car, with snow melting on her face and hair, she watched him turn the ignition.

'Why did you follow me?'

53

His eyes swivelled towards her and he said, without any discernible change of expression, 'I wanted to kiss you again.'

Of course this was the cue for her stomach to take a dramatic dive and her temperature to rise by several degrees.

Obviously he was joking. 'It wasn't that good a kiss.'

This time when he looked at her his eyes held a raw, hungry gleam. 'Oh, yes,' he said, his eyes dropping to her mouth, 'it was.'

Their journey to a country house hotel a couple of miles back was completed in total silence.

'Where's this?' she said, looking at the black-and-white-timbered Tudor Inn while she thought about how good his mouth had felt.

'Hopefully where we're spending the night. You have a problem with that?' he asked, angling a dark-eyed, questioning look at her face.

Becca read the question in his eyes and her heart skipped a beat. A sharp thrill of excitement slid through her body, bringing a flush to her cheeks and a feverish glitter to her deep blue wide-spaced eyes.

'It would probably be dangerous to try and drive any further.'

'But not impossible,' he admitted, making it difficult for her to pretend even to herself that this was anything other than what it was.

Do I know what I'm doing? God, yes. I'm playing with fire.

'We need a room.'

She snatched an uneven breath and thought, *I need my head tested.* Deep inside the liquid excitement low in her belly tightened another painful notch.

'Two rooms.'

'That seem a little excessive, but if that is what you want.'

His expression suggested that he knew perfectly well it wasn't what she wanted at all.

'One thing,' she said, catching hold of his arm as he was about to step out of the car.

'What?'

'What's your name?'

He grinned. 'I'm Christos, *yineka mou.*'

The Tudor Inn turned out to be half empty, several guests having been unable to make it because of the weather. When he heard where they had come from the proprietor expressed surprise that they had risked the drive.

He asked if they wanted a meal and Becca, with visions of candlelight, open fires, long, awkward silences and her companion's sexy eyes, said quickly, 'No—just some sandwiches, if that's all right.'

The man behind the reception desk looked at Christos, who said that sandwiches would suit him too.

'Fine. I'll leave them in the snug and you can have them when it suits you. There'll be a pot of coffee there too—just help yourselves. Up the stairs, the first two rooms on the left,' he said, handing Christos the keys.

'Nice man,' Becca said as he left.

'I could be nicer if you'd let me,' Christos said, not looking at her.

Becca was so startled that she didn't know whether to slap his face or say, *Prove it.*

The fact she had even considered the latter said a lot for her state of mind! She turned her head, expecting to see a satirical glint in his eyes or a mocking smile on his expressive lips. She was rendered breathless by the expression of driven need stamped on his dark, lean features.

Breathless she could cope with. The excitement that

swirled through her veins like a powerful narcotic was another matter.

'I'm sure that modesty is one of your most charming traits,' she said, trying for detached and faintly amused and failing horribly on both counts.

'You are ready to go up?'

Becca shook her head and pressed a hand to her throat, where she could feel a revealing pulse throbbing. She walked towards the fire blazing in the inglenook. 'I'll explore a little down here first.'

Christos nodded curtly but didn't say anything.

Becca waited five minutes and then went up. She had no problem locating the rooms the landlord had mentioned, but the question was which one Christos had taken. With no regard for security he had left both sets of keys in their corresponding locks.

Taking a deep breath, she opened the first door. The room was empty. She closed it quietly, careful to make no sound, and stepped back out into the hallway. Trembling a little, she opened the second door. The carefully prepared expression of surprise faded from her face as she stepped into the room. This room too appeared empty.

The sense of anticlimax was intense.

'Done exploring?'

Becca jumped like a startled deer and spun around. Christos stood in the doorway of the *en suite* bathroom. The moisture clinging to his golden skin and the towel looped about his waist suggested he had just that moment stepped out of the shower.

Becca stood nailed to the spot by sexual longing as she took in the details of his lean, streamlined body.

He was quite unbelievably gorgeous, she decided, as her eyes greedily explored the perfect definition of his flat belly, broad chest, and long, muscular thighs. He had the toned body of an athlete—though she could honestly say that she had never looked at an athlete with a flat stomach and imagined running her tongue across it!

The simmering silence stretched and stretched.

'I just...the door... This is your room. I'm sorry—' Her disjointed sentence faded away to nothing as she lifted her hands to her hot cheeks. 'I'll go,' she added, shaking her head.

'No!'

She turned.

A muscle along his jaw clenched. 'Don't go, Becca.' The lashes lifted from his cheeks and Becca gasped. Looking into his molten eyes made her dizzy with desire.

'Stay with me.'

Before the throaty plea had left his lips a needy moan had left her own and she was running towards him.

She felt relief as his strong arms closed around her, holding her so tight she couldn't breathe. He kissed her again and again, with a driving desperation. Becca didn't want to care about breathing, she just wanted this not to stop any time soon. She wanted to carry on feeling like this for ever. It was insane and she loved it.

This isn't love, it's sex, she told herself, and then thought, *Why give it a name? It's just incredible—and so is he.* Then she stopped thinking, because she was too busy *feeling*!

Still kissing her, Christos slid the coat from her shoulders, then peeled away her jumper. 'I have thought about taking off your clothes from the very second I saw you. Have you any idea how good you smell?'

He unclipped her bra, and as he cupped one breast in his hand rasped, 'You're totally perfect.' He picked her up and carried her to the bed.

Becca lay there, and realised that this was the first time in her entire life she had actually surrendered control. She had had no idea that it could be such a spectacularly liberating experience. The glorious contradiction made her laugh, and then she stopped, because Christos was unfastening the towel from his waist. She gave a fractured gasp as her hot, hungry eyes slid down his sleek hard body.

'Oh, my…' she whispered as he arranged his long length beside her. She touched his skin. It was like warm silk and still damp from his shower. 'I want to touch you.' As she looked at him the intimate ache between her thighs became an insistent throb.

Christos held her eyes as she laid a hand on his belly, letting one finger trail downwards, then he groaned and, leaning over, fitted his mouth to hers.

Becca's hands slid into his hair as they kissed. He touched her everywhere, his clever hands gliding over her skin. Becca groaned, feeling his cool fingers on her hot flesh, and writhed with pleasure, begging him in a husky, broken whisper not to stop.

'I won't,' he promised, pressing damp, hot kisses to her neck and eyelids before plunging into the sweet moisture of her mouth.

When he slid down her snug-fitting jeans she wriggled her hips, arching her back and lifting her bottom off the bed to help him.

She had no control over the keening cry of pleasure that was drawn from her throat as his hand slid between her thighs. 'You are *very* good at this!'

'You like this too?' he asked.

Watching his dark head as he licked his way down her stomach was the most mind-blowingly erotic thing she could have imagined. Becca could do little more than moan as she gave herself over entirely to the deep tremors of burning pleasure that passed through her body as he continued to caress her with skilled hands and lips.

When he finally parted her thighs and settled between them she entered a place she had never been before. She was beyond sanity. She just knew that if he didn't take her now she would die.

She screamed something to that effect and dug her nails in his back. In the moment before he thrust all the way into her, hard and hot, she closed her eyes, preserving for ever in her memory the image of his face drawn taut into a mask of raw and primitive need.

As he drove into her she gave a shocked little gasp and whispered *yes* against the damp skin of his neck. She dug her nails into the firm smooth skin of his shoulders. Said *yes* again as she caught the rhythm.

'Look at me!' he said thickly, and she did—just as it hit her so fast and strong that she stopped breathing. Muscles tightened, nerve-endings throbbed, all in perfect blissful, mind-blowing harmony.

Inside her she felt the heat of his pulsing release and her arms wrapped tight about him, wanting to prolong this moment for ever.

For a long time they just lay there, with his face turned into her neck, their sweat-slick bodies entwined, but finally he rolled away and gave her a sleepy, heartbreakingly gorgeous smile.

'I was tired. Next time it'll be better.'

'Then next time I will die,' she responded with total conviction. There was only so much pleasure a body could take.

Pulling her into his arms, he laughed huskily and fell almost immediately asleep.

CHAPTER SEVEN

SITTING amidst the raw ingredients that would become a Bronze Age village for Year Four's history project, despite all her best efforts Becca found it hard to concentrate on the challenge of inspiring enquiring young minds.

Christos's dark, lean face kept creeping into her head. That and a feeling of profound loss and misery—which was ridiculous, because you couldn't lose something you had never had in the first place.

Ridiculous or not, she was unwilling to release the image. Dwelling on the impossible perfection of his sensual mouth made her tummy muscles quiver, and recalling the depth of emotions his dark eyes were capable of communicating sent a jolt of neat sexual longing through her body.

She looked at her trembling outstretched hand and bit her lip. *Face it, while you're obsessing about him he's probably staring into his gorgeous fiancée's eyes. Or, more likely,* she reflected, *unscrewing a pot of glue with unwanted violence, her cleavage!*

She felt a tear of anger and misery slide slowly down her cheek and lifted a hand to blot it.

This has to stop, she told herself sternly.

For heaven's sake, anyone would think I'd fallen in love with the man! She froze and sucked in her breath… *Oh, my God…!*

She could only ignore what was so glaringly obvious for just so long, and Becca knew that her period of blissful ignorance had just come to an end. For the past months, while she'd been congratulating herself on her practicality, on her ability to face her problems head-on and come up with solutions, she had been asking the wrong questions!

This wasn't about maternity leave and childcare. This wasn't about how a dedicated single parent could make a good job of bringing up a child. This was about coming to terms with living without the man she loved.

It was stupid, no doubt about it. Criminally insane, almost certainly. But she had fallen for a man who probably didn't even remember her name!

Becca let out a strangled laugh. Maybe his PA still had it on file somewhere? Her lips twisted as she recalled the terse, typewritten note that had accompanied her lost bag when it had arrived by courier. Angrily she brushed away the tears that were flowing freely down her cheeks. It had been the sheer formality of the card that had hurt the most.

Would it have killed him to sign his own name? Even a one-night stand should be afforded that courtesy.

Instead Christos had delegated the task to one of his darned minions. After viciously tearing the note to shreds, and indulging in a crying jag that had left her face red and blotchy, Becca had reassembled the pieces and jotted down the address.

She had felt slightly better when she had shoved the sum of money she'd been forced to borrow from him into an envelope and posted it. *Closure* she had defiantly termed her action. But she hadn't yet realised that she was pregnant.

Anchoring her hair from her face, she got to her feet and caught sight of herself in the mirror.

'I'm an idiot,' she told her teary reflection. 'Only an idiot would fall in love with the enemy.' Then, as the room tilted without warning, she sank back down onto her knees and let her head flop forward.

She was back there—back in that room, at the moment

she had discovered the identity of the man who had just made love to her.

Getting out of bed by the light of the moon that had filtered through the half-closed curtains, her intention to get a glass of water, instead she had tripped on his discarded trousers. As she'd picked them up his wallet had fallen from the pocket. Dropping to her knees, she had retrieved a credit card that had spilled out.

She'd been about to slide it back in when the name had leapt out at her.

She'd frozen, an expression of horror stealing over her face, then she'd risen to her feet and gazed at the sleeping figure. *Oh, no. What have I done?*

She had gone to the bathroom, barely registering what she was doing as she'd pulled on her clothes in the dark. Going back into the bedroom, she had actually got as far as the door when a compulsion she hadn't been able to resist made her walk across the room to the bed where Christos lay.

In the half-light she'd seen his chest rise and fall, slowly and rhythmically. The sheet gathered low on his hips had revealed his lean, tightly muscled torso. His skin, warm and smooth, had invited her touch.

She could remember the tight feeling in her chest that had forced her to breathe shallow and fast, to drag enough air into her lungs, as she'd sunk to her knees beside the bed and stretched out her hand.

Her fingertips had tingled as they'd hovered a whisper away from his skin. A deep, voluptuous sigh had escaped her aching throat as her fingers had made contact with his bare flesh. She'd allowed her sensitised fingertip to draw a line down his flat belly, feeling the shift of muscle under the satiny, slightly damp skin.

She should have run then, when he had stirred and murmured throatily in his sleep, but the feeling had been addictive.

But Christos had opened his eyes and she'd no longer had that option. For a moment he'd looked at her blankly, then recognition had spread across his face and warmth and passion had stirred hotly in his eyes.

He had reached for her, touching a strand of bright hair, then seen the dampness on her face and pulled himself upright, dragging a hand through his tousled dark hair as he'd flicked on the bedside lamp.

Becca had blinked in the brightness.

'You're crying.' His thumb had brushed a shiny tear from her cheek.

Becca had closed her eyes, the tenderness and concern in his deep voice making it hard to cling to her righteous anger and disgust.

'You're dressed!'

She'd opened her eyes in time to see him swing his legs over the edge of the bed, apparently oblivious to his naked state. Becca hadn't been. She'd been a long way from oblivious. There was not an ounce of surplus flesh on his long, lean body to conceal the ripple of taut, perfectly formed muscle as he moved.

As he'd taken her face between his hands her lashes had lifted from her cheeks, their eyes had connected and a visible quiver had run through her body. Even knowing the warmth in his dark eyes was fake, that he was not, in fact, sensitive and caring, but a manipulative, lying rat, she'd had to struggle against her gut reaction.

A gut reaction that had said *This is a man you can trust with your life.* Were her instincts wrong this time!

'What is wrong, *yineka mou*?'

The endearment pierced her like an arrow aimed at her heart. 'I've never had a one-night stand in my life before.'

And what a time to start! 'I don't care if you don't believe me,' she added defiantly.

His response was immediate. 'Of course I believe you.'

She leaned back on her heels and his hands fell away. He watched, perplexed and concerned, as she covered her face with her hands.

'Becca!' he exclaimed, oozing the sort of the caressing amusement she found almost impossible not to respond to. 'You don't think I'm the sort of man who has double standards about such things, do you?' He took her wrists and drew her hands from her face. *'Do you?'*

Incapable of responding, Becca just looked back at him, thinking even at that moment, when she hated him, that she had never in her life seen anything as beautiful as this despicable man.

'I'm the last person in the world to judge.'

Becca, who was busy judging herself, bit down hard on her lip, and felt her eyes fill with angry self-recriminating tears when she heard him say, 'Besides, this wasn't a one-night stand.'

Becca knew she shouldn't even respond to such a ludicrous contention, but then this had been a night for doing things she shouldn't have!

'You mean there are going to be more nights like this?' Without allowing him time to respond to this angry question, she gave a bitter laugh and added, 'Well, there couldn't be, could there?' she reasoned.

'There couldn't?'

The indulgence in his tone made her want to scream. 'Even someone as s...stupid as me, Christos—' she heard the self-pitying quiver in her voice and lifted her chin in angry defiance '—is eventually going to catch on to the fact you're not a sexy security guard.'

She saw him stiffen and gave a triumphant little smile,

even though she'd never felt less triumphant in her life. She felt sick, used, and deeply ashamed of herself.

'Yes. I know that you're really a Carides.'

'Ah…'

Her voice rose to an accusing shriek as she yelled, 'Is that all you've got to say?'

His glance moved to his wallet, lying on floor where she had dropped it. She met his eyes and produced a disdainful sniff.

'Well, I suppose I should thank you. Not every girl can say they've slept with a Greek tycoon. *Tycoon*—is that the right term?'

'Somewhat generic, but it is one that has been used before,' he admitted, studying her flushed, tear-stained face. 'Don't you think you're overreacting slightly?'

'*Overreacting?*'

'Essentially nothing has changed. I am the same man I was an hour ago.'

'If you really think that you're insane.' Her hands balled into tight fists as she rasped in a low, driven voice, 'I'll never, *never* forgive myself for sleeping with the enemy.'

He looked startled. 'Enemy?' he repeated slowly. 'Is that what I am now?'

She met his eyes. 'You always were. I just didn't know it.' Her eyes were filled with bitter tears of self-recrimination as she lifted her head.

The golden skin of his face pulled taut against the carved contours of his darkly handsome face as he watched her. 'And you would condemn me because of my name?' he wanted to know.

'No, I condemn you by your actions—which, not to put too fine a point on it, *stink*! What's wrong?' she asked. 'Can't you get a girl into bed without lying through your teeth?'

The anger that she sensed had been building in him

seemed to drain at her jeering insult. 'My name doesn't normally act as such a hindrance when it comes to attracting the opposite sex.'

The horrid image of hordes of nubile babes all competing for his favours did not do much to improve Becca's state of mind.

'Well, I'm not so easily impressed by your money. And quite frankly,' she confided truthfully, 'the sound of your name makes me feel physically sick!'

'You would judge me by my cousin's standards?'

'As far as I can see, you're two of a kind,' she retorted, and had the satisfaction of seeing the flare of furious anger in his eyes before he vented a violent-sounding foreign expletive.

'I can understand that, after what he has done to you—'

'Not me. My sister,' she inserted, unable to meet his devouring eyes without her stomach taking a violent, quivering nosedive.

Becca endured the stunned silence that greeted her words for a full thirty seconds before her control crumbled.

'For pity's sake,' she entreated, averting her gaze and covering her hot cheeks with her hands. 'Will you put on some clothes? *P...please?*'

Christos gave no sign of having heard her fractured plea. 'You mean you and Alex never—?'

'I've never been introduced to the man,' she cut in. 'Well, I've seen him at a distance,' compulsive honesty compelled her to admit, with scrupulous accuracy. 'Dark, very little chin to speak of, and,' she added, frowning in distaste as she recalled, 'a loud voice. Not really my type.'

Christos's normally rich, expressive voice acquired a dull monotone as he tersely interrogated her. 'You haven't slept with my cousin?'

Dragging her wandering eyes back to his face, she achieved a passable shrug.

'You were never carrying his child?'

'I've never slept with a Carides before tonight.' Her eyes slid down his lean, toned body, gleaming in the subdued light, and a shiver ran through her body.

'You led me to believe that you—'

'I didn't set out to deceive you,' she cut in.

'Then as I did not set out to deceive you. We could call it quits.'

'I don't think so,' Becca retorted, shaking her head.

'We will discuss this further in the morning. Come here. You are wearing way too many clothes.'

The colour flew to Becca's cheeks. She looked at her fingers, intertwined with his, and felt despair when she couldn't summon the strength to pull free. 'You really think I'm going to come back to bed with you?'

'You're thinking about it, aren't you?' He paused and took her chin in his fingers, tilting her face up to his.

'I know you want to…you know you want to…'

A small cry of distress emerged from Becca's throat. She shook her head to dispel the lingering images and got slowly to her feet. She picked up a dry cracker from a plate on the desktop. Little and often, the doctor had advised when she had explained that she was having trouble keeping food down.

For weeks her morning sickness, which had unfortunately not been confined to the morning, had been utterly horrendous, but now things were improving.

Becca felt the familiar knot of tension in the pit of her stomach as she recognised that she couldn't delay coming clean about her prolonged bout of 'stomach flu' for much longer.

Hot tears welled up in her eyes, and she angrily dashed them away with the back of her hand. It must be due to her hormones, she decided. Certainly her emotions had never been this close to the surface before. Her hands fell to the soft mound of her belly in an instinctively protective gesture. A wobbly smile formed on her lips as a sigh shuddered through her body. Things never happened the way you anticipated they would!

The father of her child might not have had a name or face in her dreams, but one thing she had been clear about—when she told him she was carrying his child his response had been one of incredulous delight!

Something told Becca that it was never going to happen that way in real life.

CHAPTER EIGHT

THE phone ringing made Becca jump.

'Becca?'

The sound of her sister's voice made Becca smile. 'No, I'm a recording, Erica.'

'Right…yes, very funny. I was just ringing to see if you're there. And you are which is…good. See you later.'

Becca lifted the receiver from her ear as it went dead and frowned. 'Is it me?' she puzzled out loud. 'Or was that very odd?'

She had started to wonder recently if maybe her sister had guessed about the baby. Erica hadn't come right out and said anything, but on a couple of occasions she had caught her sister smiling to herself when she heard Becca blaming her recent weight loss on a bout of stomach flu.

And Erica had definitely been more understanding about her volatile mood swings than might otherwise have been expected!

She had no time to ponder the odd non-conversation with Erica, because as she put the phone down the doorbell rang. Becca glanced absently at the clock on the mantel; it was still too early to be her elderly neighbour, who often popped in after walking her dog.

Slapping her cheeks lightly, to restore a little colour to her pallid complexion, she went into the bijou hallway. Her expression set in an enquiring smile, she yanked open the door with a jerky flourish.

Her look of polite enquiry faded to slack-jawed horror as her eyes travelled up the length of her visitor—all six feet five inches of him—before connecting with a pair of mesmerising dark eyes set in a face of implacable male beauty.

For a fraction of a second Becca thought she had lost it, big-time, and was suffering from some form of hallucination. She blinked several times, but the mirage remained solid—and very real. Equally real was the great wave of enervating lust and wild longing that washed over her.

She exhaled on a big gushy sigh and grabbed the doorframe as her knees sagged.

'You shouldn't be here.'

Mixed with the fear, suspicion and disorientation she was feeling, Becca was overpoweringly conscious of an aching hunger that made her imagine putting her head against his chest and breathing in the subtle warm male fragrance of his hard body.

Shouldn't be here! It was obvious to Christos as he looked at her thin face and tired, shadowed eyes that he should have been here long before now. It was equally obvious to him that it was possible to want to wring a person's neck and protect them from even the lightest of breezes at one and the same time.

This fusion of feelings was not comfortable.

'You are going to invite me in.'

The comment was more an autocratic decree than a suggestion, and Becca, paralysed with lust and utterly terrified of what was going to come out of her mouth if she opened it again, responded by shaking her head vigorously from side to side.

His dark brows drew together as he studied her face. 'You have been crying,' he accused huskily.

At this point Becca's numbed brain finally recognised that he was inexplicably, seethingly furious! The strength of his feelings was evident in the tense lines of his coiled lean body, and underlined by the erratic muscle that clenched and relaxed like a ticking time bomb.

Becca cleared her throat and tried not to look at his mouth. Looking at his mouth made her think about fitting her own to it.

She wondered bitterly if there was some unwritten rule that only men who were very bad for you were incredible kissers.

'What was he like?' Erica had asked when, as part of her strictly expurgated version of events, Becca had explained that she had not got to confront Alex but she had bumped into his cousin, Christos.

When Becca had shrugged and looked away, to hide her blushes, her sister had added, 'I hear he's a serious hunk.'

'I suppose he is quite good-looking. If you're into all that dark, smouldering stuff.'

'Alex used to say mean things about him,' Erica had recalled. 'But thinking about it now,' she'd mused, 'I think he was actually jealous. Did you see the girl he's engaged to?'

Becca had actually felt the blood leave her face. Even though she had seen from her sister's concerned expression that her behaviour was likely to arouse suspicions, she hadn't been able to control the horror in her voice as she'd gasped, *'Christos is engaged?'*

'Oh, yes. To this stunning Greek girl. I saw her picture in that Sunday supplement.'

Feeling sick, Becca had abruptly excused herself under the pretext of making a cup of tea. When she had returned her sister had looked thoughtful, but had tactfully not commented on her elder sister's red-rimmed eyes.

Becca dragged her thoughts back to the present as an awful possibility occurred to her. 'Is she here too?' she asked, looking past Christos.

'Is who here?' Studying her expression intently, he added, 'I am quite alone, Becca.' Something that until recently had never bothered him.

As he stood to one side Becca saw a low-slung convertible parked outside her garden gate. It was about as unobtrusive as its owner! Clearly she could forget about this visit passing without notice.

Becca caught her lower lip between her teeth and suppressed a groan as she anticipated the curious questions she would be fielding from her neighbors concerning the identity of the driver of the gleaming monster for the next week at least.

Curious questions are the least of your problems, girl!

Getting him out of her head last time had been bad, so it was pretty much a given that it would be worse this time. Her eyes darkened as she recalled waking in the middle of the night, consumed with longing.

'It is cold out here.'

Becca swallowed past the constriction in her throat and continued to scan him through the dark mesh of her lowered lashes.

She had spent the last months almost convincing herself that absence had made her exaggerate his attributes. No man, she had reasoned, could be *that* good-looking. How wrong she had been!

Far from being inaccurate, the painful truth was that, no matter how true to life the mental image of him she retained in her memory, no mental image could summon up the raw sexual aura which was an integral part of him.

'There's no warm welcome waiting for you in my home, Christos.'

His mouth spasmed and a muscle in his lean cheek clenched as his dark eyes captured hers. 'This is ridiculous,' he contended.

The irritation in his husky voice brought her chin up. 'I'm extremely busy.' *Having your baby.* A tiny inarticulate gurgle escaped her lips and her eyes widened in panic. For a split second she actually thought she had said it out loud.

'We cannot have a private conversation on your doorstep.'

'I'm not about to have a conversation, private or otherwise, with you anywhere.'

'You sound like a child,' he condemned.

Becca took a deep, steadying breath and rubbed her trembling hands in a nervous gesture up and down her jogger-clad thighs. The action drew Christos's restless eyes to the soft feminine curves.

Suddenly miserably conscious that, compared to his glamorous fiancée, she must look one step removed from a bag lady, Becca wished she hadn't changed into comfy clothes when she'd got home that afternoon. Teeth clenched, she endured his narrow-eyed scrutiny. By the time his attention had moved on the tension in her body had climbed to screaming pitch.

He took his time to withdraw something from the breast pocket of his jacket. Becca, her eyes round with surprise, focused on the shiny object that swung from his fingers.

'My locket!' She reached for it and their fingertips brushed. With a tiny gasp she froze, as a shudder of sexual longing ran through her body.

Eyes downcast, she let it fall into her palm. 'Thank you.'

'We have, I think, unfinished business.'

Panic immediately engulfed her, driving every vestige of colour from her skin, as the irrational conviction that he knew about the baby gripped her.

Christos, his hand extended, stepped forward as she swayed.

Becca, unable to speak, took a deep gulp and moved her hands in a fluttery gesture to ward him off. To her relief, after a slight pause his hands fell away. But he didn't back off—a fact that Becca was overwhelmingly conscious of as she faltered.

'H...how did you know?' Half of her was actually relieved it was out in the open. The other half dreaded the recriminations that lay ahead. But at least she now had an explanation for his anger.

He gave a baffled frown, his dark brows twitching into a straight line. 'Know what?'

'Nothing.' Her eyes dropped from his. 'Just for a minute I thought…' Of course he didn't know. Nobody did except her doctor and the headmistress.

The latter had been especially supportive when they'd discussed Becca's maternity leave. She had even suggested Becca returning part-time if that suited her better after the birth.

'You thought what?'

She blinked and shook her head. 'It doesn't matter.'

'It looks to me as though it matters very much to you,' he observed, scanning her milk-pale face.

'Look…' She pinned on her best impersonal smile. 'This really isn't a very good time for me.'

His mobile lips sketched a brief cynical smile. 'I am not going away, Becca.'

'I really, *really* wish you would,' she choked.

His dark eyes narrowed on her face. 'I don't believe you.'

She gave a negligent shrug and laughed. The tinkling sound appeared to annoy him—which as far as she was concerned was a good thing.

'I can live with that.'

'You've missed me.'

The unforgivably accurate statement brought a mortified flush to her face.

'When it comes to arrogance,' she choked, 'You're in a class of your own.' *When it came to a lot of things Christos was in a class of his own.*

'There's no need to be defensive,' he soothed, as his

glance travelled over the smooth contours of her face. 'What did I say that spooked you back there?'

'I am not defensive,' she gritted back through clenched teeth. 'I was not spooked, and I do not miss you. I don't even know you!'

'True. If you did you would not resort to blatant lies.'

'So, what? Are you a mind-reader or something?' If he was she was in deep trouble.

His eyes scanned her flushed, scared face. 'I recognise the symptoms, Becca. I look in the mirror every morning,' he added, without changing expression.

'And at five-minute intervals thereafter, I expect—' Mid-crushing retort, she froze. 'What are you talking about? Recognise what symptoms?'

'Is it so impossible to imagine that I have not been able to forget you?'

Her heart was beating so fast when she managed to respond that her voice was breathy and faint. 'Quite honestly—yes.' *Outside my fantasies.* 'We had a one-night stand, Christos.'

The reminder was more for her own benefit than his. If she allowed herself to believe him she would be setting herself up for some major hurt and humiliation—which would be fine if she just had herself to consider. She ran a hand across her stomach and lifted her chin. She had the baby to think of now.

The permanently etched groove above Christos's masterful nose deepened as he retorted with chilly hauteur, 'I don't do one-night stands.'

Her temper fizzed, restoring a flush of colour to her pale cheeks. 'You're suggesting I do?'

'You owe me a goodbye.'

Becca, her brow puckered in bewilderment, shook her head. 'I don't understand.'

His eyes glittered with combustible brilliance as they

swept over her upturned features before locking down on her mouth. 'I woke and you were gone.' He swallowed and fought to contain his feelings as his voice sank to a raw rasp of outrage. 'You used me for sex and walked away.'

This last blighting accusation robbed her momentarily of the power to respond. Then she was forcibly hit by the sheer hypocrisy of his words.

'And you wanted lifelong commitment, I suppose?'

His rigid jaw tightened at the inflammatory sound of her laughter. 'It amuses you? Would you have laughed if *you* had woken and found the bed empty? Would it have been so funny then?'

'I thought you'd be relieved I'd gone. I mean the morning-afters are a bit awkward, aren't they?'

His face taut, Christos released a long fluid string of curses in his native tongue—at least they sounded like it to Becca. 'Do not be ludicrous. You know nothing about *morning-afters*… You are one of the most naïve women I have ever met.'

'So sorry if I'm too amateur for you. That I'm not *au fait* with the correct sexual etiquette for one-night stands,' she flared.

Christos gritted his teeth. 'This has nothing to do with sexual etiquette,' he growled contemptuously. 'This is about…'

About waking and reaching for someone who wasn't there. A new experience. Yes, he had been furious, and his alpha male pride had taken a body-blow, but Christos had enough self-awareness to recognise and even at some level appreciate the supreme irony.

After a lifetime of being the one to walk away, someone had walked out on Christos Carides!

And he cared. He *cared* that this woman he barely knew, with her warmth, her soft voice and softer skin, hadn't been there when he'd reached for her. No level of self-awareness was going to help him deal with that—or the fact that he had woken every morning since feeling the same way.

What would help?

'What *is* this about?' Becca asked, her voice weak.

Christos's expression lost that distant, slightly unfocused look as his eyes meshed with hers. 'Perhaps we should try it and see.'

She was almost afraid to ask. 'What do you mean?'

'I mean we should spend a night of passion and let *you* wake up alone.' He tilted his head to one side and regarded her shocked face through narrowed eyes. 'The idea doesn't appeal?'

'A night with you? Let me see…' Becca pretended to consider the idea before completing scathingly, 'That would be slightly less appealing than bubonic plague.' *Let him never know how big a lie that is.*

'You condemned my cousin for discarding your sister.'

'You're not *seriously* comparing yourself with an innocent eighteen-year-old virgin, are you?' Becca spluttered indignantly.

Dark stains of frustration appeared along the slashing curve of his cheekbones as their eyes clashed. 'You left my bed. You stole away like a thief in the night.'

Comprehension dawned in Becca's eyes. 'Sorry—I'm slow! I didn't realise why you were so hung up about this! Well don't worry—if anyone asks,' she promised, with a saccharine-sweet smile, 'I'll say *you* did the walking, so your male pride can stay intact. Not that they're likely to ask, because it's not something I'm going to boast about,' she reflected bleakly.

'Well, obviously you have told someone.' Her startled eyes flew to his face. 'Why else would your sister think it appropriate to write to me and place the blame for your fragile mental state and physical deterioration at my door?'

'My mental state isn't fragile—' She stopped as the full

import of his words hit home. 'Erica wrote to *you*?' Becca's eyes widened to their fullest extent and a dull flush of mortified colour rose up her neck until her entire face burned. Her thoughts raced. 'She knew you were coming here now?'

'I rang her to ask if you would be at home. You do realise that she is very concerned about you? She does blame me for your present condition.'

Becca barely registered what he was saying. Her thoughts were racing. It explained their odd telephone call. Erica had been checking to see if she was at home! This was nothing short of a conspiracy! What Becca couldn't understand was *why* Erica would do something like that.

'But I didn't discuss you with her—really I didn't.'

'Sometimes it is not what you say, but what you don't…'

'She shouldn't have written to you—'

Christos cut across her mortified protest. 'I had to see you anyway, to return your pendant.'

'You could have sent it with my other things. That way you could have avoided lying to your fiancée about the purpose of your visit to Yorkshire.'

Christos froze, the strong lines of his face growing taut. 'What do you know of Melina?'

'Enough to know she has my sympathy,' Becca choked.

Instead of responding to her jibe with anger, he slid his eyes from hers. This evidence of evasion confirmed Becca's suspicions.

'I despise men who cheat.' *And women who sleep with men who belong to someone else!*

'Our engagement did not work out.'

'You mean she discovered that you were a faithless bastard?'

'I mean,' he retorted, his manner abrupt, 'that we decided we did not suit. I do not wish to discuss Melina with you, Becca.'

'I don't much care *what* you wish.'

For the first time she registered that despite his definitely *not* off the peg suit, on his definitely *not* off the peg body, Christos wasn't looking his usual immaculate self. His tie was unfastened, and several buttons of his shirt had parted.

But a man who had just been dumped by his beautiful fiancée could be excused a sartorial slip or two...

'You loved her?' In her mind she saw him getting in his car and driving to forget.

Christos stared at her, his expression hard to interpret, and Becca flushed. 'It's none of my business.'

The corner of his mouth lifted, but the smile didn't reach his eyes. 'True,' he agreed.

'Did she find out about us?'

He shook his head. 'You are not the reason Melina and I are not together.'

Of course, Becca thought. I'm not important enough. Christos had just been dumped by the woman who had probably been his ideal.. maybe even the love of his life! What could have been more natural than for him to seek comfort in the first available pair of female arms?

And as I was so very available last time he probably thought... *Why not?* Well, not any more. I can't live with second best.

She lifted her chin. 'Look, you came because of something my sister wrote. But one night together hardly makes you responsible for me in any way.' Her laughter was met with stony silence. 'As you see, I'm fine.'

Becca struggled to understand his expression as he studied her in silence. The seconds ticked uncomfortably by. 'You are not fine. And I did not come because of your sister's letter.'

'Then why did you come?'

'I came because you do not belong here.'

Her nose wrinkled. 'What do you mean? Then where *do* I belong?'

His nostrils flared as smouldering velvety eyes clashed with deep blue. 'In my bed.'

CHAPTER NINE

BECCA sucked in a shaken breath and, smiling, tried to project total conviction. 'Never going to happen.'

She could avoid his eyes, but she couldn't escape the image imprinted in her mind of him lying asleep, the sheet loosely gathered around his lean hips. His chiselled features, relaxed in repose, had made him look younger, almost vulnerable.

'Why would I get back into the bed of a man who didn't even tell me his real name the first time?'

'Your outbreak of moral indignation is slightly less convincing taking into account that knowing you were sleeping with "the enemy" didn't stop you doing the same again.'

Without waiting for her to reply, he barged past her into her living room. By the time she had closed the front door and followed him he was running his finger along the spine of the paperback she had been reading.

'That's not something I'm proud of,' she said in a low, intense voice. 'And, for your information, I didn't steal away in the night. It wasn't the night, it was morning, and you were asleep. I think nothing short of an earthquake would have woken you.'

It had been two in the afternoon when Christos had woken, still jet lagged. When he'd discovered she was gone he had been consumed with anger.

'Did you even *try* and wake me?'

She turned her head and refused to answer.

'So you didn't. Why?'

'Looking at you makes me feel sick.' The childish retort made her wince, but what was she supposed to say? That she was ashamed that she had made love with a member of the detestable Carides family, not once but twice? And even more shamed that she knew she would not have had the strength to say no to a repeat performance if she had waited for him to wake?

'From what your sister tells me, you've been doing a lot of that just lately.'

'Erica exaggerates.' The colour fled her cheeks as she avoided meeting his eyes. *He can't know. He can't know.* 'Stomach flu,' she muttered. 'I've had stomach flu.'

'You are well now?'

His searching scrutiny made her feel vulnerable and exposed. 'Your concern touches me, it really does.'

'I am not stupid, Becca.'

Becca covered her mouth with her hand and mumbled, 'I don't know what you're talking about.' She had doubts about denial being the best form of defence, but at that moment she had nothing else to fall back on.

'I think you do.'

She looked into his dark, lean face and recognised that denial wasn't going to work. He's relentless, she thought, in the second before the buzzing in her ears became a dull roar and the world started to tilt.

She heard him release a string of curses in his own tongue as he pushed her down into the nearest armchair.

She didn't have the strength or the will-power—never a lot of that around Christos—to struggle as he urged her head down between her knees with the terse instruction to take some deep breaths.

'You need a doctor.'

'The only thing I need is for you not to be here,' she retorted, trying to marshal her defences. The very last thing she wanted was her doctor arriving and saying that a pregnant woman needed to take care of herself.

A few moments later the world stopped spinning quite so wildly and Becca woozily lifted her head.

Christos's hand immediately fell away. In a fluid motion he rose from his squatting position and took a step backwards. Standing with his arms folded across his chest, his expression was brooding and sombre as he studied her face.

Becca lifted her head and saw lines of strain on his face that she had not noticed earlier. Sighing, she passed a hand across her eyes and apologised.

'Sorry about that—no lunch.' Her smile was painfully forced.

'We had sex with no protection.'

This blunt comment sent the colour flying back to her pale cheeks. She pressed a hand to her chest and struggled for a semblance of composure as she felt herself immersed in the sensual fog of sexual recall.

She gave a careless shrug, relieved that she had unexpected acting abilities, and blissfully unaware that she had been staring at him with silent longing for a full thirty seconds.

'The relevance being...?'

She watched the muscles in his long brown throat work as he swallowed before replying, 'Pregnant women faint.'

'I didn't faint.'

His lip curled in a sardonic smile. 'If I had my doubts before, I no longer do. You are a very bad liar. When your sister mentioned your sickness it did cross my mind,' he admitted.

She knew a scornful laugh should be her response, but Becca could only stare at him in horror. 'That's a pretty big leap to make.'

'I believe in following my gut instincts. The first time I saw you I knew—'

'The first time you saw me you knew what?' she prompted, watching as he walked across the room and picked up a pile of exercise books balanced on the arm of a chair. He pushed them onto the floor before lowering his long, lean frame onto the overstuffed floral armchair.

'That's my marking!' she exclaimed in protest. 'It's all mixed up now!' Their eyes met and she was no longer able to pretend an interest in her essays on what Year Four had done during half-term. 'The first time you saw me?' she prompted again, huskily. 'What did you know?' She despised herself for asking.

'I knew you were trouble.' His dark eyes brushed her bright hair and travelled lower, lingering on the full curve of her lips. 'My instincts are generally right.'

His eyes captured hers, and the heat she saw smouldering in them drew a tiny gasp from Becca's raw, aching throat. Fighting the sexual tension that was crackling between them, Becca nervously ran her tongue across her lips, inadvertently drawing his attention to the soft pink outline.

'Pity for us both that you didn't listen to your instincts,' she retorted thickly as his eyes darkened.

'Do you not think I've asked myself why I didn't on more than one occasion?'

'And what are your infallible instincts telling you now? No—I really don't want to know,' she said hastily.

'They are telling me you are pregnant. Are you pregnant, Becca?'

'If I am I don't see that it's any of your business.'

Anger tightened his patrician features as he looked at her with incredulous astonishment. 'If I could be the father it's very much my business,' he retorted grimly.

His comment ignited an inexplicable flame of fury in Becca, who leapt to her feet, her hands clenched and her eyes blazing. '*If?*' she yelled. '*If?* Who else would the father be if not you?'

One brow elevated, and his expression was totally unreadable as his dark, heavily lashed eyes swept across her face. 'So you *are* pregnant?'

After a short pause Becca nodded.

Christos held her eyes for a moment, then, cursing in his native tongue, clutched his head in his hands.

Becca knew that it was foolish to allow herself to be hurt by his reaction, but she had no control over the aching pain of loss she felt.

The problem was, a girl had no control over her dreams—and Becca had foolishly allowed herself to dream. She hadn't acknowledged, not even to herself until that moment, that there was a part of her that had still secretly expected him to react like a joyous expectant father.

'Are you okay?'

Her hesitant enquiry brought his head up. He looked at her incredulously, one dark brow arched. 'Me? Am *I* okay?'

She nodded. No wonder he looked gutted—he probably thought she was going to use the baby as leverage.

It was only natural really, she conceded, that if you were Christos Carides there would be any number of women who would like to trap you into marriage. Well, on that score at least she could put his mind at rest. A marriage of convenience was not on her list of things to do with the rest of her life!

'You don't have to worry, you know.'

'I don't?'

Becca shook her head vigorously. 'I've no ambition to be the next Mrs Carides.' She gave a little laugh.

'That is unfortunate. But I'm sure you will adapt.'

'What did you say?' she whispered.

He continued as though she hadn't spoken. 'I will need to rearrange my diary, but I think a wedding in four weeks' time will be possible. And you?'

'Me?' she echoed blankly.

He looked mildly irritated by her inattention. 'Will four

weeks be sufficient for you to organise things at your end? You need not worry about the actual ceremony—I will deal with those arrangements.'

'You mean you'll delegate the task?' She skidded to an abrupt halt and gave a high laugh that she managed to cut off before it tipped over into outright hysteria. She had been about to embark on a squabble about who was to arrange a marriage that was never going to happen.

Christos slanted her a frowning look of enquiry. 'What is so funny?'

'I was just thinking that insanity must be catching.' Her response caused his frown to deepen. 'You actually expect me to marry you in four weeks' time?' Strange. To look at him nobody would suspect he was stark, staring *crazy*.

'As I said, I can be reasonably flexible.'

'You? Flexible?' She gave another laugh. 'That, I suspect, will be a first.'

'I do feel that for obvious reasons—' his glance strayed meaningfully to her stomach '—sooner would be better than later.'

'Don't you, Becca?' he prompted, when she didn't respond.

'Never would be a lot better.'

'I do not think the occasion warrants such flippancy,' he reproached her.

'You think I'm flippant? Let me tell you, Christos, I'm that far away...' she held her finger and forefinger a whisper apart to illustrate her point '...that far away from having total hysterics.' She sucked in a deep breath and made a mammoth effort to stay calm. 'Let me explain this to you— as you obviously don't inhabit the same world as the rest of us. It is the twenty-first century. People don't go around getting married because they're pregnant.'

She watched his lips twist in a derisive smile. 'I have not the faintest interest in what *people* do.'

With most men the arrogant announcement would have been made for effect. With Christos, she realised with a sinking heart, it was simply a statement of fact.

'Let me rephrase that. *I'm* not going to get married because I'm pregnant.'

He heard her out patiently, while looking as though he was fighting an urge to strangle her. 'Once you've considered the situation sensibly—'

Becca struggled to hold on to her temper. 'Do not patronise me, Christos.'

He was unable to stop his exasperation showing as he went on, 'I feel sure I can rely on your good sense—'

Becca's low-pitched squeal of sheer frustration cut across his words. 'You're forgetting I don't have good sense. If I did I wouldn't be in this situation to begin with.'

'You're emotional,' he condemned.

Her eyes opened to their widest. 'Too right I'm emotional!'

'Be calm. It cannot be good for the baby or for you to get stressed.'

Becca's hands went automatically to her stomach. His eyes followed the instinctively protective gesture. 'If you don't want me to be stressed, then please go away.'

'It doesn't work that way, Becca.'

'I have everything organised—my maternity leave, childcare. Honestly, Christos, if you really want to be helpful and feel involved you could make a contribution to the child's education when he or she is older. University can be very expensive. I'm still paying off my own student loan.'

Christos angled a dark brow and looked at her as though she had gone mad. 'And what about the eighteen years before then? Will I be allowed to send Christmas and birthday presents?' The satiric bite of his words made Becca wince, and he relapsed into a fresh stream of low, impassioned Greek.

'I'd appreciate it if you didn't use obscenities in any language in my home,' she told him frostily.

He revealed his even white teeth in a savage, mirthless grin. 'They weren't obscenities. But only because I have iron control.'

'Well, I'm going to have to take your word on that, aren't I?' Their eyes clashed, and abruptly her anger towards him guttered. Give the man his due, he was only trying to do what he thought was his duty. 'I'm sure we can work something out if we put our heads together.'

Christos didn't look mollified by her concession.

'You think my involvement with this child would be satisfied with such a paltry gesture as paying for education? I am not a distant uncle.' His eyes dropped to her belly and his voice thickened as he added, with a hint of wonder in his voice, 'I am the father.'

Becca, who was still struggling with the stubborn image in her skull of their heads close together, snapped in a high, goaded voice, 'Yes! And I'm his mother—though no doubt you wish I wasn't. And,' she added, without pausing to draw breath, '*he* might be a *she*.' Her eyes moved over the impossibly symmetrical features of his dark face and she sighed, continuing to regard him with angry loathing as she thought, *Whichever it is, I really hope this baby looks like its father.*

'*We* are this child's parents, so of course your wishes are to be considered, but I think you're forgetting that the most important person here is the child. Is it not the duty of parents to put the needs of their child before their own selfish desires?'

'You're accusing me of being selfish?' she yelled, expelling an angry gasp and clenching her hands tightly in her lap. 'I'll *love* my baby, and that's the most important thing!' she declared, with an emotional throb in her voice.

'*Our* baby,' he corrected quietly. 'And I'm sure you will.' Becca had started to relax when he added, 'But what do you think is best for a child? To be brought up by a single parent or as part of a stable family unit? Do you think you are considering our child's best interests when you connive to deprive him of a relationship with his father?'

'I'm not conniving! I just didn't think you'd want to be involved. And as for marrying me—that's...well, quite frankly, it's ludicrous!'

'*Ludicrous?*' he echoed, looking outraged. 'You think that marrying me would be ludicrous?'

Becca, who was not allowing herself to think about what being married to him might involve, because some aspects were dangerously attractive, nodded firmly. 'Yes—ludicrous. You're really not thinking straight about this. It's understandable,' she admitted. 'You've had a shock. But imagine for one minute what your family would say.'

'I do not consult my family on how I live my life.'

Becca's feelings found release in a loud groan. 'But imagine what your mother would say.' Becca, who had seen pictures of the incredibly elegant Mia Carides in a Sunday supplement, suspected it would be something along the lines of *Pay the little gold-digger off, Christos.*

Head angled to one side, Christos studied her face. The intensity of his regard began to make Becca feel uneasy. She lifted her chin, suggesting a defiance she was far from feeling.

'Will you stop looking at me like that?'

Christos carried on looking at her, and thought about how soft her body had been in his arms, how it had felt to sink into her. It took him several seconds before he had sufficient control over his breathing to respond tersely.

'I think my mother would like you. She's been trying to marry me off for years.'

'Sure—she'd welcome me with open arms,' Becca sneered. 'The girl who trapped her precious son.'

'Let me tell you something about my parents. When they met my mother was promised to someone else—the son of a close friend of her family.'

'I'm sure your family history is fascinating, but...' Despite herself, Becca's curiosity got the better of her. 'She married your father, not this other man?'

'They were in love. And as she was carrying my father's babies at the time, it seemed the best idea.'

'Babies?'

He touched his chest and nodded. 'Me and my brother, in fact.' The shocked, round-eyed expression on Becca's face caused his sardonic grin to widen. 'Are you shocked that I was once a baby?' he wondered. 'Or is it the fact that my mother was not a virgin bride that makes you sit there with your mouth unattractively open?' The latter wasn't quite true. Her mouth, open or closed, was enough to fill a man's head with steamy fantasies.

Becca closed her mouth with an audible click. 'I'm not shocked,' she lied. 'But,' she admitted, 'I suppose I did picture you born clutching a Palm Pilot computer and asking what the dollar was doing against the yen. I didn't know you had a brother.'

'Five minutes older than me. He only lived a few minutes,' he revealed.

'That's so sad. I'm sorry.'

'Thank you, Becca. Now, would you like a church wedding?'

The soft sympathy vanished from Becca's face as she gritted her teeth. 'I keep telling you—I don't want to get married.'

'And what about your parents? What is their reaction to

your pregnancy? Will they have a problem with me as a son-in-law?'

'They will want me to be happy.'

'The implication being that I cannot make you happy? Yet I seem to recall you saying that I had given you more pleasure than you thought possible.'

Hot, mortified colour suffused her cheeks and she bit her lower lip. 'How can you be sure it was me?'

'I have a very good memory, Becca.' The taunting expression faded from his face as he added thickly, 'And besides, I would never confuse you with another woman.'

'Sure—I'm *very* special.'

It would have been oh, so easy to succumb to his husky velvet drawl. But Becca knew that if she ever forgot the inescapable fact that the only thing that set her apart from any number of other women who had shared his bed was the fact she was carrying his child, she would be in serious trouble. *And you're not now?*

'Look, we spent one night together!' she told him, dabbing the tip of her tongue to the beads of moisture that had broken out along her upper lip. 'We experienced a short-lived hormonal reaction,' she diagnosed. 'Which is hardly the most scientific thing on which to base a lifelong commitment.'

'But it's a good place to start,' he retorted and watching her flush deepen, added, 'A *very* good place. I am pleased that you share my belief that marriage is not a temporary measure, Becca. But a marriage based on *science*?' he drawled contemptuously. 'Marriage is a leap of faith. A gamble!'

Becca was genuinely appalled by the contention. Of course she knew that no marriage came with an iron-clad guarantee of success, but a *gamble*...? Such recklessness was alien to her nature.

Sure—you're so not reckless you're only carrying the baby of a man you barely know.

Ignoring the ironic voice inside her head, she countered tautly, 'You're not serious!'

'Certainly I am serious. Marriage is always a gamble.' Nothing in his manner suggested he found anything wrong with this concept. 'And it is frequently a compromise.'

A compromise as in marrying a woman because you'd accidentally impregnated her? she thought, shaking her head vigorously. 'I won't compromise. And I'm not a gambler.'

'Life is a gamble, *yineka mou.*'

She stared at him. 'Your life may be a gamble, but mine isn't. My life is planned...'

'Was getting pregnant part of this grand plan?'

Becca's spine snapped to attention. 'Are you suggesting I got pregnant deliberately?'

'No, that is not what I am suggesting. I am simply pointing out that life is no more predictable than love.'

Becca wondered if the expression that flitted across his clear-cut patrician features had anything to do with Melina, the woman he had planned to marry.

Christos had lost the love of his life. What did it matter to him now if he sacrificed his freedom for the sake of his child when he had lost his true love?

And how much freedom did he intend to lose? What would his marriage vows mean to him? She didn't have the faintest idea, she realised, her thoughts racing. He might mean it to be a civilised 'arrangement'. They would lead separate lives, but present a united front for public consumption.

CHAPTER TEN

'OH NO!' she gasped, as a wave of faintness washed over her.

'You are ill?'

Becca opened her eyes and blinked, and discovered he was on his knees at her feet. As her head lifted his hands slid from her shoulders. Close to, she could see the lines radiating from the corners of his eyes…dark, velvety eyes, filled with concern at that moment.

I think you're the love of my life.

She shook her head. 'No, I'm fine.' Lies didn't get much bigger; she had never felt *less* fine in her life!

His critical scrutiny lasted. 'You don't look fine,' he said, taking her hand. It was icy cold. 'I think I should call a doctor.'

There was no doctor alive who could cure what ailed her! Becca gathered her scattered wits and forced a stiff little smile. 'That really won't be necessary.'

Christos remained openly sceptical as she pulled her fingers free of his and lifted her chin.

'Would you like me to call someone else? Maybe your mother?'

She shook her head and looked at him through a teary haze. 'No, don't do that.'

Her urgency caused his brows to lift.

'I haven't told them yet,' she admitted.

He digested this information in silence, then after an uncomfortable silence asked, 'Who have you told?'

'I haven't actually told anyone yet. Except my doctor,

93

obviously, and Gillian—the headmistress where I work,' she explained. 'Oh, and you.'

'You didn't tell me,' he reminded her drily. 'Why is it so important for you to prove you can cope alone? That you don't need anyone?'

Becca's eyes narrowed. 'No, I just don't need *you*.'

Her childish retort emerged sounding mean and spiteful. She gave a groan and buried her face in her hands.

A couple of minutes later she blotted the dampness on her cheeks with the back of her hand and lifted her head. 'I didn't mean that the way it sounded.'

'Then you do need me?'

'No—yes.' Suddenly too weary to think straight, let alone fight, she sighed. 'I don't know what I mean,' she admitted, scrubbing her eyes like a tired child.

'I think it is probably better if we tell your parents together anyway.'

Becca stared at him and laughed. 'Have you heard a word I've said?'

'I have been listening, but now I think perhaps it is your turn. Do you really expect me to permit you to bring up my child alone?' The brutal truth was hard to deliver to someone who was staring back at him with red-rimmed eyes, but it needed to be said.

Becca closed her eyes and shook her head. She was literally shaking with the force of her feelings. '*Permit?* You will not *permit* me?'

Her shrill interruption did not affect his icily calm delivery. 'Not alone.'

'I don't have a boyfriend.'

'A situation that is hardly likely to last for ever,' he contended.

Becca, her lips set in an angry straight line, folded her arms across her chest. 'Not your business,' she gritted, thinking that Christos was going to be an impossible act for any man to follow.

He bared his teeth in a white, angry smile and ripped at the collar of his shirt, revealing a small section of olive-brown skin. Becca's stomach gave a lazy flip. She closed her eyes, cursing her weakness, and for an indulgent moment imagined the touch of her lips on his heated skin.

'If you were a free, single agent I'd agree with you. But you're not. You are carrying a child. My child. I will not have my child brought up by another man, Becca.'

'I wouldn't do that!' She felt physically nauseated to discover just how low his opinion of her was.

'I intend to make sure that you don't. You are obviously a very impulsive woman.'

Pretty hard to dispute that, she thought. Eyes narrowed into tearful blue slits, she focused on his lean face. 'I will always put my baby first.'

'Then marry me, and your baby will have everything he needs—including a father.'

'It's not that simple.'

'Oh, but it is that simple. Simple, and not negotiable. You marry me, or I will contest your custody of this child.'

She went cold all over and sucked in a shaky breath. 'You're not serious,' she said, even though she could see he was. If there could ever be a physical representation of *implacable* his expression was it.

'I would suggest you do not try and test that theory.' The dark line along the crest of his sculpted cheekbones suggested he was close to losing his grip on his volatile Greek temper.

'Don't threaten me, Christos.'

Under his tan Christos was as pale as Becca was. 'You act as though marrying me would be a fate worse than death.'

'No court would give you custody.'

'It is true that the legal system favours the mother, but could you take the risk?' He watched the remaining colour drain from her cheeks and tried not to feel like a total bastard.

'If you blackmail me I'll be the wife of your nightmares.'

He sketched a grin. 'I'll take that as a yes, shall I?'

'One of these days you won't get your own way, and I hope I'll be there to see it.'

Had she been in the mood to notice such things, Becca would have seen that he looked tired and relieved rather than triumphal.

'That's all you've got to show for an entire morning's shopping?' Erica teased when she met her for lunch.

'They're nice shoes,' Becca said defensively as she replaced her purchases in the bag. The price label had seemed obscene to her, but she had succumbed when she saw how long and elegant they made her legs look.

Becca ordered fish and a salad. When the waiter had gone she noticed the price of her scallops and gasped. 'That's so expensive! I should have ordered the chicken,' she fretted.

'You're about to marry one of the richest men in Europe—if not the world, for that matter—and you're worried about not ordering the cheapest thing on the menu! As for the shoes,' Erica added, looking at the package on the empty seat. 'The man has given you an empty chequebook and you buy one pair of shoes and worry about it. You really are hopeless, Becca,' she said, looking amused.

'I don't need anything else,' Becca retorted weakly. 'Except for a dress for the wedding, and I didn't really see anything I—'

'Could afford?' Erica teased. 'I can see you need a few lessons in shopping. After lunch,' she promised. 'Now, what about some wine?' Becca looked alarmed and Erica grinned. 'Don't worry, in deference to your stress levels I'll join you and have a glass of mineral water. But you're really going to have to get used to the fact that you don't have to balance the books at the end of the month any more. You're going to be the disgustingly rich Mrs Carides. You're not paying.'

But I am, Becca thought dully. I'm paying with my freedom. So much had been crammed into the past three weeks that she had not had much time to think about the step she was taking.

At the end of the day, despite the fact that she'd successfully resisted her sister's blandishments over several purchases, there still seemed to be an awful lot of clothes lying on the hotel bed—including a genuine vintage thirties dress she had seen and fallen in love with. Sleeveless, with a scooped neckline, the heavily beaded cream silk creation reached mid-calf.

'What do you think?' she had asked Erica as she'd emerged from the changing room.

Erica had shrugged, and by way of reply had looked at the price label. 'You'll look great. But I think you could do better,' she'd said, shaking her head. 'You're marrying a billionaire. You do realise that all you have to do is pick up the phone and designers will be fighting to dress you?'

'I've been dressing myself for twenty-six years and I think I'll continue, if you don't mind.'

'You know what I mean.'

'I do. If you've got it—or in this case if Christos has got it—you should flaunt it.'

'Well, isn't it tempting?'

'No.'

Erica gave her sister a quick, affectionate hug. 'You really are the world's worst conspicuous consumer, aren't you?'

'Perhaps you should marry him yourself?' Becca suggested tartly.

Erica watched as her sister tried to see her rear view in the mirror. 'Don't think I wouldn't cut you out if I had half a chance,' she teased.

'Feel free.'

Becca's tone brought her sister's frowning regard to her face. 'You do know I'm joking, right?'

'Of course I do.'

Erica's concerned frown evaporated and she gave an impish grin. 'Well, even if I did want to steal him off you I wouldn't stand a chance. You know, the other evening I had been telling him about my nursing course, talking for ten minutes at least, when he looked at me and said, ''Did you say something?'' And,' she recounted, her mock indignation escalating as she recalled the unbelievable slight, 'On Tuesday he forgot my name! He called me Emma!' The recollection made her eyes dance with laughter.

'Christos has a lot on his mind at the moment,' Becca said. 'Maybe he's one of those people who just aren't good with names.'

'You won't be sticking up for him if he forgets *your* name,' Erica predicted with a grin. 'Not that that's likely.'

'You don't think so?' asked Becca absently as she gathered the heavy beaded skirt in one hand and prepared to go back into the changing room.

'Heavens no. He hardly takes his eyes off you. You must have noticed,' she added, giving her head an incredulous little shake when Becca looked at her with blank astonishment. 'He's clearly got a thing about redheads.' Erica could not keep a hint of wistful envy from her voice as she added ruefully, 'Or at least about you.'

There was a moment of startled silence before Becca smiled at her sister. The sparkle in her eyes faded and she said, in a voice that didn't even hint at the depth of her churning emotions, 'Aren't I the lucky one?'

It only lasted for a moment, but for that instant Becca knew what it would feel like if Christos returned her feelings.

Almost immediately common sense reasserted itself and presented an entirely more plausible explanation for Christos's constant scrutiny.

Of course the man watched her—within hours of installing her in the luxurious hotel suite she presently occupied he must have realised that he had lumbered himself with a woman who was social liability.

The man is watching you like a hawk because he's afraid you'll use the wrong fork, or offend someone important!

But she would never forget that moment when she had allowed herself to hope.

'You know,' Erica confided, her teasing expression fading as she smoothed back her long blonde hair from her face, 'I sort of feel responsible for you and Christos getting together—writing to him and everything. I mean he could have been a total bastard, like Alex, and then I'd have felt terrible.'

'But you've decided he's not, have you?'

Erica laughed. 'Are you kidding? Behind the bossiness and that dark, brooding exterior he's one of the good guys—and anyway, he's crazy about you.'

And she believed it, Becca realised. Maybe, she reflected, the younger girl was seeing what she wanted to. Not trusting herself to respond, Becca gave a quick smile and, twitching the curtain, stepped inside the changing booth.

Despite the lukewarm reception to her dress Becca had remained firm, and now, as she tried it on again, she was glad she had. She was pirouetting in front of the full-length mirror when there was a knock on the bedroom door.

A quick glance at her watch told her it was thirty minutes after the time she'd arranged to meet Christos, her parents and her future mother-in-law in the restaurant. She cursed softly under her breath.

'Hold on a minute!' she yelled.

It was several minutes later when she appeared at the door, her cheeks pink from the exertion of fighting her way out of the dress, with a hotel robe belted tightly around her middle.

Seeing Christos standing there, looking predictably gorgeous, robbed her of the ability to speak. So Becca simply stared at him, feeling a confusing mixture of antagonism and lustful longing until, looking extremely impatient, he broke the silence.

'There is a problem?' You didn't have to be particularly intuitive to notice that he was in a vile mood.

'Why would there be a problem?' she countered warily.

'You were to meet our respective parents with me.' His dark brows drew into a straight line as he consulted his watch. 'Forty-five minutes ago.'

'Thirty-five,' she couldn't help correcting.

A nerve clenched along his jaw as his glance slid to her mouth. 'I stand corrected.'

'No…' She drew a sigh and he looked expectant, in the slightly bored, supercilious way that was unique to him. With anyone else she would have been the first to cheerfully apologise if she was late, so why was apologising to him like pulling teeth?

'I lost track of time and, no, before you say anything,' she warned, 'I *didn't* forget on purpose. I was trying on my wedding dress.'

His eyes swept downwards and Becca was suddenly very conscious that she was naked beneath her robe. She clutched the lapels together at the neck.

'And is it a nice dress?'

As if he was interested. His observant eyes caught her sliding her hand down the neckline of her dressing gown, to ease the chafing of the heavy fabric against her sensitised nipples, and she snatched it away, blushing.

'It makes me look less fat than the others did.' She was almost looking forward to the stage when she was obviously pregnant, because right now she just looked—and felt—fat and shapeless.

'You're not *fat*!' Luscious and ripe were the adjectives that came to Christos as he looked at her.

His astonishment appeared genuine, which made Becca's attitude towards him thaw fractionally as she advised gruffly, 'I'd reserve judgement until you've seen me in it, if I were you.'

'I will—in a few days' time.'

The reminder sent a flash of pure panic through her body. Was it really only days away?

Calm. Be calm, she told herself sternly. *Don't think about it!*

'Let me see you in this dress now, and I'll give my informed opinion.'

Soon I'll have to think about it. Soon it will be a reality.

'You want to see me in my wedding dress?' She shook her head and made an effort to focus. 'Oh, no. It's unlucky for the groom to see it before the day,' she reminded him.

'You are superstitious?'

'Not especially, but let's face it—we need all the luck we can get.'

His dark gaze swept up from her bare toes.

She read the anger in his deepset eyes. 'It's the truth,' she insisted defiantly. 'The truth shouldn't annoy you. Though,' she added as a muttered addition, 'just about everything else I do or say does.' Which did not exactly bode well for a life of togetherness, she thought dully.

'By all means let's embrace the truth,' he retorted, flashing the sort of smile that she was learning to mistrust. 'And in that same spirit of openness and honesty, may I ask you something?'

'I suppose so,' she agreed cautiously.

Christos heard himself ask the question that had been uppermost in his mind since she had opened the door. 'Are you wearing any clothes underneath that thing?'

CHAPTER ELEVEN

OVERPOWERINGLY aware of the heat explosion in the vulnerable core of her body, she slung a hard, angry smile in his direction. 'Very funny.'

'I was not trying to be funny. I actually don't find it at all funny that I can think of very little else but having you in my bed.'

He found himself thinking about this subject at the most inappropriate moments—like during his meeting earlier that day. When he had realised that he had no recollection at all of the previous half-hour's delicate negotiations, he had had to excuse himself, much to the astonishment of the others present.

Ironically later, his second-in-command had been full of awe and admiration, assuming it had been part of some fiendishly clever strategy on his part.

This blurring of his personal and work life was something he had never before experienced—he had *never* struggled to compartmentalise his life.

'You look shocked,' he said, examining the pale contours of her delicately moulded face. 'It's hardly news that I am attracted to you, is it?'

His dark lashes swept downwards and his restless glance moved to the blue-veined pulse-spot that beat frantically at the base of her throat.

'Or that you are attracted to me.' Under his steady gaze she went bright red, a response he seemed to take as confirmation of his assertion. 'Which makes your bizarre insistence on pre-wedding night abstinence all the more baffling.'

'But you said…'

There will be no need to bolt your door. I may be prepared to blackmail you into marriage, but my bed you will come to willingly, yineka mou.

That had been what he'd said. She had played it back in her head often enough to be word-perfect.

On that occasion Becca had fired back a derisive, 'Don't hold your breath! No—on second thoughts do.' And he had laughed in a way that suggested he didn't think for a second she'd hold out.

Maybe he was right.

The trouble stemmed from the fact that she had lost control. Since she had agreed to the wedding he had been laying down the law and she had been meekly complying. At least that was the way it felt. Although she was genuinely worried about how he would react to her rapidly changing body, her ill-thought-out insistence that he wasn't going to be sharing her bed until after the wedding had been mostly an attempt to take back some control.

Of course she had shot herself in the foot—because she had been dying of frustration ever since that first night, when he had installed her in the luxury hotel suite and left without even touching her!

'I didn't think you were bothered.' She heard the resentment in her voice and bit her lip.

'Then you are wrong. I am. Very.' His lips formed a twisted grin as he used the word. 'I am so *bothered*,' he revealed from between gritted teeth, 'that I can barely function.'

Thank heavens it's not just me!

The relief she felt at not having voiced her thought out loud faded as she encountered the glitter of hot, raw desire in his gaze. She gave a ragged gasp as all the muscles low in her belly tightened.

She tried to respond with a scornful smile. But her face

felt stiff and her voice, when she spoke, was strained and shaky.

'The next thing you'll be telling me is you're marrying me because I'm so irresistible.'

Anger and frustration flashed in his dark eyes.

This was the first time he had given a hint that it concerned him one way or the other. 'Can you forget the damned marriage for one second?'

Having spent an hour that afternoon with his mother, who had talked about nothing else, he found it was not his favourite subject. He wished he had just dragged Becca off to the nearest register office

Hands set on her slim hips, breathing hard, Becca followed him inside her hotel suite. 'I'd love to forget it!' she yelled at his back.

After moving restlessly around the sitting room of her suite Christos picked up an apple from the laden fruit bowl and put it down again, his expression sour as he muttered something under his breath.

Becca felt sick. Of course he resented the fact he was being forced into marriage because of his old-fashioned belief that there was no other way to raise a child. She had no idea why she felt so hurt and shocked. Any man in his situation would feel the same.

'Don't you think I've *tried* to forget it?' she challenged. 'But it's pretty damned hard when you've got this damned rock on your finger!' she yelled, pointing at the square-cut sapphire surrounded by diamonds that he had casually produced and announced she should wear.

'You don't like the ring—fine,' he said, dismissing it with a casual shrug. 'I will get you another. When I saw it I thought that it matched your eyes.'

An expression of astonishment washed across her features. 'You chose it?' she said, shaking her head in a confused negative motion.

His brows lifted. 'Who did you think chose it?'

'I assumed you'd got one of your minions to buy it.' As someone who found it terribly hard to ask anyone to do anything, and therefore usually ended up doing it herself Becca envied his ability to delegate.

Before Christos could respond the phone in his pocket began to shrill. She stood there while he listened and then spoke into it in his own language.

'My mother,' he explained, sliding it back into his pocket. 'She and your parents were concerned that you had been taken ill when you didn't turn up as arranged. Your parents said you're never late.'

'And you weren't concerned, I suppose?' She whisked around, and found herself looking directly into the large mirror that was set on the wall.

To her dismay Christos came to stand behind her, and their reflected eyes meshed in the mirror. 'I have learnt over the past days that you are more robust than you appear,' he observed, looking at her slender ramrod-stiff back.

She swung back. 'You mean I won't agree with every decision you make?' she suggested sweetly.

'This campaign you have to retain your independence is quite unnecessary, you know,' he told her mildly.

'I don't know what you mean.'

His lips twisted into an ironic smile as their eyes locked. 'I have no taste for docile women, *agape mou.*'

Becca's heart began to thud heavy and slow in her chest as he carried on looking at her. Her eyelids felt hot as she stared back. The enervating wave of lustful longing that threatened to submerge her made it an effort not to fall over, and her knees felt strangely disconnected from the rest of her body.

Do you have a taste for me?

Before the compulsion to voice her unspoken question became too strong to resist she took a deep, restorative breath and picked up her bag from the table, pretending to search for something inside.

'Please don't run away with the idea that I care one way or the other what sort of woman does it for you.' Closing her bag, she gave an amused laugh.

His hooded eyes fixed on the back of her burnished head, he took a step towards her.

'I think you already know.'

Becca felt her control slip another fatal notch and took another deep breath before turning around. 'You really don't need to flirt with me just because we're getting married.'

'Who would you suggest I flirt with?'

'I don't care,' she snapped.

He ran a finger down her cheek. 'Liar,' he taunted, and felt her shiver.

Breathing hard, Becca turned her head away. 'Is it a total disaster?'

'What are we talking here? My lack of success in seducing my future wife?'

Well aware that her own irritability had a lot to do with frustration, Becca snapped back tetchily, 'Don't be stupid. We both know that you could seduce an iceberg with your eyes closed if you wanted to.'

Eyes gleaming with laughter, he admitted, 'I much prefer to keep my eyes open. I like to watch your face,' he confided in a raw, sexy voice that stripped her nerve-endings bare.

'I was talking about my parents and your mother,' she explained hoarsely. If ever there was a mismatch it was the glamorous widow of a Greek tycoon and her own very ordinary parents.

His eyes narrowed. 'Why would you assume it's a disaster?'

'You're not serious? Well, my parents and your mother

are hardly going to have a lot in common, are they?' she pointed out, clasping her hands together to hide the fact they were still visibly shaking as she pretended to study herself in the mirror.

'They have their future grandchild in common. And even if they didn't, they appear to be getting on very well.'

'Well, don't expect me to pretend to be something I'm not just to impress your mother,' she warned him darkly.

A bewildered expression on his face, Christos touched her shoulder and gently pulled her around until she was facing him. 'Why would I want you to be anyone but yourself?'

As if *herself* was someone who would marry a Carides!

Becca stated the obvious. 'Well, I'm hardly the sort of girl your average Greek tycoon marries, am I?' She bit down on her lower lip, disgusted by the self-pitying quiver that had entered her voice.

'You are very fond of labels, aren't you, Becca?'

The accusation made her blink. 'No, of course I'm not.'

His hands slid down her shoulders. Twisting his fingers into hers, he brought her hands up to his lips. Becca's insides melted.

'You have no need to be insecure. You will be my wife. My wife does not need anyone's approval.'

Your wife needs love, though. *Your* love, Becca thought to herself.

Adopting a businesslike attitude that gave no hint of her desperate yearning, she lifted her head and smiled.

'Will you please tell our parents that I'll be along directly?'

His lips formed a twisted smile as he saw her glance flicker significantly towards the door. 'No problem,' he said, releasing her hands. 'I will wait.'

She slung him a frustrated glare. 'Then it will take longer,' she warned him.

His broad shoulders lifted. 'How so?'

She looked at her toes. 'You make me nervous.' She lifted her head and caught a dangerously speculative expression on his face. His dark eyes brushed hers and she fled.

Inside the relative safety of the bathroom, she leaned against the door and, her eyes closed, sighed.

Two days! She seriously doubted she would last!

As she walked through the lobby with Christos at her side she was uncomfortably aware of the way people turned and stared. She was under no illusion as to who they were staring at. She looked up curiously, to see if Christos was irritated, and discovered that he appeared totally oblivious to the fact that he was the centre of attention.

When a woman about to enter a lift saw them and stopped, unashamedly staring, it was the final straw for Becca, who hissed, 'Is it always like this?' A future of being gawped at, her appearance being analysed and criticised by total strangers, because of who she was married to filled her with horror.

He slowed and looked down at her. 'Is *what* always like this?'

'Do people stare at you wherever you go?'

Before he had an opportunity to respond the hotel manager, an incredibly elegant silver-haired man, who wore extremely smart suits and had an air of calm efficiency, appeared at their side.

The manager nodded respectfully to Becca and expressed the hope that she was enjoying her stay. Clearly the fact that Christos was picking up the bill gave her VIP status in this man's eyes.

She assured him everything was marvellous, which it was, and the man turned his attention to Christos.

'Your secretary has left a message at Reception, sir,' he said.

Christos looked surprised. 'She has?'

'Apparently she wasn't able to contact you on your mobile.'

'Which is why I turned it off,' Christos observed, looking irritated. 'I should see what she wants,' he admitted. 'You go ahead, Becca, and I'll catch up. This shouldn't take a moment.'

Becca just stood there. 'No, I'll wait for you.'

Already turning, he slid her a quick impatient look, failing to identify the note of panic in her voice. 'They are waiting for you—go ahead.'

Her jaw tightened. She knew they were waiting for her—that was the problem! His mother would hate her on sight, of that she had totally convinced herself, and she was furious with herself for caring about this unknown woman's approval. Despite Christos's assertion that he didn't give a damn what anyone else thought, she felt sure his mother's disapproval, even if it was polite, would mean something.

Even if the protection his presence at her side offered was mostly in her mind, as she watched him vanish from her view Becca decided that a man with an ounce of sensitivity would have realised she was scared stiff and offered a bit of support!

Do you really think he's going to be there to hold your hand in awkward moments? Get used to it, Becca, she told herself sternly. *Being a babysitter for an insecure wife is going to be way down his list of priorities. In fact you are going to be way down his list of priorities.*

She was so lost in her angry, resentful thoughts that a man had virtually thrust his face into hers before she even noticed he was there. Becca instinctively recoiled at the sudden intrusion, and blinked.

The first explanation that offered itself to her was that the stranger was drunk. 'Excuse me,' she said pleasantly.

'Becca, isn't it?'

She looked at him blankly, wondering if she was meant to know who he was. 'Sorry—I don't think I know—?' She broke off as somewhere to her right a blinding flash went off. It was followed in quick succession by several more. Disorientated, she blinked.

'So when's the wedding, love?' the man asked, in the same chummy manner.

The shock of realising she had been waylaid by a reporter held her immobile for a moment.

'Let's have a shot of the ring, Becca.'

Becca automatically put her hand behind her back and looked around frantically. But there was no sign of Christos.

'Excuse me,' she said, adopting a nervous, frigid expression as she attempted to step past him. The man moved, effectively blocking her access to the dining room.

Becca, her temper aroused, was too angry now to be frightened when another flash went off in her face.

'Known him a long time, love? Why are you marrying him, Red?'

'Mind your own business!' she gritted.

He grinned and sneered, 'You marrying him for the money, Red?'

'No, I'm marrying him because he's very good in bed,' she snapped. 'In fact he's the best sex I've ever had!'

The guy's mouth fell open in shock, before an appreciative gleam of delight appeared in his eyes. He had no opportunity to respond, however, because the next second Christos was there, looking tall and menacing. With his face like thunder he hauled the man away from her with such force he almost jerked him off his feet.

'Not the suit, mate!' the younger man cried jokingly. Then he saw Christos's face and his smirk faded.

'Christos, don't!' Becca reached out urgently and caught his arm. 'For heaven's sake, he'd love you to take a pop at him. He'd be able to sell the story for loads!'

'Listen to the lady!' the reporter croaked.

Becca was thinking that if Christos did listen it would be a first when to her intense relief the cavalry, in the shape of hotel security, arrived on the scene. They were large, well-spoken individuals, wearing nice suits and no-nonsense expressions.

Their fortuitous arrival would, she reflected darkly, have been even more fortuitous if they had got there before she'd opened her big mouth.

There was no unseemly tussle. The reporter did not resist as he was firmly but discreetly frogmarched out of Reception.

Christos, standing with his bunched fists clenched at his sides, spat an epithet in his own tongue as he watched the reporter being expelled. Apparently sensing her eyes on his face, he looked down, making an obvious effort to control his feelings as he raked a hand through his dark hair.

'That was intolerable.'

Becca's eyes widened as he framed one side of her face with a big hand. The breath caught in her throat as his strong thumb stroked the curve of her cheek. The unexpected tenderness in his action made her eyes fill.

'You are okay?' Feeling her quiver, he frowned. 'Those people are scum.'

'I'm fine,' she said, wondering how furious he was going to be, on scale of one to ten, when he found out what she had said. *Why did I say that?* 'The man has to make a living, I suppose.' *And I just paid for his summer holiday. And maybe Christmas too.*

'From invading people's privacy and publishing lies?'

An image of the next day's tabloid headlines flashed before her eyes and she felt sick. She had already discovered that Christos guarded his privacy zealously, and that any friend of his who spoke out of turn to the press about him would no longer be considered a friend.

'I am *so* sorry that happened.' She could hear the self-reproach in his deep voice as he added, 'I am to blame. I shouldn't have left you alone.'

The slick manager appeared, looking uncharacteristically ruffled. He was extremely contrite as he drew them to the privacy of an alcove, where they were screened by a lush arrangement of plants from the prying eyes of others. 'Our guests' privacy and security is paramount to us. I assure you that this sort of thing does not happen in our hotel.'

'It did.'

The inescapable truth of Christos's blunt, unsmiling retort brought an uncomfortable flush to the older man's face. He nodded. 'And for that we are very sorry.' He turned to Becca. 'I hope the unfortunate incident has not made you think too badly of us, Miss…?'

Becca, very conscious of Christos's protective arm now encircling her waist—or what passed for her waist these days—smiled and lied with credible calm.

'No harm done.' If only that were true, she thought, dropping her chin to avoid the searching sweep of Christos's dark eyes. She was convinced that her guilt had to be written in neon letters across her forehead.

The men exchanged a few more words, but Becca didn't really pay much attention to what they were saying. She was thinking about how she was going to come clean and admit what she had said to the reporter. Considering Christos was guaranteed to go ballistic when he found out what she had said, it probably ought to be done in a public place.

After the manager had left Christos motioned her to sit down. 'Can I get you something to drink? Tea?'

She shook her head. 'No—I'm fine, thank you.'

'Do you really feel up to this meal?'

'What part of *I'm fine* didn't you understand?' she snapped, leaping to her feet.

For a moment Christos watched, the expression in his dark hooded eyes inscrutable as she paced back and forth, rubbing her hands up and down her forearms. A nerve clenched in his cheek and he muttered forcefully, 'Stop!'

Startled, Becca did as he said. She was expecting to see annoyance on his face, but the tenderness in his expression took her breath away. She didn't resist as he took her hands, which were clasped tight around her own forearms, and laid them flat against his chest. Her wide eyes locked with his and a shiver rippled through her body.

'It's an understandable reaction.' She stiffened, then relaxed slightly as he added, 'You've had a nasty experience.'

'It was a bit of a shock,' she admitted. 'What I don't understand is how he knew who I was—or about our marriage?'

Christos's eyes narrowed. 'I think I do,' he said grimly, and then, without explaining what he meant, he bent his dark head towards her. 'You're coping very well with this, you know.'

Becca almost groaned. His admiration only made her feel even more wretchedly guilty. 'Actually, I'm falling apart—and we both know it.'

Fortunately Christos didn't know the real reason for that. He didn't have the faintest idea what his closeness was doing to her. How feeling the heat of his hard male body through the layers of clothes that separated them made her dissolve inside.

Becca's eyes closed as if she could feel the slow, heavy

thud of his heartbeat under her fingers. He covered them
with his own hands, making it impossible for her to remove
them even had she wanted to. Which, needless to say, she
didn't.

CHAPTER TWELVE

'THESE people can get under your skin,' he admitted. 'Especially when you're not accustomed to the intrusion.'

'And you are?'

He nodded in response to her tentative suggestion. 'I am,' he agreed. 'I should have warned you this was likely to happen at some point. The best thing with paparazzi,' he explained, 'is not to say anything at all.'

Oh, no! 'Right.'

'Just don't react.'

'I'll remember,' she promised gravely, resisting the temptation to ask if strangling a member of the press could be termed *not reacting*.

'It doesn't actually matter what you say.' *That's all you know,* she thought. 'They will always twist it.'

'In fact,' she observed brightly, 'you might read something that you didn't say at all. At least not intentionally.'

'What did you say to him, Becca?'

She had to tell him some time, and now was as good a time as any. She opened her mouth, but as he looked at her expectantly she wimped out and shook her head.

'You know, I really don't recall. Don't you think we should go in to dinner? The parents will wonder what's happened.'

'Suddenly you're very eager.'

'I'm hungry,' she lied.

Having said goodnight to their respective parents, Christos insisted on escorting her back to her room. They reached her bedroom door.

Christos released her arm and tilted his head towards her. His attitude was that of a stranger as he said, 'Goodnight.' Before turning to leave her.

Becca turned her key in the lock, then gave a sigh and spun around. Christos was already some way down the long hotel corridor. 'No!' she called out after him 'Don't go, Christos!'

After the slightest pause in his step he carried on walking. Assuming he hadn't heard her, Becca was about to run after him when he stopped and turned.

Becca's throat dried as he stood there, his head a little to one side in a questioning attitude. Frustrated by her inability to read his expression from this distance, she took a hesitant step forward.

'You want something?'

As Becca opened her mouth the door beside him opened, and she waited until the bearded young man who'd stepped out had reached the lift before nodding.

'Yes, I want you. That is...' she corrected, relieved now that she *couldn't* see his expression '...not *want*, exactly. I—'

'That is a blow to my male ego.'

'This is no joke, Christos,' she reproached him. 'There's something I have to tell you. You're not going to like it,' she warned him, going inside her room and switching on the light.

When he came in she had already taken up a seat on the sofa. 'I hope you don't mind if I take these off. They're agony.' She could feel his eyes on her and sense his impatience as she slid off her high heels.

As a delaying tactic it didn't offer much respite.

Christos stood waiting while she tucked her feet under her.

The pause before he broke the lengthening silence had little to do with his patience and understanding, and quite a lot to do with the fact that her action had caused her skirt to ride up, revealing the lacy tops of her hold-up stockings and a section of bare flesh!

'So, what am I not going to like?' he asked, thinking about how silky her skin had felt under his hands.

Reluctance etched in every line of her face, Becca stopped avoiding looking at him and saw he seemed unusually preoccupied.

'Your mother was very nice to me.'

Her blatant procrastination caused his lips to quiver with amusement. 'They do say confession is good for the soul.' Loosening his tie, he lowered his lean frame onto the sofa beside her.

Becca, noting that he looked mellow and relaxed, felt irrationally resentful. 'Not always good for shaky relationships.'

Her tight-lipped retort caused his brows to lift as he suggested. 'So you think couples should have secrets?'

She shook her head impatiently. 'No, of course I don't. That isn't what I'm saying at all,' she retorted, missing the gleam of sardonic humour in his eyes.

'Oh? I thought for a second there you were an advocate of the ''What they don't know won't hurt them'' school of thought?' he murmured innocently.

'If you are you asking if I'll turn a blind eye if you fool around the answer is no. And,' she added darkly, 'I don't give a damn how discreet you are!' She paused for breath and continued in a more moderate tone, 'I probably should have mentioned this before,' she admitted.

'That you expect fidelity from your husband? Most people would not call that an unreasonable request. I'd go so far as to suggest that most would say you should be able to take that for granted.'

'Yes, if it were a normal marriage I expect they would. But ours will be a marriage of convenience. I suppose you thought I might not mind too much if you carried on much as before.'

'And how would that be?'

Her reproachful blue eyes met his teasing stare head-on. 'I don't have the faintest idea about the lifestyle of a playboy billionaire,' she admitted. 'But I'm assuming it involves doing pretty much what you want, when you want, and,' she added with a swallow, 'with who you want.'

'A billionaire would not stay that way very long if he lived the debauched life of unrestrained hedonism you appear to be visualising, *yineka mou*. I have been known to put in the odd fourteen-hour working day,' he observed drily, 'which actually leaves little time for carousing.'

'I know you work.' Having already observed at first hand his work ethic, she felt qualified to comment on his ability to operate when most people would have succumbed to exhaustion. 'But you're hardly a monk, are you?'

'No, I am not a monk. But what I did before we were engaged to be married does not concern you.'

This gentle remonstrance brought a militant sparkle to Becca's eyes. 'No, but what you do after we're married does.'

It wasn't as if there would be a shortage of women willing to compensate Christos for his loveless marriage. And no doubt some would dream of taking her place one day.

'Yes.'

Becca blinked and regarded him suspiciously. 'What do you mean? You agree?' She was unable to hide her astonishment.

'Certainly I agree.' He gave a shrug. 'This surprises you?'

She studied him, trying to gauge his sincerity. 'Yes, it does,' she admitted gruffly.

'You wish our marriage to be more than cosmetic? That is what you're saying?'

Am I? 'I suppose I am,' she admitted uncertainly.

'Then we are of one mind in this.'

Robbed of an argument, she had little choice but to come clean.

'Should I take this personally?' he asked, when she scooted without thinking to the other side of the sofa.

'Sorry.' She grimaced, flashing him an absent half-smile. 'I can't think when you're near me, and this is hard enough as it is.'

Unaware that she had said anything to produce the flicker of hot emotion in his eyes, she tapped her lip with her forefinger.

'I really don't know why I did it…' she faltered.

'Did what, *yineka mou*?'

Becca lifted her eyes to his and shook her head. 'Please don't be nice to me. It makes me feel even more wretched. I won't blame you for being furious.'

'I will do my best to oblige you, and be suitably furious—but don't you think you should tell me what I'm supposed to be furious about first?'

'This is so difficult—and embarrassing,' she muttered under her breath.

'I'm still living in the hope that you will tell me what you have done before I go totally grey,' he said, sounding weary.

'When you asked me about that reporter I lied.' Her eyes slid guiltily from his. Eyes closed, she took a deep breath and hunched her shoulders. 'I did say something to him…something I probably shouldn't have. No—cancel that. I *definitely* shouldn't have. I've no idea why I said it. I was angry, and he was so revolting, and it just came out.'

'What did you say?'

Her chin lifted. 'Word for word?'

'A close approximation will do.'

'He asked me why I was marrying you.'

A look of understanding spread across his face. 'So you told him about the baby? Not the way I would have chosen to announce it, but it is nothing for you to lose sleep over.'

She shook her head. 'No, I didn't tell him about the baby.'

Christos heaved a deep sigh and clamped his hand to his forehead. *'Becca—!'*

Once she started talking the words tripped over one another. 'All right. I might have said something like you're very good in bed and suggested that you're the best sex I've ever had. Which really isn't as much of a recommendation as it might sound, because frankly there isn't much competition. I know it was crude and vulgar, but I swear I didn't mean to say it. It just came out.'

The stunned silence stretched until her shredded nerve-endings began to scream.

'Thirty seconds. You were talking to him for thirty seconds, tops. I tremble to think what you'd have disclosed to the world's press if I hadn't come along when I did.'

Her startled eyes flew to his face. Her jaw dropped. She had been eaten up with remorse, beating herself up all through that interminable dinner, and he was *laughing*!

She drew herself up and dealt him a killer glare. 'You think this is *funny*?'

He shot out a hand and cupped the back of her head, sinking his fingers into the thickness of her silky curls as he splayed his long fingers to cradled her skull.

'I think you are delightful.'

His incredible eyes stayed on her face while his husky voice made her skin tingle.

She had never heard that the scalp contained any erogenous zones, but his fingers seemed to have located some anyhow. Tomorrow she might look it up…but right now she thought she might just enjoy it.

'You're not angry?'

'It was unfortunate.'

'Aren't you afraid that you'll have a wife who blabs every time someone sticks a camera in her face?'

'I'm much more concerned about having a wife who doesn't want me in her bed.'

'It's not that I don't *want* you in my bed. It's just that I'm quite big…' The books she had read all suggested that she should barely be showing at four months, whereas her bump was far from discreet. 'Clothes hide a multitude of sins, and the truth is not all men are turned on by pregnant women.'

'*That* is the reason you have put me through weeks of torture and more cold showers than can be good for any man?' He took hold of her chin and dragged her face up to his. 'I find you beautiful and desirable, and quite frankly it offends me to hear you denigrate yourself that way.'

'You haven't seen me naked recently,' she retorted.

'That can be remedied now,' he added, drawing her to her feet and looking at her in a way that made her insides dissolve.

'Christos…'

He effectively stilled her protest with his lips and led her through to the bedroom. The way he managed to strip off her clothes while not breaking eye contact for one second spoke of the sort of experience she didn't let herself think about.

She had enough body image issues as it was!

Christos, to her intense relief, did not. He was fascinated by the new heaviness and sensitivity of her breasts, and the gentle mound of her belly didn't seem to bother him at all.

Lying next to him in bed, she touched his warm skin and gave a deep sigh of pleasure. 'I'm really glad we're doing this. I've felt so…'

'Cranky?' he suggested with a smile in his voice.

'Well, yes.'

'You're amazing,' he said, propping himself up on his elbows to look down on her voluptuous curves. 'I want to taste every inch of you.'

'It might take a long time.'

'I have all night.'

She gave a slow, sultry smile and ran a hand down the flat of his belly. 'In that case maybe I could taste you?'

His eyes were filled with a feverish brilliance as they locked with hers. 'I'm all yours.'

Becca took him at his word.

It was four in the morning when the taxi drew up outside Christos's London home. Asking the driver to wait, Becca got out. Even though she was not wearing a coat, she barely noticed that the temperature had dropped below zero. She stood for a moment, with her bare fingers closed around a wrought-iron railing that was already silvered with frost, gathering her courage.

The elegant square of tall, imposing early Georgian residences was deserted, and with a heart thudding loudly in trepidation she mounted the shallow flight of steps that led to the intimidatingly large, shiny front door.

She took a deep breath and, feeling strangely disconnected from what she was doing, pressed the intercom button. A disembodied voice responded almost immediately. There was no suggestion of astonishment that she should be calling at this hour, just a polite request for her to state her name and her business.

In a tense voice she responded to the request literally.

'Name...yes, of course,' she said. 'My name is Becca Summer, and I have come to tell Christos that I can't go through with the wedding.'

Unaware that her startlingly literal response had brought about a frenetic flurry of activity within the house, she nod-

ded in response to the slightly delayed assurance that someone would be with her directly.

She nervously wrung her icy hands, unaware that a camera above her head was recording every move she made.

True to the invisible presence's promise, barely a minute
had elapsed when the front door—grand, in keeping with
the rest of the building—was pulled open.

Becca was shocked to see Christos himself standing
there, in bare feet, his dark hair deliciously tousled and with
a defined shadow on his normally cleanshaven jaw. He was
wearing a black robe that ended mid muscular brown
thigh—and, as far as she could see, nothing else whatsoever.

The focus she had fought so hard to maintain vanished
in the time it took her to draw a single gulp of cold air into
her lungs. Underneath the fabric she knew his skin would
be warm and smooth to the touch. *Do not go there, Becca!*
The stern command came far too late to halt the stab of
uncontrollable sexual desire that caused the muscles in her
abdomen to clench viciously.

After not breathing at all for the space of several heartbeats, she released a fractured sigh and croaked accusingly,
'You're not asleep.'

'I *was* asleep,' he corrected, dragging both hands through
his dark hair before pressing his fingers to the groove above
his nose. 'And I retain a faint hope that I still am. That any
minute now I will wake up and discover this is all a nightmare.'

'I'm really sorry to disturb you,' she apologized, thinking, *I'm his bad dream.* 'But I… It couldn't wait. Once I
realised, I had to tell you. The thing is, I can't go through
with this wedding.'

A muscle clenched along his strong, stubble-dusted jaw
as their eyes connected. 'Is that so?'

Becca gave a frustrated frown. Christos didn't seem to

be grasping the seriousness of what she was telling him. 'This isn't a joke. I'm totally serious.'

'So I understand from my housekeeper, who woke me to tell me your news.' The woman—clearly she had drawn the short straw—had taken very good care not to look him in the face as she did so. The memory caused the hard planes and angles of Christos's face to grow taut. 'Do you often discuss our private business with total strangers?'

A flush ran over Becca's fair skin and she grimaced. 'I didn't think,' she admitted.

And from not thinking she had tumbled headlong into thinking the wrong thing. Right now the only thoughts going through her head concerned the fabric belt which had been loosely tied around his waist. The same belt that had now slipped and come to rest on his narrow hips...

What if it slipped a little more? Rather than being shocked by the realisation that she was mentally undressing this man, Becca felt excited.

I'm sexually liberated, she thought, and began to smile— until she saw the way Christos was looking at her. He would definitely consider a giggle inappropriate. Or, worse still, he might ask her what she smiling at. And she might tell him.

That was a very sobering thought!

'Forgive me for not displaying shock, but I have already discovered that not thinking is a way of life for you. It was only three hours ago you kicked me out of your bed.' He was still stinging from that experience. 'I warn you, I don't much like to be treated like a sex toy.'

Becca giggled, and then clamped a hand over her mouth as she caught his murderous glare. 'I wanted to spend the night with you, but I didn't want to see your face when you read the tabloids this morning,' she admitted.

'I don't read the tabloids.'

Gathering the shreds of her shattered will-power, she

dragged her wandering eyes back to his face. 'Let me explain about this—'

'By all means explain,' he said, cutting across her. 'But I do not care to discuss my personal business in the street. And you appear not to be dressed for the weather.'

You have room to talk, she thought, trying not to stare too obviously at the section of hair-dusted golden chest. How could a man sound so stuffy and stern and look so incredibly sexy?

'No, of course not.' She glanced uncomfortably over her shoulder. 'The thing is…the taxi. He's waiting. Shall I tell him to go?'

'Unless you wish to include him with my household in this discussion?'

Becca clenched her teeth and recognised it might have helped her cause if she had been a little less up-front about her reason for calling.

'There is a problem?' he added, scanning her upturned features when she didn't move.

'Sort of,' she admitted, concerned about the fact he could read her so damned well even when she kept her mouth shut. 'The thing is, I think I might have…well, actually, no…I *did* come out without any money, and…'

'You came out without any money?' he repeated, in an astonished voice.

'Not deliberately,' she countered. 'I just need you to pay the man. I'll pay you back,' she heard herself add, ridiculously.

It was no surprise when, after moment's incredulous silence, he threw back his dark head and laughed. 'Just when I thought you could not get more absurd you say something to prove me wrong.'

At least his laughter had taken the edge off the simmering tension between them.

Becca responded to his gesture and entered the house. Inside the warmth of the chandelier-lit hallway, she realised that she was very cold indeed, and shivered.

CHAPTER THIRTEEN

'I WOULD offer you my robe.' Christos touched his lapel. 'But I might be left a little over-exposed.'

Becca felt the heat bloom in her cheeks. He couldn't have known what she was thinking—*could he?*

As he turned to issue an instruction to a uniformed man she studied his profile through the protective shield of her lashes. When the employee had nodded and stepped out of the front door—she presumed to pay the taxi off—Christos's attention shifted immediately back to her. Caught staring like a greedy child in a sweet shop window, she self-consciously lowered her gaze.

Christos reached out and, cupping her chin in his hand, tilted her face up to his. 'You're like ice,' he said with a frown.

'I—'

'I know,' he interceded. 'You didn't think. Do you like the marble?'

'Marble?' she echoed, wondering more how it was possible for the lightest of his touches to be so debilitating than what he was talking about.

'The floor in here—which appears to interest you so much.'

'It's very nice,' she agreed gravely as she tried to still her chattering teeth.

His expression softened. 'Come, we will go into the library. There is a fire lit there.'

She couldn't restrain her curiosity as she followed him. 'How do you know there's a fire?'

'I know because I was in there half an hour ago.'

127

'You mean you'd only just gone to bed?'

He gave a slight ironic smile in response to her exclamation, and with a hand in the small of her back propelled her ahead of him through a panelled door to the right.

'Do you always work that late?' The glow of embers revealed to Becca's interested gaze a room with wood-panelled walls, bookshelves and a large oak desk on which a laptop was open. There was more proof of recent occupancy, should his word not be proof enough, in the half-full brandy glass on the mantel of the Adam fireplace.

'I was not working.'

'But you said…' She shook her head. 'Sorry, I didn't mean to pry.'

'I could not work.'

Becca puzzled over the undercurrent in his voice as she watched him walk over to the desk. A flick of a switch and the angled reading lamp that sat there lent the masculine room a warm, subdued glow.

Christos closed the laptop with a click. 'My inability to work can hardly surprise you.'

Mutely she shook her head.

He spelt it out. 'I had just been ejected from a warm bed, and I didn't want to sleep alone.'

'Oh,' some demon made her retort spicily, 'I'm sure that could have been solved. All you had to do was pick up the phone…one word and I'm sure there would have been dozens of women eager to hotfoot it over here.' A scowl formed on her face as she brooded on those unknown over-sexed and almost certainly stunningly beautiful women.

A gleam appeared in Christos's dark hooded eyes as he watched her. 'You do know that you sound dangerously like a jealous woman, *yineka mou*?'

Becca, who did know, glared at him. 'For heaven's sake, take that smug look off your face. *Men!*' she muttered, slinging a disdainful look over her shoulder as she walked over to the fire. 'You're all the same.'

Even as she made the disgruntled claim Becca knew that it was totally false. Christos wasn't like any other man. Her Greek lover was utterly and totally unique.

'You think you're totally irresistible.'

'Well, you must take some of the blame for that—telling me there are any number of women willing to leap into my bed if I snap my fingers.'

She had lifted her icy hands to the warmth of the dying flames when a log landed with a thud amongst them, sending up a cloud of sparks.

She turned and found Christos standing very close. She brutally quashed the urge to press her head against his chest. 'You scared me.' But not as much wanting him scared her. 'I suppose you think that all you have to do is snap your fingers and *I'll* be in your bed too?'

'I don't think I will ever take having you in my bed for granted.'

'Because we're only together for the baby?'

'You know that is not the case.'

'The sex, you mean?' *Please say there's more; please say there's more,* she thought, willing him with her eyes to say what she longed to hear. He didn't have to feel the way she did; she could live with less. Less would be more than she had now.

His dark eyes moved over her slim, nervous figure and the silence between them stretched. Finally he gave an odd, twisted smile and said, 'Ah, the sex…what else…?'

Becca silently berated herself for having let herself harbour false hopes. 'You could have that without marriage.'

'You and the baby are a package deal. This light suits you.'

The driven quality to his abrupt addition made her laugh nervously. She lifted a hand to her smooth, unlined face.

'You mean it hides the bags under my eyes and the crow's feet?' Then she recognised the expression of fierce tenderness in his amazing eyes and the laughter locked tight in her throat.

As he covered the space that separated them her anticipation of his touch was so strong she was literally shaking.

'I mean,' he corrected, taking her face between his big hands, 'that it makes you look like you've just stepped out of a Titian. You're a living, breathing work of art.'

Becca's eyes half closed as he tilted her face back. An almost feline sigh of pleasure escaped her parted lips as his mouth, teasingly soft, moved up the entire length of her pale throat. He moved to the corner of her mouth and stopped.

'Your lip is bleeding.'

'It is?' she said vaguely, and lifted a not quite steady hand to her mouth. There was a spot of blood on her finger when she pulled it away. 'I bite my lip when I'm nervous.'

'And I make you feel nervous?'

The sensuous promise in his eyes made her stomach flip lazily.

'I don't know the word for what you make me feel,' she admitted in a throaty whisper.

His head bent closer, close enough for her to feel the tickle of his warm breath as it stirred the fine downy hair on her skin. 'You're still bleeding,' he rasped.

'I am?' she whispered, thinking his eyes were the hottest thing she had ever seen.

'Uhuh…' he grunted, bringing his lithe male body right up against her.

Becca's knees sagged as she felt the hardness of his erection dig into the softness of her belly. She groaned again as she felt the damp brush of his tongue against the fragile broken area on her lips.

'Oh, God!' she moaned in an agonised whisper. 'What are you doing?'

'First aid,' he rasped throatily. 'We should stop the bleeding.'

If he doesn't stop I'll need full-on resuscitation, not first aid, she thought. And if he did stop? What then? Her eyes suddenly snapped open.

'Don't stop!'

The panicky entreaty brought a gleam of male satisfaction to his smoky dark gaze.

'It was not my intention,' he admitted, sliding the soft cashmere cardigan off her shoulders to reveal the bright silk tee shirt she wore beneath. 'You are warm enough?'

Warm? She was on fire! 'I'm fine.'

She quivered as his fingers skimmed over the jewel-bright fabric before sliding underneath to touch the warm skin of her midriff.

'This feels nice,' he told her, fitting his mouth to hers.

After several moments of increasingly frantic kissing she surfaced, gasping for air.

Christos, the sharp angles of his carved cheekbones highlighted by dark bands of colour, allowed his eyes to roam over the soft contours of her face until they stilled on the swollen, full outline of her tremulous lips. '*Very* nice,' he approved throatily.

'It was a gift from your mother.'

She felt the deep rumble of his warm laughter. 'I didn't mean this,' he corrected. And to illustrate his meaning he stroked a fingertip down the length of her spine. When he reached the base he slid his fingers under the waistband of her jeans. 'Your skin is a gift, perhaps,' he conceded. 'But not from my mother.'

Her eyelids felt hot and heavy as she lifted her eyelashes from her cheek, and her senses swam as she focused on his dark face. Her expression was unselfconsciously enthralled when she reached up and trailed a finger down his strong jaw. The sprinkle of dark stubble made her fingertips tingle.

'My God!' she said, her voice thick with emotion. 'You're just so damned perfect that when I look at you I…I just want…' Closing her eyes with an inarticulate shake of her head, she pressed her face against his chest, inhaling the unique scent of his body.

She felt his lips in her hair and it no longer seemed to matter that she was unable to articulate the range and depth of emotions he aroused within her. It was enough just to be here with him.

Why can't life always be this simple?

'Becca…?'

The sound of his thickened voice brought her head up. There was an expression of fascination on his starkly beautiful features as he lifted her hair from her neck and let the burnished strands fall through his fingers.

'*Theos*, but leaving you tonight was hell!'

Her eyes widened. 'I thought you wanted to go.'

'Wanted!' he ejaculated, staring at her as though she was mad. 'Where do you get these weird ideas from? It has occurred to me that we should talk more—then maybe these things would not happen so often?'

'Talking is good. But later, not now,' she pleaded, pushing her fingers deep into his lush dark hair.

She closed her eyes as he claimed her mouth, and felt her insides shift and melt as his tongue made repeated stabbing incursions between her parted lips.

She felt rather than heard him say her name, the sound lost in her mouth as she twisted, straining to press herself closer to him. Imagining her bare skin against his was no longer enough. She reached for the tie on his robe. When the knot would not slip, she let out a frustrated little grunt.

Christos's hand came up to cover her own and she lifted her passion-glazed eyes to his.

'So you have forgotten this nonsense about not going through with the wedding?'

With a sharp cry of horror she pulled away from him.

Christos stood there, looking confused and then angry as she backed away, her hand held to her mouth and her eyes wide and accusing.

'So is that what that was all about? You make love to me and I'll just fall in with whatever you want?' The pain of thinking he could be so calculating made her feel betrayed. She had let down her defences and he had taken advantage. Her lips quivered and she added with a gulp, 'And there was me thinking you *wanted* to make love to me.'

Christos looked at her quivering lip and watched her glorious eyes fill. He swore softly under his breath and gritted in frustration, 'You think I can turn it on and off like a tap?

Reading the frustration in his angry face, she felt a flicker of uncertainty—which she swiftly repressed. She was in a position to know that when it came to getting what he wanted Christos would have no qualms about using any methods necessary. And he wanted this baby to be a Carides and thought she was threatening to call off the marriage.

'I won't be manipulated!' If only it was that easy! When he touched her she lost her mind—and her will.

'I was not trying to manipulate you,' Christos bit back, very white around the lips as he grabbed his head in both hands and groaned. *'Theos...!'* he yelled, his head lifting. 'I was trying to make love to you. I forget my own name when I make you love to you, but do I accuse you of trying to turn me into an amnesiac?'

'So you didn't think that you could make me change my mind about the wedding by making love to me?' she asked, unable to tear her eyes from the nerve that was ticking away in his lean cheek. *He forgot his own name...?*

'Look, if I wanted to use dirty tactics to coerce you into going through with this wedding I would *not* make love to you.'

Becca, her brow furrowed, watched open-mouthed as he strode back to the fireplace, picked up the half-full glass of amber liquid from the mantel and tossed it back in one gulp.

'I've no idea what you're talking about.'

He slammed the empty glass down and turned back to her. As his dark eyes travelled in a lazy, insolent fashion up and down her body his mouth twisted into a smile that was both cynical and splinteringly sensual.

When he eventually captured her eyes with his dark liquid gaze Becca shivered, and was appalled to recognise the tingle that passed through her body as excitement.

'Let me spell it out for you. You need me.' The cynicism etched in his smile became more deeply ingrained as he added, 'Even if it's only for sex, you need me.'

The heat flew to her cheeks as she finally realised that he thought the threat of *withdrawing* sexual favours could make her do anything he wanted. *And couldn't it?*

'I always knew you were an arrogant piece of work, Christos, but this really… Words fail me…' she revealed, her voice shaking with outrage.

'Not noticeably,' he inserted drily. 'Do you know how I know that you couldn't do without it?' he asked.

The crude question made her compress her lips and stare at him with loathing, while her skin began to burn with humiliated heat.

'Because *I* couldn't. I will return your compliment of earlier: you're the best sex I've ever had too.'

'I told you I wasn't being literal. The reporter just caught me off guard and made me angry and…' Her chest lifted and a deep sigh juddered through her body. 'I am?'

'Yes.' His beautiful lips quivered as he steadily held her gaze.

'And you've had quite a lot of sex,' she murmured thoughtfully. 'In fact probably loads. So that must make me pretty…well, pretty brilliant.' The choking sound that emerged from his lips made her eyes widen. 'Please tell me that I did not say that out loud!' she begged in a mortified whisper.

'It is not a good thing to base a marriage on lies.'

'It's not a good thing to base a marriage on a baby either,' she retorted, wondering if a person could die of mortification.

'And on sexual compatibility,' he reminded her. 'And before you begin a litany of denial—'

'I wasn't going to,' she said, feeling quite absurdly self-conscious as she met his eyes. 'Not being able to look at someone without wanting to rip off that someone's clothes,' she said, looking at the knot on his belt, 'is not a feeling with staying power.' *Or at least I hope not, because I don't think I can take another month of this—let alone years!*

'I am presuming I am that *someone*?'

'I only sleep with one billionaire at a time.'

A flash of annoyance highlighted the subtle shards of gold in Christos's eyes as he gritted, 'I am getting tired of your preoccupation with my financial status.'

Anger drove the colour from her face, leaving it porcelain-pale. 'You think I'm after your money?'

'That I could deal with!' he retorted.

The wrath faded from Becca's face to be replaced by a baffled frown. 'I don't understand.'

'I am not my bank balance. Would being poor make me a better person? Would wearing glasses and looking geeky make me sensitive? Has it occurred to you that whenever you want to push me away you bring up the differences in our backgrounds?'

'Well, you must admit they're quite big diff…' She caught his expression and stopped.

'You make obstacles where there are none.'

She looked at him doubtfully, recognising the point he was making but not totally convinced.

'I am assuming that the main problem is that you want romantic love,' he said, and watched the colour leave her cheeks. 'That is understandable. But we are dealing with reality, here—not fairy tales.'

CHAPTER FOURTEEN

'You think love is a fable?'

'I think we should accept that what we have is not so bad. We give each other pleasure, and we are going to be blessed with a child we will both love. Is it adult to long for some nebulous ideal?'

You are my ideal, she thought. It was ironic that she would probably never tell him.

'I am prepared to make allowances—'

'That's good of you,' she cut back sarcastically.

'Becca, I understand your caution.'

'You do?'

'The problem is, I have no idea what is going on here. Why do you come here in the middle of the night saying you cannot marry me?'

'I didn't say I couldn't marry you.'

Eyes narrowed, he stared at her. 'I think you did. And so, incidentally, do half of my staff.'

'I said that I couldn't go through with this marriage.'

'Ah, well, that is *quite* different.' Eyes closed, he let himself fall backwards onto a large leather chesterfield. Closing his eyes, he lay sprawled there for several moments before he lifted his head and looked at her. 'I feel a great deal older than when I first saw you,' he revealed in a driven voice. 'You turn up in the middle of the night, frantic—'

'I wasn't frantic.'

'It is below zero out there, and you didn't have a coat on.'

'Okay—I was frantic.'

He arched a brow. *'Was...?'*

'It's just that you said our wedding would be something simple, and I believed you. And then at dinner, when your mother started talking about the arrangements, I realised that your definition of simple is definitely not mine!'

'Why didn't you say something then?'

'I want her to like me.'

'Which involves going along with something you hate? I see.'

'It's all right for you!' she retorted, stung by his attitude. 'I was trying to make a good impression.'

'You are marrying me, not my mother, and you have never appeared to feel the need to agree with anything I say.'

'There are plenty of people falling over themselves to do that.'

Her acid retort drew an appreciative grin from him.

'When your mother started talking about the arrangements she's made and the people who are coming she was so pleased, and she's gone to so much trouble and expense...' Becca lifted her hands in a gesture of appeal. 'How could I say anything?' she asked him.

'I'm picking up the tab for the wedding, if that makes it any easier.'

'No, it doesn't.' She rolled her eyes to the ceiling in frustration. 'I only started thinking about it properly when you had gone and I couldn't sleep.'

'You couldn't?' he echoed, sounding not unhappy about her insomnia.

'This thing is totally out of control. I mean a choir?'

'Is a choir so excessive?'

'Maybe not. But a full orchestra and a soprano being flown here from the New York Met are.'

There was a degree of caution in his deepset eyes as he scanned her pale, indignant face. 'Let me get this straight.

You still agree we need to get married? It is just the manner of that marriage that concerns you?'

Need, not *want*, she thought sadly. She knew she shouldn't let it hurt, but it did, and she was pretty damn sure it always would. She took a deep, steadying breath. Nothing she could do would turn this wedding into a joyful celebration of commitment, but she could turn it into something that wouldn't give her nightmares.

'That it scares me rigid would be closer to the truth.'

He looked baffled. 'Why are you scared?'

Her expression earnest, she struggled to explain why the lavish production this wedding had turned into was filling her with utter panic and abhorrence.

'I'm not a centre stage sort of person, Christos, and when I think of all those people looking at me...' She shuddered and pressed a protective hand to the gentle mound of her stomach. 'It's not the sort of wedding I've ever wanted. I just...'

The sudden softening of Christos's expression stopped her mid-sentence. Without warning her eyes welled with tears. For a moment she looked at the hand he extended to her—a strong hand, with long tapering fingers. She gave a gusty little sigh and reached out. She felt the familiar electric shock tingle as his warm fingers closed around hers.

'I thought all girls dreamt of the full works sort of wedding,' he said, only half teasing as he drew her towards him.

Becca eased herself onto the padded arm of the chesterfield and, shaking her head, said firmly, 'Not me. Even if this wedding had been the real thing.' She winced as the long brown fingers encircling hers tightened.

'Sorry,' Christos said, his face expressionless as he watched her rub her hand.

'It just keeps getting bigger every day,' she said, nursing

her hand against her chest. 'I mean, I thought there'd be a dozen or so guests. Do you know how many are coming?'

'Should I?'

'You obviously weren't listening at dinner,' she retorted. Her irritation didn't seem to register with him at all. From his remote expression it was hard to tell if he had even heard her.

'I must have been thinking about something else.' *Like now.*

He swallowed, the muscles in his brown throat contracting as he carried on thinking about feeling her warm soft curves beneath him, her pliant limbs winding around him, pulling him close, the sound of her fractured little gasps of pleasure hot against the skin of his neck, her hot little mouth on his skin...

He drew a deep breath. It was time to take control.

'And,' she pointed out, scowling as she recalled the elaborate arrangements Mia Carides had delighted in telling her about, 'they'll all know that I'm pregnant. I mean, it is pretty obvious.'

She looked at Christos, who looked back blankly. Maybe, she thought gloomily, he was finally seeing things from her point of view. Maybe the vision of her waddling up the aisle accounted for the beads of sweat that he was dashing from his forehead with the back of his hand.

'Obvious?'

The only thing obvious to Christos was that he hadn't been in control since the moment he'd laid eyes on this redheaded witch.

'Well, even if I wear a tent I'll show. They will know we wouldn't be getting married otherwise.'

She saw something flash into Christos's eyes, but before she could quite get a handle on it his dark lashes swept downwards, forming an impenetrable shield.

'Are you ashamed of being pregnant?'

Becca sprang to her feet, her eyes flashing. 'No, of course not. I'm proud!' she exclaimed.

Christos's head came up. 'And so am I.'

The wrath died from her face. Their eyes locked, dark brown on bright blue, and slowly she realised the truth.

'I believe you are!' she exclaimed.

'You sound amazed, yet children are a blessing.'

Becca doubted very much if every man in his situation would think so. But there was no doubting Christos's sincerity. 'Even children with red hair? I don't know if you've realised, but it is a possibility.'

Her apologetic manner brought a grin to his dark face.

'You know,' she said, as it suddenly hit her, 'I think you're going to be a really good dad.' Becca suddenly felt embarrassed, and had the impression that she had succeeded in surprising him.

'And husband?'

Good, bad or indifferent—he was the only one she wanted.

Her startled eyes flickered to his face. The silence stretched until Christos gave a quick hard smile and said in a dry tone, 'It would appear that the jury is still out on that one.'

'You're the one who said marriage was a gamble,' she reminded him.

'Gambling implies that you habitually lose. I prefer to think of it as a calculated risk. Not to stray too far from the point.'

Straying was a hard thing not to do, Becca reflected, when she was looking at his mouth.

'So, do I have this right? Your problem is with the ceremony, and not the marriage.'

'I suppose so—yes.' She nodded. 'It is.'

'Then I will fix it in the morning,' he promised, sliding his hand under the neckline of her silk top.

'In the morning? Are you mad? Oh, Christos, don't do that; I can't think,' she moaned, closing her eyes as his fingers moved across the tingling peak of her right breast. He stopped doing it, and she opened her eyes and snarled, 'I didn't mean it literally.'

'You are quite demented, you know—and quite delicious.' He buried his face in her hair and inhaled the sweet fragrance. 'I will sort out the wedding arrangements in the morning. I should have known better than to give my mother a free hand,' he admitted.

'But won't she be very upset?'

'Probably,' Christos agreed, not sounding at all perturbed by the prospect. 'But not as upset as I will be if you do not kiss me within the next sixty seconds.'

'I wouldn't want to upset you…'

'This is not my room.'

Becca wasn't even aware that she had voiced her sleepy confused waking thought until a voice close by observed, 'So you are finally awake.'

Blinking sleepily, she focused on the face of the man who stood a few feet away.

'Want some?' he asked, extending a mug that contained coffee towards her.

'Oh, no!' she gasped. 'I stayed the night!'

'There wasn't much night left to stay once we finally went to sleep,' he observed, raising his cup to his lips and taking a deep swallow. 'Shall I ring for more coffee?'

She raised herself on one elbow, then fell back again as the throw that was draped over her slithered down, revealing the fact that she was stark naked beneath it.

'And have someone come in here and see me? What would they think?' she gasped, horrified.

'This display of Victorian prudery after last night is somewhat hard to take.' The amusement in his eyes deepened as a dark flush spread across her fair skin. 'As for what my staff would think if they came in here—I would say it is pretty much what they're thinking now.'

'And you don't care what they think?'

'I spent the night with my fiancée and we didn't make it up the stairs. Is there something I should feel ashamed about?'

'I suppose this is normal for you. You probably make a habit of sleeping on the sofa in here when things get too urgent to make it up the stairs.'

'I have been known to spend the odd night in here,' he admitted.

'Oh, you're disgusting!' she choked.

'That's not what you said last night,' he taunted. '*Last night* you said I was pretty much marvelous—not to mention incredible and—'

Becca rolled over and pulled the cover over her head, in the process exposing a good deal of leg. 'Go away,' she said, when he lifted the throw and uncovered her tumbled curls.

'Occasionally I work through the night. I sometimes cat-nap here.' He laid his palm flat on the leather cushion beside her. 'Alone.'

Feeling really stupid for making such a fuss, she pushed her hair off her face and, dragging the cover with her, pulled herself into an upright position.

'What you did before we were together is none of my business.'

His lips quivered. 'That is a relief to me.'

'You're dressed,' she accused, noting for the first time the grey tailored trousers, crisp white shirt and tasteful silk tie he wore. 'You're going out somewhere? Why didn't you wake me?' she fretted. Her eyes widened. 'Erica will be frantic! We arranged to meet and I didn't leave a note or anything.'

'In reply to your first question, I am not going any-where—*we* are.'

Becca, her face screwed up in suspicion, stared back at him. 'We are?'

'I just said so, didn't I? And in reply to your second question I did not wake you because had I done so we would not have gone anywhere.'

'Why not?'

'Do you have any idea how delicious you look when you wake up?'

'Me?'

His smouldering gaze lingered on the bare upper slopes of her breasts and he was shaken by a deep sigh. 'There is something very sensuous about the way you stretch.'

Becca, who looked at herself in the mirror every morning and thought she bore more of a resemblance to an unmade bed than this sex goddess he was describing, had no inten-tion of pointing out his error.

'If I had woken you earlier I would have been obliged to make love to you.'

'And that would have been a bad thing?' To be consid-ered irresistible by a man like Christos did a lot for a girl's confidence.

He responded to her provocative pout with a fierce, hun-gry grin. 'A very *good* thing. But we have things to do, so stop trying to distract me,' he told her sternly.

'Something more important than making love?' *I can't believe I just said that.*

Christos released his breath in a slow, sibilant hiss. 'Show a little mercy, Becca,' he pleaded throatily.

She looked back at him innocently.

'I am not made of steel,' he told her. 'Also your sister is likely to come in at any moment.' Taking the cover, which she had artfully allowed to slip down to reveal a teasing glimpse of rosy nipple, he tugged it firmly up to her chin.

Becca's eyes widened with shock as they swivelled to the door and back to Christos. 'Erica is here?'

'Yes, she is. When last seen she was in the kitchen, distracting my chef.'

'But why?'

'I require her help.'

Becca pulled her knees up to her chest. 'What is this about, Christos?'

'You want a simple marriage ceremony?' Becca nodded. 'So we are having a simple ceremony.' He glanced at the metal-banded watch on his wrist. 'In about two and a half hours.'

Shaking her head, Becca looked at him. 'This is a joke, right?'

'Wrong.'

'We can't be getting married this morning. Nobody can arrange a marriage in a few hours.'

'I am a man of resource, and my name impresses others more than it does you, it's all been arranged,' he revealed drily. 'When I use it some doors open that might otherwise stay closed,' he admitted.

'But how?'

'It has been arranged for some time. I rang my assistant, told her what I wanted, and said if she didn't get it she could look for another job.'

This tongue-in-cheek response drew a glare from Becca, who clicked her tongue in irritation. 'Will you be serious?'

'Things are looking up. Not long ago you would have taken me at my word.' His lips quirked as he angled a dark brow and wondered, 'Could it be that your opinion of me is improving?'

'Like you care what I think about you,' she mumbled.

'To be married to a wife who thinks one is in league with the devil would not be a comfortable experience.'

Was *comfortable* the best he thought their marriage could be? What a depressing thought. 'I have never thought you were evil,' she protested. 'Just opinionated, arrogant…'

'I think you should know that finishing that sentence could affect the harmony of our wedding day,' he told her solemnly.

Wedding day! She swallowed and drew a deep sighing breath. 'This isn't a wind-up? We really are getting married this morning?' It seemed impossible, but she was starting to appreciate that the word no just wasn't in Christos's vocabulary—in any of the five languages he was fluent in.

He nodded.

'You really don't let the grass grow, do you?' She gave a shaky laugh and raised her hand to her head rubbing her temples. 'What about all the people turning up for the wedding tomorrow?'

'They need not concern you.'

'See!' she cried, wagging a triumphant finger at him. 'Arrogant.'

A smile glimmered in his dark eyes. 'Do you want to have the last word or do you want to get married?' he asked, producing the black robe he had been wearing for a short time the previous evening and handing it to her.

Becca snatched it from him and did not deign to reply. 'Are you going to look away?' she asked.

Christos looked at her incredulously. 'You think there is any of you that I haven't seen?'

Flushing to the roots of her hair, and a lot of other places too, Becca straightened her shoulders, got to her feet and let the cover drop. It took a massive amount of will-power not to look at him—especially when she heard the unmistakable sound of his sharp intake of breath.

Lifting her chin defiantly, she chose to take her time to

pull on the robe. Actually, there was very little choice involved. Knowing his eyes were following her every move made her incredibly clumsy. By the time she had cinched the knot on the robe tightly her palms were damp and slick and her heart was thudding like a sledgehammer.

Fixing a bright enquiring smile on her face was almost as painful as stripping naked in front of him had been. 'Right—what next?'

Christos wasn't smiling. Neither did he look as though he was taking any pleasure from her discomfiture. The skin of his face was drawn taut, and the lines around his mouth and eyes were etched deeper by pressure that threatened to snap his control.

The touch of his smoky eyes made Becca shiver, and as the silence stretched so did the crackle of sexual tension that was an almost tangible presence in the room. When Christos finally broke the silence his voice was uneven and his accent thicker than normal.

'*Theos*, but you are beautiful!' he rasped rawly.

Before Becca could even think about responding to the remark he turned his head jerkily and, clearing his throat, opened the door.

'I'll get someone to take you to your sister.'

'We could stay here.' Her eyes widened with total horror as she heard the words spill from her lips. Clearly the connection between her vocal cords and her brain had been severed. *Talk about begging for it!*

She held her breath as he turned his head. Simple rejection she could deal with. If he said something cutting she would die of humiliation.

'I know we could, witch, but if you don't get out of here in the next twenty seconds we will miss our own wedding.'

She ran on legs that felt like jelly.

CHAPTER FIFTEEN

BECCA glared at her younger sister with frustration.

'It's no good looking at me like that,' Erica said, miming a zipping action across her lips. 'I've been sworn to secrecy. All you need to do is get ready. I've even run a bath,' she said, pushing open the door of the *en suite* bathroom.

The scent of subtle perfume and steam immediately filled the room.

'Go ahead,' Erica urged. 'Enjoy a soak. But remember,' she warned, wagging a finger at her sister, 'we're working to a strict schedule here.'

'Schedule!' Becca shrieked. 'This is a wedding, not a military exercise.'

'Well, don't blame me—I'm only following orders.'

Becca, who was starting to feel as if everyone was in on this conspiracy, flung up her hands in exasperation. 'After a lifetime of ignoring schedules you start taking notice now. Great! You do know that this is ridiculous...ludicrous?' She poked her head around the door and discovered an extremely decadent-looking sunken tub in a bathroom that was the size of a football pitch.

'It's *my* wedding—it can't be a secret from me,' she muttered crankily.

'That's not what Christos says.'

'And what he says matters?'

Erica repressed a grin. 'According to him it's on a strictly "need to know" basis, and you apparently don't need to know. You just need to look beautiful. If you want my opinion,' she added, 'I think it's ultra-romantic. Your problem is you always like to be in control, and now you're not.'

Pushing her open-mouthed sibling into the bathroom, she added, 'I'd offer you some champagne,' she said, filling her own glass from an open bottle, 'but you're not allowed, are you?'

'You're enjoying this, aren't you?' Becca accused, lowering herself into the sweet-scented water.

Her sister's laugh came through the open door. 'What's not to enjoy?'

Maybe she had a point, thought Becca, as the warm water lapped over her tender breasts. She sighed and felt almost mellow as some of the tension eased from between her shoulderblades. She *did* have a problem when she wasn't in control—which was about ninety-nine per cent of the time around Christos.

Before she had time to get any mellower, Erica poked her head around the door. 'Mark will be here to do your hair in fifteen minutes. Just thought I'd let you know...'

Becca opened her mouth to protest, and then closed it again. Did it really matter who Mark was? She had asked for a simple wedding, but she had to make allowances for Christos's inexperience of 'simple'.

It was an hour later when, dressed in the beaded dress she had chosen herself, and with her hair a silken mass of ringlets held off her face by a gold circlet of antique seed pearls, Becca stood at the top of the sweeping staircase.

'Don't move an inch until I get Christos,' Erica screamed, while she pelted down the stairs two at a time. 'He's got to see this!'

'This is really stupid,' Becca was muttering, when Christos, who must have been waiting, appeared in view.

He stood at the bottom of the stairs, his eyes trained on the slim figure at the top. Becca found his enigmatic expression hard to read.

'This is stupid,' she repeated under her breath as she began to descend. What she'd seen in the mirror had pleased her, but Christos had dated some of the most beautiful women in the world—women who were groomed and glossy. There was a limit to how much gloss a person could achieve in an hour, even with the help of the miraculous Mark and his equally talented make-up artist associate.

'No, it is not really stupid,' he retorted, shaking his head. 'It is a memory I shall treasure. You look very beautiful.'

The unqualified sincerity in his voice and the glow in his incredible eyes sent Becca's pulses leaping.

'Can I know where we are going now?' she asked, adding worriedly as he arranged a fur stole around her shoulders, 'I hope this isn't real fur?'

'The very best fake money can buy,' he promised. 'As to our destination—we are going to take a helicopter ride.'

Her astonished eyes flew to his face and he smiled enigmatically back at her. 'You're not going to tell me where, are you?'

'You're catching on.'

'Help!' Becca muttered. 'I hate surprises!'

As they landed on the playing field next to the school where up until a short time ago she had worked, Becca decided she had had enough.

'Right—you tell me what's going on or I don't budge from this spot.'

'Fight! Great!' approved Erica from the seat behind. 'You two are better than a trip to the cinema.'

'Shut up, Erica,' Becca said without turning her head. 'Right, you,' she added, nodding her head in Christos's direction. 'Explain.'

'I'm assuming that you didn't have a discipline problem in your classroom?'

'I never had cause to raise my voice—but then I was

never teaching above the racket a helicopter makes, or teaching an extremely arrogant man.'

Amusement flickered in his eyes. 'Your mother said that your favourite place is a ruined castle.'

'Keep,' she corrected automatically. 'The castle went a long time ago. What has that got to do with anything?'

'The celebrant is meeting us there in…' he consulted his watch '…twenty minutes. Your parents, my mother and my great-aunt Theodosia will be there. Plus your very helpful sister.'

'That's me, in case you've forgotten.'

'Shut up, Erica,' Becca said again, still staring at her future husband.

'Is this small and simple enough for you? We have a table booked at the…Pheasant?…is that correct? If you wish a religious blessing at a later date that is not a problem.'

Becca nodded, her expression dazed as he mentioned the best hotel in the district. A man who could organise all this was clearly a force to be reckoned with—but then she'd already known that.

'Why are you doing this?' she asked, angling a wary look at his dark handsome face.

'Does your wedding day have to be an unpleasant memory?'

She gave a helpless shrug. 'I suppose not.'

He nodded. 'Fine. Then, if you have no more objections, can we go?'

A limo was waiting to take them to the old keep down by the river—the last visible remnant of the fortification that had been built to protect the settlement which had been here long before the present town.

As they approached the open door of the keep Becca suffered a major attack of nerves.

She started to pull back, but the hand that gripped her own tightened fractionally.

'What am I doing?' she asked out loud.

'You are getting married,' Christos replied.

His matter-of-fact tone had a calming effect on Becca.

'Your mother said you used to come here when you were a child and pretend to be a princess.'

'You must have been riveted.'

Christos paused and allowed Erica to enter the room before them. 'And now you look like a queen.'

Before Becca could do anything but stare at him he was drawing her inside. She blinked as she took in the transformation which had been wrought on the simple room with its lofty rafters and exposed stone walls.

The transformation had been brought about mainly by filling every available space with flowers. Hundreds and thousands of sweet-smelling flowers.

The guests who were seated in a semi-circle at the far end of the room rose as they entered. With the exception of the woman with bright beady eyes, wearing pearls looped again and again around her thin wrinkled neck, they were all familiar faces. Christos's mother and her parents.

The celebrant smiled encouragingly as they approached.

Becca took a deep breath and thought, *This is it.* With a smile she stepped forward.

The ceremony had gone like a dream. The celebratory meal later was another matter.

'What's wrong?' Christos asked.

'You can't come in here!' she exclaimed, pulling a fresh tissue from the box provided.

'Why?'

'It says "Ladies' Room" on the door for a reason.'

'I'm not going until you tell me what is wrong,' he countered. 'It was something Theodosia said, wasn't it?'

'She hates me,' Becca said, biting back a sob. 'Sorry,' she added with a grimace. 'Hormones.'

'Of course she doesn't hate you! What exactly did she say?'

'She asked me how far gone I was. I said f...four months, and she looked at me and said I'm far too big for four months. She obviously thinks I'm trying to pass off someone else's baby as yours.' She shook her head. 'I'm not!'

'Hush,' Christos said, laying his hands on her shoulders. 'I'm sure she thinks nothing of the sort—and does it even matter what she thinks?'

'She thinks,' came a loud voice from behind a stall door, 'that twins run in this family. In my opinion you're big because you're carrying two Carides. Now, will you two go away and leave an old lady some privacy?'

'Twins?' Becca gulped. 'Is that possible, do you think?'

'I don't know,' Christos admitted. 'We need to find out. But now I think we should join the party,' he said, taking her hand.

Despite this advice, when they did join the others Christos did not seem in a party mood. As Becca herself was feeling pretty stunned by the possibility that she might be carrying two babies she could appreciate his mood.

As they were driven back to the helicopter he remained withdrawn and aloof. It was only when the car came to a halt he turned to her.

'Do you regret marrying me?'

Startled by the question, Becca responded without thinking. 'No, I don't.'

His intense expression didn't alter, but she saw something flicker in the back of his dark eyes at her response.

'You didn't marry me because I threatened to contest your custody, did you, Becca?'

Becca shook her head.

'Then why?'

'Maybe I thought you were right.' She looked at his mouth and thought of it against her skin. 'Maybe,' she admitted huskily, 'I think that a baby needs both parents too.'

'And maybe,' he suggested silkily, 'you didn't hate the idea of being married to me as much as you suggested?'

Her eyes lowered. 'I suppose there are some benefits to being married to you.'

He took her chin in his hand and lifted her face to his. 'And as soon as we get back to the house I will show you some of them,' he promised, in a sensuous growl that made her shiver with anticipation. 'But first I will delay our flight for twenty-four hours.'

'Flight?'

'We are going to Venice for our honeymoon. But first I think that after what Aunt Theodosia said we should make a visit to your doctor.'

CHAPTER SIXTEEN

FROM the moment the doctor said cheerfully, 'Yes—definitely two heartbeats there,' Becca's life changed.

She had no problem with Christos being protective. In fact for five minutes she actually thought it might be quite nice to be spoiled a little and to feel cherished. But she swiftly learned that the advantages were outweighed by the disadvantages.

The news that she was carrying two babies brought out the autocratic side of Christos's nature with a vengeance! To Becca's initial amusement, and then her increasing dismay, he went totally overboard and acted as though a puff of wind was going to damage her.

The first thing he did was cancel their honeymoon plans for Venice. But, since almost overnight Christos appeared to have stopped looking at her as though she was a sexually desirable female, maybe, Becca reflected bitterly, that was not such a bad thing.

She told herself that a lot of men didn't find pregnant women sexually attractive, and that things would go back to how they had been after the babies were born. But sometimes she secretly wondered if this was wishful thinking on her part.

Things might have been easier to bear if she had gone to Greece with him as they had originally planned, but he had decreed that impossible.

'The stress of the journey…the heat,' he said, looking astonished that she should even suggest it. 'There would be no network of support from close family, and that is very important at a time like this.'

'What would you know about *a time like this*?' she was goaded into retorting childishly.

'I am learning.' The expression on his face said loud and clear that she should be too. 'No flitting back and forth to Greece. It is out of the question.'

Despite her continued protests, and her obstetrician saying that as far as he was concerned she could fly up until the last weeks of her pregnancy, Christos remained immovable on the subject. And, as he was in the middle of delicate negotiations which required him to be not just in Athens but several other European locations, Becca was frequently left alone at home in London.

She tried to put a brave face on it. When he cursed the timing and asked if she was lonely she lied and told him she enjoyed the time alone. In reality she missed him more than she would have thought possible. Far from becoming part of his life, as she had hoped, she felt further away from him than ever.

Several times when he *was* there she almost lost her temper when he remonstrated with her for doing something he considered too physically taxing—there was very little, it seemed to her, that he *didn't* consider too taxing—but each time she bit her tongue and kept quiet.

She knew that his attitude stemmed from a deep-seated fear that history would repeat itself, and she couldn't be mad with the man for worrying about the health of their babies. But understanding his motivation didn't stop her wanting to take a swing at him when she accidentally learnt that the staff had instructions to spy on her and report to him if she did anything reckless—like opening a packet of biscuits!

When she had challenged him about this he had not displayed any repentance. 'Do not be paranoid, Becca. It is not a question of *spying*,' he had retorted, his lips spasming in distaste at the emotive terminology. 'I simply need to

know that in my absence you are taking care of yourself.'
He'd angled a questioning brow. 'Of course if you'd agreed
to have a maternity nurse live in, as I suggested—'

'I am pregnant—not sick!' Becca had flared back, even
more exasperated than the last time he had tabled this ridiculous notion. 'As I told you last time, when you came
up with that totally daft idea, I do *not* need a keeper, a
nurse, or staff spying on me.'

Christos hadn't pressed the idea, but she had come away
feeling irrationally guilty that she was the cause of the lines
of strain around his eyes, and it did not feel like a triumph.

Thirty-six weeks into her pregnancy Christos returned unexpectedly, looking exhausted after a three-night absence,
and casually announced that he had taken a sabbatical and
would not be leaving her side again until some time after
the birth.

'Can you do that?' she wondered, thinking of the awesome responsibilities he shouldered.

'I can do anything I wish,' he replied, sounding
astounded that she should think otherwise. A hard expression filtered into his eyes as he added, 'Afraid having me
around will cramp your style?'

Becca stared at him, not understanding the peculiar inflection in his voice. Maybe the thought of months of do-
mestic bliss was responsible for his cranky mood. *'Style?'*
she echoed with a derisive hoot. 'What style? A ten-ton
truck has more style than I do,' she reflected as she eased
her bulk into a chair.

'You look just as an expectant mother should.' The tact-
ful response caused her to smile as she met his eyes.
'Though a little tired.'

'For that matter, so do you,' Becca retorted, noting the
grey tinge under his tan and the lines of strain bracketing

his mouth. 'I'm carrying a bit of extra weight—what's your excuse? You know what I think your problem is, Christos?'

She was trying to figure out why her innocuous remark should cause him to stiffen and look at her so oddly when he prompted in a harsh, almost driven voice, 'What is my problem, then?'

'You're a total workaholic.'

For some reason she couldn't fathom he found her response amusing.

'It's true,' she protested. 'You are.'

She looked at him, wanting to rub away the frown lines from between his eyes. But she no longer thought it was a coincidence that every time she initiated physical contact he made some excuse and left the room, so she repressed her impulse rather than risk the pain of rejection.

'Will you be glad to have me around?' he asked, studying her face with an intensity she found unnerving.

'Of course.' The sheer frustration of being unable to tell him how glad she was made Becca's guarded response emerge sounding stilted.

'Or maybe you have got used to having the place to yourself?' he suggested.

'It will take some adjusting to,' Becca admitted.

'You won't be alone for much longer,' Christos observed, his strong dark features clenched taut as he looked at her belly.

'I hope not. I feel as though this has been the longest pregnancy in history,' she sighed.

When he left to shower and change before a late dinner, Becca dashed down to the kitchen and conspired with the very compliant chef to produce all the things Christos liked best for their meal together.

Sitting there later, looking at her plate, Becca wondered how she could have been so pathetically eager to please him—Christos was so 'glad' to be home that he had dashed away at the first half-legitimate pretence.

They had barely sat down when his mobile had rung.

'*Kyria…?*'

Becca looked up from her moody contemplation of her untouched food and forced a smile for the benefit of Spyros, the butler.

'Would you like some dessert? A little of the lemon pudding you like so much, *kyria…*?' he suggested tentatively.

Becca shook her head. 'No, thanks. It doesn't look as though Christos will be home. Say sorry to Fabien for me, will you? And tell him the food was delicious, as usual.'

Upstairs, she showered and changed and went to bed, planning the things she was going to say to Christos when he finally deigned to come home.

She re-ran in her head the events that had led to her yelling recklessly as he had walked out of the door, 'Well, if you walk out now don't expect me to be here when you get back!'

The expression on his face as he had swung back, his dark eyes narrowed to slits, even now had the power to make her shiver. 'Do not make childish threats you have no intention of following through.'

'How do you know I won't walk out?'

'If I didn't know it was your hormones talking I would seriously worry about your mental health.' He had narrowed his dark eyes on her flushed face and added incredulously, 'You don't actually think that I would allow you to leave, do you?'

'You wouldn't notice if I wasn't here,' she'd flung back childishly.

Christos, his expression taut and irritated, had passed a hand across his eyes. 'We will talk when I get back.'

'Maybe I won't want to talk then.'

Going over it in her head, she recognised that her sulky

retort hadn't been her finest hour—but how was she supposed to behave? Her husband had only just told her he was never going to leave her side, and then straight off had dropped everything because the cousin he loathed had a problem only he could sort out.

Was she being totally paranoid, or did that sound slightly less plausible than world peace?

Later that night, slipping beneath the silken sheets of the bed they shared—or were meant to—she realised how often Christos used the excuse of not wanting to wake her for sleeping on the sofa in the dressing room.

Erotic recollections of past times were generally the only thing she had to keep her warm at night. And if there had been something other than glorious head-banging sex to bind them—at least on his side—Becca might not have been haunted by the possibility that a highly sexed man like Christos was satisfying his hunger elsewhere.

She sat up suddenly, her face a mask of resolution as she sniffed and brushed the tears of self-pity from her cheeks. Maybe it was time to find out one way or the other if her anxieties were founded!

And if they are…?

Becca shook her head in silent denial. She didn't want to think about what she would do if they were.

Her fingers trembled as she dialled Alex's number. The phone was picked up almost immediately—which in other circumstances might have struck her as strange at two in the morning.

'Sally, this is Becca. I'm really sorry to disturb you, but could I speak to Christos?'

There was a short pause, and what might have been a sniff, before the other woman replied, 'I'm sorry, Becca. He isn't here.'

He'd lied…!

Why am I so shocked? she asked herself?

'Becca? Are you there? He shou—'

The phone dropped from her nerveless fingers onto the carpet. She pressed her hand across her mouth and let out a strangled cry of utter misery from her aching throat.

She had thought it would be better to know one way or the other. Now she knew how wrong she had been! She knew she ought to be feeling something—she wasn't sure what, but *something*.

Instead she just felt strangely numb and unnaturally calm as she set about packing a bag, her actions slow and methodical as she moved around the room, shaking out a crease or smoothing a fold.

'Inevitable, really,' she said to the empty room. 'He never loved me—never even pretended to.' She gave a dry-eyed sniff and bit down hard on her trembling lip.

But he had promised to be faithful, and he had broken that promise. She couldn't live with his infidelity—not even for the sake of her unborn babies.

She sat on the end of the bed and formulated her plans. She would stay with her mum and dad until the present tenant's lease on her cottage ran out, in six months' time. Getting her job back was unfortunately not an option but if she was lucky she might get some supply work.

Her lip quivered and she started to cry. She was still crying two hours later when, totally exhausted by the emotional outpouring, she fell into a deep, dreamless sleep.

When she awoke the first thing she saw was Christos's face, inches from her own. Her initial sleepy pleasure at seeing him was quickly replaced by a potent mix of anger and loss—immense, incapacitating loss.

Carefully, without taking her eyes from his sleeping face, she edged her body away from his and levered herself with utmost care off the bed. She stood there holding her breath when he stirred and murmured in his sleep, but after a moment his breathing became even and heavy again.

Like her, he had fallen asleep wearing his clothes—the same clothes he had left the house in the previous night. She looked down at him, the expression on her face an accurate reflection of the confusing mixture of emotions that were tearing her in disparate directions.

A terrible surge of longing welled up in her as she gazed down. She tried to block the images that entered her head. Images of him over her, the muscles in his powerful shoulders and arms bunched with tension as his lean, streamlined body, slick with sweat, slid... She inhaled sharply, sucking in air through flared nostrils as she fought to free herself of the erotic memories.

For a moment she had almost followed the voice in her head that told her it would be all right to lie down beside him, to feel the strength of his long, lean body next to her for the last time.

Have you no pride, woman? she asked herself.

Holding back the tears, Becca stumbled towards the door, not trusting herself to be in the same room as him. In the hallway she leant against the wall and, eyes closed, took several deep, restorative breaths.

The world is full of cheating men; you married one—get over it, she told herself. Feeling not even slightly over it, and doubting she ever would, she raked her fingers through her disordered curls. You have some choices to make, she told herself, and remembered the bag she had packed the previous night, wondering if she could risk going back in to get it.

'Kyria...?'

Becca opened her eyes and found the normally impassive butler looking at her with some concern.

'You are well?'

She nodded. 'Just getting my breath. Is something wrong?' *Apart from my life being messed up beyond belief.*

He glance swivelled pointedly towards the bedroom door. 'Is—?'

'He's asleep,' Becca cut in quickly. 'We probably shouldn't disturb him. Can I help?'

'There is a visitor,' the butler explained hesitantly, quite clearly not convinced by her attempt to appear normal.

'Well, you'll have to tell them that Christos is not available just now.'

'The visitor is asking for you, *kyria*...'

Something in the man's strange manner sent a premonitory shudder through her body and she asked, 'Just who is this visitor?'

'It is Miss Karas. She was...'

'She was engaged to my husband,' Becca inserted, in a calm voice that gave no hint of the fact that she felt as though she was dying inside.

Her thoughts were racing. Could this be the answer to the question she had not dared ask herself yet? Was Melina Karas the woman Christos had spent last night with? And heaven knew how many other nights when he was allegedly away on business?

'She is waiting?'

'It was difficult to stop her, *kyria*. She was insistent. I think perhaps I should waken Mr Carides—' he began doubtfully.

Becca straightened her shoulders decisively. 'No, I'll deal with this.'

CHAPTER SEVENTEEN

THE woman in the small salon turned as Becca entered, her demeanour, and the edge of condescension in her smile as she looked Becca up and down very much that of the mistress of the house and not the visitor.

Becca returned the scrutiny of those almond-shaped eyes, their exotic brilliance enhanced by expertly applied colour, with a steadiness that seemed to unnerve the other woman slightly.

'You don't know who I am—'

'Yes,' Becca cut in. 'I do.'

'Why don't you sit down?' the older woman suggested, still in the manner of a gracious, concerned hostess.

Becca, who needed quite badly to sit down, immediately decided she'd die before she did so now. The sympathy and consideration of her husband's mistress was more of a salt-in-the-wound situation than she was prepared to tolerate.

If she was his mistress?

Was this really the sort of woman Christos would be unable to live without? For the first time Becca questioned her own conviction as she observed the malicious light shining in the dark beauty's eyes.

Christos was normally such an instinctively good judge of character, but love had quite obviously dimmed his normal powers of perception. Becca could tell at a glance that this woman, despite her stunning looks, was cold and shallow. Of course she would still have hated her with a vengeance even if she had turned out to be delightful and warm.

Becca lifted her chin and shook her head, a frown forming between her brows as she studied her beautiful visitor.

'I've seen you before, haven't I?'

She frowned as she made the mental connection between this tall, elegant and very beautiful brunette in her home and the woman who had offered her opinion on fluffy bunnies versus cartoon cats when it came to mobiles for babies' cots.

'You were in the shop—and then in the café I went to the other day.' Comprehension flickered in her eyes. 'And it wasn't a coincidence, was it? You were following me!' she accused in horror.

'I admit I was curious,' the other woman responded, with a careless shrug of her narrow shoulders. 'Curious to see what sort of woman had trapped Christos into marriage.'

'I didn't trap Christos into anything.'

'Of course you did. But that really doesn't matter now,' she conceded with a generous smile. 'At first I admit I was angry with you—for taking advantage when he was vulnerable. But then I realised that you were clearly besotted with him and therefore not entirely to blame for your actions. You know, of course, that Christos loves *me*?'

A few minutes earlier this statement would have made Becca want to crawl away into a corner and lick her wounds. She had walked into the room prepared to see the woman Christos preferred to her, his wife. The woman who could make him happy.

But then, as she had listened to this incredibly beautiful creature, who was everything Becca was not, she'd become more and more convinced that she wasn't looking at that woman.

This woman could never make Christos happy. She could never love him the way he deserved to be loved! She was hard, selfish and mean. Not the most objective conclusion in the world, but Becca's gut instincts told her she was right on this one.

Becca lifted her chin and smiled. 'He married me.'

The other woman's smile wavered slightly as this quietly confident response threw her off-balance. 'I feel sorry for you.'

'Because Christos married me?' Becca shook her head. 'I don't think so,' she mused. 'I think you're actually as jealous as hell of me.'

A unattractive mottled tide of angry colour rose up Melina's neck as the remark found its intended target. 'His family will never accept you. You'll always be an outsider!' she hissed.

'And what would you know about it?'

'We've been seeing each other for months!' she yelled shrilly. With a triumphant grin she pulled out a notebook from her bag and began to flick through the pages. 'Athens, Rome, Paris—I have all the dates and hotels.'

Watching her, it dawned on Becca that her visitor was far from stable. She glanced towards the door. 'My husband's travel arrangements are not a secret.'

'And last night he was with me.' She saw the colour fade from Becca's face and smiled. *'All night,'* she emphasised with malice. 'And look at yourself,' she invited with a sneer. 'Do you honestly blame him? You look as though you slept in those clothes.'

Before Becca could confirm that she had, the door burst open and Christos, who had definitely slept in his, stood there. His expression belligerent, he locked his dark explosive eyes with Becca's. Eyes still glued to hers, he stepped inside and, after slamming the door behind him, tipped the contents of the suitcase she had so carefully packed the previous night over the floor. The bag followed it.

'What the hell does this mean?' he demanded.

'It means you'll have to pick them up, because when I

get down it takes a crane to get me up again.' She patted her distended belly and sighed.

Her response threw him slightly. 'If you think you are going anywhere without me—*Theos. Melina...?*' He looked from one woman to the other. 'What the hell are you doing here?'

Melina tore her startled glance from the pile of clothes on the floor and lifted her melting eyes to Christos's face.

Christos's response to her passionate flood of Greek was a cold terse instruction. 'Speak English in front of my wife.' He turned his head to Becca. 'Melina appears to think that she has saved me the painful task of *telling you*.' He turned back to the other woman. 'Telling her what, exactly, Melina?'

His voice was filled with icy disdain. This was Christos at his most cold and cutting. Becca almost started to feel sorry for the other woman.

Melina looked flustered, and gave a light laugh. 'That we still love one another, darling. That our breaking up was just a silly mistake. It's understandable that you didn't want to say anything, with her being pregnant.' Her thin lips formed a *moue* of pained distaste as she glanced at Becca's distended waistline.

'I take it that you had no such qualms?' Christos suggested drily.

If Becca or the babies suffered because of this he would personally strangle the woman. Even if the balance of her mind was quite definitely seriously disturbed!

'I thought she deserved to know.'

This pious statement wrenched a strangled expletive from a grim-looking Christos.

'I love you, Christos.'

'Then I can live without your brand of love.' His eyes flickered towards Becca. 'Are you okay?'

'That would be overstating it,' Becca admitted. 'But I'm hanging in there, fighting.'

'She's in denial,' said Melina compassionately.

Christos gave her a frowning, impatient glance. 'She has nothing to be in denial about. I don't love you and I never did.'

Melina flinched, then shook her head. Her eyes held a feral gleam of determination as she gazed at him. 'You don't mean that. We are meant to be together. You're only being like this because of her!' she hissed, throwing a malevolent glance towards Becca.

Intercepting that look, Christos moved to interpose his body protectively between that of his wife and his ex.

As Melina advanced towards him Christos held up his hands and shook his head. Something in his manner must have finally pierced the fantasy she had constructed, because Melina stopped dead, the colour draining from her face.

Becca looked away, embarrassed, as her rival quivered. 'But you love me.'

'I am married—and even if I wasn't I have no feelings for you.'

The brutally honest response drew a sharp gasp from Melina.

'I think you should leave,' Christos said, and warned in the same devastating soft voice, 'If you come anywhere near my family again there will be consequences, Melina.' He picked up the phone.

Becca, who was watching him, had no doubt he meant it. And it seemed from the way Melina straightened her shoulders and picked up her designer bag that she believed him too.

'I'll call you a cab.'

'Don't bother,' Melina snapped. 'I know my way out.' At the door she turned back, and her smile as she looked at Becca was vicious. 'Tell her where you were last night if you weren't with me, Christos.'

The door slammed and her parting shot hung in the air between them.

Becca sat down heavily on the sofa. After looking down at her glossy bowed head for a moment, Christos released a strong expletive and fell onto his knees beside her.

He lifted a gentle hand to her cheek and Becca looked back at him blankly, still trying to make sense of what had just happened.

'I'm really sorry you had to go through that. I had no idea she'd pull a stunt like that,' he admitted, with a self-recriminatory grimace as their eyes meshed. 'You coped remarkably well, you know.'

Becca stilled, then with an ironic laugh turned her head away. 'You thought that was coping?' She swallowed and shook her head. 'I thought you were having an affair, Christos.' She turned back and caught a look of shocked devastation on his handsome face that could not have been feigned.

'You thought I was having an affair?' She nodded and he shook his dark head. 'I don't know what to say.'

'*No, I'm not* would be good…' She paused. 'If it's true?' she added huskily.

He flinched as if she had struck him. '*If?*' he echoed hoarsely. 'If?' he said again, then, visibly restraining himself, sucked in air through flared nostrils. 'That was why you packed the bag? You were going to leave me? You were serious last night?'

'Yes… No… I don't know,' she admitted, bowing her head.

Christos looked at the top of her glossy head for a long time before he spoke. 'I could not bear to lose you.'

Her head lifted. His face was filled with the same depth of aching sincerity and pain she had heard in his voice.

This is about the babies, she cautioned her hopeful heart. But of course it didn't listen.

'And I couldn't bear to think of you making love to someone else,' she admitted bluntly.

'How could you think such a thing?'

She stared at him. 'Well you haven't been making love to *me* have you?' She watched a telltale flush of colour run up under his olive-toned skin and her heart sank.

The skin was drawn tight across his face, lending stark prominence to each perfect contour and angle as he said, 'I've been worried about the babies.'

'Don't use them as an excuse,' she recommended, in no mood at that moment to be sympathetic to his concerns. 'I may be the size of a small mountain now,' she admitted, with a rueful glance down at her girth, 'but I wasn't when you stopped touching me,' she reminded him bitterly. 'Why don't you just admit you can't stand the sight of me?' she yelled, clamping a hand over her mouth to contain the self-pitying sob in her throat.

He looked at her incredulously. 'Is that what you think?'

'It's what I know,' she contended stubbornly.

'Theos!' He lifted both hands and dragged them through his already disordered dark hair. When his hands fell back to his sides Becca saw he was laughing.

Her chest swelled with indignation. 'You think this is funny!' she shrieked, and seriously considered hitting him.

Christos stopped laughing and suddenly grabbed her by the shoulders. There was no trace of the humour that had offended her in his face as he leaned in close to her.

'No,' he said as she lowered her chin. 'Look at me, *pethu mou.*'

Her heart beating very fast, Becca did as he demanded—and when his fierce gaze locked with hers what she saw glittering in his fabulous eyes made her heart beat even faster.

'I stopped touching you because I was afraid.'

'I…I don't understand,' she faltered.

'Two babies…'

At that point Becca lost her temper with him. 'Do you think I would do or encourage *you* to do anything that would harm the babies?' she demanded indignantly. 'I know your mother had a hard time, and things went badly, but I'm not your mother. In fact I'm not a mother at all yet. And when I am I'd like to feel like a woman too. But at the moment I can't ever imagine…'

Her emotional tirade ran out of impetus at about the same time she ran out of breath. Tears flowing freely down her face, she sat there, her bosom heaving as she gasped for air.

'Feel like a woman? Of course you're a woman—a warm, desirable woman. This is not about me not finding you attractive.'

His response had soothed her feelings slightly, but her eyes still held hostility as she asked, 'Then what is it about?'

'Do you have any idea how much higher the maternal mortality rate is with multiple births?' he demanded. When she shook her head he said grimly, 'I do.'

'If a pregnancy has ever been more carefully monitored than mine, I have yet to hear about it,' she retorted grimly.

'I have always prided myself on my self-control, but when I touch you…' A deep sigh lifted his chest and his lips twisted in a self-derisory grimace. 'You must admit that our lovemaking was never tame, *pethu mou*.' The gentle flush that ran up her neck until her face was bathed in colour brought a wicked glint to his eyes.

Becca realised how much she had missed that glint.

'I have a vague recollection,' she admitted huskily. She turned her exasperated glare on him. 'Fair enough, you're worried about sex—but that doesn't mean you can't hug me, or show me a little bit of affection or…'

'But you never appeared to need—'

'I didn't need what?' she asked, when he stopped mid-sentence.

'Me.'

Becca looked at him in staggered silence. That Christos could feel any form of insecurity about her needing him had never even crossed her mind.

'You appeared to enjoy the time we spent apart. You never displayed any sign of missing me,' he recalled accusingly. 'I felt…' He swallowed. 'I felt at times irrelevant,' he admitted.

The concept of Christos Carides ever being *irrelevant* made her blink. It had never occurred to her that he was capable of feeling this sort of insecurity.

'You're the least irrelevant person I have ever met, Christos.'

'What if I lost control and—?'

'Rubbish!'

He looked at her in startled enquiry and Becca spelt out her meaning.

'Christos, you could never hurt me.' She shook her head to emphasise her total conviction. 'You're a passionate lover, not some sort of selfish brute, and I won't have you think about yourself that way.'

Before he had a chance to respond she took his face between her hands and pressed her mouth to his. For a moment there was no response, and then a deep sigh vibrated through him and he was kissing her back, with a tenderness that went bone-deep.

When they broke apart Christos looked as shaken as Becca felt.

He blotted a tear that was running down her cheek. 'It has been hell not to touch you,' he confessed huskily.

Tell me about it, Becca thought, and sniffed.

'But with us it never stops with a touch, does it?' There was fascination in his eyes as he raised a hand to her burnished curls. 'I catch fire when I touch you.'

It seemed to a mesmerised Becca that there was a flame deep in his eyes as he looked at her. 'There's nothing wrong with a bit of combustion.' She slanted him a sultry look from under the sweep of her lashes and confided huskily, 'I rather enjoy it.'

'You know that my twin brother was stillborn?'

The fear she saw lurking in his eyes made her heart ache with empathy. 'Our babies are healthy, Christos.' She pressed her hands to her belly. 'Feel, if you don't believe me. They're right here.'

He looked startled for a moment. Then his strong, masculine features relaxed into an excited, almost boyish smile of anticipation as he raised his hand. He still hesitated. 'May I...?'

Becca took his hand and pressed it to her stomach.

His eyes widened as he felt the vigorous movement within. 'Do they do that all the time?' he asked in an awed whisper.

'Pretty much,' she confirmed. 'So, you see, they are a tough pair.'

His eyes blazing, he took her small hand and pressed it to his lips. 'And they will remain that way,' he promised.

'Of course they will.' Becca studied his face, trying to understand the source of the tension that was emanating from him.

'After I was born my mother became ill. Obviously I have no memory of the time, and it is not spoken of, but children hear things...'

Becca nodded. She was a teacher—she was only too aware of children's ability to hear things they weren't meant to.

'And they make an impression…stay with the child.'

Clearly whatever he was about to tell her had made an impression on the young Christos. Becca waited, knowing that this wasn't the time to rush him, even though the anguish in his face made her want to weep with frustration because she wasn't able to stop him hurting.

'After the trauma of the birth and…' he paused slightly before he said the name of the brother he had never known 'Vasilis's death, my mother suffered from a form of what I assume would be called post-natal depression today. These things were not so readily recognised then.

'For a long time,' he continued, 'she was hard to reach. My parents' marriage suffered greatly. She became angry and resentful, and, in her grief she came to believe that it was my father's fault that my brother died.'

'People need someone to blame.'

He nodded agreement. 'She accused him of putting his pleasure first and killing her baby.'

'Oh, the poor man!' Becca exclaimed. 'And how your mother must have regretted it later.'

'I'm sure she did,' Christos agreed. 'But this tragedy cast a shadow over my parents' marriage for many years. That, and the fact that the birth left her unable to have more children. If you ever said such a thing to me, Becca…' He shook his head and swallowed.

Becca knew she would never forget the terrible haunted light in his eyes as he looked at her. 'For an intelligent man you are pretty dim—do you know that?' she told him huskily.

To be called dim was obviously a new experience for Christos, who looked so astonished she almost laughed.

'If you had these worries why didn't you share them with me?'

A bemused frown formed between his dark brows. 'Share…?'

This time she did laugh. 'Married people do—and we are married, you know.'

'Are we?' His glance slid significantly to the clothes on the floor. 'But you were going to leave me.'

'When I rang Alex's last night you weren't there.'

'You rang…?' He looked aghast, which a short time ago Becca would have translated as guilty, but now she was seeing things more clearly.

'I kind of put two and two together, as you do…' she admitted, trying to block that devastating moment from her memory. 'Now I realise I was being stupid. If you were going to cheat you'd tell me. You're much too up-front to sneak around.' And she was pretty sure that if he had it would not have been with Melina, who had a smile like a snake and was ever so slightly mad.

'Melina was stalking me, you know.'

This casual revelation caused Christos to stop grinding his teeth and stare at her.

'She was what?' he exclaimed, and Becca went on the explain about the shop and the café.

Christos rubbed his jaw and looked shaken and angry. 'I wish you'd told me.'

'I didn't know she was your ex-fiancée when I saw her.' Her eyes slid from his. '*Were* you at Melina's place last night?'

His jaw tightened. 'Yes. But not doing what you think.'

Her eyes flew to his face. 'You don't know what I think,' she protested.

'You will have no argument from me on that score,' he retorted, with feeling. 'Your thought processes remain a total mystery to me. Am I meant to take it as a *compliment* that you think I will be ''up-front'' when I choose to cheat on you?' One dark brow lifted as he enquired with heavy irony, 'With my cheating apparently being taken as some sort of given? *Theos!*' he breathed. 'I never know what you're going to say next.'

'I didn't—'

'No,' he said cutting across her with an impatient movement of his hand. 'For the sake of my sanity I think it best you don't go there.' He drew a deep breath. 'I was telling you about last night.'

'You don't have to.'

He studied her face in silence for a moment. 'Oh, I think I do. Sally has suspected for a few weeks that Alex has resumed his affair with Melina—'

'Melina and Alex!' Becca gasped.

Christos nodded. 'Well, I'm not sure that it can be termed an "affair"—but Alex could never resist the opportunity to get one over on me—and Melina was bitter when I broke off our engagement.'

Becca lifted a hand to his cheek. '*You* broke off the engagement? But I thought...'

Christos's dark gaze moved across her flushed face. 'I hardly dare ask,' he revealed drily, 'but what did you think, *yineka mou*?'

'I thought that she dumped you, and you slept with me on the rebound.'

His dark brows lifted as an expression of incredulity spread across his face. 'Your readiness to believe that other women are as ready to reject me as you does wonders for my fragile ego. And this extraordinary conclusion was based on what evidence, exactly?'

'Imagination and jealousy.' Easy to recognise in retrospect, but not at the time.

'My engagement to Melina was over almost before it began. It never was a planned thing,' he revealed. 'She got drunk at her parents' anniversary party and had her father announce to the entire world that we were engaged. I should have stopped it then. But I thought, Why not...?'

His shoulders lifted in an expressive shrug, and his voice contained a large dose of self-derision as he explained his reasoning.

'We had a lot in common, and we'd had an on-off thing for some years…' he admitted. 'I wanted a family. It was not difficult to convince myself that it would be enough of a marriage for me. You see, in my defence, at that point in my life I had never seen a particular redhead. So I didn't know how much better than *all right* and *workable* things could be.'

Becca's eyes misted with emotional tears as she brought his hand to her face.

'I started to regret it straight away,' he admitted.

'What did she do when you called it off?'

'She knew I was coming over to return her keys, so she arranged a little…floorshow. Which involved Alex and her with very few clothes and a rug.'

Becca gasped, trying hard not to imagine the scene he described. 'And you walked in?'

He nodded, amused by her shocked expression.

'What did you do?'

'Nothing.'

Becca stared at him. *'Nothing?'* she echoed in a bemused voice. 'That doesn't seem very in character.'

'Why should I have done anything when I didn't give a damn? It may interest you to know that five minutes after I'd met you—maybe less—I punched my cousin on the nose. Twice, actually.'

'Why?'

'Because I thought he had done to you what he did to Erica.'

Choking back an emotional sob, Becca flung her arms around his neck and kissed him several times, interspersing the kisses with fervent thank-yous. 'Not,' she added when she eventually drew back, 'that I approve of violence.'

'Of course not,' he concurred gravely.

'But Alex is the most horrible man.'

'No arguments there.'

'It's poor Sally I feel for.'

Christos nodded. 'A nice girl—she deserves a lot better than my cousin. Last night when she confronted him he apparently admitted that he was spending the night with Melina. When she rang me she was in a terrible state. She begged me to use my influence…said if I told Melina to leave him alone she would. I thought that was unlikely, but she was so desperate that I went round there to remind my cousin that he had wife and a baby at home.'

'Just as Melina planned you would.'

'You caught on to that faster than I did,' he admitted, a glint of startled admiration in his dark eyes as they met her own. 'When I got there Alex was very drunk,' he recalled. 'But he was not actually the problem.'

'It was *you* Melina was after.'

'I will not go into details,' he said, his lips twisting into a grimace of fastidious distaste as he recalled the previous evening, 'but when I said thanks, but no thanks, she became…*unpleasant*.' Only his very quick reflexes had stopped her raking his face with her nails.

Becca, who had seen for herself how 'unpleasant' Melina could be, could imagine how horrendous it must have been. 'You got Alex home?'

Christos nodded. 'Eventually—and I think I got through to him.'

'You did?'

Christos nodded. 'I told him what the rumour mill says his father-in-law did to a guy who tried to embezzle from him. I think it made an impression. The one thing that Carl cares about more than making money is his daughter.'

'I know I shouldn't have jumped to conclusions,' Becca admitted, her eyes sliding guiltily from his.

'I should have appreciated how it looked from your point of view.'

Sighing with pleasure as she felt the touch of his fingers in her hair, Becca mused thoughtfully, 'I suppose it makes you a little insecure, loving someone so much when you know they don't love you back.'

The hand that had been stroking her hair stilled. 'You love me?'

For a split second she considered denying it, and then thought—What the hell? It wasn't as if she was going to be able to hide it for ever.

There was a hint of defiance in her face as she levelled her eyes with his. 'So what if I love you? It doesn't change anything.'

'You being in love with me doesn't change anything?' He stared at her as if she was totally insane. 'The hell it doesn't!' he growled, a split second before his mouth came down on hers, hard and hungry.

When he lifted his head and put her carefully from him, as though she was breakable, they were both breathing hard.

If this is a dream I definitely don't want to wake up, she thought, looking at his lean, dark face with eyes that glowed with love. 'I take it you don't mind about...you know...?'

'Mind?' He gave a grin of fierce relief, the tension visibly seeping from his body. 'My dear, delicious lunatic— why should I mind my wife loving me?'

Becca blinked up at him.

'You look like a confused baby owl,' he told her lovingly.

'Men do not fall in love with confused owls of any age.'

He gave a complacent laugh and, after running a loving hand over her stomach, let it remain there. 'I've been crazy in love with you from the first moment I laid eyes on that red head of yours. I knew I couldn't let you get away from me.'

Becca started to shake. 'You only married me because I was pregnant!' she protested weakly.

'I married you because I can't live without you,' Christos corrected, nibbling his way reverently along the smooth curve of her shoulder.

'And it didn't occur to you to tell me?' she moaned, laying her head against his chest and thinking of all the miserable nights she had spent.

'Now, why am I thinking pot, black and kettle?' he teased, tilting her face up to his.

'I thought you wanted a marriage of convenience, Christos.'

'Despite appearances, I was never that much of a fool. I want and always have wanted a marriage with you in it,' he said simply. 'It's the only way it works for me.'

She smiled up at him, love shimmering in her eyes. 'Good—because I'm in this for the long haul.'

'And I intend to make it a pleasurable journey for us all,' he promised, laying a protective hand on her stomach.

Her throat thick with emotion, she covered his hand with her own and intertwined her fingers with his. 'Any place you go, I'll quite happily follow.'

EPILOGUE

WHEN Becca returned from her appointment she ran straight out onto the terrace, impatient to share her news with Christos. It was the sort of news that deserved to be shouted from the roof—and here that was an option.

That was why she loved their beach villa here on the island so much. There were no servants to be guarded or circumspect around, no formality, no ringing phones—just them: the family.

And she knew that Christos treasured the time they spent here as much as she did.

She gave a sigh of sheer pleasure as she looked out to the beach and the sea beyond. And—right in the middle— the three people that made it very, *very* good to be Becca Carides! She lifted her hand and waved wildly.

Down on the beach, Christos caught his breath at the sight of the slim figure with her hand above her head. As he lifted his own hand to shade his eyes the soft summer breeze caught the full skirt of the dress she wore. He smiled and felt the familiar lick of lust as he watched her strenuous efforts to subdue the billowing fabric as it lifted.

Becca gave up on controlling her dress and, slipping the straps over her shoulders, let it fall to the ground. Underneath she wore a bright red bikini, which she had brought along for the long weekend because Christos liked the way it clashed with her hair. *She* liked what he said it did to his blood pressure!

She bent over to unfasten the ankle straps on her sandals, and saw the tall, tanned figure loping up the beach to meet her.

There had to be very few men who looked as good as her husband in a pair of swimming shorts, Becca reflected. Long legs, broad shoulders, and a taut, toned body that carried not an ounce of excess flesh to hide the perfect musculature she never tired of looking at.

I just love the way he moves.

Becca smiled as she realised anyone hearing her panting would assume she had been the one doing the running.

'Where have you been?' Christos demanded, placing the giggling bundles he carried, one under each arm, on the tiled terrace floor.

He lifted his head and, grinning at his wife, adopted a long-suffering tone as he added, 'And before you ask—yes, I did keep them out of the midday sun, smother them with suncream and keep their hats on at all times… Well, *almost* all times,' he corrected, pulling a frilled sunhat from the auburn curls of their eleven-month-old daughter. With a gummy grin she immediately snatched it from his hand with her chubby baby fingers.

'How like a woman,' he observed, straightening up and pressing a hungry kiss on his wife's lips. 'Mmm—you taste good,' he said, before wagging a finger at their daughter and complaining, 'She spends all morning pulling it off. Now she decides she wants it.' He tapped their daughter's tip-tilted nose playfully and looked around for her brother.

'Vasilis!' he called. 'Where is that boy?'

Laughing as she gathered her grubby, rosy-cheeked daughter into her arms, Becca pointed across the terrace.

She would imagine there were many people who would have difficulty connecting this figure with sand in his hair and a relaxed grin on his face with the man who wore designer suits and never had a hair out of place. That man could sway a boardroom with a well-chosen sentence and one of his signature looks.

'*Theos!*' Christos exclaimed. 'Imagine how fast he's going to move when he finally decides to walk!' Christos moved to retrieve Vasilis before he managed to catch the cat he was pursuing. 'When are you going to catch up with your sister, Vasilis?' Christos demanded of their son, who had yet to take his first step.

'He'll get there,' Becca said comfortably, as she watched Christos heave the struggling little boy into his arms. The similarity between father and son was marked—the only real difference being that Vasilis had deep blue eyes...her eyes. It was his twin sister who had inherited their father's dark brown eyes.

'Girls mature much faster. You remember that, Effy,' she told her daughter, who was attempting to eat her hat. 'You know, I think she's teething again.'

Christos rolled his eyes to the ceiling and groaned. 'Will there ever be a time when one of them isn't?'

Becca laughed. At moments like this it hit her just how lucky she was. A deep sense of contentment washed over her as Christos joined her.

'You look very pleased with yourself,' he observed.

'Actually, I *am* pretty pleased with myself,' she said, offering her lips for the lingering kiss her husband planted on them.

'Yes, *very* good—like strawberries.' He studied her bright eyes and prettily flushed cheeks with narrowed eyes. 'Has this smugness and sparkle got something to do with your mysterious appointment this morning?'

'You could say that,' she confirmed. Then, unable to stretch out the tension another second, she blurted, 'The doctor confirmed what I already knew...I'm pregnant, Christos. We're going to have another baby!'

Christos stilled, his eyes dropping down her slim body. 'We've only just started trying,' he protested hoarsely. 'I thought these things took time.'

'You of all people should know that isn't always so.'

Her shoulder lifted in a shrug. 'I suppose we just have to accept that you're a regular superstud.'

'A baby...' he said, still looking stunned.

Becca nodded, then blinked as without a word he took the placid Effy from her arms and planted both twins in their toy-filled playpen. Striding urgently back to his wife's side, he took her face between his hands.

There was a shade of anxiety in his face as he asked, 'This is what you want, *yineka mou*?'

Becca covered his hands with her own. 'I've never been happier in my life, Christos,' she admitted. 'And you?'

Christos's eyes were suspiciously bright as he brought her hands to his lips and pressed a fervent kiss on first one small palm and then the other. 'If you find a happier man than me he is lying—because it simply is not possible.'

The depth of sincerity shining in his eyes brought an emotional lump to her throat.

'I love you so much it hurts,' she admitted thickly.

His eyes burning, Christos bent his head and kissed her with a passion that made Becca's toes curl.

When he lifted his head she released a shuddering sigh. 'You have no idea how glad I am that you came back for Alex's wedding... When I think about not meeting you...'

His strong hands closed possessively over the rounded contours of her firm bottom and Becca leaned into him, loving the lean, male hardness of his body.

'There was no chance of that not happening.'

'No...?'

He shook his head and said, with total conviction, 'You and I were fated to be together.'

Becca blinked away the emotional tears that sprang to her eyes. 'You really believe that, don't you?' she said, wonder in her eyes as she stroked the strong curve of his lean cheek.

'Don't you?' he challenged.

A smile of sheer happiness illuminated her flushed face as she dragged his head down to hers. 'I think there's a special someone for everyone, but only the lucky few find each other. And I'm the luckiest—to have found you.'

* * * *

Kim Lawrence brings you more hot-blooded Mediterranean romance in
Mistress: Pregnant by the Spanish Billionaire, *available August 2009, in Mills & Boon® Modern™ romance*

Sale or Return Bride

SARAH MORGAN

Sarah Morgan trained as a nurse, and has since worked in a variety of health-related jobs. Married to a gorgeous businessman, who still makes her knees knock, she spends most of her time trying to keep up with their two little boys, but manages to sneak off occasionally to indulge her passion for writing romance. Sarah loves outdoor life, and is an enthusiastic skier and walker. Whatever she is doing, her head is full of new characters, and she is addicted to happy endings.

CHAPTER ONE

'SEBASTIEN FIORUKIS?' Alesia gaped at her grandfather, the grandfather who had been a stranger to her in all but reputation for her whole life. 'In exchange for the money I need, you expect me to marry *Sebastien Fiorukis*?'

'Precisely.' Alesia's grandfather smiled an unpleasant smile as she struggled to find her voice and fought to control the torrent of emotion that surged up inside her. Whatever she'd expected when she'd been working up the courage to tackle her grandfather, it hadn't been that.

Fiorukis. The Greek tycoon who had taken his father's moderately successful business and built it into a corporation that rivalled that of her grandfather; the billionaire reputed to be every bit as ruthless as her grandfather; the man who moved between women at a speed faster than the cars he drove and the jets he flew. The man who—

'You can't be serious!' She looked up, her teeth gritted and her eyes stinging. The very thought made her feel *sick*. 'The Fiorukis family was responsible for the death of my father—'

And she despised them as much as she despised her grandfather.

As much as she despised everything Greek.

'And because of that, my blood-line died out,' her grandfather said harshly. 'Now I shall ensure the same fate for the Fiorukis family. If he marries you then it will end with the son, just as mine did.'

Alesia stopped breathing, rigid with shock. *He knew.*
Somehow he knew.

The file she was holding dropped from her nerveless fin-

5

gers and papers scattered across the marble floor. She didn't notice.

As the full implication of his words sank into her shocked brain, her face paled and her voice was little more than a whisper. 'You know that I can't have children—?'

How could he know? How could he be party to such an intimate, personal detail?

All her life she'd kept that information private. The only slight salve to her pain had been that her anguish was her own—*that no one would pity her.*

She stared at him, her breathing rapid. She'd arrived strong and full of purpose. Now suddenly she felt vulnerable and exposed. Stripped naked in front of a man who, despite their shared blood-line, had been a stranger from her childhood.

That man was watching her now, an expression of smug satisfaction in his hard eyes.

Her grandfather, Dimitrios Philipos.

'I make it my business to know everything about everyone.' His tone was brittle and unsympathetic as he observed her distress with evident satisfaction. 'Information is the key to success in life.'

Alesia swallowed back the lump building in her throat. How could such personal agony ever be considered 'success'?

Marriage.

It was the cruellest taunt. She'd long ago been forced to come to terms with the fact that, no matter what her future held, it wouldn't be marriage. How could it? How could a woman in her position ever marry?

Her mind raced ahead, trying to keep up with the evil genius of her grandfather. 'If you *truly* know everything about me then you must also know the reason I'm here. You must know that my mother is getting sicker, that she needs an operation—'

His smile was unpleasant. 'Let's just say I've been expecting you. You didn't disappoint me.'

Fury shot through her, driving out the weakness induced by his reminder of her own limitations as a woman.

She hated him.

Alesia stared at the grandfather she'd never even met before this moment and gave a shiver of revulsion. Her head throbbed with a tension headache that had been plaguing her since she'd stepped off the plane at Athens Airport and she felt a dull ache in the pit of her stomach, a reminder that she'd been too nervous to eat for the past few days.

So much was at stake. Her mother's future lay in her hands, in her ability to negotiate some sort of deal with a man who was nothing short of a monster.

He presided over the room like a king, seated in an enormous gilded chair with ornately curved handles, barking out orders to terrified staff who hovered within shouting distance.

Alesia glanced around the opulent room with distaste. Such a blatant display of wealth sickened her.

Did the man have no shame? Did he know that she held down three jobs in order to give her mother the care that she needed?

Care that *he* should have been providing for the past fifteen years.

Alesia took a deep breath and tried to calm herself. Temper would get her nowhere. It took enormous effort not to just turn and walk from the room, leaving the old man to his piles of money and lonely existence. But she couldn't do that. She had to ignore the fact that he was the most selfish, shallow individual she'd ever laid eyes on and she had to ignore the fact that if it hadn't been for her mother she wouldn't be standing here now. She had to stay focused on the task in hand.

Nothing—*nothing*—was going to distract her from her reason for being here. He'd ignored her mother's needs for fif-

teen years, denied her very existence, but Alesia wasn't going
to let him ignore *her*. Not any longer. It was time that he
remembered what family was supposed to be about.

'Wipe that expression off your face. You came to me, remember? You're the one who wants the money.' Dimitrios's
voice was harsh and heavily accented and Alesia stiffened
defensively.

'For my mother.'

He gave a grunt of contempt. 'She could have asked me
herself if she had any backbone.'

Alesia felt the anger rise inside her again and squashed it
down with ruthless determination. She sensed that if she let
her emotions rule then he'd show her the door. 'My mother
is very unwell—'

He watched her closely, a nasty smile on his face. 'And
that's the only reason you're here, isn't it? Nothing else
would induce you to step over my threshold. You hate me.
She's taught you to hate me.' He leaned forward. 'You're
furiously angry and you're trying to hide it because you don't
want to risk antagonizing me in case I say no. In case I slam
the lid of my coffer shut and catch your fingers.'

He threw back his head and laughed, obviously enjoying
the situation enormously.

Refusing to believe that anyone could be so totally lacking
in conscience, Alesia spread her hands and tried to appeal to
his sense of reason. 'She was *your son's wife*—'

'Don't remind me.' The laughter faded and he sat back in
his chair watching her without a flicker of remorse or regret.
'It's a shame you weren't a boy. You look as though you've
inherited his spirit. You even look a little like him, apart from
that blonde hair and those blue eyes. You should have had
dark hair and dark eyes and if my son hadn't been seduced
by that woman you would have had the pedigree you deserve
and you wouldn't have lived the last fifteen years of your
life in exile. All this could have been yours.'

Alesia glanced round the room at 'all this'. The contrast between her own circumstances and those of her grandfather couldn't have been more marked. Evidence of his wealth was everywhere, from the ostentatious statues that guarded the entrance of virtually every doorway in his mansion to the enormous fountain that gushed forth in the elaborate courtyard.

Alesia thought of her own home in a rough area of London—a small ground-floor flat which she'd had converted to accommodate her mother's disability—all that she could afford after she'd paid for the help her mother needed.

Then she thought of her mother and her long struggle for survival. *A struggle which this man could have lessened.*

She gritted her teeth and doubled the effort required not to walk from the room. 'I'm perfectly happy with my pedigree,' she said stiffly, 'and I love England.'

'Don't answer me back!' He turned on her with an enraged growl and for a moment she tensed, sure that he was going to hit her. 'If you answer back, he'll never marry you. You may not look Greek but I want your behaviour to be totally Greek. You will be meek and obedient and you will not venture an opinion on any subject unless asked. *Do you hear me?*'

Alesia stared at him in disbelief. 'You're serious about this? You really think I'm going to marry a Fiorukis?'

Her grandfather gave an ugly smile. 'If you want the money, then yes. You'll marry Sebastien Fiorukis and you'll make sure he doesn't find out about your infertility. I will make sure that the terms of the deal will tie him to you in marriage until you produce an heir. Seeing as you will never produce an heir, then he will be locked in a childless marriage for ever, unable to extract himself.' Dimitrios Philipos threw back his head and gave a nasty laugh. 'The perfect retribution. They always say that revenge is a dish best eaten cold. I've waited fifteen years for this moment but it was worth the wait. It's masterly. You are the tool of my revenge.'

Alesia stared at him in undisguised horror, so shocked by his vindictive plan that she was unable to hide her distaste.

No wonder her mother had warned her that the man was evil. He didn't have an ounce of compassion in his body.

'I can't do that.' She lifted a hand to her throat. Suddenly she couldn't breathe. The room was totally airless. 'You can't ask me to do that.'

She couldn't marry Sebastien Fiorukis. He had all the characteristics she despised in a man. To be asked to spend her life with him—

Alesia closed her eyes and tried to remember how she'd got into this situation. She'd never believed in feuds and vengeance.

She was English!

Her grandfather's smile was unpleasant. 'If you want the money then you'll do it.'

Alesia bit her lip hard, her mind racing in all directions.

She wanted the money. *She had to have the money.* 'It's wrong—'

'It's justice,' her grandfather said, his voice icy-cold. 'Justice that we should have meted out to the Fiorukis family a long time ago. The Greek always avenge their dead and you, even though you are only *half* Greek, should know this.'

Alesia stared at him helplessly.

Was this the time to tell him that she hated everything Greek? *That she didn't feel at all Greek and never would?*

She stayed silent, she couldn't risk alienating her grandfather.

Anything.

That was what she'd told herself before she'd arrived at her grandfather's villa today. She'd do *anything* to get the money she needed.

But she'd underestimated her grandfather's ability to turn her desperation to his own advantage.

She studied him carefully, noting the chill in his eyes and the ugly set of his fleshy mouth. The thought flashed through her brain that to intentionally make an enemy of this man would be foolish in the extreme. Then she almost laughed at her own naïvety. They were enemies already. Had been from the day that her mother had smiled up at her father and captured his heart, shattering Dimitrios's plans for a wedding to a good Greek girl.

'Fiorukis will never agree to marry me,' she said calmly. 'He'll refuse.'

And then she wouldn't have to spend the rest of her life with a man she'd been bred to hate. There was no way he'd agree to marry her, she consoled herself. Sebastien Fiorukis discarded women with ruthless efficiency and with a casual disregard for their feelings. It was common knowledge that marriage was right at the bottom of his agenda.

Why would he marry *her*, when their families were virtually at war?

'Sebastien Fiorukis is first and foremost a businessman,' her grandfather said in derisive tones, 'and the inducement I have offered him to marry my granddaughter will prove too tempting for him to pass up.'

'What inducement?'

Her grandfather gave a nasty smile. 'Let's just say that I have something he wants—which is the basis of all successful business negotiations. He is also a man who can't pass an attractive woman and not make a move on her. For some reason he favours blonde women, so you're in luck—or you will be once we've got you out of those tatty jeans and dressed you in something decent. And if you want that money then you won't do anything to put him off. Now clear up the mess you made on my floor.'

In luck? Her grandfather truly thought that attracting the attentions of that arrogant, ruthless Greek was lucky?

Functioning on automatic, Alesia stooped and gathered together the papers with shaking hands, her mind working quickly. What choice did she have? There was no other possible source for the money she needed. If there had been then she wouldn't be standing here now. And it wouldn't be marriage in the true sense of the word. They probably wouldn't even need to speak to each other very often—

'If I do it—if I say yes, you'll give me the money?'

'No—' her grandfather gave a grunt '—but Fiorukis will. It will be part of the agreement. He will give you an allowance every month. How you spend that will be up to you.'

Alesia's mouth fell open. Her grandfather had managed to construct a deal where he didn't even have to part with his money—

Sebastien Fiorukis was not only going to have to marry the granddaughter of his greatest enemy but he was going to have to pay for the privilege.

Why would he agree to such an outrageous idea?

What exactly was the inducement that her grandfather had referred to?

She raised a shaking hand to her temple, wishing that her head would stop aching. Wishing that she could think clearly.

She knew enough about her grandfather to assume that, for whatever reason, Sebastien Fiorukis would agree to the deal.

Which meant that if she wanted the money then she was going to have to do the one thing she'd promised herself that she'd never do.

She was going to have to marry.

And marry not just anyone, but the man whose family had been responsible for the death of her father.

A man she hated.

*   *   *

'Why would Dimitrios Philipos come to us?' Sebastien Fiorukis paced the terrace that ran the length of his luxury Athenian villa and then paused to study his father, his handsome face devoid of expression. He'd learned at an early age the advantage of inscrutability and he practised the art to perfection. 'The feud between our families goes back for three generations.'

'Apparently that's the reason for his approach,' Leandros Fiorukis said cautiously. 'He thinks it's time to mend fences. Publicly.'

'*Mend fences?*' Sebastien raised an eyebrow, incredulity lighting his expressive dark eyes. 'Since when did Dimitrios Philipos ever want to mend fences? The man is evil and totally without conscience.'

The fact that his father was even *considering* meeting with the man astonished him. But his father was growing old, Sebastien acknowledged with a tinge of regret, and the loss of the family company so many years earlier had been a thorn in his side for too long.

His father sighed. 'I want this feud to end, Sebastien. I want to retire in peace with your mother, knowing that what is rightfully ours has been returned. I no longer have the stomach for a fight.'

At the prospect of finally going head to head with his lifelong enemy, Sebastien gave a dangerous smile. Fortunately he had no such reservations. In fact he positively thrived on confrontation and animosity. If Dimitrios Philipos thought that he could play his usual game of bullying and intimidation then he was going to discover that he'd finally met his match.

His father picked up some papers. 'The deal he is offering is astonishing.'

'All the more reason to be suspicious of his motives,' Sebastien drawled in cool tones and Leandros Fiorukis eyed his son cautiously.

'You would be a fool not to listen and I know you're not a fool,' his father said carefully. 'Whatever else he may be, Dimitrios Philipos is still a Greek. He pays you a compliment by offering to meet.'

'The day Dimitrios Philipos pays me a compliment is the day I reach for a weapon,' Sebastien drawled lazily, his gaze lingering on his father's face, registering the lines of worry and the dark shadows.

Suddenly he realized that his father had aged. That the strain of the ongoing feud had been too much for him.

'I have agreed to the meeting on your behalf—' His father looked at him wearily and Sebastien gritted his teeth and vowed that, whatever it took, he would end this feud once and for all, even if he had to take Philipos down with his bare hands.

'Good.' His tone was curt. 'It's time to end this. Tell me what he's offering.'

'He's returning your birthright. He's handing over his company.' His father gave a harsh laugh and dropped the papers on to the table. 'Or should I say ''our company'' since that is how it started out before Philipos defrauded your grandfather?'

Philipos was offering back the company? Sebastien hid his shock, his dark eyes veiled as he watched his father. *It couldn't be that easy.* 'And in return?'

His father's gaze slid from his. 'You marry his grand-daughter.'

'You're joking!' Stunning dark eyes alight with incredulity and more than a trace of amusement, Sebastien stared at his father in disbelief. 'What century are we in?'

Without meeting his gaze, his father shuffled the papers in front of him. 'Unfortunately those are his terms.'

Sebastien stilled. 'You're *not* joking.' The humour faded from his tone and suddenly his voice was lethally soft. 'In which case you ought to know that I can't think of anyone who would be less appealing as a potential consort than a blood relative of Philipos.'

His father lifted a hand and rubbed the back of his neck to relieve the tension. 'You are thirty-four, Sebastien. At some point you have to marry someone. Unless you wish to spend your life alone and childless.'

'I want children,' Sebastien said flatly, 'very much. It's the wife that gives me a problem. Unfortunately I require certain qualities in a woman that don't appear to exist.'

He thought about the extremely beautiful gymnast he'd spent the last few evenings with. And before that the dancer. None of them held his attention for more than a few weeks at a time.

'Well, if you can't marry for love, then why not for sound business reasons?' his father said gruffly. 'If you marry the girl, the company is ours.'

Sebastien's mind was racing at speed. 'That's it?' His eyes narrowed. 'It can't be that simple.'

His father relaxed slightly, his expression suddenly hopeful. 'He's an old man. The company is in trouble. There are few men skilled enough to sort out the problems and Philipos knows that you are one of them. Even he acknowledges that you are a brilliant businessman. By insisting on the marriage he ensures that his granddaughter will be financially secure in the event that the company folds. And it won't with you at the helm. It's a generous offer.'

'That's what concerns me,' Sebastien drawled softly. 'Dimitrios Philipos is not renowned for his generous offers.'

'He is offering a considerable inducement to marry the girl.'

'I'd need a considerable inducement to agree to marry a woman that I haven't ever laid eyes on,' Sebastien said tightly, his razor-sharp brain working quickly.

Why would Philipos be offering him the company?

And why would he want him to marry his granddaughter?

His father looked at him wearily. 'It's time to put aside suspicion and learn to trust. Philipos started that business with my father and then took it from him. He claims that he regrets the past and wants to put it right before he dies.'

Sebastien stilled, his mind racing ahead, asking one key question. *Why?* 'And you believe him?'

His father shrugged. 'Our lawyers are in possession of a draft agreement as we speak. What reason do I have not to believe him?'

'Perhaps because Dimitrios Philipos is an evil megalomaniac who only ever acts in his own interests,' Sebastien said caustically, wrenching the silk tie away from his neck and dropping it over the nearest chair. He felt the tension rise inside him. Suddenly the stakes were high and he felt the familiar rush of adrenalin. The higher the stakes the more satisfaction was to be gained by playing. 'Do I really need to remind you of his sins towards our family?'

'He's an old man. Perhaps he's repenting.'

Sebastien threw back his head and laughed but his dark eyes glittered dangerously. 'Repent? The old bastard wouldn't know the meaning of the word. I'm almost tempted to go along with the idea just to see what game he's playing this time.' Sebastien undid the top two buttons of his shirt and gestured to one of his discreetly hovering staff to bring drinks. The heat in Athens in July was punishing. 'So why can't the granddaughter find her own husband? Philipos certainly keeps her existence quiet. No one ever sees or hears of her. Is she just ugly or does she have some vile disease that would be passed on to my offspring?'

'They would be her offspring too,' his father pointed out, 'and you haven't managed to find a wife.'

'I haven't been looking for a wife,' Sebastien said silkily, 'and I certainly don't need one hand-picked by my greatest enemy.'

The thought almost had him laughing. There was little

doubt in his mind that the Philipos heiress must have some *very* unfortunate traits or she would have been married long before now.

'I'm sure she's a lovely girl,' his father muttered and Sebastien lifted a dark eyebrow in mockery.

'On the contrary, I am expecting her to have two heads and no personality. If she *were* lovely then Philipos wouldn't hide her away and the press would have tracked her the way they track me. She is, after all, an extremely wealthy young woman.'

'The press track you because you give them plenty to write about,' his father said dryly, 'whereas the Philipos heiress has been in England.'

'And England has the most intrusive tabloid press of all,' Sebastien murmured, a frown touching his handsome features. 'Which makes the situation even more interesting. If they have left her alone then she undoubtedly has two heads and no personality.'

His father sighed in exasperation. 'Evidently she leads a discreet life. Unlike you. The girl went to an English boarding school. Her mother was English, if you remember.'

'Of course I remember.' Sebastien drained his glass, vivid memories clouding his brain. 'I also remember that she was killed when our boat exploded. Along with her husband, who was Dimitrios Philipos's only son.' Memories flickered across his brain… *A child, limp and lifeless in his arms as he dragged her to the surface of the water; chaos, blood, people screaming…* Sebastien gritted his teeth. 'She lost both her parents and Philipos blames us for their deaths. And now he wants me to marry his granddaughter?' He lifted an eyebrow, his expression sardonic. 'Given her genealogy, I will have to sleep with a dagger under my pillow. I'm amazed that you accept the suggestion with such equanimity.'

'We too lost family in that explosion,' his father said

heavily. 'And time has passed. Enough time. He's an old man.'

'He's an evil man.'

'We were not responsible for his son's death. Perhaps time has given him the opportunity to reflect and he realizes that now.' Leandros ran his fingers over his brow, visibly disturbed by the memories of that terrible time. 'He wants her to have a Greek husband. He wants his line rebuilt.'

Sebastien narrowed his eyes and wondered when his father had grown so soft. If Philipos wanted his half-English granddaughter to have a Greek husband then there was undoubtedly a reason. *And he intended to discover that reason.*

'What about the girl? Why would she agree to such a marriage? She is the granddaughter of Dimitrios Philipos. As such she is unlikely to be possessed of the emotional stability I would want in a wife.'

'At least meet her.' His father tried a different approach. 'You can always say no.'

Sebastien surveyed him thoughtfully. It was true that he wanted children. And he'd always wanted to restore Philipos Industries to his family, where it belonged.

'What is in it for her?' His voice was sharp. 'Philipos gets his grandchild, I gain a son and a company that is rightfully ours—what does she gain?'

His father hesitated and shuffled the papers in front of him. 'Sebastien—'

Sebastien inhaled sharply. '*Tell* me.'

His father glanced at him warily. 'On the day of your wedding you are to pay money into her personal account.' He shifted awkwardly as he studied the papers again. 'A substantial sum. That sum is to be repeated every month during your marriage.'

There was a long silence. Then Sebastien gave a disbelieving laugh. 'Are you seriously telling me that the Philipos heiress wants *money* for marrying me?'

'The financial settlement is an important part of the deal.'

'The woman is already richer than Midas himself,' Sebastien launched, his volatile Mediterranean temperament rising to the surface with the force of an erupting volcano. 'And yet she wants *more*?'

His father cleared his throat. 'The terms of the deal are very clear. She receives money.'

Sebastien strode to the edge of the terrace and stared down across the city he loved so deeply.

'Sebastien—'

He turned quickly, the expression in his dark eyes cynical and hard. 'Why do I even hesitate?' He shrugged broad shoulders in a dismissive gesture. 'All women are gold-diggers, the fact that this one chooses to dig deeper than most changes nothing. At least she is honest about it, which is to her credit. As you rightly say, this is a business arrangement where both parties understand the score.'

'You make her sound hard and money-grabbing but why not reserve judgement?' his father urged. He looked at his son helplessly. 'Any relative of Philipos is going to be accustomed to an extremely extravagant lifestyle. Her requirement for funds may not be a reflection on her character. She might be sweet.'

Sebastien winced and refrained from pointing out that his taste didn't run to 'sweet' girls. 'Sweet girls don't demand huge sums of money from prospective husbands. And if she's a Philipos then she will have horns and a tail,' he said drily. 'And I'll do well to remember not to turn my back on her.'

'Sebastien—'

'Like you, I want the business restored to the family, so I'll see her because I'm intrigued. But I'm making no promises,' Sebastien warned grimly, depositing his empty glass on the table. 'If she's to be the mother of my children then I at least have to be able to stomach the sight of her.'

* * *

'You are not to speak.' Dimitrios Philipos glared at Alesia as the helicopter hovered over the landing pad. 'And you are to keep those flashing eyes of yours fixed on the ground. You are to be meek and obedient like a good Greek girl. If you keep your mouth shut until the wedding takes place, everything will be fine. By then it will be too late for Fiorukis to change his mind.'

At that precise moment Alesia was more concerned with her own state of mind than that of her prospective groom.

Why did they have to visit him on his private island? What was wrong with the mainland?

Satisfying herself that the helicopter was safely down, Alesia relaxed her death grip on her seat and forced herself to draw some much-needed oxygen into her starving lungs. Even the supposed safety of the helicopter hadn't distracted her from the vast expanse of azure-blue ocean beneath them. She was terrified of the water and always had been. And she still couldn't believe that she'd actually agreed to this meeting.

Suddenly she felt terrified. Terrified that her hatred of her grandfather would show along with her contempt for the entire Fiorukis family. 'What if he knows that I can't have children?'

If her grandfather had discovered that the childhood accident had left her unable to bear children, then how did she know that Sebastien Fiorukis hadn't discovered the same thing?

'He doesn't know. Until recently he didn't even know of your existence. He will never know until you are safely married and he discovers that you are unable to provide him with a son.' Dimitrios Philipos gave a nasty smile and Alesia flinched.

This was all wrong.

She shouldn't be doing this.

And then she remembered the money. She *had* to have

that money. She would do anything for that money. And anyway, was what she was doing really so bad? If Sebastien Fiorukis was a gentle, decent man then it would have been different and her strong sense of right and wrong would never have allowed her to go ahead with a wedding, knowing what she knew. But he wasn't like that.

The whole Fiorukis family was every bit as corrupt as her grandfather and Sebastien was at the helm. From what she'd heard, he was Greek to the very core. He was utterly without conscience and as cold and ruthless as her grandfather. Judging from his total lack of interest in commitment, he'd never had any great desire to become a father. Undoubtedly he would be a terrible father. To give a man like that an innocent child would be wrong. Perhaps it would be a good thing for everyone if both lines ended, she thought grimly. Philipos and Fiorukis. At least the feud would be buried with them.

And both men owed her. Between them they were responsible for the accident that had wrecked her family. It was time for them to pay.

On the day of the wedding, Fiorukis would transfer a lump sum into her account and continue to do so for the remainder of their marriage. Which meant that her mother could have the operation she so desperately needed. No more worries, no more holding down three jobs and worrying that the money wouldn't stretch.

As long as Fiorukis didn't discover that her mother was still alive.

Alesia bit her lip. If he found *that* out then it wouldn't take a man of his intelligence two minutes to realize that her grandfather had no love for her whatsoever and that this entire deal was suspicious.

She paused in the doorway of the helicopter and gave a soft gasp as the heat thumped into her. It was on the tip of her tongue to ask her grandfather how, if she was truly half

Greek, she found the heat so intolerable but she held the words back. Over the past few days she'd learned that the best way of dealing with her grandfather was to stay silent.

'Don't forget.' Her grandfather jerked her back roughly and glared at her. 'You are now a Philipos.'

Alesia hid her distaste. 'You refused to let my mother use that name,' she said thickly, 'but now, when it suits you, you expect *me* to use it.'

'Fiorukis is to marry you because you're a Philipos,' he reminded her with an evil smile. 'If he knew you were a nobody he wouldn't touch you with a bargepole. And stop tugging at that dress.'

Alesia gritted her teeth and released her grip on the hemline. 'It is positively indecent. It barely covers anything.'

'Precisely.' Her grandfather glanced over her and gave a satisfied grunt. 'A man likes to know what he's buying. Remember everything I said. Fiorukis has a brain as sharp as the business end of a razor but he's still a red-blooded Greek. One look at you in that and he won't be thinking business, I can assure you. You wear the dress as if you dress like that every day. You do not mention the existence of your mother. You do not say *why* you want the money.'

'He'll want to know why I'm marrying him,' Alesia said defiantly and her grandfather gave an unpleasant smile.

'Sebastien Fiorukis has an ego as large as Greece. And for some unfathomable reason women can't seem to leave him alone. Probably because he's rich and good-looking and women are usually too stupid to resist that combination.' Her grandfather gave a snort of derision. 'He'll assume you're just another in a long line of admirers who want access to his millions.'

Alesia shuddered. The man must be arrogant beyond belief. To be considered so brainless and shallow as to judge a man by his looks and his wallet seemed to her the ultimate insult. 'I don't think—'

'Good!' Her grandfather glared at her as he interrupted her stammered protest. 'I don't want you to think. And neither does he. You are not required to think. You are merely required to lie down for him whenever he pleases. And if he asks you, then you desire this marriage simply because Sebastien Fiorukis is one of the most eligible bachelors in the world and you are keen to rediscover your Greek roots. And try not to flash those eyes at him. A Greek man does not like confrontation in the marriage bed.'

Marriage bed?

Alesia felt her stomach lurch. Somehow she'd managed to avoid thinking about the deeper implications of this marriage. That they would have to become physically intimate. But then she remembered everything she'd read about Sebastien Fiorukis. If reports were correct, then he had at least three mistresses on the go at once. Given his complete lack of interest in commitment, he was hardly likely to weld himself to her bed, was he? He'd be a wandering husband and that suited her perfectly. As long as he deposited the right amount of money in her account every month, she'd be more than happy never to lay eyes on the man.

She swayed slightly and, if it hadn't been for her grandfather urging her forward down the steps, she would have backed into the helicopter and begged the pilot to take them back to the mainland.

As it was she was forced to take those few steps on to the Tarmac, forced to blink in the dazzling sunlight, dimly aware of a powerful figure watching her from a safe distance.

The situation suddenly overwhelmed her and she would have paused again had her grandfather not pushed her hard. Unprepared for the unexpected force of that push and unused to wearing such ridiculously high heels, she would have lost her balance had strong arms not reached out and steadied her.

Shocked and embarrassed, Alesia gasped out her thanks,

her fingers curling into rock-hard biceps as she tried to regain her balance. A dark male face swam in front of her and for a brief moment she collided with night-black eyes. A strange sensation curled deep in her pelvis and she felt the colour seep into her cheeks.

'Miss Philipos?'

It took a moment for Alesia to realize that he was addressing her because the name was so unfamiliar.

'Stand up, girl!' Her grandfather's impatient tones cut through her thoughts. 'A man can't stand a woman who clings. And for goodness' sake speak when you're spoken to! What was the point of that expensive education if you can't even string a sentence together?'

Her face hot with embarrassment and humiliation, Alesia regained her balance and cast an agonized glance at her rescuer. 'I'm sorry, I—'

'No apology is needed.' Sebastien spoke in cool, measured tones but the expression in his eyes as he studied her grandfather made her shiver.

These two men were sworn enemies—

'Clumsy—' Her grandfather shot her an impatient look and then turned to his host. 'Believe it or not, my granddaughter can walk when she applies her mind to the task. But like most women she's empty-headed.'

Alesia dipped her head rather than risk displaying the flash of anger that she knew must be visible in her eyes. Only by focusing on thoughts of her beloved mother did she prevent herself from stalking back to the helicopter and demanding return passage to the mainland.

She had to forget how much she hated her grandfather.

She had to forget how much she loathed the whole Fiorukis family.

She had to forget all of it.

The only thing that mattered was getting Sebastien Fiorukis to marry her.

No matter what happened, she would save her mother.

CHAPTER TWO

SHE was stunning.

Sebastien watched the silken blonde hair fall forward, obscuring her features, but not before he'd caught a glimpse of eyes the colour of violets in a perfect heart-shaped face. His gaze fixed on her smooth, creamy skin and then drifted down to her lush pink mouth. Her face alone was amazing, but combined with the body…

His eyes drifted lower. *Obvious*, he thought to himself scathingly, as he scanned the obscenely short dress that revealed tantalizingly long legs and fabulously generous breasts. Nothing was left to the imagination. Clearly the Philipos heiress had no reservations about displaying *exactly* what was on offer, he mused as his eyes settled on the temptingly full curves of her cleavage. But then she was selling herself for a ridiculously high price, he reminded himself cynically, so perhaps it was understandable that she felt he should be able to view the goods.

And view them he did.

Lust, basic and primitive, slammed through him, astonishing him by its very force. He was a man who had been fed a diet of beautiful women since he was a teenager and these days it took a lot to hold his attention.

But this girl was *definitely* holding his attention…

Suddenly the deal on the table before him took on new dimensions. Whatever Dimitrios Philipos had in mind, marrying his granddaughter could hardly be considered a hardship. Whatever else might be wrong with her, she certainly wasn't ugly and he *certainly* wouldn't have a problem being confined to bed with her on the occasions when it suited him.

25

Accustomed to being on the receiving end of non-stop female admiration and flirtation and confident of her response to him, Sebastien relaxed and waited for her to notice him in the way he'd *definitely* been noticing her.

It came as a considerable surprise to realize that she didn't seem remotely interested in his opinion of her attributes. Instead she stared at the ground, her chest rising and falling, her slim fingers digging hard into her palms, her knuckles white.

Scared?

Angry?

Sebastien attempted to read the body language and his speculative gaze slid to her grandfather, searching for answers. His body stilled as he caught the ugly expression on the older man's face. *The man was a bully and a thug.* And in this case the object of his aggression was undoubtedly the girl. Struggling with a base instinct that erupted from nowhere and surprised him with its intensity, Sebastien ruthlessly subdued the impulse to violently floor the man.

Was he forcing her into this marriage?

Experienced enough to know that women were complex creatures at the best of times, Sebastien decided to reserve judgement. He already knew that she'd inherited her grandfather's obscene thirst for wealth—why else would she be demanding such ridiculous sums from him on a monthly basis when she was already in possession of an indecent fortune?

And he couldn't even blame that aspect of the deal on her grandfather because she was to be the only recipient. Apparently her grandfather stood to gain nothing financially from a merger between their two families except a longed-for grandchild.

Torn between irritation with his father for creating this situation and fascination with the mind of his enemy, Sebastien tried to open a dialogue between them.

'Your journey was good, Miss Philipos?'

She displayed not a flicker of a response. It was as if she hadn't recognized her own name, he thought grimly, contemplating her complete lack of reaction with a deepening frown. Perhaps she preferred informality. 'Alesia?'

Immediately her eyes flew to his, astonishment lighting the blue depths, as if she were surprised that he was addressing her. 'Yes?'

Finally he had her attention. 'I asked whether your journey was good.' He dealt her a smile that never failed to gain female attention but she missed it because her gaze had returned to a point somewhere near his feet.

Sebastien hid his frustration. It was as if she couldn't bear to look at him. She was a complete contradiction. Her dress shrieked attention-seeking and yet her body language said something entirely different.

'It was fine, thank you.' She kept her eyes fixed firmly on the Tarmac and he noticed that her breathing was rapid, as if she was under immense strain.

Deciding that his first priority was to remove her from the presence of her grandfather, Sebastien took control. 'Walk with me while the lawyers argue the details. There are things we need to talk about.'

Immediately on the defensive, Dimitrios Philipos hunched his shoulders aggressively and stepped forward. 'She stays with me.'

Not budging an inch, Sebastien arched a dark eyebrow expressively. 'Is this proposed marriage to take place between three people or two?' His tone was dangerously soft. 'Are you intending to be present on our wedding night?'

He heard a soft gasp of shock from the girl standing by his side but ignored her, all his attention focused on the grandfather whose stance was now blatantly confrontational.

'If you knew my reputation you wouldn't choose to pick a fight with me, Fiorukis.'

Undeterred by his threatening tone, Sebastien gave a cool smile, ignoring his father's warning glance. 'I've never been afraid of a fight. And if you knew *my* reputation, you'd know that I choose to conduct my personal relationships in private. I've never been into groups.'

At that less than subtle reference to his own sordid reputation, Dimitrios Philipos glared at his rival for a long moment and then gave a grunt. 'Very well.' He gave a brief nod of assent, his expression grim. 'She might as well see her new home.'

Given that the deal was yet to be signed by either party, the statement was decidedly premature but Sebastien's natural instinct to deny such an assumption was stifled by a gasp of horror from the girl in question.

'My new home?' She glanced around her with naked alarm, suddenly roused from silence by her grandfather's statement. 'This would be our home? You'd want me to live *here*?'

Dragging his eyes from her slim legs, Sebastien gritted his teeth, barely able to hide his impatience.

Familiar with women who lived to shop, he rarely if ever brought his female companions to his island, accustomed to that very reaction from other members of her sex. It would seem that his prospective bride was no different. But, given the size of the financial deal her grandfather had negotiated on her behalf, that shouldn't have come as a surprise. What would a woman do with such an exorbitant sum if she didn't have access to a significant number of designer boutiques?

Sebastien narrowed his eyes, something about the whole situation jarring uncomfortably in his sharp brain.

His innate business sense warned him that this deal didn't feel quite right and he mentally shifted through different angles, seeking answers to the questions stacking up in his mind. And the main question was: *What did the Philipos heiress stand to gain from a union with a Fiorukis?*

Why would the granddaughter of the richest man on the planet need to marry him for money? Still pondering that question, Sebastien studied Dimitrios Philipos and caught the cold, avaricious gleam in the older man's eyes. Remembering his reputation for being the ultimate miser, Sebastien decided that he probably restricted her spending, which was why she was looking for other sources of income. He'd known loads of women who made a career out of marrying rich men. If granddaddy was no longer a soft touch then she'd need to look for some other sucker to pick up her bills. And, judging from her horrified reaction to the idea of being sequestered on an island without a boutique in sight, those bills were going to be *big*.

A flicker of contempt shot through him but he dismissed it with almost bored indifference. So she was greedy. He gave a mental shrug. That didn't come as a surprise.

Reminding himself that her motives had never been in question, he hid his distaste. 'I also have houses in Athens, Paris and New York,' he drawled lazily, 'so if you're concerned about the opportunity to exercise my credit card, then you can relax.'

Her eyes were fixed on the sea and she seemed not to have heard him.

Sebastien suppressed his irritation. Clearly he had been right in his assessment that she would have no personality. Even though he'd invariably thought that women generally talked *far* too much about very little of interest, he was finding the reverse considerably less satisfying than he would have imagined. Why on earth didn't the woman say something? Unaccustomed to such a lack of interest Sebastien decided that the sooner he got her on her own, the better.

'You don't like the island?' His tone was conversational and she shot him an agonized glance.

'There's lots of sea.'

That was most definitely *not* the answer he'd expected.

'There generally is when you live on an island. All the bed-rooms in my villa open on to the beach or the pool.'

If he'd expected an enthusiastic response to that announce-ment then he was again disappointed. Instead of the delight he'd anticipated, her face seemed to pale dramatically.

Sebastien frowned. Was there something wrong with her?

'My granddaughter feels sick after the journey,' her grand-father grunted and Sebastien felt another surge of irritation with the older man.

Did he never let the girl speak for herself?

And surely if she'd been brought up in England she was used to expressing her own opinions?

Aware that the deal could not be concluded without his signature on the document, Sebastien focused on the girl. 'I will take Miss Philipos and show her the island while you two begin the meeting—I'll join you shortly.'

Dimitrios Philipos glanced at his watch. 'I have to be back in Athens in two hours. I want the deal signed before I leave.'

Sebastien watched him closely. The older man was defi-nitely up to something. *Why the hurry?*

He was nothing like she'd expected.

Alesia stared in frozen silence at the man standing in front of her, her gaze resting on the width of his shoulders before lifting to his cool black eyes. Bold brows framed night-dark eyes and his strong nose accentuated the perfect symmetry of his staggeringly handsome face.

She'd been bred to hate this man.

In vain she searched for some evidence that he was as unsettled by this bizarre, awkward situation as she was but she found none. She sensed without even speaking to him that he was a man who would never find himself discomfited by any situation. Instead he studied her through narrowed eyes, the expression on his sinfully masculine face revealing nothing of his inner thoughts. He wore authority with the ease of a man who'd been born with a ferocious talent at business and had proceeded to exercise it at every opportunity.

Alesia looked at him helplessly.

How could this ever work out?

Ludicrously rich and breathtakingly good-looking, he was *totally*, totally out of her league and it was utterly mortifying to know that if her grandfather hadn't offered him a significant 'inducement' and dressed her in such a ridiculous dress he wouldn't have looked twice in her direction.

She felt like a total fraud.

Alesia bit back a burst of hysterical laughter. What would he do if he knew that she lived in a tiny damp flat? That she held down three jobs in an attempt to make ends meet? *That the dress she was wearing was the only one she had and even that was on loan?*

The thought of being alone with this man quite simply terrified her. What on earth would they talk about? What did they have in common?

Nothing.

And, to make matters worse, he clearly loved the sea.

Alesia kept her eyes fixed on the ocean and for a moment it all came rushing back. The sudden force of the explosion, the horrified screams of the injured and the sudden plunge into freezing water which buried her in a darkness so frightening that the memories still kept her awake at night. And then there were the memories of a man, dark-haired and strong, lifting her. Saving her—

Suddenly the price of saving her mother seemed almost too high.

She would have to live here, on an island, surrounded by sea that terrified her, living with a man she despised.

She gave herself a mental shake and dragged her gaze away from the water. She didn't have to swim or even to paddle, she reminded herself firmly. All she needed to do was remember the reason she was here. To play the part she'd schooled herself to play.

And she knew *exactly* why her grandfather had given the Fiorukis family a deadline of two hours to complete the deal. He was afraid that, left on her own with the man, she'd blow it. That she'd do something to put Sebastien Fiorukis off marrying her.

And he was right. She was so different from his usual choice of woman that the comparison was laughable. She couldn't even do a decent job of walking in the shoes.

'As far as I'm aware there is no language barrier between us,' he said smoothly, his dark gaze resting on her face with a significant degree of speculation, 'and yet so far you have uttered barely a word and cast barely a glance in my direction.'

Clearly she'd dented his monumental ego.

Alesia stifled a cynical laugh. *Was that all he cared about?* That she hadn't gazed into his eyes and fallen for him like the other brainless women he mixed with? He was *unbelievably* shallow and, as far as she was concerned, Sebastien Fiorukis deserved everything that was coming to him.

'You must forgive me—' her voice sounded stilted '—I—I'm finding this situation rather difficult—'

'Me, too. And that's hardly surprising given the circumstances. It's not every day you are expected to agree to a marriage to someone you have only just met. But this proposed marriage between us is going to be somewhat heavy weather if you can't bring yourself to speak to me,' he drawled lightly, and she met his gaze full-on.

'Am I supposed to speak honestly?'

'Why else did I just get rid of your grandfather?'

She almost smiled at the reminder of how neatly he'd dismissed her relative. Whatever else he might be, Sebastien Fiorukis was evidently *not* a coward. In fact he was the first person she'd met who didn't seem remotely intimidated by her grandfather, which was at least something in his favour. But nevertheless she was agonizingly aware that one wrong word from her could blow the whole deal.

'My grandfather is afraid that I'll say the wrong thing. He wants this deal very badly.'

'And you, Miss Philipos?' There was something dangerously soothing about his voice. Like a lethal predator stalking his prey. 'How badly do you want this deal?'

Being called 'Miss Philipos' felt totally alien. It was as if he was addressing a stranger. But it was all part of this act she was expected to maintain.

She lifted her chin. 'I want to marry you, if that's what you're asking.'

That at least was true. She *did* want to marry him. It would solve all her problems.

And all her mother's problems.

There was a sardonic gleam in his dark eyes as he watched her carefully. 'Don't tell me—' his voice was a deep, dark drawl '—you have been madly in love with me for your whole life? You have dreamed of this moment from your cradle, perhaps?'

She'd dreamed of having access to enough money to finally help her mother.

'I'm not in love with you, Mr Fiorukis, any more than you are in love with me,' she said calmly, 'and we both know that love is not the only reason for marriage.'

His spectacular eyes narrowed. 'Nevertheless, since we are the two people who will be forced to live together as a result of this deal, I think it's important to discover whether we can at least tolerate each other's company, don't you?' He gestured towards a narrow path that led down to the beach. 'Let's walk.'

She followed his gaze. The sea stretched into the distance like a cruel, forbidding monster, mocking her. The breath jammed in her throat and the panic rose.

'Can't we just stand here?'

'You wish to conduct a conversation on my helicopter pad?' His dark drawl dripped sarcasm and she flushed, still struggling as cold fingers of panic threatened to drag her down into darkness.

'I just don't see why we need to walk down to the sea.' This was close enough. *Too close.*

He glanced at her with barely concealed irritation. 'I refuse to conduct a conversation with your bodyguards hovering in the background.'

Her *bodyguards*?

Alesia glanced over her shoulder. She hadn't even *noticed* the three burly men until this moment, even though they must have been on the helicopter. She'd been too busy concentrating on not looking at the ocean. 'Oh—they work for my grandfather.'

'You don't need to explain. As the Philipos heiress you are entitled to protection.'

Momentarily forgetting her concerns about the sea and her shoes, Alesia almost laughed aloud. Protection from what? Who would be interested in a penniless, gawky student who spent every waking hour working herself to the bone? But clearly he knew nothing of her real life. Glancing around her, she noticed two other men hovering close by. 'Who are they?'

His smile mocked her. 'I'm afraid my own security team is naturally suspicious. Let's just say that a Philipos landing on the island creates a certain level of tension.'

She glanced briefly at his powerful shoulders and wondered why he needed a security team. He looked capable of taking on an entire army single-handed should the need arise. For a man who spent his days involved in business, he was supremely fit and athletic. Perhaps it was the hours he spent in bed with women, she mused idly, stepping to one side to avoid a dip in the path.

'My grandfather creates tension wherever he goes.' She spoke without thinking and then remembered too late who she was talking to and coloured. 'I mean to say—'

'Don't feel you have to excuse yourself to me,' he drawled softly. 'Grown men shiver in their shoes when your grandfather enters a room. It is part of the reputation he has built for himself. He manages by fear.'

But didn't Sebastien have the same reputation?

Wasn't she about to marry a man *exactly* like her grandfather?

Looking at the hovering bodyguards, she gave a shiver and made a decision. 'All right, let's walk on the beach.' She stooped to remove the shoes her grandfather had insisted she wear. 'Three-inch heels and sand don't go together.'

She saw the brief flash of astonishment in his beautiful dark eyes and realized her mistake immediately. Doubtless the women that he dated would be capable of climbing Everest in stilettos if the need arose.

'I like to feel the sand between my toes,' she improvised quickly, cursing her stupidity and making a mental note to take a crash course in suitable footwear as a matter of urgency.

'Be careful not to cut your feet on the rocks,' he said smoothly, reaching out a hand and taking hers in a strong grasp. Long fingers curled over hers and she felt an almost irresistible urge to drag her hand away. 'Those shoes are stunning and do amazing things for your legs. But on reflection I agree that they're probably better suited to a nightclub. I have several favourites so I can promise you that you'll have ample opportunity to wear them in a more suitable setting.'

Nightclubs?

Alesia glanced at him blankly, realising with no small degree of consternation that he clearly believed her to be a real party-girl. What would he say if she confessed that she'd never actually been to a nightclub in her life? That her demanding working pattern ensured that she rarely if ever had an evening off to enjoy such indulgences?

Quickly she steered the conversation away from such dangerous subjects. 'So, if you don't trust my grandfather, why did you invite him to your island—?'

They had negotiated the rock successfully and yet strong fingers still held her securely. 'This deal is important to me for many reasons.' He glanced at her thoughtfully. 'You are surely not pretending to know nothing about the feud that exists between our families?'

Her breathing quickened and she snatched her hand away. 'Of course I'm aware of the feud—'

My father was killed on your father's boat; my mother and I were both injured.

Emotion rose inside her until she could hardly breathe. *Until it threatened to choke her.* She felt him watching her and struggled for control.

Alesia turned away in distaste, still clutching her shoes in her hand. Only the most rigid self-discipline allowed her to continue the conversation with this man.

'I think before we go any further you should know that, despite the fact that my grandfather would want me to, I don't play games. I can't pretend something I don't feel,' she said coldly. 'I don't flirt and I refuse to pretend that this marriage is anything other than a business arrangement between two parties. We each get something we want.'

'And what exactly is that, Miss Philipos?'

'Money,' she said succinctly, lifting her chin and looking him in the eye. 'I get money.'

'Straight to the point. You are the only living relative of the richest man on the planet and yet still you want more,' Sebastien drawled, his gaze suddenly speculative, 'which probably makes you the biggest gold-digger in history. Tell me, Alesia—' he said her name with mocking emphasis '—just how much money is enough?'

By now they were standing on a stretch of perfect golden sand. Alesia concentrated on the man next to her, keeping her back to the azure-blue sea which sparkled and shone in the intense heat of the Greek summer sun. To her it represented nothing but terror.

'Given your own wealth, I could ask you the same question. You already have a company that nets you billions and still you want what belongs to my grandfather.'

'That's right, I do.' His smile was sardonic. 'But I'm not going to *quite* the lengths that you are to achieve that goal. For money you are prepared to tie yourself to your greatest enemy. A man that you clearly hate—'

A sudden attack of panic assailed her. She'd revealed too much. *He mustn't back out of the deal.* 'I didn't say that—'

'You didn't need to,' he said drily. 'It is apparent from every flash of your eyes, from the way you hold yourself and from all the things that you *don't* say, that you hate me with every bone in your body.'

Alesia could barely breathe as she cursed her stupidity.

Her grandfather had warned her that the man was clever and she'd ignored him. Had dismissed everything he'd said as yet another part of his plan. But in this case he was right. Sebastien Fiorukis *was* clever.

He was clever, dangerous and every bit a match for her grandfather.

'I don't hate you,' she lied hastily and he lifted a winged brow.

'I should warn you that I am a man who prefers honesty,' he said softly, 'even when it is distasteful. You've just admitted that you're prepared to marry a man that you hate for money. Now, what sort of person does that make you, I wonder?'

She almost choked with outrage. He made her sound

dreadful. If only he knew why she wanted the money, he might not be so swift to judge her.

She stared him in the eye. 'Let's just say that I'm more than satisfied with the financial arrangements that are to be a part of this contract.'

The accusation was so false, *so far from reality*, that for a wild, uncontrolled moment she almost blurted out the truth. But to confess the truth would be to blow the whole deal. And she needed this deal for her mother. What did it matter what he thought of her? What did it matter if he thought she was a money-grabbing gold-digger? If he discovered her grandfather's shoddy treatment of both her and her mother then he would *never* believe that her grandfather wanted this deal for her benefit. He'd realize that her grandfather was so far from being the 'family man' that he was pretending to be that something more sinister was afoot.

He'd sense that her grandfather was after revenge.

'Well, you're prepared to marry the granddaughter of your greatest enemy just to get his company. And you already have your own company that makes you *billions*. So what sort of a person does that make *you*?'

'Rich enough to afford you,' he responded in cool tones, his eyes hard as they scanned her pale face. 'Your opinion of me is as low as mine is of you, which should make us extremely well-matched. It will be a pleasant change not to have to charm a woman when I come home tired from a day in the office. I think marriage may suit me after all.'

'You wouldn't be able to charm me if you tried,' she said stiffly, made *furious* by his overwhelming arrogance. 'And, just for the record, I'm not remotely interested in experiencing your *superior* bedroom technique. That isn't what this marriage is about.'

'Is that so?' He smiled and stepped closer to her and suddenly she was aware of nothing but heat and she wondered how on *earth* she was going to be able to stand living in

Greece. The atmosphere was so still and oppressive that she could barely draw breath. Her skin tingled and buzzed and she felt *strange*.

'This is a business arrangement,' she reminded him coldly, and his dark eyes gleamed.

'A business arrangement—' He repeated her words thoughtfully, his eyes fixed on her face as he studied her every reaction. 'Tell me—do you know how babies are made, Miss Philipos?'

The temperature of the air surrounding her seemed to increase dramatically.

Colour flared in her cheeks and her toes dug into the sand. 'What sort of a question is that?'

'A sensible one,' he replied smoothly, 'given that the production of a baby is generally preceded by sexual activity, with or without "*superior bedroom technique*". Tell me, does your "business arrangement" include sexual activity, Miss Philipos?'

Totally shocked by the lethal intimacy of his tone and the sudden shift in the focus of the discussion, her eyes widened and she gave a soft gasp.

'I—I don't—'

'No?' His tone hardened and his gaze was unsympathetic. 'And yet that is what this deal is all about. Tell me, Miss Philipos, just how exactly do you envisage this "business arrangement" taking place? Do you intend to bring your briefcase to my bed?'

She inhaled sharply as all sorts of uncomfortably blatant images assailed her brain.

Somehow she'd managed to convince herself that this whole thing could be a relatively straightforward arrangement. He could live his life. She could live hers. The issue of a sexual relationship had crossed her mind briefly, of course, but somehow the notion of sex with a man she'd never met had seemed abstract. Unreal.

But face to face there was nothing unreal about Sebastien Fiorukis. He was six foot two of full-on, sexual, adult male.

Suddenly the sex aspect of their agreement didn't seem quite so straightforward as she'd previously imagined it to be.

For a moment she forgot about the sea and her grandfather and focused on the appalling reality of sliding between the sheets with this hot-blooded volatile Greek.

'Not a briefcase.' Struggling to pull herself together, she answered his sardonic question as calmly as she could, ignoring the kick of her heart and the strange buzz in the pit of her stomach. 'But clearly there will be no emotional involvement between us. I will have sex with you because that is what the contract demands, but nowhere does it say that I am required to enjoy the experience.' She caught his incredulous gaze. 'And that's fine,' she added hastily, suddenly extremely anxious to reassure him that her enjoyment was *not* on his list of objectives.

'You'll "have sex" with me?' Sebastien stared at her in fascination, night-black eyes raking her face as he repeated her words.

Alesia closed her eyes. The problem was, he was used to women who expected to be seduced. She didn't. In fact she couldn't think of anything worse. She wasn't remotely interested in sex and never had been. Once she'd discovered that she'd never be able to have children, she'd buried that part of herself away. And it no longer mattered to her. The few kisses she'd experienced since reaching adolescence had proved to her that she just wasn't interested.

Realising that the situation was rapidly sliding out of control, she gave a frustrated sigh and tried one more time to make him see logic. 'Look—this isn't about you.' She tried clumsily to rescue his ego from any damage inflicted by her remark. 'This isn't personal. We just won't have that sort of marriage. And that's fine. I mean really—' she spread her hands in a nervous gesture, wondering how on earth this conversation had begun '—it's how I want it.'

He stirred, his gaze still fixed on her face. 'Clearly you have always had lousy sex.'

Hot colour flooded her cheeks and she looked away quickly, trying to regain some semblance of control.

Perhaps this was the point where she was supposed to tell him that she'd *never* had sex before but there was no way she was doing that! It was too embarrassing to have reached the grand old age of twenty-two and still be a virgin and she was totally confident that when the time came she could successfully hide her massive lack of experience in that department.

'So you're prepared to marry me and have "businesslike sex"—' his tone was dangerously casual '—and I pay you for the privilege. Interesting concept and one that I confess I'm unfamiliar with. I've never before found myself in a position where I had to pay for sex.'

'Of course you have.' She responded without thinking. 'Women hang round you hoping that you'll spend your billions on them and in return they fawn over you and pretend to find you attractive—if that's not paying for sex, I don't know what is. And in this case you're not paying for sex, you're paying for my grandfather's company.'

He looked totally stunned by this less than flattering interpretation of his love life and Alesia struggled not to roll her eyes in exasperation. His ego was positively monumental! He obviously thought that women wanted to be with him because he was completely irresistible. He was *so* sad!

'You're a rich man, Sebastien,' she said impatiently, using his given name as he had used hers. 'You can't be telling me that I'm the first woman to be interested in your money.'

His dark eyes narrowed and he finally found his voice. 'Let's just say that you're the first *seriously rich* woman to be interested in my money. Why would you need it so much, I wonder?'

If only he knew.

Alesia dangled the shoes under his nose, her gaze intentionally provocative. 'Perhaps I just have *enormous* spending powers.'

She almost laughed as she listened to herself. The truth was that she wouldn't have a clue how to spend money if she had it. Apart from her time at boarding school, she'd lived in virtual poverty for her entire life and economizing came as naturally to her as breathing. If she *was* pointed in the direction of a designer boutique, she'd probably just drop to her knees and start scrubbing the floor.

The dress she was wearing was the first new item of clothing she'd had for as long as she could remember and she only had that because her grandfather had taken one look at her ancient pair of faded jeans and almost burst a blood vessel. When she'd pointed out tartly that she didn't have the money for a dress, he'd barked out a series of orders to one of his staff and three dresses had duly been chosen. But even then she hadn't been given the option of selecting her favourite. Instead she'd been subjected to the humiliation of modelling all three in front of her grandfather, and had the added humiliation of being forced to wear the most revealing garment she'd ever laid eyes on.

'You need to show the man what he's getting,' he'd grunted when she'd protested that there was no way she could wear a dress that was that low-cut. 'Wear it or the deal is off.'

So she'd forced herself into the offending garment and tried not to show how utterly self-conscious she was to be wearing such a totally unsuitable dress. As far as she was concerned, the dress said one thing, *'Pull me',* and she had the sense to realize that, given her appearance, mentioning her virginity to Sebastien Fiorukis at this point would do nothing but engender laughter.

'I can see that my honesty offends you,' she said smoothly, lifting her chin to hide her discomfort, 'but perhaps I can remind you that you yourself are entering this marriage for sound business reasons. Why else would you agree to sacrifice your bachelor lifestyle for marriage?'

'Who said anything about sacrificing my bachelor lifestyle?' His firm mouth shifted slightly at the corners. 'It's only fair to warn you that I have an *exceedingly* high sex drive. Since our sex life is clearly going to be extremely tedious, then I'll need to seek diversion elsewhere. But I'm prepared to pay that price in order to regain possession of Philipos Industries. The company that your grandfather stole from my family.'

She frowned. 'I don't know what you're talking about. Philipos Industries belongs to my grandfather and always has.'

'Not true.' His gaze was hard. 'And if you expect me to believe that you don't know the history of our little family feud, Miss Philipos, then you seriously underestimate me. You wanted honesty, then let's have it.'

She swallowed hard. She didn't underestimate him. Not for a moment. She was just thrown by his unexpected announcement. 'Are you telling me that our grandparents were in business together?'

His eyes narrowed. 'Are you telling me that you weren't aware of that fact?'

She shook her head. 'My grandfather refuses to discuss business with a woman.' At least that wasn't a lie, she thought ruefully. Her grandfather despised women. Especially English women. It was the reason he'd disowned her mother and herself. He'd wanted nothing to do with either of them. 'I've heard rumours, of course, but nothing concrete.

Are you saying that he took the business from your grand-father?'

'It is how the feud began.' Sebastien looked at her, his dark gaze suddenly speculative. 'He lied and cheated until my grandfather was forced to sign the company over to him,' he bit out, his expression grim. 'So you see, Alesia, I want to marry you because I intend to reclaim what is rightfully mine. And the feud ends here.'

Alesia stared at him, for once totally mute.

What would he say when he discovered the truth? That the feud hadn't ended at all.

That her grandfather was about to strike a master blow.

And she was the tool of his revenge.

CHAPTER THREE

PALE-FACED and utterly miserable, Alesia sat shivering in her white silk wedding dress, feeling *nothing* like a bride.

Despite the gold band on her finger, part of her still couldn't believe that she'd actually gone through with the wedding.

Oblivious to the elaborate celebrations taking place around her, she stared blankly at her plate and tried to focus her mind.

She'd actually married Sebastien Fiorukis.

It seemed hard to believe that only two weeks had passed since their meeting on his private island. Since then everything had been a blur of frantic activity. Lawyers had worked overtime, papers had been signed and wedding planners had burned the midnight oil to put together the wedding of the decade.

To Alesia the ceremony had been a nightmare.

Why hadn't she anticipated the attention that such a high-profile wedding would attract? For the press, who were eternally fascinated by Sebastien Fiorukis, the fact that he'd finally chosen to marry the granddaughter of his greatest enemy had sent an explosion of excitement and speculation through the gossip-hungry media. Knowing that personal details of the handsome Greek billionaire sold newspapers, the press had been everywhere, flashes going off in her face and people yelling at her to smile and glance in their direction.

And of course the wedding attracted even more attention because of the presence of her notorious grandfather. Dimitrios Philipos so rarely appeared in public that his presence alone was enough to draw a crowd of fascinated onlookers. Everyone wanted to witness a public meeting between Fiorukis and Philipos. Everyone was anticipating fireworks.

Sebastien had handled the attention and simmering speculation with an air of almost bored disdain, ignoring reporters, greeting guests with just the right amount of attention and interest, as comfortable and confident as he'd been during that first awful meeting.

In contrast, Alesia had taken one horrified look at the jostling, over-excited paparazzi and kept her eyes firmly fixed on the ground in an attempt to blot out what was happening.

She didn't want people to be interested in her.

She knew that journalists had a way of digging up secrets. *What if they dug up hers?*

What if something happened to stop the wedding? To prevent her mother from having the operation she so badly needed?

Terrified that someone would say something to halt the ceremony, she'd stood at the front of the church like a frightened rabbit, hardly daring to breathe in case she drew attention to herself, *in case someone recognized her for the impostor that she was.*

She'd worn the long white wedding dress that her grandfather had presented her with, pulled the veil over her face and hoped that none of the guests would notice her wan face or the fact that she was *seriously* out of her depth. Playing the role of rich heiress was totally new to her.

When she realized that they were safely married the relief had been so great that she'd almost passed out.

Once or twice it had crossed her mind that this wasn't the way weddings were supposed to be, that this was supposed to be a happy day. But then she reminded herself firmly that she'd never been one to dream and fantasize about weddings, so it wasn't possible for her to be disappointed that hers hadn't lived up to expectation. She didn't have any expectation.

'You could try and look a little more like an excited bride and less like someone being led to torture,' Sebastien suggested silkily, snapping his fingers at the waiter and indicating that he should top up their glasses. 'This is, after all, what you wanted. You've landed yourself a billionaire. Smile.'

Alesia grabbed the glass gratefully and drank deeply, her loathing for Sebastien Fiorukis increasing by the minute. He was cold, unfeeling and just *horrid*. At least she was thoroughly uncomfortable with the situation but he just didn't seem to care that they didn't even like each other.

All right, so she *was* marrying him for the money, she conceded, but that was completely different because she was *desperate*. Unlike him. He was already a billionaire. He already had one company. Only someone who was impossibly greedy could want *two*!

Alesia shivered as she contemplated the man she'd married.

He was just like her grandfather. Rich, successful, restless and never satisfied.

Maybe champagne would help. She didn't normally drink but wasn't alcohol supposed to numb the senses? She sincerely hoped so. The way she was feeling, she needed her senses rendered unconscious. Returning the empty glass to the table, she sucked several breaths into her lungs and tried hard to forget that everyone was watching her. Speculating. Why hadn't someone warned her that Sebastien had such a large family? And so many friends—

'I wasn't expecting all this—'

'It's called a wedding,' Sebastien said helpfully, smiling briefly at a stunning woman who cast a longing glance towards him as she slid past on the arm of a male guest, 'and it's what you signed up for when you agreed to marry me for my money. Enjoy it. It's costing enough. Look on it as retail therapy.'

Money.

Grateful for the reminder, Alesia took another slug of champagne and forced herself to focus. All she had to do was remember the money. The reason she was doing this. It didn't matter that everyone was staring at her. It didn't matter that everyone was wondering why Sebastien Fiorukis had chosen to marry her. *It didn't matter that she felt lonelier than she had in her whole life.* All that mattered was that at last—*finally*—her beloved mother would get the treatment she needed so badly.

She glanced sideways at the man sitting next to her. *The man she'd married.* He lounged beside her, totally relaxed and well within his comfort zone, as if marrying a total stranger was something he did every day of his life. Outwardly he was the type of man women the world round drooled over. Sophisticated, spoiled and so ridiculously wealthy that he could never have understood in a million years how it felt to be poor. How it felt to be so desperate for money that you'd do *anything*—even marry a man you'd been raised to hate.

His suit was dark and accentuated every inch of masculine perfection. His shoulders were wide, his frame powerful and athletic and he wore his looks with the ease and assurance of a man who'd been born with the entire silver cutlery set in his mouth.

He'd never known poverty and he'd never known hardship.

How could he ever understand what had driven her to this moment? A flash of panic suddenly assailed her. What if he backed out of their agreement? The man was every bit as ruthless and money-mad as her grandfather. She'd been naïve and stupid to trust him. She should have checked. She should have rung the bank—

She turned to him, her heart pounding uncomfortably in her chest as she contemplated the various scenarios, all of them awful.

'Has the money been transferred to my account?' The question flew from her lips unbidden and she immediately clamped her mouth shut and wished it unsaid as spectacular dark eyes fixed on hers with unconcealed disdain.

'Even as we speak,' he drawled softly, his firm mouth tightening into a grim line. 'I'm surprised you're not begging to miss the reception so that you can go and spend, spend, spend.'

Feeling relief wash over her she relaxed slightly, telling herself that his opinion of her really didn't matter. All that mattered was her mother. And anyway, Sebastien Fiorukis was hardly in a position to criticize her for wanting money. She glanced down at the gold watch that nestled in the dark hairs of his wrist. The watch alone was probably worth more than she spent in a year.

'And my grandfather's company?'

'Now belongs to me,' he said dryly, reaching for his glass, 'along with a substantial quantity of debts and enough labour-relation problems to ensure that my time is fully occupied for the foreseeable future. I'm afraid it's going to delay our honeymoon, *pethi mou.*'

Honeymoon?

Her eyes flew to his, startled. She hadn't thought any further than the wedding day. She certainly hadn't contemplated the fact that he might be planning a honeymoon. Panic knotted deep in her stomach. 'I—I didn't think we'd be having a honeymoon—'

'Honeymoons are for lovers,' he slotted in with a grim smile, 'which is what we are supposed to be. But at the moment I haven't got time for a wife. So there's no honeymoon.'

Alesia closed her eyes briefly and breathed a sigh of relief.

A honeymoon would have been unbearable. As it was, hopefully he'd be too busy to spend any time with her. They could lead separate lives.

Alesia sucked in a breath and forced herself to relax. It would be fine, she assured herself. They barely needed to see each other. This was her life now. She really had to try and adapt.

Her eyes scanned the enormous garden that was the setting for the reception, taking in the glitz and the glamour. Guests had flown in from all over the globe to witness the wedding of Sebastien Fiorukis and everywhere she looked there were elegant women and rich, confident men.

Alesia bit her lip and dug her short, unmanicured nails into her palms.

Could they see through her? Did they realize that, despite being the 'Philipos heiress', she didn't move in these circles and never had? What would they say if they knew that normally she dressed in jeans and waited on tables to earn extra money? What would they say if they knew she didn't have a penny to her name?

Except that now, she reminded herself as she lifted her glass to her lips, she *did* have a penny to her name. Thanks to her new husband, she was now an extremely wealthy woman. On paper. In reality the money was already spent. She'd set up an agreement with the bank so that the money was automatically transferred into her mother's medical fund.

'What are you planning, I wonder,' Sebastien purred, surveying her with a dangerous glint in his eyes. 'You look alarmingly like a woman who is plotting.'

Her eyes widened in alarm. 'I—I'm not plotting—'

'No? Then you'll be the first member of your sex who isn't.'

Before she could think of a suitable reply, he lifted a hand to her head and removed the elaborate clip with a decisive movement.

She gave a gasp of surprise and protest as her blonde hair unwound itself, slid down and settled over her shoulders. 'What are you doing?'

'I paid for you,' he said succinctly, his eyes fastened to her hair with undisguised masculine interest, 'and you were *very* expensive, *agape mou*. I therefore have the right to use you in any way I see fit.'

Alesia almost choked with outrage. 'You don't own me—'

'Oh, yes, I do.' He leaned towards her. 'I do own you, Alesia. Every single delectable part of you. I own your long silky hair and those amazing eyes that can almost convince me you're innocent even though I know you're a conniving, greedy little gold-digger. I own that fabulous body which you've doubtless used on countless occasions to persuade men to part with their money. I own the lot, Alesia. The deal we both signed was nothing short of a purchase on my part.'

She closed her eyes. 'You make me feel like a—like a—'

'Whore? Prostitute?' he supplied helpfully. 'I can see that the distinction might be difficult to make but you're obviously perfectly satisfied with your career choice and who can blame you? There are far worse ways of earning a substantial sum of money.'

She gave a gasp of outrage and her eyes flew open. 'Whatever you may think of me, I'm *not* promiscuous!'

'At the price that you charge, that is hardly surprising,' he drawled, a sardonic gleam in his dark eyes as they swept over her flushed cheeks. 'Clearly you know how to keep yourself exclusive. Only the richest can afford you.'

Deeply offended, her eyes flashed her distaste. 'I *hate* you,' she said passionately and he smiled.

'Maybe. But you need my money, *pethi mou*, which says a lot about your character, don't you agree?'

Overwhelmed by a sudden impulse to tell him exactly why

she needed the money, Alesia stared helplessly into his arrogant, handsome face and fought the impulse to slap it.

She couldn't tell him.

She'd come this far—

And she didn't need to defend herself to a man she didn't like or respect.

She rose to her feet, determined to put distance between them, but lean brown fingers closed around her slender wrist.

'If you're about to make an exhibition of yourself then think again,' he advised silkily, the expression in his eyes like a building thunderstorm. 'You're now my wife and I expect you to behave as such. This is not the time or the place for female tantrums. Everyone is looking at you. Sit down.'

Alesia tried to jerk her hand away but his grip tightened mercilessly and she sank back into her chair wondering how on earth she was going to get through the next hour with this man, let alone a lifetime.

Awash with hatred for him, she glanced up and saw a sultry-looking brunette staring at her with a stricken expression on her lovely face.

Alesia frowned. 'Now I see what you meant about people staring. She looks pretty upset,' she muttered, glancing sideways at Sebastien who was lounging in the chair next to her. 'Am I to assume she wanted to be sitting where I am?'

Part of her found it hard to believe that anyone would *choose* to marry Sebastien Fiorukis but there was no missing the misery in the other woman's gaze.

Sebastien fastened night-black eyes on the girl in question and gave the ghost of a smile. 'Quite a few women wanted to be sitting where you are, *pethi mou*,' he drawled, 'so you should just count yourself lucky.'

Lucky?

'Don't you even care that she's upset?' Alesia made a

sound of disgust. 'You are *totally* unfeeling. Perhaps she was in love with you. She might be heartbroken.'

'Heartbroken.' He studied her, his gaze speculative. 'Funny—I never would have thought you were a romantic. After all, you're the woman who just married for yet more money. Are you telling me you believe in love?'

Alesia bit her lip. 'She's *obviously* upset—'

He gave a cynical smile. 'So would you be if you saw your glamorous lifestyle threatened. Relax. Her affection is no more than wallet-deep. Her wounds will be healed by the next rich man foolish enough to glance in her direction.'

Alesia stared at him in appalled disbelief. 'Who have you spent your life mixing with? Where did you get *such* a low opinion of women?'

'From people like you, perhaps?' His tone was lethally smooth and she flushed deeply, knowing that she was in no position to contradict him.

How could she? She *did* want his money, even though it wasn't for her benefit.

'Let's not pretend that either of us believes in fairy tales or love.' His eyes fastened on hers. 'You certainly don't or you wouldn't be sitting here now.'

Love.

Glancing at the girl one more time, Alesia saw raw jealousy in her eyes and almost laughed at the irony of the situation.

Whatever the emotion driving her, the girl clearly wanted to be sitting where she was sitting. She was probably the envy of at least half the women in the world.

And she'd never felt more miserable in her life.

Alesia returned her gaze to her plate and almost jumped as she felt Sebastien cover her hand with his own.

Startled by his unexpected touch, she lifted her gaze to his and was instantly mesmerized by the look in his seductive dark eyes. It was a look that teased and tantalized, a promise of things to come, and for a moment she just stared, held captive by the sheer sexuality of his presence.

He had something that she'd never encountered before—

A magnetism. A—

He leaned towards her and she stopped breathing, waiting for him to speak. Waiting to hear what he suddenly wanted to say to her—

'My mother is about to come and speak to you,' Sebastien murmured softly in her ear, lean, bronzed fingers toying idly with a strand of her hair, 'and you are to say nothing which upsets her in any way, do I make myself clear? As far as she is concerned, we are crazy about each other. One wrong move on your part and the money stops.'

Crazy about each other?

Her heart thudding uncomfortably, Alesia froze. She was totally thrown by the contrast between the seduction in his eyes and the lethal tone of his voice.

There was no missing the warning in his tone.

'Surely she knows this is a business arrangement—' Her own voice was little more than a croak and she struggled to breathe. 'We only met two weeks ago.'

'My mother is a romantic,' he murmured, smiling down at her with what must have seemed to a casual observer a flattering degree of attentiveness. 'She believes that we were destined to meet and fall in love. The feud has come full circle. Your parents died and now we are together.'

Finding that she just couldn't think straight when he was leaning so close to her, Alesia swallowed hard and then turned to greet the woman who had approached while they'd been talking. They'd been introduced briefly before the ceremony but that was all and Alesia had barely paid attention. As far as she was concerned his mother was just another Fiorukis. Another member of the family who had been directly responsible for her father's death. She ought to hate her. She was the enemy.

Alesia stared up at Diandra Fiorukis, saw the warmth in her eyes and the pride in her expression and suddenly found she couldn't hate her. Nor could she see her as the enemy. She was just someone's mother.

A mother attending her beloved son's wedding. Proud. Nervous.

Drawn. *Strained.*

'You look beautiful, Alesia,' the older woman said wistfully. 'Your own mother would have been so proud of you if she could see you now.'

The reminder that her own mother didn't even know she was getting married tore at Alesia's heart. Her mother would have been *horrified* had she known that she was getting married. And to whom.

Unable to speak for a moment, knowing she couldn't reveal that her mother was alive, she struggled with the emotion that threatened to erupt inside her.

'This is a happy day for our two families. I'm pleased that your grandfather agreed to come today.' His mother settled herself in the chair next to her. 'Everyone wants family around them when they marry.'

Family?

Alesia remembered that his mother had no idea that she and her grandfather had only met two weeks earlier. That they had no relationship at all and never would.

That her grandfather had brutally cut both her mother and herself out of his life.

It was on the tip of her tongue to protest that she didn't consider her grandfather to be family, but fortunately she realized in time that such a statement would reveal far too much about the true situation and she couldn't risk that. There was still too much at stake. If they discovered that her mother was alive and that her grandfather had disowned both of them then they would guess that this wedding was about revenge, not unity.

Feeling guilty for deceiving the other woman, she changed the subject.

'I never realized Sebastien was part of such a large family,' she said stiffly, watching as yet another giggling teenager fought for his attention. Everywhere she turned there seemed to be sisters, cousins and aunts hugging him, small children waiting to crawl on to his lap.

His mother smiled serenely. 'They are your family too now.' She reached out and took Alesia's hand in hers. 'You've no idea how much I've longed for this moment. I thought Sebastien would never be willing to sacrifice his bachelor life for a girl. I'd given up hoping that he'd ever find anyone good enough for him.'

Seeing that the woman was genuinely moved, Alesia squirmed uncomfortably. She couldn't pretend—she just couldn't.

'My mother is a romantic,' Sebastien drawled, turning his attention from the younger members of his family to the older. 'She dreams only of happy endings.'

There was a clear warning in his eyes and Alesia clamped her lips together, holding back the words that she wanted to speak, reminding herself that she didn't have to apologise to these people. That she didn't have to explain herself.

'I dream of grandchildren,' his mother confessed, her eyes sparkling as she looked at Alesia. 'As I'm sure your grandfather does.'

Appalled by his mother's innocent expectations, Alesia felt a sick feeling build in the pit of her stomach.

Grandchildren.

And that, of course, was the one thing she was never going to be able to provide. She closed her eyes and told herself firmly that it didn't bother her what the Fiorukis family wanted. She *hated* them. She hated her grandfather and she hated their stupid feud. In fact she hated everything Greek because it embodied everything that had ruined her mother's life.

So why was she suddenly struck by conscience?

Sebastien lounged in his seat, watching his new bride through veiled eyes.

He considered himself something of an expert on the avarice of women, but even he was astonished by her almost indecent desire to get her hands on his money.

He was used to women who at least pretended to be interested in something other than his wallet but Alesia, it seemed, couldn't even be bothered to pretend. It was the *only* question she'd asked him. The only piece of information it seemed she needed of him. *'Has the money been transferred to my account?'*

Her total desperation shone through. All through the ceremony she'd been pale and anxious, her agitation so palpable that he'd started to wonder whether something was seriously the matter with his bride.

Anyone looking at her would think she *needed* the money.

He gave a grim smile, knowing full well that 'need' was a relative term and to the Philipos heiress need clearly encompassed greed of a magnitude that even he had failed to encounter in the past.

Aware that his mother was still watching them, he tried to find a mutually satisfying topic of conversation and drew a blank. 'So tell me,' he breathed sarcastically, relieved that his mother was not skilled in lip-reading, 'what will be your first purchase with your newfound wealth? A thousand pairs of designer shoes or something bigger? A yacht, maybe? A racehorse or two?'

She lifted her eyes from the contemplation of her untouched plate of food and stared at him blankly. 'Pardon?'

He frowned down at her, noticing for the first time the dark smudges under her eyes. Clearly she hadn't slept for nights. Probably worrying that the deal would fall through, he mused.

'I was asking how you plan to spend my money,' he repeated, realizing with a flash of surprise that she was paying him not the slightest bit of attention. He almost smiled at the irony of the situation. He was accustomed to employing a variety of skills designed to keep women at a distance and yet the woman he'd just married was having trouble remembering that he existed. 'I think I should at least know something about my wife.'

'Oh.' She frowned as if she were thrown by the question. There was a brief hesitation and something close to panic flashed in her eyes. 'I—I don't know yet—I expect I'll go—shopping?'

Sebastien refrained from pointing out that she truly would have to shop until she dropped if she stood even the faintest chance of spending even a fraction of the money he'd just delivered into her account.

Clearly he wouldn't be seeing much of his new wife, he mused grimly. To spend that volume of money was going to take a considerable length of time and serious application on her part.

Consumed by an irritation that he didn't begin to understand, he rose to his feet and extended a hand. 'Time to earn that money. We're expected to begin the dancing.'

She stared at him stupidly. 'Dance? You and I—together?'

He ground his teeth. 'It's tradition for man and wife to dance.' Without giving her time to argue, he hauled her against him and flashed a smile into her shocked face. 'Time to give the crowd what they've been waiting for, *pethi mou*.'

He strode purposefully on to the dance floor, his arm round her waist in what must have seemed to the wedding guests an affectionate gesture. In fact he was keeping her from running because he knew for a fact that if he released her she would *definitely* run.

She was staring up at him as if he'd gone completely mad. And perhaps he had, he reflected. After all, he had just married a woman whose values he despised. Hardly the action of a sane man.

'Smile up at me as if I'm the only man in the world,' he ordered softly as he stopped in the middle of the dance floor and curved an arm round her waist. 'We are the focus of attention and I would hate to disappoint our guests.'

'This is ridiculous.' Sebastien felt her stiffen, saw her teeth clench. 'I thought we agreed that we weren't going to play games. That we were going to be honest with each other.'

'In private, yes.' He lowered his face closer to hers so that there was no chance of being overheard. 'But to the outside world we have to create the right impression. My mother needs to think this marriage is real, the financial markets need to think this marriage is real. So we're going to make them think it's real.'

His attention was suddenly caught by her perfectly shaped mouth and for a moment he couldn't quite remember what was so important about the financial markets. Mesmerized by the soft curve of her lips, Sebastien watched as they parted slightly and a delicate pink tongue darted out nervously.

His whole body tightened in a primitive male response to the gesture of vulnerability.

'You're deluding yourself,' Alesia said shakily, her eyes darkening in consternation. 'No one looking at us can possibly think this marriage is anything other than a business arrangement.'

Reminding himself that there was nothing vulnerable about a wealthy woman who'd just married someone she clearly loathed, he dragged his eyes from her mouth.

'Then it's up to us to prove them wrong.' Without thinking, he pulled her hard against him in a gesture of pure possession and felt her quiver of shock as her body came into contact with his for the first time.

Awareness exploded between them and Sebastien stopped breathing. Shocked into stillness by the unexpected power of their mutual response. It was as if their bodies had recognized something that both of them had failed to notice. Alesia's subtle scent oozed over his senses and seduced his mind and body into forgetting everything except the woman in his arms.

Neither of them spoke but he saw her breathing go shallow, watched the pupils dilate in those amazing violet eyes as she acknowledged the throbbing tension in the atmosphere.

He felt her tremble against him and frowned slightly, registering for the first time just how delicate she was. She'd revealed enough of her full cleavage during that first meeting with her grandfather for him to have formed an impression that she was generously built, but now he realized how totally wrong he'd been in that initial assessment. With predictable masculine focus, he'd been seriously distracted. The rest of her was impossibly slender. *Fragile.*

Still shocked by the power of his response to her, Sebastien curved a hand over the base of her spine in brooding contemplation and gave a wry smile as he acknowledged the eternal weakness of man. His libido was clearly indifferent to the fact that she was a self-confessed gold-digger. But then what was wrong with that? Gold-digger or not, she was *incredibly* beautiful and he should be rejoicing that his new bride might well prove to have her compensations. Providing they didn't have to indulge in conversation, the forthcoming night promised to be *far* from boring.

Since he'd removed her hairclip, her blonde tresses poured down her back in a shiny silken sheet and he found himself resisting the temptation to bury his face in its scented mass.

She tried to pull away but he held her firmly, his gaze faintly mocking as he looked down at her.

'Amazing is it not,' he murmured softly, curving her

against him as they swayed in time to the music, 'that our bodies can feel something that our minds tell us not to?'

She planted a hand in the centre of his chest, panic in her eyes as she tried to hold him at a distance. 'I don't know what you're talking about.'

He removed her hand in a deliberate movement, pulled her closer still and lowered his head so that his mouth was only inches from hers. Her unexpectedly seductive scent made his head swim. 'Oh, yes, you do, you know *exactly* what I'm talking about.'

'What are you doing? Everyone is staring—'

So was he. He'd never seen eyes such an unusual shade of blue, he mused, his gaze still fixed on her face. The colour of English violets.

'For a self-confessed gold-digger you are extraordinarily sensitive,' he murmured in her ear, sliding his other arm round her and pulling her closer still. 'Why would you care what people think?'

'I just don't like being stared at.'

He gave a short laugh. She was an heiress, albeit a ridiculously protected one. 'Then you'd better get used to it fast, *pethi mou*. I spend my life being stared at.'

Other couples joined them on the dance floor and Sebastien suddenly realized that she was barely moving in his arms. Instead she was holding on to him tightly as if he were the only solid, dependable thing in her life. *As if she were afraid of letting him go.*

He frowned down at the blonde head which was only inches away from his chest.

Where did it come from, this vulnerability that flowed from her?

His mouth hardened as he reminded himself forcibly that this marriage had come about because she didn't have a principled bone in her body. If she seemed vulnerable then it was probably all part of an elaborate act to attract wealthy men.

The truth was that she was a ruthless, manipulative woman, who was willing to go to distasteful lengths to swell her already swollen bank account.

'I'm not letting go,' he drawled lazily, wondering why she was always so conscious of people staring. Having been on the receiving end of public attention since he'd outgrown the privacy of his pram, it was something he no longer noticed. Surely she was the same? 'You signed on for this when you agreed to marry for money.'

Her eyes held a hint of reproach. 'I *didn't* sign on for public performances—'

'You agreed to be my wife,' he responded smoothly, 'with all that entails. Do you know what I think, *pethi mou*? I think you were so blinded by the money you didn't see the rest of it. I don't think you thought further than the cash.'

He felt her stiffen.

He could see a tiny pulse beating in her throat, feel the extraordinary tension throbbing from her delicious body and his own body tightened in an instantaneous response that almost made him groan aloud.

How could he ever have thought that the Philipos heiress was cold?

English and reserved though she may be on the surface, there was now no doubt in his mind that she had enough hot-blooded Greek blood in her to ensure that their sex life would be far from boring.

His head bent lower, his mouth so close to hers that they were almost touching. 'You've got what you wanted. The cheque. Now it's my turn.'

She was staring at him like an animal in a trap. 'You got what you wanted too—my grandfather's company.'

'*My* father's company,' Sebastien corrected her softly, his free hand sliding up her spine and settling on the back of her neck. 'And that was only part of what I wanted. Now it's time to help myself to the rest.'

His gaze mocking, he dipped his head with lazy arrogance and claimed the mouth that had been tempting him ever since she'd first set foot on the island, intending to demonstrate to the Philipos heiress just *exactly* what she'd let herself in for when she'd traded herself for money. Intending to show her that greed had a price.

Her mouth was warm and sweet and his senses exploded, propelling him out of control.

Heat and fire spread through his lower body and he was consumed by a sexual need so powerful that he dragged her closer still in an attempt to satisfy the sudden grinding ache in his loins, but the action simply inflamed him still further.

They were so close that he felt every tiny tremor of her body, felt her shiver as he held her. He saw the shock in her violet eyes before they drifted shut and her fingers curled into the front of his shirt for support.

His last coherent thought was that *this* wasn't what he'd planned.

A small part of his brain told him to pull away, to end it now, but her soft, delicious mouth drugged his senses and prevented him from doing anything except help himself to more.

He filled himself with her. The scent of her slithered over him like a suffocating cloak, the blood in his head raged and pounded, clouding thought and reason. Lust ravaged his body as he plunged into a raging heat totally new to him. The fire burned red then gold and he fanned the flames by taking more and more of her.

As if from a distance he heard a soft whimper of shock and desire and that tiny sound was enough to break the sensual spell that she'd wrapped around him.

He dragged his mouth from hers with supreme difficulty, discovering for the first time what it felt like to be completely out of control.

What the hell was he playing at?

He'd always considered himself to be a ruthlessly disci-
plined man. Whatever the situation, be it provocation or
temptation, he *never* lost control. *So why, once his mouth
had taken possession of hers, had he suddenly lost all ability
to think rationally?* In fact he'd stopped thinking altogether,
his actions driven by an instinct so raw and primitive that
he'd been well past control.

His body still hummed with unfulfilled tension, his nerves
sizzled and his manhood ached and throbbed.

The realization that she'd succeeded in affecting him so
strongly irritated him in the extreme and he struggled to rationalize his own behaviour. To find some explanation for
such an uncharacteristic reaction.

Was it really so surprising? he wondered, surveying her
flushed, shocked face with grim concentration.

Whatever else she may be, there was no denying that his
new wife was a stunningly beautiful woman who managed
to project just the right amount of innocence and vulnerability
to tempt a very traditionally minded Greek male.

He wouldn't be human if he didn't respond.

And the cure was to take her to bed, he decided with characteristic decisiveness. Women, however beautiful, never
held his attention for long. One night, maybe two, would be
all it would take to get his fill of her. After that he'd be able
to start thinking clearly again and move on.

Decision made, he grabbed Alesia's wrist and virtually
hauled her off the dance floor towards the exit without ut-
tering a word.

And just to be sure that the staring guests were left in no
doubt as to how he felt about his new bride, he swept her up
into his arms and planted another swift kiss on her shocked
mouth.

With a smile at his mother, who was shedding tears of
undisguised delight on the arm of his father, he strode out of
the garden towards the waiting limousine.

Alesia didn't wriggle in his arms, didn't move. It was almost as if she wanted him to take her away from there. Which couldn't possibly be the case, he reflected grimly, because another thing he knew about women was that the whole point of spend, spend, spend was to allow them to party, party, party.

Her head lay against his shoulder in almost weary resignation and he felt something pull inside him. *A feeling which he instantly dismissed with a sharp frown.*

She was good, he had to hand it to her. She was already trying to tie him in knots. A less experienced man might have thought that she was glad he was holding her.

Fortunately he knew better—

One night, he promised himself as he dropped her in the seat of the limo as if she was infectious.

He'd make her pregnant that first night and that would be it.

He wouldn't have to touch her again.

He could get on with his life and she could get on with spending his money.

CHAPTER FOUR

ALESIA huddled into the leather seat, trying to control the tiny tremors that still attacked her body. Sebastien's skilled assault on her senses had left her shattered by the discovery that she didn't know herself at all.

Stunned by her own reaction, she struggled to rationalize what had happened.

Nothing had prepared her for that kiss.

It had been dark, terrifying, *exciting* and he'd unveiled a part of herself that she hadn't known existed.

Everything about her felt different.

She wanted to lift her fingers to her lips and see what had changed but she didn't dare with him seated beside her.

She didn't want him to know what he'd done to her—

What he'd made her feel—

She closed her eyes and gave a whimper of self-disgust. What an irony. She'd kissed men before and felt nothing. Why was it that the first man to show her what a kiss could mean had to be a man she despised?

'You can open your eyes now.' Sebastien sounded bored, as if he'd rather be anywhere than sitting next to her. 'We've left the crowds behind. It's just you and me. No more pretending.'

Still struggling with the humiliating knowledge that she hadn't even tried to push him away, Alesia opened her eyes and swallowed hard.

'Where exactly are we going?' Her voice was a nervous croak and he gave a grim smile.

'Somewhere more private. The time has come to take our

''business deal'' to another level, *pethi mou*, and for that I do *not* need an audience.'

How could he speak like that when he clearly wished he were with anyone but her? How could he even be contemplating spending the night with her?

Suddenly she understood the true meaning of the phrase 'out of the frying-pan into the fire' and wished they were back at the reception. She'd thought that being in crowds of people was bad but it was nothing compared to being alone with Sebastien Fiorukis. 'Is it far? I'm very tired—'

'We're going to my Athens home,' he returned, shrugging off his jacket and removing his tie. 'And it isn't far. But you won't be sleeping, *pethi mou*, no matter how exhausted you are. You still have the rest of your bargain to keep. And after that kiss I think we're both going to have a *very* interesting evening.'

His blunt reminder of what they'd shared sent tingles through her already sensitized body and a slow, insidious warmth uncurled low in her pelvis. Desire, hot, restless and totally unfamiliar, tangled and pumped inside her.

She saw the sardonic gleam in his black eyes and swallowed hard. 'I don't know what you mean—'

'No?' Sebastien was hard, tough and uncompromising but his voice was silky smooth as he undid the top few buttons of his shirt. 'Need a reminder?'

Dark hairs nestled in the dip of his bronzed throat, a tantalizing hint of what he kept concealed.

Alesia flattened herself in the furthest corner of the car, enveloped by a sudden rush of panic and something altogether more complicated that she couldn't begin to name.

Up until this moment she hadn't even considered Sebastien as a man. She'd seen him as the enemy and as the answer to her mother's problems. Never as a man.

Until that kiss.

The kiss had wakened something in her. Taken her by storm. *Changed her.*

Suddenly she was aware of him as a man. *And for the first time in her life she was aware of herself as a woman.*

Like a rabbit in a trap, she stared at him. He lounged with careless ease in the seat next to her, long legs stretched out in front of him, an air of almost bored indifference on his handsome face. It was the first time she'd seen him anything less than rigidly formal and her eyes were drawn first to his powerful shoulders, the strong line of his hard jaw, blue-black with stubble.

She realized with a sudden lurch of her stomach that the trappings of wealth and success disguised the essence of the man he was. Underneath his sophisticated exterior lay man at his most primitive and basic. Dark and dangerous. Raw and untamed. *A hunter.* She was just contemplating what that meant for her when she realized that they'd driven through electric gates and were approaching a large and very beautiful villa set in acres of grounds.

Momentarily distracted, she just gazed in silence. 'It's *huge*,' she mumbled finally. 'And there's only one of you.'

He gave a short laugh. 'And, as you've just discovered, I have an extremely large extended family,' he said drily, 'all of whom frequently decide to descend on me at once and need to be accommodated. I also do a great deal of business entertaining. I need the space.'

Alesia stared at him in disbelief and then back at the house. He needed this much space? She was used to living in a room where she could virtually touch all four walls from her bed.

'I hope the house comes with a map,' she muttered as she stepped out of the car. Immediately she realized her mistake as Sebastien stared at her with brooding concentration.

'You are the granddaughter of a man who is richer than Midas. Your grandfather is well-known for keeping elaborate homes. Why would you be so surprised at mine?'

Alesia bit her tongue.

She'd slipped up again.

Stupid stupid stupid.

Warning herself that she *had* to concentrate, she tried to recover her mistake.

'I've never been that great at finding my way around new places,' she muttered vaguely as he took her arm and led her towards the door.

'Fortunately there's only one room that you need to find,' he advised in cool tones, 'and that's the bedroom.'

Alesia flushed to the roots of her glossy blonde hair and would have stopped walking but he swept her up in his arms and carried her across a spacious marble hallway and up a beautifully curved staircase.

'I can walk—' she said through gritted teeth and he flashed her a grim smile.

'This isn't for your benefit, *agape mou*, but for the benefit of my staff who are at this moment peeping discreetly round corners hoping for a glimpse of my new bride. Unfortunately for us, they are as romantically inclined as my mother so I intend to give them the show they're expecting.'

Staff?

Her mouth fell open and she closed it again quickly. Of course a man like him would have staff. How else could he run a house on this scale?

He strode into a room, kicked the door shut behind him and dropped her with little in the way of warning before striding over to the full-length windows and opening them.

His need for fresh air and distance caused a shaft of pain that she couldn't decipher.

So the 'show' was over, she thought wryly, struggling to regain her balance and maintain some shred of dignity.

Now what?

Glancing at the tension in those broad shoulders, her heart sank. He certainly did not look lover-like.

'Look—' her voice was weary '—we both know that this whole situation is ridiculous. We don't have to do this—'

'*This* was part of our agreement.'

He turned, his dark eyes glittering with intent. 'What's the matter?' He strolled towards her with all the grace of a jungle animal stalking its prey. 'Having second thoughts? Suddenly realizing what it is you agreed to?'

His tone was clipped and hard and her heart leaped into her throat. Distant, cold and monumentally intimidating, Sebastien was totally out of her league and it was useless pretending otherwise.

'What *we* agreed to,' she corrected, taking a step backwards and then wishing she hadn't as he registered the defensive movement on her part with a cool smile.

'*We* agreed to a marriage,' he reminded her softly, lifting his hands and unbuttoning the rest of his shirt with slow, deliberate flicks of his long fingers, each movement taunting her. 'And that is what we're going to have, *Mrs* Fiorukis.'

He peeled off his shirt and let it fall to the floor with casual disregard. But then he was probably never going to wear it again, Alesia thought hysterically as she took another step back and suddenly realized that there was nowhere else for her to go. Her back was against the wall. Literally.

With considerable difficulty, she moved her gaze from the tantalizing vision of bronzed skin and rough chest hair clustered against rock-solid muscle. Heart thudding hard, mouth dry, she stared defiantly into the corner of the room, just *refusing* to look at him. Perhaps if she didn't look, then she wouldn't feel. *Wouldn't want.*

The sound of a zip being undone made her flinch, the rustle of silk sliding to the floor made her nerve-endings tingle, and at that point she closed her eyes, just *knowing* that he was naked and absolutely determined not to look.

'Well, Mrs Fiorukis?' His rough masculine voice taunted

her and she sensed him moving closer. *And closer.* 'Are you ready to close this particular part of the deal?'

Eyes still closed, heart still hammering, she tried to reason with him. 'You can't possibly want me and I *certainly* don't want you—'

He was too close.

His raw masculine scent surrounded her and oozed into her senses, making her stomach drop and her legs weaken.

'On the contrary, I paid an indecent sum of money for you,' he reminded her coldly, 'and I expect you to earn that money.'

Her eyes flew open and she gave a disbelieving laugh. 'In the bedroom?'

'Where else?' He gave a bored shrug. 'I'm certainly not in need of your assistance in the boardroom.'

Her mind searched frantically for an escape from the building sexual tension which was threatening her ability to think or function.

'You already have a mistress—'

'Several,' he confirmed helpfully, 'but you needn't worry that it will affect my performance in bed.'

She didn't even want to think about bed.

Every inch of her throbbed. Her senses danced and pirouetted in a crazy response to the man in front of her.

'Look—I'm trying to be honest,' she said desperately, 'and the truth is we just don't have to do this. You can go to your mistress—I don't care—'

She didn't need this. Didn't want this. She wanted freedom from these feelings that she didn't recognize. Hadn't felt before.

'But my mistress won't give me children,' he reminded her silkily, 'and I want children. And *this* is the way children are made, remember?'

Her gaze, showing a glimmer of guilt, flew to his. It was a mistake. Slumberous dark eyes captured and trapped her, drawing her in. Those eyes alone were enough to make a woman lose herself, she thought dizzily, struggling to remember why it was that she didn't want to go to bed with him. His eyelashes were long and dark and ridiculously thick and his hard jaw was covered in blue-black stubble that made him look even more dangerous.

'If you're nervous then you needn't be,' he said. 'I may not like you but that kiss alone was enough to prove to both of us that, despite our emotions, physically at least there is a powerful chemistry between us.'

Alesia felt dizzy and drugged and her mouth was so dry she could barely speak.

She gaped at him. 'Chemistry? You think there's chemistry between us?'

'I know there is—' he curved a hand round her waist and drew her against him '—and so do you. Stop pretending you don't feel it too.'

Alesia was so busy trying to understand his belief that there was chemistry between them that she somehow managed to miss the fact that his hand was moving down her back. With a swift, purposeful movement he undid her dress and she gave a soft gasp of shock as it pooled at her feet, leaving her dressed in only a pair of silk panties.

Consumed by embarrassment, she lifted her arms to cover her naked breasts but Sebastien caught her hands and drew them around his neck before scooping her up in his arms.

'This is definitely *not* the time to cover up your best assets,' he urged thickly, carrying her to the bed and depositing her in the centre.

Before she could move a muscle, he came down on top of her, his weight pinning her to the bed.

'Whatever your faults, you have a *fabulous* body,' he said huskily, sliding a lean bronzed hand over her body with maddening slowness as he surveyed her with raw male appreciation. 'I'll be honest about one thing, *pethi mou*, I was all ready to refuse this deal whatever the incentive and then I saw you.'

Her breath jammed in her throat. 'You were going to refuse?'

'Of course.' He raised his head to look at her and there was a flicker of dry amusement in his dark eyes. 'We are expected to make babies for our respective families, *agape mou*, and that requires a certain activity on my part. If I had found you unattractive there was no way I would have agreed to this marriage. Despite rumours to the contrary, I'm *extremely* particular about who I take to my bed.'

She stared up at him, her heart pounding, her resistance crumbling to dust under the hot sexuality of his gaze. 'You find me attractive—really?'

No man had ever looked twice at her before but then she'd gone out of her way to avoid all but platonic relationships with the opposite sex.

'Really.' His tone of self-mockery drew her attention to his body for the first time and her colour deepened. It was the first time she'd seen a naked man. A naked aroused man. The sight was nothing short of daunting.

Now that the moment had come, panic assailed her. He was right, she thought, closing her eyes with a helpless moan as his mouth traced the line of her jaw. She hadn't really thought this through. How could she ever have thought she'd be able to pretend that she was experienced? She didn't have a *clue* and there was no way she'd ever be able to convince him otherwise.

'You loathe me,' she moaned, moving her head away from his clever mouth with a gasp of disbelief. 'You despise me. You can't possibly want me.'

She was wondering frantically what to do when Sebastien took control and, with a smooth shift of his powerful frame, he rolled her under him and lowered his mouth to hers. Instantly her body erupted and with a whimper of helpless excitement she realized that he was so used to being in charge that all she had to do was to lie there and he'd make all the moves. He'd show her the way.

It was her last logical thought before she fell deep into his kiss—

Just like the time before, she forgot everything. She felt the erotic slide of his tongue in her mouth, the hotly sexual exploration that sent shivers through her whole body and had her arching against him. She felt his hand move downwards, dragging over one sensitized nipple and resting on her hip.

And her head started to spin. Nothing felt straight or clear.

Her heart hammered, her pelvis burned and her senses tangled and swirled in an exotic dance, fired by the sensual thrust of his tongue.

Just when she thought she was definitely going to pass out, he dragged his mouth away from hers. With a reluctant groan he trailed his mouth down over her neck, her throat, until finally he lingered on her breast.

At the first casual flick of his tongue she cried out in shock, driven wild by the intensity of the sensation, and as he sucked her into his mouth she shifted her hips in a desperate attempt to soothe the wild burning in her pelvis.

'You have amazing breasts,' he groaned, turning his attention to the other one. 'It was virtually the only thing I noticed about you when we first met.'

Some deeper part of her brain registered that remark but she wasn't capable of any reaction other than a pleading whimper.

She wanted more—*something*—

'Sebastien—' She breathed his name on a sob of desperation and he gave a wolfish smile of male triumph.

'And the other thing I like about you,' he murmured huskily as he slid further down her frantically writhing and excited body, 'is that underneath that prim, restrained exterior you are *so* hot. How could I ever have thought that you were cold and English?'

Alesia couldn't even respond because at that moment he spread her legs in a ruthlessly possessive gesture and concentrated his attentions on an entirely different part of her body.

Torn between shock at being exposed to a man's gaze for the first time and a sensual pleasure so terrifying in its intensity that she could hardly breathe let alone think, Alesia bit back a moan of denial. Resisting her feeble attempts to close her legs, he held her firm and used his tongue with an erotic mastery that made her writhe and sob in an ecstasy that she hadn't even dreamed existed before this moment. She just couldn't believe that he was doing these things to her and that she was *encouraging* him.

'Sebastien—' Confused and overwhelmed by the sudden explosion of sexual need that she didn't properly understand, she arched her back and curled her fingers into the sheets. *'Sebastien—'*

He slid up the bed in a fluid movement, his eyes scanning her flushed cheeks with ill-disguised satisfaction. 'Definitely *not* cold,' he murmured, his hand closing over her wrist as she reached to pull the sheet up. 'No way. You never cover up until I say so and I haven't finished looking at you yet.'

His gaze made her feel hotter still and he slid a hair-roughened thigh over her legs as she writhed against the sheets in an attempt to relieve the burning need that threatened to consume her whole body.

'Something the matter?' he taunted her softly, his eyes shimmering dark with barely restrained passion. 'Is there something you want from me other than my money, *agape mou*?'

Her body throbbed and ached from his all too skilled seduction and she was just *desperate* for him to finish what he'd started.

'Say it,' he said harshly, shifting his weight so that his powerful body covered hers, teasing her further. She felt his silken arousal hard against her and curled her legs round him, arching in mute invitation.

Still he held himself back, his gaze faintly mocking as he looked down at her.

'Lose that English reserve. Tell me what you want, *agape mou*,' he commanded and she lay looking up at him, totally in his control, her heart beating rapidly and her body consumed by a powerful craving that she just had to satisfy.

'You,' she groaned softly, writhing under him in a wanton attempt to get closer. 'You. I want you. *Please.*'

With a growl of masculine satisfaction, Sebastien slid an arm under her hips, lifted her in a decisive movement and thrust into her with barely restrained masculine force.

Shocked by the power of that alien invasion, Alesia gave a sharp cry and her eyes flew wide and clashed with his.

She saw the sudden speculation in his sultry, sexy gaze and kept her expression blank. She didn't want him to know. The brief pain faded, extinguished by her driving need for physical satisfaction, and she moved her hips under his. His eyes still holding hers, he lowered his head and captured her mouth, teasing and tasting with his tongue until her whole body was burning hot and writhing under his.

Only then did he move again, this time incredibly gently as if he was trying not to hurt her. And his unexpected tenderness made the whole experience unbearably erotic. Alesia clutched at his broad shoulders and slid her hands down his muscular back, feeling the degree of strength and power that he'd so carefully leashed on her account.

Without moving his mouth from hers, he lifted her with a strong arm, shifting her position, and ripples of excitement exploded through her sensitized body as he changed the angle.

How did he know?

How did he know to move in a certain way, touch her in a certain way?

How could he make her feel like this?

She gasped his name against his mouth and he gave a growl of satisfaction low in his throat and thrust hard, each stroke long and deep as he controlled her and drove her to completion. She shot into orgasm with a strangled cry of disbelief, her body convulsing around his in waves and waves of pulsing ecstasy that refused to end.

It was wild and uninhibited and totally outside her control, her body just exploding in a frenzy of raw sexual excitement.

She heard him mutter something rough in Greek and then with a harsh groan he grabbed her hips and buried himself deeper still, not even giving her a chance to escape from the storm that was overtaking them.

She felt his hardness and his heat and then felt his muscles bunch as her frantic convulsions propelled him to his own climax. She felt his fingers dig into her scalp, felt the liquid pulse of his release as he powered into her, driven over the edge by the living force they'd created between them.

Locked in the throes of pleasure which refused to diminish, Alesia slid a hand over his muscled back, feeling the heat of his skin, the vital masculinity of the man, as he struggled to control his breathing.

His weight crushed her to the bed, his body still locked with hers in the most intimate way possible, and it crossed her mind that this was the closest she'd ever felt to anyone in her life. They were connected in every sense of the word.

For a long moment Alesia lay still, utterly stunned by what had happened.

Never in her wildest dreams or fantasies had she imagined that it would be like that.

That two human beings could be so close.

With a brief frown of confusion she lifted a hand hesitantly and touched his bronzed shoulder.

What had happened?

She'd started out hating him, and now—

She swallowed hard and tried to make sense of what had just happened. Sifting through her tangled emotions, suddenly she couldn't find the hatred any more. How could you share such intimacies with someone and hate them?

And surely he couldn't hate her, either? How could something so perfect have been created out of hate? It wasn't possible—

She felt something inside her melt away, leaving her exposed and vulnerable but she didn't care. She'd discovered something that she hadn't known existed. Something amazing.

Guilt and confusion mingled inside her. They'd shared something really honest and yet she'd told him such *lies*. What would he say if he knew the extent to which she was deceiving him?

Maybe she should tell him—

After what they'd shared, she needed to be honest.

Sebastien lifted his dark head and stared down at her flushed cheeks and bruised mouth for a long moment. Then he rolled on to his back and covered his face with a bronzed forearm.

Feeling suddenly awkward, Alesia lay still, suddenly impossibly shy, not wanting to be the first to speak. For a short time they'd been as close as two people could be. They'd shared something special and the whole world had shifted. Everything seemed different. He *had* to feel it too.

They had to speak about it. *She had to tell him the truth.*

Surely he'd say something in a moment.

'It looks as though I'm going to get my money's worth.' His tone was cool and matter-of-fact.

Without so much as a glance in her direction, he sprang

out of bed with the lithe grace of a jungle cat and strolled into the bathroom, slamming the door behind him, leaving her rigid with shock.

Sebastien stood under the shower trying to recover from what had proved to be the most explosive sexual encounter of his entire life. His usually sharp mind was foggy and his body throbbed in a state of almost agonized arousal. Breathing heavily, he eyed the door of the bathroom, torn between a primitive need to satisfy his libido and a desire to regain some sort of control over his unusually scattered emotions.

He wasn't used to feeling like this.

With an exclamation of disbelief he thumped the button on the wall and turned the water into an icy blast. He gritted his teeth and let the water sluice over his thoroughly over-heated body, seeking relief from his state of almost intolerable discomfort.

It was either that or return to the bed and make love to her again and again and again and that *wasn't* what this marriage was about.

He hadn't expected to derive much pleasure from the experience.

Irritated beyond belief by her total obsession with money, he'd taken her to bed to make her feel cheap, to see if he could trigger any signs of conscience.

He hadn't expected her reaction to him to be so totally uninhibited. Hadn't expected the chemistry between them to be so powerful.

And he hadn't expected her to be a virgin.

Cursing fluently he turned off the water, swept a bronzed hand over his face to clear his vision and reached for a towel. He was a man who was used to always being in control and while he'd been in bed with Alesia he *definitely* hadn't been. The knowledge that his loss of control had been with a woman whose values he despised made his response even more reprehensible in his opinion.

Or did it? Was it really so surprising that he'd found the encounter almost unbelievably erotic? he wondered. The women he usually spent time with moved in the same circles as him, were sophisticated and sexually experienced. Sebastien gave a wry smile of self-mockery as he wrapped the towel around his lean hips. At what point had he lost sight of the truth? That, when all was said and done, he was, in fact, a *very* traditional Greek male and like all traditional men he preferred exclusivity when it came to women.

It hadn't occurred to him that his new wife might be a virgin and the truth was that her innocence in the bedroom had somehow served to heighten the emotional and physical experience. Given that it wasn't an encounter he intended to repeat in the near future, he didn't need to worry.

Having rationalized his response to his satisfaction, Sebastien glanced warily at the door that led to the bedroom.

He'd get on with his own life, leaving her to spend his money. And if she wasn't already pregnant then he'd sleep with her again at some point.

It was a good job that he was likely to be kept extremely busy for the foreseeable future.

Alesia lay still, eyes tightly closed, physically drained and enveloped by a humiliation so acute that she could barely bring herself to address what had happened.

How could he be so *hurtful*?

And to think she'd almost told him the truth.

She groaned as she remembered her own reaction to him. *She'd had no idea it would be like that.* That she was capable of such intensity of feeling. None of the limited experience she'd had before had prepared her for such a scenario.

How could she have responded so wildly to a man that she didn't even *like*?

She covered her face with her arms.

And how was she ever going to look him in the face again?

For him it had clearly just been sex, whereas for her—
Remembering how she'd sobbed his name and virtually
begged, she gave another whimper of disbelief. There was
no escaping the fact that she'd inadvertently given him yet
more ammunition to feed his already monumental ego.

She lay in the bed, listening to the sound of the shower,
dreading the moment when the water stopped. She didn't
want to be here when he came back. *Didn't want to give him
the chance to humiliate her still further.*

But before she could move the bathroom door opened and
he strolled out, wearing nothing but a narrow towel tucked
loosely around his lean hips.

Now what?

Was he planning on returning to the marital bed?

Against her will, her eyes fastened on the dark hair on his
chest and travelled downwards, knowing exactly what exciting secrets the towel concealed.

Her mouth dried and she felt the immediate response of
her own body.

She ached in places she'd never ached before and when
he casually dropped the towel on the floor and strolled towards her, a vision of bronzed, masculine perfection, her
heart thundered in delicious anticipation.

Unable to drag her eyes away from his magnificent body,
Alesia struggled to breathe. How could she not have noticed
before how staggeringly good-looking he was?

And how could he be so relaxed and at ease when her
entire body was humming with tension?

Didn't he feel it too?

He strolled to the edge of the bed, cast her a sweeping
glance from under thick black lashes and then reached for
his Rolex which he'd left on the bedside table.

It was only when he turned away from her that she realized
she'd been holding her breath.

She stared at him as he walked back across the room and

started to dress and the question spilled out before she could stop it. 'Are you coming back to bed?'

'For what purpose?' His tone was bored and he didn't even glance in her direction as he finished dressing. 'This was business, remember, and for now at least that part of our business is concluded.'

'And that's it?' Her voice was barely a whisper as she sat up, clutching the silk sheets to her breasts. 'That's all you're going to say?'

He paused in the doorway, his lean, strong face displaying not one flicker of emotion as he studied her in brooding contemplation. 'Let me know if you're pregnant.'

With that he strolled out of the room and let the door swing closed behind him.

Soaked in humiliation, Alesia sank back against the pillows.

How could he be so totally cold and unfeeling? Such an utter bastard?

Almost screaming with anger and frustration, she rolled over to try and ease the maddening ache in her body and gritted her teeth.

It didn't matter what he said or how he touched her, she was *never* letting him back in her bed again!

CHAPTER FIVE

Two weeks later Alesia was in the enormous kitchen at the far end of the house when Sebastien came striding into the room, simmering with barely restrained masculine aggression, a thunderous look on his handsome face.

'What the *hell* are you doing in here?' In raw frustration he raked lean bronzed fingers through sleek, dark hair and inhaled deeply. 'I have been searching *everywhere* for you. No one had a clue where you were.'

Sexual awareness shot through her body and Alesia dug her nails into her palms.

Two weeks.

It had been two whole weeks since she'd last laid eyes on him and, like a young puppy seeing his master after a long separation, her quivering, yearning body just exploded with excitement.

One greedy, tentative glance at that lean, handsome face with its fierce, dark eyes and blue-shadowed jaw was enough to make Alesia's stomach drop and her pulse rate double. One glance and she remembered every frantic, hot, seductive moment of the way this man made love. And, if that wasn't bad enough, her whole being just lifted with happiness because he was finally, finally *home*.

Appalled by the strength of her reaction to him, she turned towards the fridge, hiding her face. She couldn't help the way she felt about him but at least she refused to give him the satisfaction of showing him, she thought grimly. He'd already made his thoughts on the subject clear, having slept with her once and then absented himself for two whole weeks. Clearly their one sexual encounter had bored him in the extreme, whereas her complete lack of experience and sophistication meant that she'd left him in no doubt whatsoever that he was a God in the bedroom. The knowledge that she'd held nothing back made her *squirm* with bonedeep humiliation.

She wished she could put the clock back. Two weeks ago she hadn't even noticed his firm, sexy mouth, the seductive glint in his Mediterranean dark eyes or the perfect musculature of his powerful body. She hadn't noticed the superb bone structure or the slightly cynical smile that turned heads everywhere he went. *She hadn't noticed him as a man.* Now she noticed *everything* and every feminine part of her shrieked in recognition of his raw, untamed masculinity.

'Naturally I didn't know that you were searching for me,' she said coolly, poking around in the fridge until she was confident that her betraying colour had subsided. Only when she was sure that she was in control did she remove some cheese and a bowl of glossy dark olives from the fridge and place them on the table. 'And in answer to your question, I'm making myself lunch.'

He strolled into the room and glanced at her with naked incredulity. 'Why?'

Because she'd never had access to so much delicious food in her life and it was just marvellous not to go hungry in order to save money.

She shrugged. 'Why not?'

'Because I have an extensive and well-rewarded staff,' he said slowly, enunciating his words as if he were addressing a child, his astonishment palpable, 'and their job is to produce meals for you so that you don't have to take an inconvenient break in your shopping schedule.'

She flinched at his cutting remark. His opinion of her was just *so* low. But could she really blame him for that? After all, she was the one who'd given him that impression and had to continue to do so. 'I have all the time I need to shop,' she said idly, 'given that I haven't seen you since our wedding day. And your staff have got better things to do than make me lunch.'

He was looking at her with a stunned expression on his handsome face.

'I don't know why you're looking at me like that.' She glanced impatiently in his direction. 'Have you never made yourself lunch before?'

'Frankly, no,' he confessed drily, a strange expression in his eyes as he looked at her. 'And I hadn't exactly expected you to either. Do you often waltz into your grandfather's kitchen and make yourself lunch?'

Alesia froze. She'd done it again. Had forgotten that she was supposed to be rich and pampered. Then she gave a mental shrug.

'I don't expect people to wait on me.' Aware that he was looking at her curiously, she sighed and rolled her eyes. 'Now what?'

'It's just that you constantly surprise me,' he drawled softly, his gaze speculative. 'Just when I think I have you all worked out, you do something that is totally out of character.'

She cast him a look of contempt. 'You know *nothing* about my character.'

'Evidently not,' he murmured, his shimmering dark eyes narrowed as he surveyed her thoughtfully. 'However, I think our staff might be a little shocked if they discover you in here, making lunch.'

Alesia bit her lip and refrained from telling him that she was already on first-name terms with his head chef and that they'd swapped Greek and English recipes. 'They're *your* staff.'

'You're *my* wife.'

Her body tingled at his silky reminder. 'Forgive me for forgetting that fact,' she said acidly. 'I haven't seen you since our wedding day two weeks ago. I assumed you'd taken up residence elsewhere.'

And she just *hated* him for not even bothering to show his face.

'I didn't realize you were going to miss me so much and it was our wedding *night*,' he corrected softly, studying her through narrowed eyes. 'You saw me on our wedding night. Another occasion when you surprised me. I wasn't expecting a virgin in my bed.'

Her cheeks flamed. 'I don't know what you mean—'

'You should have told me,' he said smoothly. 'Greek men are very possessive, *agape mou*. I might have been prepared to raise the purchase price still further had I realized the unique value of the goods. You missed out.'

She winced at his mercenary assessment of her character. 'I was satisfied with the deal.'

His eyes glittered in his handsome face. 'I'm beginning to think that I might be too,' he drawled, stepping closer to her. 'You were *amazingly* responsive.'

Graphic images flashed through her brain and her legs started to tremble as the memories came crashing back.

'You paid me to perform in your bed,' she said unsteadily, 'so that's what I did.'

He gave a short laugh and moved closer still. 'You were *totally* out of control, *agape mou*, and you expect me to believe that you were acting?'

He was too close. She couldn't breathe. *Couldn't think.*

She wasn't used to dealing with men like him. She wasn't used to talking about sex.

Careful not to look at him, she sliced the cheese into chunks and laid it in a bowl. 'It wasn't my choice to introduce sex into our marriage. I was perfectly happy to have a very different sort of marriage.'

'One where I pay you to do nothing?'

'You weren't paying me for sex,' she said steadily, adding

olives to the bowl. 'You were paying me for the "privilege" of taking over my grandfather's company.'

'It might interest you to know that that particular "privilege" has taken up every daylight hour since our wedding,' he drawled, his eyes raking over her in frowning contemplation. 'Your grandfather is an appalling businessman. You can blame him for the fact that you haven't seen me.'

'I'd rather thank him,' she said, putting the finishing touches to her salad and lifting the bowl. 'I had no desire to spend any time with you at all. And now, if you'll excuse me, I'm planning to go and eat my lunch.'

And phone her mother.

That had been one of the major benefits of Sebastien's long absence. She'd been in daily contact and was following her mother's progress anxiously.

'No.' His voice was lethally soft as he lifted the bowl from her clutching fingers and returned it to the table. 'I do *not* excuse you.'

She made the mistake of looking at him. Stormy blue eyes clashed with smouldering black and instantly the breath caught in her chest.

The look in his eyes was intensely sexual and she could see that his mind most certainly wasn't on anything as boring as lunch.

His eyes moved from hers, lingering on the full curve of her breasts and then sliding down to rest on her smooth, flat stomach exposed by her hipster jeans. 'Don't wear trousers again. You have great legs. I want to see them—'

'You are such a chauvinist,' she flung at him, her cheeks flaming with colour at his remark. 'Do you always tell women what to wear?'

'Women don't usually go out with me looking as though they're about to unblock a drain.'

'I like my jeans. They're comfortable.'

'So is underwear,' he said silkily, his lashes lowering as

he gave her a look of pure sexual speculation. 'And that would be my preference.'

Knees shaking, she put a hand on the table for support. 'I'll wear what I want to wear—'

'Not in my company,' he said, his tone suddenly icy. 'You'll wear what I want to see you in.'

She bit her lip. 'That's ridiculous.'

'You should have thought of that before you sold yourself.'

She gave him an incredulous look. 'You want me wander round your house in my underwear?'

'If I tell you to.' His gaze was mocking. 'I pay enough for you. I might as well see what I'm buying.'

She turned her head so he wouldn't see the tears that stung her eyes. He made her feel so *cheap*. 'Fine.' Pulling herself together, she threw him a tight smile. 'I'll wear my jeans when you're not here, which is most of the time, fortunately. Now, if you don't mind, I'd like to eat my lunch.'

Before she could guess his intention, he curved a lean brown hand around the strip of flesh exposed by her top and hauled her against him.

Trapped by the expression in his eyes, her heart began to hammer against her chest and her head swam alarmingly.

He lifted lean bronzed hands and cupped her face, forcing her to look at him. 'Are you pregnant?'

The question threw her and she gazed up at him in total shock. 'No.'

'Good.' He gave a devilish smile and scooped her into his arms. 'And you know what they say—if at first you don't succeed—'

'What are you doing?' She started to wriggle out of his arms but then his mouth fastened on hers in the most erotic kiss imaginable and, like a starving man finally facing the prospect of a meal, she sobbed with relief and fell into that kiss.

His tongue delved into her mouth in an explicit gesture of masculine intent that sent her pulse racing and her head spinning. Her arms slid round his strong neck, her fingers tangled with his silky dark hair and she wriggled in his arms just desperate for more.

Mouths locked, they ravaged each other, biting, licking, exchanging gasps and groans, stoking the heat between them to almost intolerable levels.

His mouth still fastened to hers, he lowered her back to the ground and thrust her back against the wall, every inch of his powerful body hard against hers.

Alesia sucked in some much-needed air, her stomach tumbling frantically as she felt the heavy throb of his arousal against her.

A sound in the corridor outside made them both freeze.

'*Theos mou*, what are we doing?' He glanced around him in naked disbelief. 'This is my *kitchen*, a room I have only visited a few times in my whole life.'

She closed her eyes in embarrassment. 'Someone could have walked in—'

'No chance. If they had I would have fired them,' Sebastien announced raggedly, closing long fingers around her wrist and virtually dragging her out of the room. 'I value my privacy above everything else and my staff are fully aware of that fact.'

Hoping the staff in question were nowhere nearby to witness her surrender to caveman tactics, Alesia struggled to keep up with his long stride. 'Where are we going?'

'Somewhere I will not have to stare at pots and pans when I have finished with you,' he said silkily, striding towards the stairs so rapidly that she virtually had to run to keep up with him.

'*Sebastien—*'

Once in the bedroom he kicked the door shut behind them, lifted her up and deposited her in the middle of his bed.

She'd promised herself that if he ever came near her again she'd slap his arrogant face and walk in the opposite direction. So why was it that she couldn't move?

She watched in hypnotized fascination as he lifted a lean brown hand and removed his tie with a few skilled flicks of those clever fingers. His eyes never leaving hers, he undid the buttons on his shirt and yanked it off, revealing a bronzed muscular chest covered in curling dark hairs.

'Time to lose the jeans,' he suggested helpfully, his shimmering dark gaze fastened on her flushed face as he dispensed with the rest of his clothes with single-minded purpose. 'Do it yourself, or I'll do it for you.'

Alesia lay frozen, helpless to look away from his fabulous body. No wonder he was totally unselfconscious about parading around naked, she thought numbly. He was as near perfect as a man could get and just looking at him made her mouth dry.

Without the outward trappings of sophistication he was revealed in all his masculine glory.

Desire heated and coiled low in her pelvis and her breathing quickened in anticipation.

Lithe and athletic, he came down on the bed next to her, one arm sliding under her and stripping off her clothes in a series of deft, decisive moves.

'That's how I prefer you, *pethi mou*,' he growled, his heated gaze sliding down her naked, trembling length in blatant sexual appraisal.

Alesia squirmed with anticipation and forgot her resolve not to let him touch her again. Every part of her burned for him and the worst thing was that he knew it. He gave a low, satisfied laugh and teased the tip of one breast with slow flicks of his tongue.

She gasped and arched towards him and he answered her unspoken plea for more by sliding his hand downwards, his strong fingers finding her slick warmth.

He gave a groan of acknowledgement. 'Waiting two weeks clearly has its benefits,' he said hoarsely. 'It's amazingly gratifying to have a wife who is so willing.'

The barely veiled insult went straight over her head and, with a shocking degree of masculine purpose, Sebastien raised her hips and thrust into her hard.

'Is this what you want?' He shifted her position and drove deeper still and Alesia let out a thickened moan, swamped by an almost intolerable sexual excitement.

Her body exploded into orgasm and Sebastien brought his mouth down on hers and kissed her hard, smothering her sobs with the pressure of his mouth and stealing her breath with the intimate lick of his tongue.

He thrust into her with rhythmic force, his powerful body shuddering over hers as he reached his own completion. Finally he dragged his mouth from hers and inhaled unsteadily.

Stormy black eyes clashed with hers and then he rolled on to his side and gathered her against him, curving her slim, trembling body against his powerful frame.

'That was simply amazing,' he said huskily, sliding a leisurely hand down her back and between her legs, 'if a little quick. So now we'll do it again. Slowly.'

Still trembling from the force of her own climax, she gave a gasp of shock which turned to a moan of disbelief and longing as his skilled fingers slid into her already hotly excited body. He stroked and teased her in the most intimate way possible and then rolled her on to her stomach with the supreme confidence of a man with a single purpose in mind.

Battling with the realization that he intended to do it again and that she had no intention of stopping him, Alesia buried her burning face in the pillow and gave a moan of denial as he lifted her on to her knees and positioned himself behind her.

She opened her mouth on a shocked gasp, intending to

protest that he couldn't—*they couldn't*—and then felt the silken pressure of his masculine arousal against her most intimate place. Unconsciously she moved her hips in feminine invitation and heard him mutter something in Greek before his strong hands grasped her writhing hips and anchored her for his powerful thrust.

Alesia went up in flames. Never in her whole life had she ever imagined a sensation so indescribably, unbelievably, *wickedly* good. Still sensitized from her first climax, her body started to contract immediately and she heard him utter a shocked exclamation as she exploded into orgasm within seconds of his penetration.

No longer in control of any part of herself, Alesia cried out and sobbed, begged and moaned, so totally uninhibited and driven by passion that her whole body was a quivering mass of sensation.

She felt the unrestrained power of driving masculine thrusts, heard his hoarse exclamation of disbelief and then lost touch with reality as his own pulsing release sent her over the edge into ecstasy yet again.

For a moment they were both held suspended in a place of such exquisite excitement that reality no longer existed for either of them. And then finally the wildness subsided, leaving them both shuddering in the aftermath of an unbelievable experience.

Eventually Sebastien moved, but only to roll both of them back on to the bed with a very male groan of undiluted sexual satisfaction.

Alesia lay with her eyes closed, shell-shocked and totally exhausted. She couldn't believe that she could have behaved in such a way. Couldn't believe she was capable of being so shameless and abandoned. *And she couldn't believe that it had been even better than last time.* This time she'd known what he was capable of doing to her, what she was capable of feeling, and that knowledge had heightened her excitement to intolerable levels.

'Well, that was definitely an improvement on an afternoon of meetings,' he drawled, his eyes still closed as he lay on his back, one bronzed arm resting across his face, the other holding her firmly against him. 'Had I known how hot you were when I signed those papers I wouldn't have hesitated. You are worth every penny of the money you charge.'

Plunged back into the stark reality of her life by his harsh words, Alesia kept her eyes tightly shut, wishing that he'd stayed in the meetings. At least then she wouldn't have had to cope with the knowledge that she'd once more abandoned herself totally to a man who clearly despised her.

'I don't know how you can make love to me when you so clearly hate me,' she murmured, careful to keep the shake out of her voice as she struggled to forget all the things she'd begged him to do to her while she'd been under the influence of his superior seduction technique.

'Because we don't make love,' he drawled flatly, his eyes hard as they locked with hers. 'We have sex, Alesia. And, fortunately for you, having sex does not require emotional attachment. If it did then men would never use the services of prostitutes.'

She gave a gasp of pain and curled her fingers into the sheets. 'Are you comparing me to a prostitute?'

'Not at all.' He gave her a cool smile and sprang out of bed, lithe and energetic, as if he hadn't just spent an entire afternoon engaged in extremely physical activity. 'You're much more expensive.'

'I really, really hate you, do you know that?' Wounded and humiliated, she curled up in the bed and pulled the sheet over her for protection, consumed by a self-loathing so powerful that the pain of it was almost physical. How could she respond to a man who clearly had absolutely no respect for her? 'I don't want you to come near me again.'

It was said for her benefit as much as his but he merely smiled.

'Yes, you do.' He strolled back to the bed and leaned over, planting both arms on the mattress so that his face was only inches from hers. 'Do you think I don't know how much you ache for me? You may want to hate me but, fortunately for both of us, your hot little body is totally lacking in scruples and the moment I flick the switch you're mine.'

She lifted a hand to slap his face but he caught it with a warning glance.

'Not nice, my little wife,' he purred softly. 'You made your bed and now you're lying in it. Or rather, you're lying in mine. On your front, on your back, whichever way I choose to position you. And that's where you're going to stay.'

Her eyes clouded with pain. 'I want you to leave me alone—'

'Not a chance.' With a final lingering glance at her lush mouth, Sebastien straightened and picked up the phone by the bed, his eyes fixed on hers as he spoke in rapid Greek. Minutes later there was a discreet tap on the door and he answered it and came back to bed carrying a tray. 'Sit up. You need to eat or you'll collapse on me later.'

She stayed stubbornly under the sheet. 'I'm not hungry.'

'We've just had sex without stopping for six hours,' he said in a conversational tone. 'You didn't eat that lunch and you're going to miss dinner. I don't want you fainting on me in the nightclub.'

Six hours? She stared at him in mute astonishment and then glanced at the darkened windows. The knowledge that she'd been so sexually transported that she'd lost all track of time made her want to sink deeper in the bed. It took her a moment to register the rest of his statement.

'Nightclub?' Her voice shook. 'What nightclub—?'

'The one I'm taking you to this evening,' he said smoothly.

'It is a new business venture of a *very* good friend of mine. Athens society will be deciding whether it is the ''in'' place to be seen.'

And doubtless if Sebastien Fiorukis were there then it would be considered the 'in' place to be seen, she thought helplessly. He was a man who set trends, a man who others followed.

She clutched the sheet. 'I don't feel like going out.'

'Your feelings on the matter are completely irrelevant,' he informed her in a bored tone. 'I wish to make an appearance with my new wife.'

'I'm not getting dressed.'

He didn't hesitate. 'Then I take you naked,' he promised softly, his dark eyes glittering dangerously as he surveyed her. 'It's your decision, *pethi mou*. You're my wife and part of your role is to entertain.'

'I thought I just did,' she said tartly and he gave an appreciative smile.

'That sort of entertainment is for me alone, *agape mou*,' he drawled lazily. 'What I had in mind was something more formal. I am meeting some *very* important guests. I need you to charm them.'

Her jaw lifted stubbornly and she tried a different tack. 'I don't have a single thing to wear—'

He gave the sigh of a male vastly experienced in the challenges presented by female attire. 'On the day of our wedding two weeks ago I furnished you with an indecent sum of money to add to your already *indecent* fortune,' he reminded her in a silky tone. 'Doubtless you have spent the last two entire weeks shopping. Pick something suitable and wear it.'

She swallowed painfully. What was she supposed to say? That she hadn't been near a shop in the two weeks since their wedding?

'I—I haven't bought anything—'

His eyes narrowed and his mouth tightened. 'Every single

penny of the money I gave you has gone from your account,' he said softly. 'You withdrew the whole lot, my hot, sexy wife, so don't tell me that you haven't been spending because I won't believe you.'

Panic slithered over her bones as she realized that he was obviously tracking her spending. How could she have been so naïve as to think he wouldn't know? Did he know where the money had gone? No, or he would have said something.

'I—I bought different things,' she hedged, sitting upright and grabbing at the sheet before it slid to her waist.

With a disbelieving glance in her direction, he prowled into the enormous dressing room that adjoined their bedroom.

Alesia closed her eyes and waited in a state of unbelievable tension for the inevitable explosion.

There was a long, pulsing silence and then he strolled back to the bedroom and picked up the phone again, barking out a set of commands in rapid Greek.

Resolving to learn Greek as soon as possible, Alesia discovered that she was still holding her breath and released it suddenly.

He must have seen that her wardrobes were totally empty and yet he hadn't said a word.

What was going on?

'Use the shower,' he ordered, lifting a bottle of champagne out of an ice bucket and handing it to her. 'By the time you've finished, the clothes will have arrived.'

'What clothes?'

'The clothes I have just ordered for you,' he said with all the casual assurance of someone with a bottomless bank account. She looked at him nervously. Suddenly he seemed very intimidating.

What was she going to say to him when he finally demanded answers on how she'd spent the money?

Her mind in overdrive, searching for plausible excuses, she stumbled into the luxurious bathroom and stood under the revitalizing spray of the shower. Suddenly she had a new awareness of her body and, after five minutes of searing-hot water and several applications of various luxurious shower foams, she realized that nothing was going to wash away the memory of Sebastien's own heady brand of lovemaking.

Filled with a self-loathing that all the water in the world couldn't quench, Alesia turned off the shower, dried herself quickly and wrapped herself in a large fluffy towel that virtually covered her from neck to toe.

Suitably concealed, she lifted her chin and strolled back into the bedroom with as much aloof dignity as she could muster.

Immediately her eyes were drawn to a rail packed with clothes and she stared at the rail and then back at him in amazement. 'Where did these come from? You didn't have time to go to a shop—'

'If you're rich then the shop comes to you,' he informed her smoothly, 'but, as the pampered granddaughter of Dimitrios Philipos, I'm sure you don't need me to tell you that.'

She swallowed, her eyes still on the rail.

Stores brought the clothes to him?

Noticing a selection of expensive cosmetics laid out on a nearby table, she blinked in amazement. It seemed that nothing had been left to chance.

She strolled over to the rail, trying to look as though this sort of thing happened to her every day. She'd never had the opportunity to even look at clothes of this quality and style before, let alone wear them. In awe she fingered a silk skirt so short that it was almost indecent.

'Good choice,' he said cynically from immediately behind her. 'That skirt has "slut" written all over it, and seeing as that's what you are you might as well advertise the fact.'

She turned on him, eyes flashing with hurt, her blonde hair

tumbling over her shoulders. 'And if I'm a slut, what does that make you?'

'Sexually satisfied,' he mocked, removing her towel with a single, purposeful jerk of his bronzed hand.

She gave a gasp of shock and grabbed at the towel but he held it out of reach, his eyes slightly narrowed as they swept over her naked body.

'You really do have the most amazing body,' he murmured, skimming a hand over one full breast. Immediately Alesia's nipples peaked and he gave a low laugh. 'And you really, *really* want me, don't you? If we weren't pushed for time I'd take you straight back to bed and try yet another position.'

Her face scarlet with mortification, Alesia tried to turn away from him but he swung her round to face him, his hands holding her firmly.

'Just don't be tempted to flirt with anyone else tonight,' he warned. 'You may be a slut but you're mine alone. I *never* share.'

Flirt?

Still horribly conscious of her nudity, Alesia stared at him in disbelief, reminding herself that this man knew absolutely *nothing* about her. She'd never flirted in her life and wouldn't even know where to begin. Because of her situation she'd always avoided that sort of contact with men. Had avoided relationships deeper than friendship.

Sebastien reached out a hand and grabbed a top from the rail. 'Wear this with the skirt,' he ordered, 'and no bra.'

She stared at the clothes in dismay. She'd never worn anything like them in her life. 'I c-can't go braless,' she stammered. 'I'm too—'

'Curvaceous?' he taunted her. 'Plenty of people out there are wondering why I married you. I intend to show them.'

Goaded beyond reason by his taunts, she turned on him. 'Are you sure you wouldn't prefer me to just go out in my underwear?' Her tone dripped sarcasm and he gave a slow smile.

'This is going to be even sexier than underwear, trust me.'

Alesia closed her eyes. She couldn't believe this was happening. 'You can't make me wear that outfit.'

'Don't test me, Alesia,' he warned softly.

'Fine.' She yanked the outfit out of his hand, grabbed a handful of the cosmetics and shot him a defiant look. 'If you want the whole world to know you married a slut, then that's up to you. Let's broadcast it, shall we?'

She stalked into the bathroom and slammed the door behind her.

CHAPTER SIX

SEBASTIEN checked his watch and paced the length of his bedroom one more time.

Never before had he had reason to question his mental acuity, but nothing about his new wife was making sense. She was an heiress in her own right, had demanded an extortionate sum of money from him on her wedding day, *a sum which he knew had already vanished from her account*—and yet there were no visible signs of profligate spending. She'd led a pampered and privileged existence from the day she was born, and yet she'd been in the kitchen making her own lunch as if she did it every day. And she'd been wearing a pair of ancient jeans that no previous woman of his acquaintance would have been seen dead in. It did not add up.

When he'd married Alesia Philipos he'd expected rich, pampered, shallow and boring. In his eyes her only redeeming feature had been her incredible face and body and her apparent willingness to display it. What he *hadn't* expected was complex—and his new wife was definitely complex.

Realising that she'd been in the bathroom for the best part of an hour, Sebastien stared at the closed door in brooding contemplation. What could she be doing in there that was taking so long?

Never good at waiting at the best of times, he was at the point of breaking down the bathroom door in search of an answer when the lock finally clicked and Alesia stepped back into the bedroom.

Sebastien stilled, his usually restless gaze arrested by the girl standing in front of him.

Only years of experience in controlling his facial expression prevented his jaw from hitting the ground.

Whatever she'd been doing in the bathroom all that time, the end result was spectacular.

She was drop dead gorgeous. Beautiful.

Her skin was pale and flawless, the faint brush of colour on her cheeks simply emphasizing the perfect shape of her face. Her incredible violet eyes looked larger than ever and the subtle sheen of colour applied to her lips simply accentuated the tempting curve of her mouth.

Sebastian bit back a groan of lust as his eyes raked every delectable inch of her in unashamed masculine appreciation.

She shouldn't have looked like that in the outfit he'd chosen.

She should have looked like a cheap tart. Instead she managed to look innocent and seductively feminine at the same time, although how a woman could contrive to look innocent in a skirt barely wider than a belt, he couldn't imagine. Her slender legs went on for ever, the miniskirt skimmed her perfectly shaped bottom and the tiny top exposed a tantalizing stretch of feminine midriff. It was just tight enough to offer support to her full breasts and Sebastien's body hardened in urgent and immediate response. For a brief but distinctly unsettling moment he struggled to remember why they had to leave the bedroom.

It was just as well he had a reliable team of bodyguards, he reflected grimly as he wrestled his emotions under control, because otherwise he'd have trouble keeping people away from her. *Men* away from her.

Sebastien ground his teeth, astonished by how possessive he felt over a woman he didn't even like.

'You insisted on this outfit so you can stop staring,' she said stiffly, 'and I probably ought to warn you that I'm not used to walking in heels this high, so unless you want me to break an ankle I'm gong to have to hold your arm.'

Taken aback by her candid admission that she'd rarely worn heels before and mentally adding that muttered confession to a growing list of facts that just didn't add up, Sebastien frowned as he felt her hand slide over his biceps.

'It's hold you or fall over. Otherwise, believe me, I wouldn't touch you with a bargepole. I hope you're well insured,' she muttered, stooping with a pained frown and sliding a finger along the strap. 'If I tread on anyone's foot while I'm dancing in these I'm going to cause *serious* damage.'

He gritted his teeth and refrained from pointing out that she wouldn't be dancing with anyone but him. Not given to making mistakes, Sebastien was forced to admit that in this case he'd made a serious error of judgement.

He'd intended her to dress like a tart to remind him of the woman she really was, because he was finding those huge eyes and that innocent expression profoundly distracting. Instead he'd turned her into nothing short of a walking temptation.

Staring down into her beautiful face, he suddenly realized that the glow of almost childlike innocence came from inside her. Nothing she wore would ever make her look cheap because she just exuded class.

A well-disguised gold-digger, he reminded himself grimly, reaching for his jacket and striding towards the door.

No matter how stunning she was or how exciting his new wife was in bed, there was no way that he'd be forgetting what had brought her there in the first place.

His money.

In the back of the limousine Alesia felt the slide of expensive leather under her bare thighs and stared down at her glamorously shod feet with almost childish fascination. A bubble of laughter threatened to erupt inside her and she struggled to hold it back. She just *loved* the shoes. They were sexy and glamorous and totally frivolous and she'd never owned anything frivolous before in her life. *And she loved the clothes.* And the make-up. She'd never had the money to spend on cosmetics before so she had absolutely no experience of applying them, which was why she'd taken so long in the bathroom.

After the first effort she'd looked like a clown, and after the second she'd managed to look as though she had a cold. Finally, after her face had been given time to settle down from all the washing and scrubbing, she'd managed to master the art of subtle enhancement and she'd been delighted with the result. And, although she felt hideously self-conscious in such revealing clothes, she also felt beautiful. Was this what it was like to be seriously rich? She wrapped one long leg over the other and felt a flash of satisfaction as she saw Sebastien's molten gaze settle on the length of thigh exposed by the ridiculous skirt.

He wanted her.

She resisted the temptation to smile and smile. He might loathe and despise her but he *definitely* wanted her. And he might pretend to be ultra cool about it, but surely no man could spend six hours in bed with a woman if he were as bored and indifferent as he pretended to be?

Lost in her own private thoughts, a sudden flash of light in her face made her jump and she gave a gasp and shrank back in her seat while Sebastien gave a soft curse.

'Paparazzi,' he muttered by way of explanation as the car slid to a halt outside a glitzy-looking building. 'They won't be allowed in the club so just smile and don't speak.'

'What is it about Greek men that keeps them well and truly stuck in the Stone Age? I'm *always* being told not to speak.' Alesia reached for her bag, hoping that she could manage to walk as far as the door of the nightclub without twisting her ankle. 'Someone ought to tell you that these days women are supposed to have a voice.'

Sebastien caught her arm and prevented her from leaving the car. 'Carlo will open the door. It prevents the press getting too close,' he said smoothly. 'And, for your information, I have a totally modern outlook when it comes to the role of women. You can speak whenever you choose. But not to the press.'

Totally modern?

Alesia gaped at him, wondering if he truly knew himself at all. This was a man who told her how to wear her hair and how to dress and who clearly saw her prime role as being to satisfy his rampant sexual needs. And he thought he was modern?

Before she could enlighten him as to the true meaning of the word, the car door opened and she was ushered into the nightclub amidst an explosion of flashbulbs and photographers yelling for her to look this way and that.

One photographer came in too close and was instantly blocked by two of Sebastien's security team.

Alesia glanced around her in confusion and astonishment. 'I can't think why they're suddenly so interested in me,' she muttered and Sebastien flashed her a seductive smile that seriously threatened her ability to walk in a straight line.

'Because I married you, *agape mou*,' he drawled lazily, 'and our two families have been at war for three generations. Newspaper editors the world over are loving it and so are the gossip magazines. Photographs of us will sell for a small fortune.'

People would *pay* for photographs of them?

Why? She was just an ordinary girl dressed up in designer clothes!

Casting a shimmering glance in her direction, Sebastien lifted an eyebrow. '*How* did your grandfather manage to keep you hidden from the media for all those years, tell me that?'

Alesia dragged her fascinated gaze away from the banks of photographers jolting for her attention. 'I—er—I led a

very private life,' she muttered vaguely, wondering again
why anyone would be remotely interested in staring at a photograph of her. The outfit was nice, but still…

Alesia allowed herself to be ushered into the sleek, ultra-
modern club and gazed around in awe. The club was crowded
with beautiful people and she realized suddenly that her impossibly tiny skirt didn't look remotely out of place in this
setting.

'This place is crowded with people wearing nothing but
underwear.' She raised her voice to be heard above the music
and Sebastien raised a dark eyebrow in response to her comment and then gave a reluctant smile.

'Dancing is hot work.'

Watching the gyrations on the dance floor, Alesia opened
her mouth to confess that she'd never been to a nightclub in
her life before and then realized that such a confession would
betray far too much about her.

Evidently he believed her to be a real party animal: a rich,
pampered heiress who spent her entire life shopping and then
modelling the results. This was supposed to be her natural
habitat.

She stared around in fascination, drinking it all in. She'd
never been *anywhere* like this.

Coloured lights swirled and flashed, various effects shimmered and smoked and through it all the pounding, pulsing
beat of the music tempted more and more people on to the
exotically lit dance floor.

Alesia felt a thrill of excitement that she couldn't quite
identify. Suddenly, more than anything, she wanted to be on
that dance floor. She wanted to let her body move to the
compelling, hypnotic rhythm. *She wanted to enjoy herself.*

She turned to Sebastien, her eyes bright and her lips parted.
'I want to dance.'

And dance and dance…

Night-black eyes clashed with hers and his hard mouth lifted in mockery. 'With or without the shoes?'

She didn't care. She just wanted to *move*.

'I'll start with shoes and then we'll see—' Aware that they were still attracting a significant degree of interest, she glanced around with a frown. 'Do people *never* stop staring?'

'You are the granddaughter of one of the richest men in the world,' he drawled, casting a cynical glance over his broad shoulder. 'Like me, you must be used to it. People always stare. You know that.'

She bit her lip and tried to look casual and confident, as though being the object of everyone's attention was an everyday occurrence.

With an air of bored cool that reflected his total lack of interest in the people gawping at them, Sebastien threaded his fingers through hers and led her on to the dance floor, retaining his possessive grip on her as they moved together.

The music pounded and pulsed and Alesia closed her eyes and discovered for the first time in her life that she just *loved* to dance. She loved the silken brush of her hair as it swished from side to side, loved the sinuous sway of her body as she moved her hips and arms to the addictive rhythm of the music. In fact she loved it *all*.

She danced to record after record, her body seduced by the hectic rhythm of the music and the relative anonymity of the crowded dance floor.

Finally the music slowed and Sebastien hauled her against him in a characteristically possessive gesture which should have annoyed her but for some reason made her already wide smile widen even further.

He was easily the best-looking guy in the room and all the women were staring at him. And she was willing to bet that they would have been staring even if he hadn't been rich and famous and useful for selling newspapers to a public hungry for a diet of celebrity gossip. Sebastien Fiorukis was a man who would stand out in the densest crowd. It was like parking a sleek Ferrari in a bicycle shed. He just looked *expensive* and he had an air of power and command that would always draw women like moths to a bright flame.

But for tonight he was with *her*, she thought, gleeful as a child as she intercepted the envious glances cast in her direction.

Trying to see him as a stranger would, her eyes skimmed over his glossy dark hair and slid to the hint of bronzed skin visible at the neck of his shirt. He looked every inch the multi-millionaire that he was. Vibrant, driven and successful at everything he touched. A man who didn't know the meaning of the word failure. He was part of her new costume and every bit as glamorous and sophisticated as the shoes and the designer outfit.

They danced until her feet ached and her throat was parched and finally she agreed to his suggestion that they break for a drink.

Responding to an impulse that she didn't understand, she wound her arms around him and gave him a spontaneous hug before they left the dance floor. 'Oh, Sebastien, thank you.' Breathless and laughing, her eyes shone as she looked up at him. 'This is fantastic and I'm having the *best* time—' She felt him stiffen and watched as stunned dark eyes swept her flushed cheeks.

'You're behaving as though you've never been to a night-club before.'

'I haven't. I mean, not one like this,' she corrected herself quickly, wincing at her own mistake. Aware that he was studying her with a curious expression on his face, she tilted her head questioningly, still breathless from wild dancing, her eyes shining with an excitement that she couldn't even begin to conceal.

She knew she should be playing it cool, looking bored and indifferent as if she spent her life in places like this, but she just couldn't. There was too much adrenalin flowing through her veins, too much excitement—

In fact, she wanted the evening never to end—

'What?' She tried to slow her breathing. 'You're staring at me because I've got a red face, aren't you?'

His eyes narrowed. 'I'm staring at you because I've never seen you smile before.'

'Well, I'm having a nice time.' Forgetting to be guarded, she glanced back at the dance floor regretfully. 'Do you think we could—'

'No,' Sebastian drawled immediately, taking her hand and leading her to a vacant table with a prime view of the dance floor. 'We definitely couldn't. I'm a man in need of a drink.'

Alesia registered that her shoes were digging into her feet and plopped gratefully on to one of the chairs, wondering why this table was free when the rest of the club was heaving with people. She felt tired and just *ridiculously* happy. She was uncovering a whole new side to herself that she'd never even known existed. She'd always assumed that she wasn't like other girls. That she didn't enjoy partying, clothes or other 'girly' pursuits. But now she realized that she'd never actually been given a chance to experience those things. And the truth was she loved them. For the first time in her life she could be self-indulgent and just *enjoy* herself.

She was just wondering at exactly what point she dared suggest venturing back on the dance floor when the crowds pressing in on their table parted.

'Sebastien! You came!' A tall, slender woman wearing an indecently low-cut black dress shimmered up to their table, her glossy mouth curved into a predatory smile. 'I'm *so* pleased.'

'Ariadne.' Sebastien rose to his feet and kissed the woman on both cheeks. 'You've surpassed yourself. I predict a massive success.'

The woman threw a satisfied glance at the heaving dance

floor. 'Captivating, isn't it? And stylish. We're already having to restrict membership.' Her slim fingers curled possessively over his forearm, the scarlet nails gleaming like a warning. 'I'm glad you came. I reserved you the best table.'

Sebastien's gaze fastened on those reddened lips and he smiled. 'Thanks.'

'I *really* need the benefit of your business brain.' Ariadne slid into the vacant seat next to him, not glancing once in Alesia's direction. 'We've come up against a couple of problems and I might need you to use your influence—' Ariadne's voice lowered and she leaned closer to Sebastien, her hand snaking around his strong neck, drawing his head towards her reddened lips ostensibly so that she could keep the conversation private.

Watching this interaction with frowning dismay, Alesia felt her newly discovered happiness drain out of her. It was quite clear that his relationship with this woman was far more intimate than simple friendship. Was she one of his mistresses? And, if so, past or current? The thought that he'd shared with other women what he'd shared with her made her feel physically ill. If she needed any more evidence that to him it was just sex then she had it now.

And, to make matters worse, the woman hadn't even glanced in her direction. It was as if she didn't exist.

Feeling as miserable as she had been happy only moments earlier, Alesia reached for the drink that had been placed by her hand and took several large mouthfuls.

She sat and drank, waiting to be included in the conversation, waiting for Sebastien to introduce her, but he lounged easily in the chair, his handsome face giving nothing away as he listened attentively to the woman who was all but wrapped around him in an attempt to exclude Alesia.

She couldn't help being aware of the curious stares being cast in her direction. It was hardly surprising that people were looking, she thought gloomily. They were supposed to be newly married and yet Sebastien had clearly forgotten her existence.

Ignored and abandoned, Alesia felt her temper begin to rise as she finished her drink.

Why should she sit there pretending to be invisible?

Too disgusted to watch them any longer and feeling unaccountably light-headed, she fixed her gaze back on the dance floor, feeling a stab of envy as she watched the dancing. On the dance floor she'd had fun. She'd lost herself in the moment. So why shouldn't she do so again? She held her breath, checking out the number of women dancing alone. There were plenty.

So why shouldn't she join them?

Without so much as a glance towards her companions, Alesia lifted her chin and stood up, clutching at the table for a moment to gain her balance and then walking purposefully on to the dance floor, looking neither left or right. If anyone was staring, she didn't want to know.

Once again the music slid into her soul and she closed her eyes and tipped her head back, feeling the rhythm flow over her and letting her body move in time. She spun and gyrated, her hair flying across her face, her arms above her head, her hips swaying.

After several minutes a tall blonde man joined her and it was so much fun to be dancing with someone again that she just smiled and matched her movements to his. Nothing mattered, she thought happily, except having fun *right now*.

She lowered her eyelashes in mute invitation, spun closer and then felt hard fingers digging into her shoulder, hauling her back in a gesture of pure masculine possession. Caught off balance, she staggered and would have collapsed in a heap had not she been held firmly against rock-solid muscle. Dizzily she glanced upwards and clashed with stormy dark eyes shimmering with barely restrained anger. Keeping her clamped against him in an iron grip, Sebastien spoke in

Greek to her dance partner and, although Alesia didn't understand a word of what he said, there was no misunderstanding his icy tone or the barely veiled threat in those midnight-black eyes. She frowned as the blond man cast a nervous glance at the width of Sebastien's shoulders and melted back into the crowd.

'What a wimp—' Alesia muttered with disdain. 'He might at least have stayed to finish the dance.'

'He had more sense,' Sebastien observed harshly, all the volatility of his Mediterranean heritage revealed in his glittering dark gaze. 'Which is more than can be said for you. We are in a public place and you are *not* supposed to be part of the entertainment. If you want to dance then you dance with me.'

She glared at him and tried to pull away. 'You were busy.'

'Then you should have waited.'

'For what? For you to decide you'd had enough of *that woman*?'

His eyes narrowed. '*That woman* happens to be the owner of this club. She is the reason we came here tonight. She needed my advice.'

'*Don't* treat me as if I'm stupid,' Alesia advised hotly, stabbing a finger into his broad chest. 'She was all over you like wrapping paper. And if *you're* going to seduce other women in public then *I'll* dance with who I like.'

Sebastien's hand curled over hers. Every inch of her body was locked against his and the feel of his hard, muscular frame made her head spin with longing.

Oh, help—

'Flirt again,' he warned, his tone lethally soft, 'and you'll discover *exactly* what it's like to be married to a Greek man.'

Heart thumping, knees shaking, Alesia stared at him helplessly and gave a tiny moan of self-disgust. How could she find this man so attractive? Trying to halt the insidious warmth that was spreading through her body, she made an attempt to pull away but he simply tightened his grip. Reminding herself that he'd just spent the best part of the evening stuck to another woman, Alesia gritted her teeth. 'I already know what it's like to be married to a Greek man, Sebastien. It's lonely and frustrating. You marry me, then you vanish for two weeks without telling me where you're going and then you take me out for an evening and proceed to flirt with someone else. I *hate* you.'

And what she hated most was the fact that she *cared*.

Colour streaked his magnificent cheekbones. 'I was not "flirting".'

'You were,' Alesia informed him unsteadily. 'Your eyes were all over her and she couldn't stop touching you and you forgot I was even there. Well, I refuse to be ignored! You chose to bring me here and then you were *rude*. And, what's more, everyone was watching.' Suddenly she felt horribly dizzy and clutched at him for support. 'And now I feel a bit sick.'

The breath hissed through his teeth and he muttered under his breath. 'Have you been drinking?'

She frowned, wondering why her head was swimming. 'I never drink.'

His mouth tightened. 'You downed most of your drink in one mouthful.'

'I was thirsty.'

'Then you should have drunk water,' he suggested helpfully, holding her firmly when her legs would have given way. 'For the record, alcohol is not the best thirst quencher.'

She leaned her forehead against his chest and wished the room would stop spinning. 'All I've drunk is the lemonade you gave me. I've probably just been twirled around too many times. That man was a very good dancer.'

'The drink was vodka with a dash of lemonade,' he said grimly, 'and I think you're not safe to be left for five minutes unattended. You're like a child at its first party.'

'And you're horrible,' she muttered, lifting her face to his, struggling to focus as she tried to remember exactly what it was that she hated about him. 'You do all those things to me in bed and then you just walk out and never say *anything* nice. Not one single thing. I just don't understand why women think you're so amazing. You don't make sense and I can't keep up with you. And I don't think I can pretend to be the person you think I am any more. It's just *exhausting*.'

Sebastien stilled, every muscle in his powerful body suddenly tense as he focused all his attention on her. 'Run that past me again?'

There was something in his tone that rang alarm bells but her head was too fuzzy to work it all out. 'You never say anything nice to me when we're in bed—'

'Not that bit—the other bit.' Thick dark lashes swooped downwards, concealing his expression. 'The bit about not being able to pretend any more.'

'Well, I'm not this stupid, brainless heiress and frankly it's a struggle to pretend that I am,' she muttered. 'I've never worn a designer dress in my life, I've never had time to party and you think I'm some sort of *mammoth* slut and yet I've never even—' She broke off and he raised a dark eyebrow in question.

'Yes?' he prompted her helpfully, his dark gaze still fixed on her face. 'Never even—?'

The loosening effects of the drink were fading and she was suddenly swamped by a horrid, horrid feeling that she'd just said totally the wrong thing but she couldn't exactly work out what. Suddenly all she wanted to do was sleep.

'Well, I'm not a slut,' she repeated vaguely, 'although I like the clothes they wear. Except the shoes hurt.'

Her head thudded back against his chest and she heard him swear softly and then felt him scoop her into his arms.

She wanted to tell him that he had to get out of the habit of carrying her everywhere but it felt so nice being back in his arms that she just gave a sigh and nestled her head into his shoulder.

'You smell *so* good,' she muttered dreamily, 'but I'm absolutely *not* getting back into bed with you until you learn to say something *nice*. It makes me feel horrid.'

He didn't answer but she saw his jaw tighten and felt him lengthen his stride.

Cool air brushed her bare legs as he emerged from the nightclub and seconds later he deposited her on the back seat of the limo before leaning forward and hitting a button. He delivered a set of instructions to his driver in terse, clipped Greek and then sank back against the seat with a grim expression on his handsome face.

Alesia curled up on the seat like a baby and struggled not to be sick. 'I'm never dancing again,' she groaned, closing her eyes and then opening them again quickly as the dizziness intensified. 'The whole world is still spinning.'

'That's the alcohol, *not* the dancing,' he informed her, shooting her a glance of naked exasperation, 'and I can't *believe* you've reached the age of twenty-two without knowing how it feels to get drunk.'

'I've reached the age of twenty-two without knowing how a lot of things feel,' she confessed sleepily, her words slurring as her head dropped back against the leather seat. 'These last few weeks have been one long new experience for me. Some of them good, some of them not so good. The worst by far was when you—'

'—didn't say anything nice to you in bed,' he finished for her, inhaling deeply like a man at the extreme limits of his patience. 'You've already told me that several times. I get the message.'

Alesia shifted her head slightly so that she could focus on him. 'Actually, I was going to say when you flirted with another woman in front of me,' she murmured, studying the harsh lines of his bronzed face and deciding that he really was shockingly handsome. 'As new experiences go, that really was the pits. But I love the clothes and the shoes. And dancing was amazing. I want you to take me again. Maybe tomorrow.'

He studied her through narrowed dark eyes, his gaze suddenly disturbingly intent. 'Tomorrow,' he warned in a soft voice, 'I have other plans for you.'

Alesia groaned. At the moment she just wanted to be left to sleep. 'Well, I expect you will have done one of your vanishing acts again by the morning,' she muttered hopefully as her eyes drifted shut again.

'No chance,' Sebastien murmured, leaning across to catch her before she sprawled on to the seat. 'I'm going to start getting to the bottom of the person you really are, *agape mou*. Tomorrow, you and I are going to start really getting to know each other.'

Alesia woke with a pounding headache.

'Drink this.' The deep, masculine drawl came from right beside her and she groaned and kept her eyes firmly closed.

'I can't drink anything—'

'It will help.' He slid an arm under her shoulders, lifted her as if she weighed nothing and put the glass to her lips.

Alesia took a tentative sip and wrinkled her nose. 'It tastes disgusting.'

'Then maybe your education regarding the effects of alcohol is truly complete,' he said drily. 'Trust me, it will help.'

She sipped from the glass, froze for a moment while her churning stomach protested and then relaxed. 'You're right. I feel better.'

'Good. Because you have less than an hour to get ready.' He straightened and she realized that he was already showered and dressed.

She stared at him in disbelief. 'Not more nightclubs.'

'It's lunchtime,' he informed her helpfully, gesturing towards the window with a sweep of his bronzed hand, 'so no, not more nightclubs. They don't generally open until midnight but you wouldn't know that, would you, given that you'd never been to one before?'

There was something in his silky tone that smelt of danger and she looked at him anxiously. Much of the previous night was a blur. Had she really told him that? 'I—er—' She cleared her throat awkwardly as she tried to work out how to rescue herself from the current situation. 'I didn't exactly say I hadn't been in a nightclub.'

'Yes, you did. Along with a great number of other fascinating revelations which I can't wait to explore in greater detail.' Sebastien glanced at his watch and then strode towards the door. 'I have some important calls to make before we leave, so take advantage of the time to have a shower but don't fall asleep again. My pilot will pick us up in less than an hour.'

The sickness returned. 'Your pilot?'

'That's right.' He opened the door and glanced back at her. 'We're going on our honeymoon. Better late than never, as the saying goes.'

'Honeymoon?' She gaped at him. 'But we weren't going to have a honeymoon. You said you didn't want to spend that much time with me.'

'That was because I thought one night with you would be enough. I was wrong. I've tried cold water and I've tried avoiding you,' he told her frankly. 'Nothing works. So we'll try a different approach.'

Her mouth fell open. 'You tried avoiding me? That's why you vanished for two weeks? You were avoiding me?'

'Yes, but it didn't work. I've accepted the way things are. We're married. It's perfectly acceptable for us to spend time together and I need to get you out of my system if I'm ever to stand a chance of concentrating again.'

She stared at him, feeling slightly faint. 'And how do you propose to do that?'

'By having endless, uninterrupted sex, *agape mou*.' He flashed her a smile. 'In less than an hour it will be just you and I and a very private island. You won't even have to dress in underwear—so don't bother to pack.'

CHAPTER SEVEN

THEY were flying over the sea again.

Was Greece nothing but ocean?

Alesia closed her eyes and tried to visualize land. Tried to control the almost frantic panic that erupted inside her.

'You can open your eyes,' Sebastien said, his voice tinged with amusement as he lounged in the seat next to her. 'We land in less than five minutes and you're missing the best view in Greece.'

Alesia kept her eyes shut. She wasn't interested in the view. She was thinking about the water. Fathoms and fathoms of ocean laid out beneath her just waiting to claim the unwary—

'*Theos mou*, you are white as a sheet.' His voice was suddenly sharp with concern. 'Is this still a consequence of last night?'

She couldn't speak, fighting her own private battle against the terror that threatened to engulf her.

There was a moment's silence and then strong fingers wrapped themselves around her cold hand. 'I remember now that you were the same colour the first time I met you. I didn't know you were so afraid of flying,' he said quietly. 'Forgive me. Next time we use the boat. It makes the journey a little longer but at least it will be more comfortable for you.'

At that her eyes flew open in shock. The fact that he seemed to care whether or not she liked the helicopter surprised her.

Why would he care?

Perhaps he was just afraid that she might be ill. Didn't

118

men hate it when women were ill? Should she confess that it was the water, not the flying?

That a boat would be even worse.

'There's no need to look at me like that,' he drawled softly. 'Everyone has a weakness. It's almost a relief to know that you have something other than just greed. You can relax now. We've landed. Welcome to my private hideaway.'

Remembering how close the helicopter pad was to the sea from their first meeting, Alesia was tempted to shut her eyes again but she forced them to stay open, knowing that she somehow had to get herself to the villa.

The sea wasn't going to leap up and grab her, she reminded herself firmly as she descended quickly and stood on the Tarmac. This fear of hers was totally irrational and it was time she tried to conquer it.

'You are still very pale.' Sebastien surveyed her with frowning contemplation and then spoke several words in Greek to his pilot, who melted into the background. 'You should lie down before dinner. Or perhaps you would prefer a swim?'

Should she confess that she never swam?

Should she tell him—?

She licked dry lips, her heart suddenly racing with fear. 'Maybe later.'

'After a few days in Athens most people can't wait to dive into the ocean,' he said, amusement flickering in his dark eyes as he glanced in her direction. 'But there's plenty of time. I have no plans to rush back to the city.'

Alesia hid her dismay.

How long exactly was he planning on staying?

It would be harder for her to phone her mother from here and if she didn't receive a call, she'd worry.

Sebastien frowned. 'You are unbelievably tense and the whole point of this trip is for you to unwind. There is nothing to do here but relax. You must still be tired after last night.'

He sounded as if he cared that she was tired and she stared at him in confusion. Why was he being nice to her all of a sudden?

Alesia gave a stiff smile. 'I am tired, you're right.'

'Have a lie down before dinner—'

They walked into the villa and Alesia's eyes widened as she glanced around her. When they'd visited the island for that first meeting, she hadn't actually set foot inside the house itself.

The living area was huge and light, decorated in blues and whites with acres of cool creamy marble. Exotic plants nestled in the corner of the room and on the walls hung several huge, brightly coloured canvases. 'It's *beautiful*—'

'My cousin designed it,' he told her, pausing by her side. 'She has her own interior design business. She is responsible for the paintings as well.'

'She's very talented,' Alesia breathed and then her eye settled on the grand piano in the corner of the room and she gave a gasp of pleasure and surprise. 'Oh!'

He followed the direction of her gaze with a quizzical frown. 'You play?'

Alesia hurried over to the piano and ran a hand lovingly over the wood. 'Yes.'

His eyes narrowed and he gestured towards the piano. 'Be my guest.'

She flushed and shook her head. 'No—it's fine. I don't— well—'

'You don't what?' His voice was soft. 'You don't want to tell me that much about yourself? Was that what your grandfather told you, Alesia? To hide the person you really are?'

Her gaze flew to his and she stared at him in consternation. 'I—'

'We're married now, *agape mou*,' he said calmly. 'The deal is signed and sealed. Nothing you do or say can change that. It's time to relax and be yourself.'

'I am myself.'

He gave a wry smile. 'No. You're back to being the zipped-up version of yourself. Last night, I suspect, I had a glimpse of the real person.'

Dismay flickered through her. 'I had too much to drink—'

'And clearly that lowered your inhibitions sufficiently for you to reveal your true self,' he drawled, dark eyes glittering as he surveyed her with no small degree of amusement. 'I discovered last night that my little kitten has claws.'

She flushed and bit her lip. 'You upset me—'

'A lapse that won't occur again,' he slotted in smoothly, reaching out a hand and pulling her towards him. 'I discovered that my wife has a personality which I suspect she obediently buried on the orders of her grandfather.'

Alesia swallowed. 'I—'

'From now on I want you to be yourself,' he commanded, sliding a strong hand around her waist and pulling her against him. 'I want to know everything about you. No secrets.'

No secrets.

Alesia closed her eyes. He still believed that her mother was dead, killed alongside her father. But to have told him the truth would have revealed that her grandfather *hated* her and that this marriage had nothing to do with mending fences and everything to do with revenge.

If he discovered the extent of her deception—if he discovered *everything*—then there would be no containing his anger—

At some point he was bound to find out and the thought of his reaction just sickened her.

'I need to lie down—'

Sebastien muttered something under his breath in Greek. 'You are never touching alcohol again,' he vowed, taking her hand and leading her through to the master-bedroom suite.

Like the rest of the villa it was an elegant and simply

decorated room and Alesia glanced around and then looked through the open glass doors on to the shady vine-covered terrace and beyond that to the large swimming pool. 'It's amazing.'

Apart from the pool, of course, but she intended to ignore that.

Suddenly she realized that the villa was a home in the way that his Athenian mansion never could be. It was full of personal touches that revealed secrets about the owner. And it was wonderfully private and quiet.

Quiet.

'Where is everyone?'

He frowned. 'Everyone?'

She waved a hand. 'Usually you are surrounded by staff—'

He gave a wry smile. 'This is my retreat. My private bolt-hole. I don't think it would fit into that category if I filled it full of staff, do you? This is the place I come to forget my responsibilities as an employer.'

She stared at him. 'We're on our own here? Just us?'

'Just us.' His voice was velvety smooth and she felt her heart miss a beat.

Suddenly she was aware of every vibrant, masculine inch of him.

Reminding herself that only last night he'd been wrapped around another woman, she lifted her chin and met his eyes with a challenging gaze.

'So who cooks, Sebastien?'

'We share it,' he said smoothly, his glance not flickering from her face. 'A boat delivers fresh produce on a daily basis. Discovering what is in the parcel is half the fun.'

Her mouth fell open. 'You cook? But Greek men never cook—'

Her grandfather didn't so much as make a cup of coffee.

'I frequently come here alone,' he told her calmly, 'so it was learn to cook or starve.'

Alesia stared at him in confusion, realizing that perhaps she didn't know him as well as she thought she did. But just exactly how much time had she spent with her new husband? she reminded herself. Virtually none. Apart from their wedding day, when they had barely been on speaking terms, the only time they'd spent together up until the nightclub had been spent in bed. They hadn't even shared a meal since their wedding.

Sebastien walked over to the glass doors and slid them open. 'Lie down for a few hours. I'll be on the terrace if you need anything.'

Alesia waited for him to go and then stripped down to her underwear and slid between the cool sheets with a sigh of relief.

Her head was still pounding from lack of sleep and the alcohol she'd unwittingly consumed the night before and suddenly nothing seemed clear any more.

Telling herself that she'd work it all out later, she drifted into a deep sleep.

When she awoke it was sunset and she sat up feeling guilty. How long had she slept? Too long—

And there was no sign of Sebastien.

She slid out of bed and searched for her jeans.

'They have been disposed of,' came a dark drawl from the doorway and she gave a start and shot back into bed, pulling the sheet up to her neck.

'You scared me—'

He surveyed her with no small degree of amusement. 'Since we are the only two people on the island, I couldn't have been anyone else. And your schoolgirl modesty is totally unnecessary, *agape mou*. I'm perfectly happy for you to walk around naked.'

She flushed to the roots of her hair. 'Well, I'm *not* happy,' she muttered, wondering if she'd ever feel comfortable with her body in the way that he did. 'And what do you mean, you've disposed of my jeans? You told me not to pack anything. The only clothes I have are the ones I was wearing earlier.'

'And you won't be wearing them again,' he said smoothly, strolling into the room. He'd changed into a pair of cool linen trousers, the sleeves of his casual shirt rolled up to reveal bronzed forearms dusted with dark hairs. 'Since you didn't appear to have purchased anything suitable for a hot climate, I took the liberty of arranging a suitable wardrobe for you.'

Still clutching the sheet, she gazed at him warily. 'A wardrobe?'

He knew she hadn't bought anything. He knew—

She closed her eyes. Well, of course he knew. He'd been into her dressing room in Athens and seen it empty apart from her wedding dress, her jeans and a few tops and, whatever else he might be, the man wasn't stupid.

'You're not used to shopping, are you?' His tone conversational, he walked into her dressing room and returned carrying a narrow sheath of peacock-blue silk. 'An intriguing quality in someone who clearly requires such a large income to support her lifestyle.'

Alesia froze and waited in horrified stillness for him to ask the obvious question—*why* she'd demanded so much money when she didn't even seem to spend it.

Frantically rummaging around in her brain for a suitable answer and coming up with none, she almost cried with relief when he simply dropped the dress in her lap.

'Get dressed,' he ordered quietly, strolling back towards the terrace with a thoughtful glance in her direction, 'and then meet me on the terrace. We'll have supper and talk.'

Talk?

Alesia fingered the beautiful dress and stared after him in dismay. It had been easier when Sebastien had done his vanishing act, she conceded. At least then she hadn't had to worry about giving anything away.

Suddenly he seemed to have developed a desire to get to know her and that was going to present her with a big problem.

Fresh from the discovery that his new wife was certainly *not* lacking in personality, Sebastien lounged on the sun-baked terrace, staring at the azure-blue pool in brooding contemplation.

Never before had he felt confused by a woman. Out of control.

In his experience their behaviour followed a totally predictable pattern. They shopped, they lunched, they partied. Even when he switched one woman for another, which he did with monotonous regularity, the pattern didn't change.

So he'd never had any expectations that his new wife would prove to be different. Hadn't she, sole heiress to the Philipos fortune, demanded an enormous sum of money to marry him?

Once in possession of such generous funds, he'd expected her to shop and shop until her feet were blistered and yet it was rapidly becoming clear to him that she hadn't purchased a single item of clothing since their wedding day.

And maybe not before then, either.

When confronted with a selection of exclusive designer outfits, she didn't behave like any woman he'd ever met before.

In fact, her frank delight at the clothes he'd produced for her trip to the nightclub suggested that she'd virtually never purchased an item of clothing in her life.

As a male with endless experience in the art of pleasing the opposite sex, Sebastien had been forced to endure countless shopping sessions with women who contrived to look suitably bored by the whole procedure. Never had he known a woman to display such undisguised enthusiasm for clothes. Alesia had behaved like a child who'd just discovered the fun of dressing up.

Which left him with the intriguing and puzzling question of just *how* she'd spent his money. And he knew that she *had* spent it because her account was empty, but so far no one had been able to give him an answer to the question of exactly where the money had gone.

None of it made sense. And neither did his own reaction to her.

He gave a soft curse as hot molten lust thudded through him and the force of his own hunger once more threatened to overwhelm him. *Never* before had he felt this out of control around a woman. Only moments ago he'd been forced to leave the room because the sight of her lying there, sleepy-eyed and pink-cheeked, had made him want to pin her to the bed and keep her horizontal using the most basic and satisfying method known to man.

Even six hours in bed with her the previous afternoon hadn't cooled his ravenous libido. He'd had no intention of patronizing the opening of Ariadne's nightclub but he'd needed to do something to take his mind off his mounting sexual hunger for his new bride.

For a man whose attention span with women had always been alarmingly short, his reaction was as mystifying as it was frustrating and it didn't help to acknowledge that seeing her dancing with another man had forced him to exercise a restraint previously untested. For a brief moment he'd been furious that she'd chosen to dress in such a provocative manner and then he'd been forced to recall that her attire had been his selection, chosen in a desire to remind himself that he'd married a woman prepared to sell herself. Instead he'd succeeded in making her achingly sexy. With those huge, innocent eyes and those endless legs she'd caught the attention of every man in the club. Not used to dealing with jealousy, Sebastien had gritted his teeth and wrestled with the totally baffling impulse to cover her from head to foot in a giant bin bag before transporting her home in an armoured vehicle with blacked-out windows.

It had taken every ounce of self-control for him not to grab the man who'd been dancing and smiling at Alesia and knock him unconscious.

Faced with the fact that he'd married a woman who was a walking temptation, Sebastien vowed that if he ever displayed her in public again then she'd be wearing a sack.

Perhaps it was just that he now viewed Alesia as his property, he mused, and he'd never been that great at sharing. And discovering that his bride was every bit as hot-blooded as himself made him even more inclined to lock her in his tower and throw away the key.

His body heating to boiling point at the mere memory of her uninhibited response to him, Sebastien inhaled deeply and forced himself to acknowledge that although he usually considered himself exceptionally broad-minded about many things, his new wife didn't fall into that category. When it came to Alesia his attitude was completely and unashamedly Greek.

Dressed in a shimmer of silk that she guessed must have cost a fortune, Alesia stepped out on to the terrace and blinked in surprise.

The table was laid, candles flickered in the darkness and the air smelt enticingly of heat and summer. And she knew Sebastien had done it all for her.

'Drink?' Sebastien strolled towards her and handed her a glass, which she took with a wary smile.

'I'm not sure if I should—'

'It's not alcoholic,' he drawled lightly. 'I may be many things, *agape mou*, but stupid isn't one of them, although I have to confess that you become a different person under the influence of alcohol.'

She flushed. 'I enjoyed dancing—'

'So I observed.' He surveyed her steadily. 'I want to know why last night was your first visit to a nightclub. I want to know why you haven't shopped.'

She searched for inspiration. 'Do you spend everything you earn?'

A ghost of a smile touched his firm mouth. 'Hardly.'

'Precisely.' She gave a shrug. 'I don't know where you get this idea that money is all about shopping.'

'Perhaps because to the female sex it usually is,' he drawled, 'but you're teaching me that women are even more complex than I first thought.' He waved a hand at the table. 'Let's sit down.'

He was being so polite and she just wasn't used to it. Up until now their relationship had consisted of nothing but insults followed by hot sex.

She settled into her seat and her eyes scanned the various dishes laid out on the table. 'Did you cook?'

'Not exactly.' He gave a rueful smile. 'I confess that most of the dishes are delivered ready-made.'

'They look good.' She leaned forward and took a closer look in the dish nearest to her. 'Jannis makes the same thing. It's my favourite—'

Sebastien stilled, his powerful frame suddenly rigid with tension, stunning dark eyes suddenly icy-cold. '*Who* is Jannis?'

Alesia stared at him in surprise, wondering why he suddenly sounded so angry. 'Jannis is your chef.'

The tension left him. 'Of course.'

'He's been teaching me to cook Greek dishes,' Alesia told him, wondering what was the matter with him. 'I enjoy it.'

She just loved cooking and it was wonderful not to have to think about the cost of the ingredients.

Dark eyes swept over her. 'How else have you been spending your time in my absence?'

She shrugged. 'I explored Athens.'

'And?' His gaze was quizzical. 'Did you enjoy the experience?'

She smiled. 'It's an amazing city. Fascinating.'

He took a deep breath. 'How is it that you have never visited Athens before? Your grandfather has a home very near to mine. Surely you have visited him there?'

Alesia froze. 'I—no,' she said finally. 'I only ever saw him at his home on Corfu.'

Just the once.

Her heart started to beat faster. Would he think that was suspicious? Would he question her further?

'What about you?' Taking the initiative, she started to question him. 'I know you have several different homes.'

He gave a smile. 'Several different houses, *agape mou*, but only one home. This one.' He was silent for a moment, staring out across the lit terrace towards the sea. 'Home should be somewhere that you can be yourself. Somewhere private, a place where you don't have to answer to other people.'

'But you're rich,' she blurted out impulsively. 'You don't have to answer to anyone—'

He topped up her glass, a gleam of amusement in his eyes as he looked at her. 'I run an extremely complex, billion-dollar corporation,' he drawled, 'and on most days it feels as though I answer to the world. Decisions that I make have an effect on other people's employment—on their lives.'

And did that really matter to him? Did he really care? Alesia stared at him. 'My grandfather just made lots of people redundant—'

His mouth tightened and the amusement in his eyes faded, to be replaced by a steely expression. 'And those people had families and responsibilities of their own. Redundancy is a reflection of poor business planning. If you look into the future you can anticipate market changes and respond in time. Redeploy people if necessary, offer training. My company has never been forced to make redundancies.'

'And yet you have a reputation every bit as ruthless as my grandfather,' she replied unthinkingly and to her surprise he laughed.

'Well, I'm certainly no soft touch, *agape mou*,' he drawled lightly. 'I reward people well and in return I expect them to work hard. It's a fairly simple formula.'

And yet the financial pages of all the newspapers described him as a business genius. Alesia recalled the things she'd read about him following that first meeting with her grandfather.

'I read that when you left university you didn't join your father's business,' she said and he gave a shrug.

'It is never comfortable stepping into someone else's shoes. I was hotheaded. I wanted to prove myself on my own ground.'

'So you started your own business?'

'My father's business is very traditional,' he explained, leaning forward and filling her plate. 'I wanted to test other areas so I developed computer software with a friend from university and then we sold it to companies. In our first year we turned over fifty million dollars. We developed the company for several years and then sold it and by then I was ready to join my father. And that's enough about me. I want to hear about you. I have heard about English boarding schools.'

Alesia smiled and helped herself to more food. 'Actually, I loved it.' It was the only home she'd ever known.

He frowned sharply. 'It is true that you went there from the age of seven?'

'That's right.'

'That seems a very young age for a child.'

But she hadn't had a home. Her father had been killed.

*Her mother was seriously ill in hospital and her grandfather
had disowned her.*

'I liked it.'

'You were never tempted to live with your grandfather?'

She almost laughed. *Live with her grandfather?* Did he
really know so little about the man?

'I enjoyed my time at school.'

'And then you went straight to university?'

She nodded. 'I read music and French.'

He refilled her plate for the third time. 'You have an amazingly healthy appetite,' he observed with a faint smile and it
was on the tip of her tongue to confess that she'd never seen
so much food in her life before but she stopped herself in
time.

Instead she smiled. 'I love Greek food.'

He looked at her with a curious expression in his eyes.
'I'm pleased.' He lounged back in his chair and questioned
her more about her music and her courses and when she
finally put her fork down he stood up and extended a hand.

'I want you to play my piano, *pethi mou.*' He hauled her
to her feet and flashed her a smile. 'A private concert with
only me in the audience.'

Her gaze collided with his and for a breathless moment
she couldn't think about music or the piano. She couldn't
think about anything except the sudden explosion of sexual
need which engulfed her.

Sebastien gave a sensuous smile of all-male understanding.
'Later,' he breathed softly, leading her back into the main
living area towards the piano. 'Now I want you to play for
me.'

It was an order and she sat down at the piano stool and
automatically flicked her hair so that it flowed down her back
and not over the keys.

For a moment she sat in silence, staring at the familiar
keys, her mind slightly detached.

And then she started to play. First Chopin, then Mozart, then Beethoven and finally Rachmaninov. Her fingers flew over the keys, fluent and nimble, stroking each note lovingly, drawing the best from the piano until eventually the final piece ended and her hands fell into her lap.

Silence followed.

Suddenly horribly aware that she hadn't even questioned him on his tastes, hadn't even thought to ask what he wanted to listen to, she risked a glance in his direction.

He was sprawled on the sofa, eyes closed, dense lashes brushing his sculpted cheekbones, long, powerful legs stretched out in front of him.

Alesia bit her lip in consternation. Had he fallen asleep?

'That was amazing.' His eyes opened reluctantly and she connected with blazing black. 'Truly amazing. I had no idea you could play like that. Why aren't you charging millions for public recitals?'

She swallowed and dragged her eyes away from his. 'I'm not famous—'

'But you *could* be,' he asserted, coming upright in a fluid movement and walking towards her. 'You could be world-famous.'

'I don't think so.' She looked away, embarrassed and *pleased* that he'd enjoyed her playing so much.

'You've just finished your degree—what now?' Sebastien enquired with the single-minded focus of someone who has his entire life clearly mapped out in front of him. 'Before you agreed to this marriage—what were your plans?'

To carry on holding down three jobs so that her mother could have the care she needed—

'I hadn't really thought—'

'Your grandfather didn't mention your talent,' Sebastien mused and Alesia clamped her jaws together and refrained from pointing out that her grandfather knew less than nothing about her. To him she was just a pawn. *You are the tool of my revenge.*

'I don't think my grandfather is very interested in music.'

'I adore your playing,' Sebastien said huskily, pulling her to her feet and framing her face with his hands. 'You are intensely passionate and sensitive—all the things that make you so wildly exciting in bed—'

Colour flew into her cheeks. 'Sebastien—'

'And I love the fact that you blush so easily,' he murmured, bending his dark head and capturing her mouth in a drugging kiss that sent a flash of the most intense sexual desire shooting through her.

She gave a soft moan and moved invitingly against his hard, powerful frame and as he whispered to her in Greek he swept her into his arms.

He was always doing this, she thought vaguely, her head still spinning from the after-effects of his erotic kiss, her limbs trembling as he strode through to the bedroom and lowered her into the middle of the bed.

'I can't get enough of you,' he groaned, sliding the tiny straps of her dress down her arms and fastening a burning kiss on her shoulder, 'and we're not leaving this island until I can go through at least five minutes in a business meeting without thinking of you.'

Fleetingly she remembered that she'd resolved not to let him do this to her again, and then his skilled fingers stripped her naked and his mouth found the sensitive jut of her nipple and the thought vanished, obliterated in an explosion of sexual excitement so intense that she sobbed his name.

'No woman has *ever* excited me the way you do,' he asserted in a raw tone, as his clever fingers proceeded to plot an erotic path down her quivering, hopelessly sensitized body. 'It is so hard to hold back.'

'Then *don't*,' she breathed unsteadily, her blue eyes glazed as she collided with his burning dark gaze.

'I don't want to hurt you—'

She closed her eyes, suffocated by the building desire, needing him so badly that her whole body ached and shivered. 'Sebastien, please—'

He gave a rough exclamation and rolled her under him in a swift, powerful movement, positioning himself between her thighs before he covered her mouth with his once more and took her.

The hot, hard strength of him deep inside her made her cry out in shameful abandon and he smothered the cry with his mouth, his own harsh grunt of male satisfaction mingling with her soft gasps.

He drove them both forward with powerful thrusts, smashing down any barriers that remained between them, an animal mating that culminated in explosive fulfilment for both of them.

In the aftermath Alesia lay with her eyes closed, waiting for him to release her, braced for his usual dismissive comment.

Instead he rolled on to his back, taking her with him, smoothing her tangled blonde hair away from her flushed cheeks with a hand that was far from steady.

'That was amazing,' he said hoarsely, studying her face. 'You are amazing. We can make this marriage work, Alesia.'

She swallowed. 'Because the sex is good—?'

'Not just because of that, but of course that is one reason,' he said, delivering a smile so sexy that she felt her whole body quiver. 'But I am fast discovering more and more about you. And I like what I discover.'

Suddenly consumed by guilt at the enormity of her deception, Alesia tried to wriggle away from him but he held her firm.

'No, this time I am not going to walk away. Nor will I say

anything horrible. We are going to spend the night together. In the same bed. I believe that children deserve parents who are happy together.' He dropped a lingering kiss on her mouth. 'I believe that we can be happy together.'

Guilt shot through her with the force of a bullet.

They couldn't be happy together. She couldn't give him children, and when he found that out... How could she tell him?

'You think I'm a gold-digger—'

He gave a dismissive shrug. 'At least you were honest about it. I can respect honesty. And what we share in bed is nothing to do with money, *agape mou*—'

He respected honesty.

Alesia closed her eyes, sick with dread at the thought of him discovering the truth.

That she'd been anything but honest with him.

But did he really need to find out? a tiny voice murmured inside her. She wouldn't be the first woman in the world who couldn't have children. Maybe he wouldn't discover that she'd always known...

CHAPTER EIGHT

THE week that followed was the most blissful time of Alesia's life.

They made love for most of the night and much of the day and when they weren't sleeping off the exhaustion induced by endless mind-blowing sex, they were talking or eating meals out on the terrace that overlooked the gentle curve of sand. And, to her surprise, Alesia discovered that she *loved* Greece. Even the constant view of the sea stretching into the distance couldn't spoil her delight at waking every morning to blazing sunshine. She adored exploring the island, adored picking oranges fresh from the tree and loved the feel of the sun on her skin.

And she also discovered that she *loved* talking to Sebastien.

He was astonishingly entertaining company and for the first time in her life she experienced what it was like to be close to another human being and it felt amazing.

On one occasion they didn't leave the bed but made love, slept and then just talked and talked while they lay wrapped around each other.

Sebastien proved to have a sharp wit, a brilliant mind and a good sense of humour as well as being astonishingly astute about the world. He was also charming and so incredibly sexy that Alesia found herself just gazing and gazing at his handsome face, unable to believe that this man was actually in bed with *her*.

Alone on the island, they were cocooned in their own sensual nest, protected from the interfering gaze of the outside world.

Protected from the looming clouds of reality.

Swamped with a quite unfamiliar feeling of happiness, Alesia drifted through each day on a cloud of pure bliss, dimly aware that this wasn't real—that this idyllic life they were sharing couldn't continue.

She was dozing in bed late one morning exactly one week after they'd first arrived on the island when Sebastien strolled into the room, vibrant and masculine and just pulsing with his usual energy.

Alesia forced herself awake, wishing that she had even a fraction of his apparently limitless energy. 'Sorry—' she yawned, brushing her hair away from her face and rubbing her eyes '—couldn't wake up this morning.'

'That's because of last night,' he teased, the sensual flash of his dark eyes a heated reminder of the intimacies they'd shared.

As she held his gaze, Alesia felt her stomach roll over and wondered if she'd ever be able to look at him without experiencing that intense burst of sexual excitement deep inside her. He only had to walk into a room and her insides fell away. Especially now when he was wearing only a pair of swimming shorts. He maintained a punishing exercise regime and the results showed in every pulsing inch of his impressive physique. From the broad, muscular shoulders to his lean, flat stomach and long legs, he had the most amazing body she'd ever seen and she couldn't look at him without wanting him to take her back to bed. It didn't matter that he didn't love her. It didn't matter that he thought she was a gold-digger. She was just *desperate* for him.

She was a *hopeless* case.

'I'll get up in a minute,' she promised, wishing that he'd suggest they spend yet another day in bed. It was the only place she wanted to be with him.

He surveyed her with amused eyes. 'I'm feeling shame-fully guilty that we've been here for an entire week and you haven't swum in the pool once,' he teased, scooping her up and carrying her on to the terrace. 'I've kept you pinned to the bed and that isn't exactly fair.'

Staring dreamily at his staggeringly handsome face, it took a moment for Alesia to realize what he had in mind.

And by then it was too late to stop him.

She experienced a second of heart-stopping panic and then he dropped her into the pool and darkness closed around her.

Guilt-ridden and seriously worried for the first time in his life, Sebastien paced backwards and forwards across the marble floor while the doctor he'd had flown in examined a white-faced Alesia.

It had been little consolation to him when she'd recovered consciousness because she'd proceeded to shiver so violently that no amount of blankets seemed to warm her. It was as if the chill came from the inside.

'She's suffering from shock,' the doctor said calmly, finishing his examination and closing his bag. 'Physically she's fine. Swallowed a bit of water when she went under so she might be feeling a bit sick, but apart from that no lasting effects. Mentally it's another matter. At a guess I'd say that she suffers from a phobia about water. Probably wasn't such a good idea to drop her in the pool.'

Unaccustomed to being lectured or to being in the wrong, Sebastien gritted his teeth and took the criticism levelled at him with remarkable restraint.

Never in his life had he felt so utterly remorseful and if a sound telling off was what it took to make him feel better, then he was more than willing to take it on the chin.

He didn't care.

All he cared about was the fact that Alesia still looked as pale as the marble on his floors and that her eyes were haunted. And he *truly* wished the shivering would stop.

Reluctant to leave her alone for more than a few minutes,

he walked the doctor back to the waiting helicopter, a frown in his eyes. 'You're sure I shouldn't fly her back to Athens tonight?'

'My advice?' The doctor handed his bag to the pilot and looked Sebastien straight in the eye. 'She needs rest. I think you should keep her here tonight, give her time to get over the shock, then fly back tomorrow when she's feeling better.'

Pausing on the threshold of his living room, Sebastien noted grimly that her skin exactly matched his white sofas and decided to take the matter of her recovery into his own hands.

He strode over to a tray of drinks and closed lean bronzed fingers around a curving bottle.

Moments later he slipped an arm under Alesia's shoulders and scooped her up, making a mental note to instruct his chef to stuff her full of food on their return to Athens. She was far too fragile.

He lifted the glass to her dry lips. 'Drink.'

Obediently she took a sip and then choked and pulled a face.

'It's disgusting.'

'On the contrary, it's an extremely expensive brandy,' Sebastien informed her, his voice thick with strain as he lifted the glass to her lips again. 'You are still suffering from shock. Please drink.'

She took a few sips and then flopped back against the pillow, totally drained.

'I'm sorry—'

Laden with guilt that she was the one apologizing when it had been he who'd thrown her in the water, Sebastien raked shaking fingers through his still-damp dark hair.

'I'm the one who's sorry,' he said stiffly, unaccustomed to apologizing but determined to do so at the earliest possible minute in the hope that the incredible discomfort inside him

would ease. 'But why didn't you tell me that you didn't
swim—?'

She closed her eyes. 'I didn't go near the water—'

He gritted his teeth. All right, so he should have noticed
that fact. 'It just didn't occur to me that it was because you
were afraid—'

Her eyes stayed closed. 'Doesn't matter now.'

It mattered to him.

Driven by a need to put right a wrong, Sebastien disposed
of the glass and scooped her on to his lap. 'I wish you would
stop shivering,' he groaned but no matter how tightly he held
her the shivering continued.

'Sorry—'

'Stop saying that,' he breathed in a raw tone, stroking her
damp hair away from her face. 'I'm the one who is sorry but
you should have told me how you felt. That first day when
you were so afraid. I thought it was the flying, but I was
barking up the wrong tree, wasn't I? It was the water—'

Her teeth chattering, she gave a reluctant nod and he
cursed softly.

She closed her eyes. 'I'm being stupid—'

'You are not being stupid,' he said quietly. 'You are
clearly reacting to something that happened in your past. I
want to know what it was.'

There was a brief silence.

'I was on the boat—'

Sebastien tensed, unsure that he'd heard her correctly.
'What boat?'

'Your father's boat. The day it exploded. I was there. I
almost drowned.'

Shattered by her unexpected confession, Sebastien found
himself lost for words. 'That's not true,' he said finally, his
voice sounding nothing like his own. 'There were no children
invited on the boat that day—'

'I wasn't invited.' Still shivering, Alesia huddled deeper

in the blankets, her blue eyes blank of expression. 'I went on board only moments before the explosion. I was supposed to have stayed at the hotel in Athens with my nanny but I was desperate to show my mother a new doll I'd been given.'

Memories crowded into his brain. *A young child badly injured—*

'You were on board when the boat exploded?' His voice was hoarse and she lifted her head and nodded, her beautiful heart-shaped face so white that Sebastien momentarily toyed with instructing his pilot to return with the doctor immediately.

'I'd barely set foot on the boat,' she said softly, 'and my parents didn't know that I'd arrived.' She swallowed. 'I don't remember much, to be honest. I was only seven. I just remember standing on the gangplank one minute and then being plunged into water. It was everywhere—I thrashed and thrashed.' Her fingers clenched into her palms and she had to force herself to stay calm. 'I couldn't breathe, couldn't find air, felt terrible pain and then everything went black.'

Sebastien's breath hissed through his teeth and his face was pale under his tan. 'Someone rescued you—do you know who?'

'No.' She gave a wan smile. 'It was just a deckhand.'

'You were the only child on the boat that day—?'

She frowned. 'Yes—I suppose so.'

'*Theos mou*—' His voice was hoarse and he raked an unsteady hand through his glossy dark hair. 'I didn't know—'

'Didn't know what? What difference does it make?'

'You were injured? And you lost both of your parents.'

Her gaze slid guiltily away from his. 'I'm fine now.'

Sebastien surveyed her in frowning contemplation, sure that she wasn't telling him the truth. But why would she lie? Having confessed as much as she had, why would she now choose to conceal the truth about the accident?

'Sebastien?'

Aware that her teeth were still chattering, Sebastien's frown deepened. 'What?'

'Could we just go to bed?'

Faced with a potential solution which was well within his sphere of experience, Sebastien seized on the suggestion with enthusiasm and immediately lifted her into his arms.

'I could probably walk,' she murmured into his neck and he tightened his grip.

'Probably is not good enough,' he growled, lowering her on to the bed as if she were made of something extremely fragile and covering her with a sheet.

Her eyes flew to his. 'Aren't you joining me?'

Humbled by the question, Sebastien inhaled deeply. 'Do you want me to? I dropped you in the water—'

She gave a tired smile. 'You didn't know—'

'But I know now and from now on nothing is going to hurt you, *agape mou*,' Sebastien vowed, stripping off and joining her in the bed with a flattering degree of speed.

With characteristic decisiveness he hauled her against him and rearranged her so that every shivering inch of her was pressed against his own body.

'Feels nice,' she mumbled, her eyes closing as she nestled against his shoulder.

Discovering feelings of protectiveness which he hadn't known he was capable of, Sebastien lay still, afraid to move in case the shivering started again.

No wonder she'd hated his family, he mused grimly, breathing in her warm, tantalizing scent and forcing himself to ignore it.

And no wonder Dimitrios Philipos blamed the Fiorukis family for everything. Not only had his beloved only son been killed on the Fiorukis yacht along with his wife, but the last remaining member of his family, his precious grand-daughter, had been injured.

Was that why he'd had her educated in England? Sebastien mused.

Had Philipos removed her from Greece for her own safety?

Clearly he'd misjudged Dimitrios Philipos, Sebastien conceded, stroking aside a strand of blonde hair from Alesia's face and noting with relief that her colour was showing a definite improvement. In choosing to link their two families then he was indeed healing a rift that had been painful for both parties.

And, once he'd consulted experts and cured her of her water phobia, their marriage could begin properly.

Starting from tomorrow, Sebastien vowed, they were going to be a proper family.

Alesia held tightly to Sebastien's hand, grateful for the distraction that his conversation offered. He'd already apologized about a hundred times for the fact that they had to board the helicopter in order to return to Athens but he'd assured her that the alternative boat trip was much longer and would be more agonizing for her.

Touched by his concern and feeling much safer than she could have imagined possible, Alesia kept hold of his hand and forced herself to concentrate on other things as the azure-blue Mediterranean blurred beneath them.

Traumatic though the incident had been, she was glad that he knew. In a way she'd revealed an important part of herself. And if anything they were closer than ever and she knew now that she loved Sebastien Fiorukis with a wild passion that she hadn't believed possible.

Never had she thought she'd share this with a man and if, deep down, part of her was constantly reminding her that she wasn't being totally honest with him, she was managing to ignore it.

For the first time in her life she was *truly* happy and she wasn't going to allow anything to spoil it.

Sebastien's mobile phone rang as soon as they landed and he gave a frustrated sigh. 'End of our peace and quiet,' he drawled as he shot her a look of apology and took the call.

Alesia smiled. She didn't mind that he took the call. She understood his dedication to his business, the fact that he cared what happened to his employees, the fact that he took his responsibilities so seriously. It was one of the many qualities that she'd grown to love about him.

Sebastien ended the call and looked at her, indecision evident in every plane of his handsome face.

'What's the matter?' Relieved to finally be on dry land, Alesia relaxed.

'That was the office.' He gave a rueful smile. 'A crisis awaits—'

'Then you should go.'

'I don't want to leave you,' he confessed, his dark eyes sweeping her face with visible concern. 'You were so unwell yesterday and I feel totally responsible.'

Basking in the totally new experience of having someone who wanted to take care of her, Alesia smiled at him happily. 'I'm fine now. I'll just rest and wait for you to come home,' she assured him, thinking that his absence would give her time to phone her mother and experiment with all those wonderful new cosmetics he'd presented her with. Hopefully the rack of clothes would still be there too, and she'd be able to wow him with an amazing outfit on his return from the office.

'I won't be long,' he promised, bending his dark head to deliver a drugging kiss to her parted lips, 'and if you feel at all ill you're to call me on my mobile.'

'I don't know the number.'

He looked startled, as if it hadn't occurred to him before now that she'd had no way of getting in touch with him. 'I'll get you a phone straight away, with my number programmed into it. The slightest problem, I want you to call.'

With visible reluctance he strode back towards the waiting helicopter without bothering to change.

That must be one of the benefits of being the boss, Alesia mused, watching in a fog of total infatuation as he boarded the helicopter again. You could dress any way you liked. Not that Sebastien needed clothes to give him stature. He oozed confidence from every taut muscle of his amazing body. He could have been dressed in a bin bag and it still would have been obvious who was in charge.

Recalling just how long it had taken her to apply her make-up on the previous occasion, Alesia hurried up to their bedroom and walked into the dressing room, noticing with considerable disappointment that the rack of clothes had disappeared. The only outfit remaining was the skimpy skirt and top she'd worn for the nightclub.

She studied it thoughtfully. She'd loved that outfit and she was pretty sure that Sebastien had loved it too. Why not wear it again? First they'd have dinner, then perhaps he'd take her to another nightclub and they could dance and dance and after that—

Delighted with her own idea, Alesia virtually skipped down the stairs to discuss suitable dinner menus with Jannis, Sebastien's head chef, and then returned to their bedroom suite to begin the transformation she had planned.

She bathed in richly scented water, daydreamed about Sebastien and smiled at the thought of the evening ahead. This time she managed her make-up in half the time and was reasonably pleased with the result. Feeling transformed and extremely feminine, she slipped her feet into the same pair of shoes that she'd worn for dancing, vowing that this evening she'd remove them and dance in bare feet.

Once she was ready she settled down to wait for Sebastien. And she waited.

Twice she picked up the phone he'd had delivered to her and stood with her finger poised over the right button only to return the phone to the table with a sigh of frustration. She wasn't going to phone him to ask him when he was coming home. He'd said that he'd be as quick as he could. She didn't want him to think she was clingy.

More time passed and Alesia chewed her lip and paced backwards and forwards in their bedroom. He was an important man, she reasoned, and he'd been away for an entire week. It was only natural that he needed some time in the office. Loads of people probably needed to talk to him.

By the time the sun went down her fingers were once again itching to pick up the phone. Why didn't he at least *call*? Had she misunderstood his desire to be home early?

Then she heard footsteps outside and the bedroom door crashed open. Sebastien stood there, dark stubble grazing his hard jaw, his dark eyes glittering dangerously in the dim light.

He looked remote, distant and thoroughly intimidating and nothing like the man she'd spent the last week with.

Alesia looked at him warily. 'Y-you don't look as though you had a great day,' she said nervously and in response he strode into the room and slammed the door shut behind him.

Alesia winced. 'If you're hungry, then—'

'I'm not hungry.' His voice was lethally smooth and he paced towards her, his shimmering dark gaze never leaving her face. 'Aren't you going to ask me if I had an interesting day at the office, *agape mou*?'

She shivered slightly at his tone and instinctively took a step backwards. 'You're very late so I expect you were busy—'

'Extremely busy.' His tone was almost conversational. 'Busy discovering plenty of interesting facts about my new wife. Facts which she hadn't thought to reveal herself even though we've just spent a week getting to know each other.'

Alesia felt the colour drain out of her face.

How much did he know?

'Sebastien—'

She couldn't believe how different he was from the man who'd been so concerned about leaving her only half a day earlier. Gone was the warmth and consideration that she'd enjoyed so much. In its place was cold disdain.

But was that really so surprising?

How could she have thought that this fairy-tale existence could continue when it was built on such shaky foundations? A good relationship needed trust and honesty and she'd given him lies and falsehoods. Nothing built on that could be sustained. It was inevitable that it would come crashing down in spectacular style.

'Perhaps you'd better tell me what you're talking about,' she said stiffly and he gave a cynical laugh.

'Why? So you can work out what I already know so that you don't reveal more than you have to? Don't worry, *agape mou*, I already know just how good you are at keeping secrets. I learned today a number of interesting facts about your life. Like the fact that up until two weeks before our wedding you have had no contact with your grandfather since you were *seven years old*.' His expression grim, he fixed her with his chilly dark gaze. 'So who paid the fees for that expensive school you attended?'

Feeling sicker by the minute, Alesia forced her voice to work. 'I won a music scholarship,' she croaked. 'There were no fees.'

He registered that admission by a tensing of his broad shoulders. 'And, according to my sources, once you were at university you held down no fewer than *three* jobs. You had two waitress jobs and you played the piano in a bar. *How* did you achieve your degree? When did you do any studying?'

'I was often exhausted,' she confessed with a glimmer of a smile that faded as soon as she registered his blackening expression. He was *furiously* angry with her. 'I'm not afraid of hard work.'

'Well, that, at least, is one thing in your favour,' he bit out harshly and she shrank slightly. Clearly he didn't think there was much else.

'Most students take one job,' he growled, pacing across the floor like a man at the very limits of his patience, 'and I can understand that you needed money because you had no parents to provide for you and a grandfather who refused to acknowledge your existence, but why *three*? What did you do with the money?' His eyes slid over her in silent question. 'All the clothes you possess, I bought you with the exception of your wedding dress. You don't shop and you're so fragile that you *clearly* don't eat much.'

Her gaze shifted from his and she swallowed. 'General living costs—'

'General living costs?' He stopped dead and repeated her words slowly, as if he were struggling with his English, and the tone he used revealed just how ridiculous he found her mumbled statement. 'Presumably this is why you went along with this deception and agreed to the marriage. Why should you struggle financially when a simpler, more lucrative option was available to you?'

She winced. Once again he made her sound just *awful*, as though the only thing she ever thought of was money. She wanted to tell him about her mother but she just couldn't; it wasn't her secret to divulge.

Sebastien started pacing again, the growing tension in his powerful frame clearly making it impossible for him to stand still. 'But the question I really want answered is why your grandfather wanted this marriage,' he growled. 'As I suspected at the beginning, he was *not* playing Happy Families by pursuing the idea of a match between us. Clearly he has no concern for your welfare whatsoever. You are merely a pawn in his evil game, although clearly a very willing pawn.

And now I want to know what the game is, Alesia. For once
I want the truth.'

Alesia stared at him, appalled. Her life was collapsing in
front of her eyes. To tell him would ruin everything that
they'd built over the last few weeks and she just didn't want
that to happen. She knew now that Sebastien was *nothing*
like her grandfather. He was a responsible man with a strong
sense of family and duty and fairness. And above all else he
respected honesty. How could she confess that she'd deceived him in the cruellest way possible?

So how did she confess the enormity of her crime to a man
like that?

The irony made her eyes sting with tears.

She loved him.

She loved him and she had to tell him probably the worst
thing that a wife could tell a Greek man. He would never
understand the desperation that had driven her to such a distasteful action. Their short, bittersweet relationship would be
over virtually before it had started.

She started to shake so badly that she could no longer
stand up. 'Sebastien—'

'Just one look at your ashen face warns me that I'm not
going to like what you're about to tell me,' he bit out grimly,
striding over to a small table and pouring himself a large
whisky. 'I knew there was something more behind this
"deal" but my father is an old man and was determined to
end the feud once and for all. Stupidly, I went against my
better judgement and decided to trust him.'

Alesia closed her eyes and wished she was somewhere
else. Anywhere else.

Sebastien downed the drink in one and strode back over
to her, the expression on his handsome face utterly forbidding. 'Since he clearly wasn't bothered whether you lived or
died,' he said harshly, 'presumably your caring, devoted
grandfather never wanted great-grandchildren either. And,

since that was his stated reason for desiring this marriage, then I assume that his method of revenge must be somehow linked. Am I right?'

Alesia felt the nausea rise in her stomach. She was going to have to tell him. She was going to—

'Alesia—?' His tone was a sharp command and her eyes flew open and she lifted her chin.

This was her crime. Indefensible, but still her crime. She had to stand by what she'd done.

'The explosion left me badly injured,' she told him, just hating the fact that her voice was shaking so badly. 'The doctors said I would never be able to have children.'

Registering that announcement, Sebastien stood in rigid stillness, every muscle in his powerful body tense as he watched her. 'Just what exactly are you saying?' he asked hoarsely and she felt a lump building in her throat as she forced the words out.

'I can't give you children, Sebastien. Ever. It isn't possible.'

He inhaled deeply. 'And your grandfather somehow knew this?'

She nodded bleakly. 'My grandfather knows everything—'

Sebastien gave a harsh laugh and ran a hand over the back of his neck in a visible effort to relieve the tension. 'This, then, was his latest revenge. To deprive my parents of the grandchildren they long for so badly and to deprive me of a child.' He paced the length of the room one more time and made a sound of disbelief before he turned and fastened her with incredulous eyes. 'And you agreed to this? Your grandfather is renowned as an evil, manipulative man with no morals. But you? For the right sum of money, you were prepared to go ahead with this deception?'

Alesia shrank inside herself and stared at the floor in utter misery.

What could she say? The answer was quite obviously yes and she wasn't in a position to explain why the money had been so very important to her.

He made a sound of derision. 'Whatever my family may have done to yours, there is no excuse for that level of dishonesty.' His voice was thick with barely contained anger, streaks of colour accentuating his fabulous bone structure. It was as if something was about to explode inside him. 'How could I ever have thought a relationship was possible? Not only are you a gold-digger but you are also a liar and a cheat.'

'You can divorce me,' she whispered in anguish and he turned on her, raw anger blazing from his dark eyes.

'I *cannot* divorce you,' he contradicted her savagely, one lean brown hand slicing through the air to emphasize his point. 'Your scheming grandfather ensured that. The contract we both signed binds us together until you produce a child.'

Alesia swallowed painfully. 'I know I did wrong, but you have to understand—'

'Understand what?' He cut through her whispered attempt to defend herself with ill-concealed derision. 'That I married a woman completely bereft of human decency? I should have been more wary of your lineage. The Philipos blood runs in your veins and you have clearly inherited his complete lack of moral code.'

Driven by disgust that he didn't even attempt to hide, he strode out of the room, slamming the door shut behind him, leaving Alesia numb with horror.

CHAPTER NINE

ALESIA spent a sleepless night feeling sicker and sicker and *totally* miserable. Remembering what the doctor had said about her swallowing water when she'd fallen in the swimming pool, she assumed the nausea would go away at some point and tried to ignore it.

She longed to find Sebastien but she had no idea where to look for him and she wouldn't have known what to say even if she found him.

She was guilty as charged.

She had deceived him. She had lied. She had married him for money.

He was right. How could she possibly defend the indefensible?

His opinion of her shouldn't have mattered, but somewhere along the way she'd fallen crazily in love with him and the knowledge that he clearly hated her depressed her in the extreme.

The situation was irretrievably bad and she'd already decided that she might as well leave and go back to London when he stalked into her bedroom, dressed in a sleek designer suit, looking every inch the successful billionaire businessman that he was.

Struggling with nausea that refused to shift, Alesia sat up in bed, trying not to let the longing show in her face. The fact that she wanted him so badly that she ached wasn't relevant. He didn't want her.

'I'll leave today,' she said shakily, unable to hold that penetrating dark gaze for more than a few painful seconds. 'You can't divorce me but you don't have to live with me and I promise I'll—'

'I came to apologize,' he muttered stiffly, cutting through her awkward attempt to bridge the silence between them with his customary impatience. 'Last night I lost my temper. There's no excuse for that.'

He was apologizing to *her*?

She blinked. 'You have every right to be angry—'

'Last night you looked very ill—' His gaze swept over her and a frown touched his bronzed forehead. 'You still look ill.'

She gave a wan smile. 'I think it was just swallowing the water—I feel a bit sick, but I'm fine—'

His eyes slid back to hers but the frown remained. 'Today you must rest. Spend the day in bed,' he ordered, his tone cool and formal. 'We'll talk later.'

She gave a sigh. She felt flattened and exhausted by the intense outpouring of emotion. 'There's nothing to talk about, Sebastien,' she said quietly. 'We both know that. You clearly can't bear being in the same room as me, so I'll leave today.'

For some reason his tension seemed to increase. 'I don't want you to leave,' he breathed, tension spreading through his powerful frame and making the air throb and sizzle. 'You are my wife.'

'A wife who can't give you children,' she reminded him painfully, and he inhaled deeply.

'That may be true, but you are still my wife and you will *not* leave.'

Alesia felt her insides give a leap. Was he thinking about how happy their week together had been? Was he growing fond of her? Was he—

'Last night I was so angered by what I had heard I wasn't thinking clearly,' he confessed in a raw tone, turning away from her and pacing towards the window. 'But on reflection I can see that you have led an extraordinarily difficult life.

Because of the accident on my parents' boat you were left orphaned at a shockingly young age with no means of financial support. All your life you have worked and slaved to keep a roof over your head and food on the table. It is hardly surprising that, presented with an opportunity to improve your circumstances, you took it. You blamed my family for the death of your parents and for your own injuries.'

'Sebastien—'

'Let me finish,' Sebastien interrupted. He turned and dark eyes collided with hers. 'Whatever caused the explosion, my family was ultimately responsible for what happened that day and we should take responsibility for that.'

She swallowed painfully. 'What are you saying?'

'That you have a right to the life you have chosen,' he said stiffly, turning again and staring out of the window. 'My family owes you and I intend to honour that debt. You will remain as my wife and you will continue to receive the allowance we agreed. How you spend it is entirely your decision.'

Flayed by the knowledge that his desire for her to remain as his wife was driven totally by his sense of responsibility rather than anything deeper or more personal, Alesia flopped back against the pillows.

She didn't want to stay here under those circumstances and yet how could she do anything else? She needed Sebastien's money to support her mother. She had no choice but to stay. And if he hated her for what she'd done—well, she'd just have to live with that.

The next few weeks dragged by.

Sebastien spent most of his time at the office and returned home after she'd fallen asleep. He slept in a different room, as if to emphasize the fact that he could no longer stand the sight of her.

Days passed without them laying eyes on each other and,

on the rare occasions that they met at a meal table, he was polite and courteous but kept a distance that filled Alesia with utter misery. His tense civility was worse than his anger.

And, to make matters worse, the sickness hadn't passed as the doctor had predicted. If anything it was worse but she hid the fact from Sebastien because she knew that he already felt ridden with guilt for having thrown her in the swimming pool.

The final straw came when she rang the hospital to check on her mother only to be told that she'd developed a rare infection and was dangerously ill.

Stricken with guilt that she hadn't somehow contrived to visit her mother before now, Alesia packed a bag and asked Sebastien's driver to take her to the airport.

The chances were he wouldn't miss her, she reasoned as she watched Athens slide past from the comfort of the passenger seat. She knew he had a business meeting in Paris because she'd watched him board the helicopter that morning from the window in the drawing room.

Like a lovesick teenager, she often stared out of the windows of his Athenian villa, hoping for a glimpse of him.

How had this happened?

How had she managed to fall in love with him?

But she knew the answer to that, of course. From the moment she'd first laid eyes on him the extraordinary tension had been there between them. She'd entered the marriage full of contempt and determined to hate him, but those feelings had rapidly grown into something very different.

When she'd sorted out this latest crisis with her mother, she'd find a way of getting over Sebastien, she vowed as she slid out of the car with her small bag and quickly dismissed the bodyguard who had insisted on accompanying her to the airport.

She spent the whole flight to London trying not to be sick and decided that as soon as she got the chance she was going to have to consult a doctor. She must have picked up some bug or other from the water she'd swallowed.

When she arrived in London it was pouring with rain, the sky cloudy and ominously grey. Thinking bleakly that the weather suited her mood, she took a taxi into London and arrived at the top hospital in time to talk to the doctor who was in charge of her mother's care.

'How is she?' she asked anxiously and he gave her a sympathetic smile.

'It was a big operation, as you know, but she came through it well until the last few days. Unfortunately she's picked up a bug and we're running a series of tests to identify the cause.'

'Can I see her?'

'If you're Alesia then you are more than welcome,' the doctor said immediately. 'She talks about you constantly. I understand you've been working abroad?'

Alesia flushed. That was the story she'd given her mother as an excuse for not visiting before but suddenly she felt torn by guilt. She should have tried to come sooner—

But how could she? In order to fulfil the contract and get the money she'd had to play a role and without that money her mother couldn't have had the operation.

Deciding that life was one long round of impossible decisions, Alesia followed the nurse to her mother's room, tugging off her wedding ring as an afterthought and dropping it into her pocket.

At this moment in time her mother didn't need to know that she'd married a Fiorukis.

Her first sight of the fragile, pale woman in the hospital bed made her choke back tears and she struggled for control. Her mother had enough to worry about without having to comfort her.

'Mum?'

Her mother's eyes flew open at the sound of Alesia's voice

and a wonderful smile spread across her pale face. 'Darling! I didn't expect you to visit.' Her voice was so weak it was barely audible. 'You thought you might not be able to for a while.'

'It's fine.' Alesia swallowed hard and hurried across the room to give her mother a hug. 'You've lost so much weight.'

'Hospital food,' her mother joked weakly, lifting a hand to stroke her daughter's hair. 'You look tired. And pale. Have you been working too hard? How's the new job working out?'

'It's great,' Alesia said, avoiding eye-contact and settling herself in a chair that had been placed beside the bed.

Her mother gave a sigh and her eyes drifted shut again. 'Well, it was lucky for both of us that you got yourself that job when you did. And that it pays so well. If it weren't for you—'

'Don't. I love you.' Alesia gave a wobbly smile. 'And I *hated* not being able to visit you—'

'But you phoned every day,' her mother murmured, 'and you gave me the greatest gift that there is. The chance to walk again. Now we just have to wait and see whether the doctors have succeeded. Until this infection they were optimistic.'

'They're still optimistic.' Alesia felt her eyes fill and struggled to hold back the tears.

'Don't cry.' Her mother's voice was gruff. 'I rely on you to be strong. You've always been so strong. Even as a little girl you were fiercely determined.'

Alesia forced a smile. She didn't feel strong or determined. She felt sliced into pieces after the events of the last few weeks, but she knew she couldn't unburden herself on her mother. 'I'm fine. Just a bit tired.'

And ill. She felt *so* sick.

'How much time off have you been given?'

'As much as she needs.' A deep masculine drawl came from the doorway of the hospital room and Alesia sprang to her feet in shock, her heart suddenly thudding at an alarming rate as she stared at Sebastien.

He stood in the doorway, grim-faced and almost unbearably handsome, his lean, dark features set in anger. Gone was his characteristic cool. With one flash of those molten black eyes he told her everything she needed to know. That he was furious with her.

And then he dragged his gaze away from her, focused on her mother and the air hissed between his teeth. '*Theos mou*—I had no idea. You are *alive*. You survived the explosion.'

Alesia felt her insides plummet in panic. This was one scenario that she hadn't prepared herself for. 'I thought you were in Paris—'

'Tracking my moves, Alesia?' His eyes locked with hers, the derision in his gaze intensifying her guilt. 'Well, now I'm back—'

Before she could find a suitable answer, her mother gave a strangled moan and covered her mouth with her hand.

Immediately Alesia forgot about Sebastien. 'Mum?' She leaned forward and felt her mother's forehead, just frantic with worry. 'Are you feeling worse? Are you sick? I'll call a nurse.' She reached for the buzzer but her mother caught her hand.

'No.' Her voice sounded scratchy and her eyes were fixed on Sebastien. 'For years I've thought about you. In my dreams. In my darkest moments. You were always there.'

Alesia looked at her mother in consternation. She hadn't expected her to recognize Sebastien but clearly she did and it was equally clear that she *hated* him. The last thing she needed now was this sort of shock and it was all Alesia's fault.

She should have guessed that Sebastien would follow her.

She never should have come.

She turned to Sebastien, desperate to rescue such a disastrous situation. 'You're upsetting her. I think you should leave,' she pleaded urgently, taking her mother's hand in her own and squeezing it tightly. 'We can talk later—'

'If that is what your mother wants, then of course I will respect her wishes,' Sebastien said roughly, walking into the room with his customary air of purpose. 'But there are clearly things that need to be said.' He turned to Alesia's mother. 'I had no idea you were alive.'

Alesia closed her eyes. They just didn't talk about the accident any more. Her mother found it all too distressing. '*Please*, will you go—?'

'I don't want him to go.' Instead her mother stretched out a hand towards Sebastien, her blue eyes so like her daughter's brimming with unshed tears. 'Not until I've thanked him. If you only knew how much I've longed to thank him but I had no way of discovering who he was and tracing him. I didn't know his name—'

At that confusing declaration Alesia stared in astonishment and, to her surprise, Sebastien stepped up to the bed and took the hand that was offered, enveloping slender fingers with his own large, strong hand. 'No thanks are needed. Not then and not now—and I had no idea who *you* were until very recently.'

'There were so many people on the yacht that day—'

Alesia glanced between them in confusion. 'Mum—?'

'How did you make contact with him?' Her mother turned towards her and the tears spilled over and trickled down her pale cheeks. 'You knew how much I wanted to find the man who rescued me. Without a name, how did you ever find him, you clever girl?'

The man who had rescued her?

Stunned into silence, Alesia sat still, unable to speak or move for a long moment. When she finally managed to produce words, her voice was croaky. 'This was the man who rescued you when the boat exploded?'

That couldn't be true.

It couldn't have been Sebastien.

'And you. He rescued you too,' her mother said, a tremulous smile on her face as she looked at Sebastien. 'He risked his life so many times going under the water to find you. I saw you on the gangplank only seconds before the explosion. I knew you were in the water, probably too badly injured to help yourself. I was screaming and screaming for someone to save my baby.'

'Your mother was trapped under wreckage on the boat,' Sebastien said gruffly, his dark eyes shadowed by the memory. 'She refused to cooperate with any sort of rescue until I'd found her daughter.'

Alesia was in shock. The vision in her head. The man she remembered. 'It was you?' Her voice was barely audible. 'The man who rescued me—the man I remember—*that was you?*'

His jaw tightened. 'I didn't realize myself until the night when you told me your story,' Sebastien confessed, lines of tension visible around his dark eyes. 'I realized then that it had to have been your mother that I'd rescued but I had no idea that she was still alive. Philipos informed everyone that she had died along with Costas.'

'That's what he wanted people to believe. He wanted me out of his life. You went back on to the boat to rescue others,' Alesia's mother said quietly, 'and the ambulance took the two of us to hospital. I asked everyone about you but no one knew anything. Then Dimitrios had us flown to England and I was forbidden from ever visiting Greece again. We kept our identity secret under his instructions.'

Sebastien frowned, every inch of him suddenly alert. 'How could he make such a threat? How could he prevent you from visiting? And why?'

Her mother closed her eyes. 'He hated me from the first moment that Costas brought me home to Corfu. When Costas was killed there was no one to defend me. He threatened to take Alesia from me,' she said wearily, 'and bring her up as a Greek. As his own. He didn't really want her. It was just a threat to punish me. Few people know just how evil that man is. There was no way I wanted him near my daughter. I agreed to disappear. To break all contact. It suited him. It was what he always wanted.'

'He paid you to disappear?' Sebastien's eyes darkened with shock and disapproval and Charlotte Rawlings gave a tired laugh.

'Pay? Dimitrios? That shows how little you know him. No, he didn't pay me a penny.'

Sebastien stilled. 'But you were severely injured with a young daughter to support—how did you manage? You had family of your own to care for you?'

'I had no family, and I managed because my daughter is a unique and very special person,' Charlotte said in a gruff voice and Alesia coloured.

'Mum, I think you should rest now—'

'Not yet.' Sebastien tightened his hand around her mother's. 'Please—if you can manage it, I really need to hear the rest of this story.'

'Alesia recovered remarkably quickly from her injuries and she was a bright little thing.' Charlotte smiled lovingly at her daughter. 'One of the doctors who was treating me and knew our circumstances suggested she try for a scholarship at a top boarding school. She was accepted. It was a difficult decision but the right one. I was having endless operations. In the holidays she stayed with one of her tutors and they brought her to see me all the time.'

Sebastien was listening intently, all his attention focused on her face. 'Go on—'

'By the time she went to university I needed all sorts of

care that we had to pay for.' Charlotte shot her daughter a tortured look. 'Alesia worked night and day to provide for me. She would do *anything*. And when she discovered that there was a chance that this operation could help me walk again she got herself this amazing job in Greece—'

A tense silence followed that announcement and Alesia closed her eyes, waiting for Sebastien to tell her mother the truth.

'You should rest now,' he said calmly, standing up and arranging the sheets more comfortably around her mother, 'but before we leave you for a while, I have one more question. Why, when Alesia grew up and he could no longer take her away, did you not ask Philipos for money once again? You are his only family. He had a duty to provide for you.'

'Dimitrios knows nothing about duty and he never gives away money,' her mother said with quiet dignity. 'And he doesn't know the meaning of family.'

Something dark and dangerous flickered in Sebastien's eyes. 'Then it's time he was educated on that subject,' he said grimly, straightening to his full height, dominating the small hospital room with his powerful presence. 'And I can assure you that he will be a willing pupil. He *will* live up to his responsibilities.'

Charlotte Rawlings closed her eyes wearily. 'No. I want no contact with that man. I never want to hear the names Philipos or Fiorukis again.'

Alesia froze in horror. Although her mother obviously recognized Sebastien as the man who'd rescued her from the explosion, she clearly didn't know his identity. What would her mother say when she realized that her daughter had married a Fiorukis? And that she'd approached her grandfather for money?

Sebastien gave a calm, reassuring smile. 'I want you to rest and stop worrying,' he instructed firmly, 'and I will bring Alesia back tomorrow.'

Her mother opened her eyes and smiled. 'You can stay another day?' Her eyes brightened. 'When do you have to go back?'

Sebastien frowned. 'She can stay as long as she needs to,' he said roughly and then walked out of the room.

Alesia gave her mother a hug and then hurried after him, virtually running so that she could match his long stride.

'Sebastien, *wait*!' Breathless, she caught his arm, forcing him to stop. '*Please* don't just walk off. I know you're still angry with me but we have to talk. You saved my life. *I can't believe it was you.*'

Burning dark eyes collided with hers and he caught her arms and backed her against the nearest wall, his whole body throbbing with barely contained fury. 'And we would have discovered that fact a whole lot sooner if you'd been honest with me. *When* will you learn to trust me and tell me the truth?' he demanded in a raw undertone, his strong fingers biting into her soft flesh as he kept her pinned against the wall. 'On a daily basis I learn something new about my wife and the process is exhausting. Each time the phone rings I wonder what amazing fact I am about to discover that you have kept hidden. Until I met you I thought that I had an incredibly effective intelligence network. Suddenly I discover that I know *nothing*.'

'You probably weren't looking in the right place,' Alesia muttered awkwardly, realizing that for a man accustomed to being in control all these revelations must be difficult to cope with. 'You didn't know my mother was alive.'

'That's right, I didn't.' He stared at her with naked exasperation. '*Why* did you hide that fact from me? And the fact that *you* were on the boat too?'

She lifted a hand to her throbbing forehead, desperate to make him understand. 'Because if I'd told you the truth you would have known that we were anything but a happy family. And if you'd known that my grandfather *despised* me, then you would have known that his desire for a union between us was driven by a desire for revenge, not grandchildren to bounce on his knee. I was too scared to tell you the truth.' She swallowed hard, breathlessly aware of every inch of his hard body pressed against hers. *She'd missed him so much.* 'And then you wouldn't have married me. And I needed you to marry me. It was the only way I could see to get the money for my mother's operation. It's a really new procedure and the NHS wouldn't fund it. I was *desperate.*'

She'd been totally out of her depth.

'I should have picked up the signals at that first meeting,' Sebastien growled, his brows locked in an ominous frown as he listened to her. 'You were so clearly afraid of him but my father was longing to have the company returned to him and I was distracted by certain other matters. Otherwise I would have realized that something wasn't right.'

Wondering what other matters had distracted him, Alesia gave a tired smile. 'Well, you know it all now,' she said, her head swimming as his familiar male scent wrapped itself around her brain and teased her senses. When he stood this close she couldn't concentrate. 'I *did* marry you for the money but I wanted the money for my mother. There was no other way. My grandfather has refused to acknowledge her existence since the day she married my father.'

'Your grandfather has a great deal to answer for,' Sebastien said grimly, inhaling deeply as he struggled for control. Aware that several nurses were glancing in their direction, he released her. 'This is not the place to have the discussion we need to have. Let's get out of here.'

He closed long, strong fingers around her wrist and virtually dragged her towards the nearest lift. With disbelief he scanned the ancient lift and instead opted for the stairs. 'If that thing breaks down we'll be in it for ever,' he growled. 'And what *is* this hospital? It looks as though it is about to fall down.'

'It is a very old building,' Alesia agreed breathlessly, wishing she had legs as long as his, 'but the surgeon here has an amazing reputation and he wanted to try something that had never been tried before. That's how I spent your money.'

'*Your* money,' he corrected her, a strange expression in his eyes as he shouldered open the door and held it for her to pass through. 'It was your money. And finally I understand why you didn't go shopping. You didn't have any left to buy anything for yourself.'

She blushed. 'I didn't need anything. And the hospital is very expensive—'

He looked around with an ironic gleam in his eyes. 'I can't understand why,' he drawled, leading her across the foyer and straight into his car, which was parked directly outside. 'It looks as though it should have been demolished years ago.'

'How did you know where to find me?'

'You were followed,' he told her grimly, leaning across to fasten her seat belt. 'My security team were under strict instructions not to let you out of their sight.'

She gazed at him in astonishment. 'Why?'

'Because you are a Fiorukis now,' he reminded her in a dry tone, the exasperated gleam in his dark gaze revealing just how naïve he found her question, 'and there are plenty of people willing to cash in on that.'

Her eyes widened. 'You think someone might kidnap me?'

'The possibility is always there but you needn't worry too much,' he drawled with a faint smile. 'They would release you soon enough when they discover how much you eat.'

She bit her lip as she studied his tense expression. 'Are you very angry with me?'

'You have driven me to the extreme of emotion since the day we met, so this is nothing new,' he murmured huskily. 'And, for future reference, the next time you wish to fly, use my plane. Like it or not, you are my wife and I won't have my wife taking a commercial flight.'

A warm feeling spread through her. She should have felt angry that he was giving orders again but after a lifetime of making her own decisions it felt wonderful for someone else to take charge. Part of her loved the fact that he was so possessive. And she basked in his determination to take care of her, even though she knew that it was only driven by his sense of responsibility towards her.

Cocooned in the luxury of Sebastien's car, Alesia stared out of the window, watching the sights of London pass by. 'Oh, look! There's the Monument. It was built to commemorate the Great Fire of London.' She gazed upwards to the viewing area. 'I remember my mother taking me there on one of her rare periods out of the hospital. I climbed all the way up to the top, all three hundred and eleven steps, while she waited in the street and waved.'

Slightly choked by the memory, she met Sebastien's eye and gave a wobbly smile.

He hesitated and then reached out and took her hand in his. 'You must have missed her dreadfully.'

She gave a tiny shrug. 'To be honest, I was so young when it all happened that I just grew up with it all. I just accepted that my mum wasn't like other people's—that our lives were different.'

'How did the press never discover that your mother was alive?' he demanded with blatant incredulity. 'How did they never find out about you? You are the only living relatives of one of the richest men on the planet and yet everyone seems unaware of your existence.'

'Like you, they weren't looking,' Alesia said simply. 'We returned to London. My grandfather insisted that my mother reverted to her maiden name and I used the same name. We were called Rawlings. And that was that.'

The beginning of years of hardship that she couldn't even begin to describe.

'That explains why you didn't respond when I addressed you as Philipos at our first meeting,' Sebastien mused. 'Presumably you took that name at your grandfather's insistence?'

Alesia couldn't hide her distaste. 'I *hated* using his name but it was all part of my grandfather's plan to make me seem part of his family,' she said bleakly. 'When you called me Miss Philipos, it used to take me a while to realize that you were talking to me. All my life I'd been Rawlings.'

'Your mother is a brave woman.'

'Don't tell her.' Alesia snatched her hand away from his, her expression urgent. She had to make him understand. 'All her life she has blamed the feud between our two families. We can't tell her I married a Fiorukis; it would kill her.'

His expression didn't alter by so much as a flicker. 'I want you to stop worrying,' he commanded, lounging back in his seat with a complete lack of concern. 'You are looking very pale. You need to rest.'

Alesia wished she could be half as relaxed. Her mind was racing through all the possibilities and none of them seemed attractive. 'I can't rest until we decide what we're going to say to her,' she said breathlessly, her brow lined with worry. 'I didn't know what to say to explain my absence so I told her that I'd taken a job in Greece and—'

He leaned forward in a swift movement, his dark eyes clashing with hers. '*Stop* worrying,' he instructed firmly. 'I will take over from here.'

She chewed on her lower lip. 'But—'

'Rest assured that I will do nothing to hurt your mother further,' he said quietly and she stared at him for a long moment.

'Why would you do that?'

His gaze was suddenly hooded. 'All sorts of reasons,

agape mou. Trust me,' he said quietly. 'And because I have already had ample opportunity to tell your mother the truth.'

It was true. He could have told her mother everything. Instead he'd been calm and reassuring and had revealed nothing that would have caused further upset.

She relaxed back in her seat and closed her eyes. 'I'm sorry.'

'Don't be.' His voice was gruff. 'I understand that you have had to make nothing but difficult decisions from an age when most children were interested in nothing but toys. But you are no longer alone in this, Alesia. The problem is mine. I will deal with it.'

For a moment she felt as though an enormous burden had been lifted from her and then she remembered that he was only doing it because he felt responsible for what had happened. Because the explosion had taken place on his family's boat.

She opened her eyes and glanced at him and then looked away quickly to hide the naked longing that she knew must be visible in her face. Her whole body just *burned* for him. 'Where are we going?'

'My suite at the Dorchester,' he replied tightly, 'where we won't be interrupted. We have rather a lot to talk about, *agape mou.*'

She didn't want to talk.

Wondering how she'd managed to develop into a person who thought about nothing but sex, Alesia crossed her legs to try and relieve the throbbing heat building between her thighs.

'A hotel?' Trying to lighten the tense atmosphere, she managed a smile as she glanced in his direction. 'I've always wanted to order room service. Is it a smart hotel?'

His eyes gleamed with amusement. 'Very,' he replied in his dark drawl. 'It will be another new experience for you. And a new experience for their room service, I suspect.

They've probably never come across anyone with an appetite the size of yours.'

'It's just so nice not to have to economize on food. But I'm actually not that hungry at the moment.' Alesia wondered how anyone could feel sick and starving hungry at the same time.

His sharp gaze was suddenly searching. 'You are still feeling ill? You do look very pale—'

She gave a self-conscious smile. 'It's been a tough day— seeing her lying there in that bed and then you turning up—'

He inhaled deeply. 'I can't believe the sacrifices you made for your mother—'

'She's my only family,' Alesia said simply, turning back to look out of the window again, 'and she made huge sacrifices for me too. She would have preferred me to stay with her but she sent me to boarding school because she thought that would give me my best chance.'

'Your grandfather has a great deal to answer for,' Sebastien said in driven tones and she shrugged helplessly.

'It's just the man he is. He'll never change.'

Sebastien's hard mouth tightened. 'We'll see.'

Their car stopped outside a back entrance to the hotel and within minutes they were inside Sebastien's suite.

Alesia flopped on to one of the beautiful cream sofas in the living area and glanced around her in awe. 'It's amazing—'

'Up until now I've just considered it somewhere to stay when I'm in London,' Sebastien confessed, gesturing towards a phone with a sardonic gleam in his dark eyes. 'Feel free to contact room service. I'm sure they'll appreciate the challenge.'

Her sense of fun flickering to life, Alesia gave a giggle. 'Can I order anything I like?'

'Of course.' He shrugged off his jacket and removed his

tie and their eyes locked, the tension that had been simmering between them suddenly flaring to life.

She could see the hint of dark body hair visible at his throat and the breath jammed in her lungs. 'Sebastien—'

'I promised myself I was going to stay away from you,' he groaned thickly, dragging her to her feet and framing her face with strong hands.

'I don't want you to stay away—' Her heart was thudding against her chest and she gazed into his eyes with something approaching awe. 'I still can't believe it was you. *You saved my life.*'

'A good move on my part,' he murmured, delivering her a sexy smile as he lowered his dark head.

Without lifting his mouth from hers, he stripped her in a few economical movements and lifted her in his arms.

'I can walk—'

'I like to carry you,' he said huskily, his dark head buried in her soft throat as he strode through to the bedroom.

'You mean you like to dominate me,' she teased, gasping as he dropped her on to the bed and came down over her with the arrogant assurance of a man who knew he was irresistible.

'I love the fact that I am the only man who has ever done this to you—' He kissed his way down her helplessly writhing body and proceeded to control her so completely that she lost her ability to think straight.

'Sebastien, please, now—'

He slid a searching, clever finger deep inside her and she arched in shock at his erotic touch.

'You are *so* hot,' he groaned and she whimpered and shifted on the bed in mute desperation.

He continued to drive her wild, to ignore her tiny sobs and moans, subjecting her to almost impossible intimacies until she was totally at the whim of her body.

And when she thought she couldn't stand it any longer he

lifted her and sheathed himself deep inside her with an earthy groan.

Her eyes flew wide and her breathing stopped but then he flashed her a dangerously sexual smile and started to move. With each forceful thrust he drove her higher, capturing her soft gasps with his mouth, urging her forward until she wasn't aware of anything except the explosive excitement building within her own body and his. When her climax hit it was so shockingly good that she clung to him, riding a tidal wave of delicious sensation so powerful that it threatened to engulf her.

He rolled on to his back and took her with him, smoothing her blonde hair away from her face with a gentle hand.

'That was amazing—' he muttered hoarsely. 'The best sex ever.'

Alesia closed her eyes and tried to convince herself that it didn't matter that he didn't love her as long as he wanted her.

Sebastien curved her body against his and then gave a soft curse as his mobile phone rang. 'I left instructions that we were not to be disturbed.'

With barely concealed irritation he reached out a hand and picked up the phone, ending the shrill tone with an impatient stab of his finger.

He listened for several seconds and then said a few words in Greek before severing the connection and inhaling deeply.

'We have to return to the hospital,' he said grimly. 'Apparently your grandfather has decided to pay your mother a visit.'

CHAPTER TEN

WHITE-FACED and anguished, Alesia would have run the length of the corridor that led to her mother's room had Sebastien not caught her arm in a vice-like grip.

'No.' His tone was firm and decisive. 'I know you're worried but I want you to leave this to me.'

Panic in her eyes, Alesia tried to yank her arm away from him. 'You don't understand what he's like. I have to go to her—'

'I understand exactly what he's like,' Sebastien said harshly. 'Trust me when I say that I am better equipped to deal with his particular brand of ruthlessness than you are.'

'But—'

'*Theos mou*, what do I have to do to get you to trust me?' Sebastien growled, jerking her against his hard, muscular body. 'How many times do I have to tell you that I will *not* hurt your mother. But the longer we argue about it, the more damage will be done.'

Alesia felt tears threaten and closed her eyes. 'I didn't know he'd come here,' she whispered and Sebastien's mouth tightened.

'I'm glad he did. It saves me having to go to him although, given the choice, I would have spared your mother this additional stress.' He relaxed his grip on her arm and gave her a smile as breathtakingly sexy as it was unexpected. 'Courage. You have been so brave this far, you can be brave a little longer. And whatever I say, Alesia, I want you to agree with me. Is that clear?'

'Whatever happened to modern?'

He flashed her a smile. 'Gone, but just for today. Do you promise?'

172

She gave a wan smile in return. 'Has anyone ever told you that you're a bully?'

'Frequently,' he replied calmly. 'Do I have your promise?'

'All right.'

What else could she do?

To her surprise, Sebastien took her hand and escorted her into her mother's room. As she saw the hunched figure of her grandfather Alesia started to shake and she felt Sebastien's hand tighten on hers in silent comfort.

Her mother was lying in the bed, her face white, her eyes fixed on the man who had made her life such a misery.

'I'm astonished that you choose to visit someone whose very existence you have denied,' Sebastien said icily, his dark eyes hard as granite as he surveyed the man standing in front of him with nothing short of contempt.

'It's none of your business,' Dimitrios growled angrily.

Alesia felt her knees quiver but Sebastien's gaze didn't flicker.

'You made it my business when you joined the fortunes of our two families. Let me make something very clear,' he said silkily. 'We have this one conversation and then you are no longer welcome near any member of my family. Particularly my wife and her mother.'

'Ah, yes—how is your *wife*?' The older man gave Alesia a nasty smile. 'I set you up, Fiorukis.'

'And for that I will be eternally grateful.' Sebastien slid a possessive arm around Alesia's waist. 'Had it not been for your relentless scheming, I never would have met Alesia.' He glanced at her briefly and a curious smile touched his firm mouth. 'And that would have been a pity because she has enriched my life.'

Alesia stared at him, momentarily transfixed by the look in his eyes, and then came back down to earth with a bump as Dimitrios Philipos gave a harsh laugh.

'If you're looking at her like that then you obviously haven't seen further than her body. It's time to tell you the truth. She can't give you children. No more Fiorukises.'

Alesia flinched and then felt herself hauled into the protective circle of Sebastien's arms.

'My feelings for Alesia have nothing whatsoever to do with her ability to bear children,' he said, his tone dangerously soft. 'And if you insult my wife one more time you'll regret it, Philipos. Unlike you, I know how to protect my own.'

Alesia held her breath. No one had ever fought in her corner or protected her before. All her life she'd been the one fighting for her mother, she'd been on her own against the world, and then suddenly this man, this man she'd deceived, was standing up for her—

A lump formed in her throat. She loved him so much and she just hated the fact that he felt obliged to look after her.

Lacking her sensibilities, Dimitrios Philipos gave a derisive laugh. 'Face it, Fiorukis, I've won. You may have the company back but you must know by now that nothing can save it and you may pretend that you don't care about children, but we both know the truth about that. You're Greek. Enough said.'

Alesia was frozen to the spot in shock. She stared at Sebastien, waiting to see signs that he was intimidated by the man in front of him, but Sebastien merely studied the older man in grim-faced silence and then, when he finally spoke, his voice was scathing. 'Firstly, the company has been returned to its rightful owner—the Fiorukis family. Your poor business decisions may have virtually brought the company down but my skills will rescue it and rebuild its reputation. As for Alesia—' he tightened his grip on her waist '—she has proved herself to be loyal, strong and loving—the three most important characteristics in a Greek wife.'

Dimitrios gave a snort. 'She can't give you a son and the contract you signed means that you can't get yourself a new wife.'

'Then it's fortunate that I have no desire for a new wife,' Sebastien drawled, his sharp gaze resting on Charlotte's shocked face for a moment before returning to his enemy. 'I think the strain of seeing you has exhausted Alesia's mother. So I want you to leave. Now. It's over. Finished. You are no longer welcome near my family.'

Dimitrios's lip curled. 'They're my family too, Fiorukis. If I choose to stay, I stay.'

'I think not. And it's time to look at some facts.' Sebastien's tone was gritty and hard. 'You lost the right to call them family when you exiled them from Greece and denied their existence. You lost the right to call them family when you failed to offer any provision for them, even though Charlotte's only crime was loving your son. You lost the right to call them family when you shamefully used Alesia as a tool of your own revenge. They are no longer your family, Philipos, *they're mine*.' His dark eyes gave a dangerous flash. 'And I always protect what's mine. Unlike you.'

Dimitrios looked at him warily. 'What's that supposed to mean?'

'You blamed my family for the explosion on our boat,' Sebastien delivered softly, 'but we both know that you—and you alone—arranged that explosion. You were responsible for the death of your own son.'

There was a hideous silence and Alesia heard her mother give a soft gasp of disbelief and shock.

Dimitrios glanced at her, a brief flash of panic in his eyes, and then he turned back to Sebastien, his eyes blazing. 'You think I was trying to kill my own son?'

'No.' Sebastien's gaze was hard. 'I think you were trying to kill my father because he'd been trying to persuade Costas to bury the ridiculous feud between our families once and for all and merge the businesses.'

'It was a ridiculous idea! My son should not have been on that boat!'

Sebastien inhaled sharply. 'The explosion was meant for my family but circumstances changed and when they finally boarded the boat your son and his wife were with them. And it was your son who died along with my uncle. And *you* were responsible. Don't you think it's time to end this feud, Philipos?'

Breathing rapidly, his eyes wild, Dimitrios rushed for the door, but it was blocked by several men.

'The Greek authorities wish to speak to you,' Sebastien said in a tone of utter disgust. 'They're very interested in several events that have taken place, including some of the recent investments you've made.'

Dimitrios paused in the doorway and glared at Sebastien. 'She's going to cost you a fortune.'

At that, Sebastien gave a flicker of a smile. 'I live in hope. I keep giving her my credit card and she refuses to use it. She is utterly unique. Again, I thank you for the introduction. I'd given up hope of ever finding a woman like her.'

As Dimitrios was led from the room Alesia sank on to a chair, her legs shaking too badly to support her weight.

'Is it true?' Charlotte's voice was a croak. '*He* planted the bomb?'

Sebastien nodded, closing the door to ensure privacy. 'We always suspected that he was responsible but there was never any proof.'

'And now?'

Sebastien shrugged. 'There is still very little actual proof, but he has been conducting some extremely shady business deals over the past few years. I think his place of abode for the foreseeable future will be behind bars. Perhaps the reason for putting him there no longer matters.'

Charlotte closed her eyes. 'He is a truly evil man. I think even Costas saw it. It was the reason he wanted to join your father in the business. He wanted a fresh start. I tried to persuade him not to. I was always afraid of what Dimitrios would do. It seems I was right.'

'You paid a high price,' Sebastien agreed quietly and Charlotte's eyes flew open.

'And you paid a high price too. You were forced to marry Alesia in order to return the company to your father.'

Sebastien gave a lopsided smile. 'It was no hardship, I can

assure you,' he drawled softly. 'Your daughter is stunning in every way. Beautiful and brave.'

Charlotte looked at him for a long moment and then turned to Alesia. 'This was the job you mentioned to me? You married for money?'

'There was no other way of getting you the operation,' Alesia said desperately and Sebastien covered her hand with his own.

'She did totally the right thing,' he said smoothly, 'and I would urge that you don't trouble yourself over our relationship. I love your daughter very much and I'm eternally grateful that she chose to marry me.'

Alesia shot him a grateful look. Even though she knew he was just protecting her mother from the truth, even though she knew he didn't really love her—

'And now you must rest.' Sebastien straightened in a lithe movement and glanced towards the door, where a doctor was hovering. 'I understand that you have made improvements today. I want you to know that as soon as you are well enough I intend to fly you to my home in Athens. Sunshine can be very restorative and you don't see enough of it in London.'

'Greece?' Charlotte gave a tremulous smile. 'I never thought to see Greece again, even though it was once my home—'

In a gesture that surprised Alesia, Sebastien stooped to kiss her forehead. 'And, rest assured, it will be your home again.'

Back in the hotel, Alesia collapsed on the white sofa feeling utterly drained. Her head swam and she felt totally washed out. 'Thank you,' she said hoarsely. 'For all the things you said to her, thank you. And for standing up to my grandfather. I suspect you're the only person to ever do that.'

'We are well rid of him,' Sebastien said, dark eyes surveying her with visible concern. 'You look on the point of collapse. I should *not* have taken you with me. It was too much for you.'

'I'm fine,' Alesia muttered, rubbing fingers across her fore-head. 'Just tired, I suppose.'

Sebastien gave a brief nod. 'Eat something,' he ordered roughly, 'and then you can sleep.'

He reached for the phone to order room service just as Alesia stood up to use the bathroom.

Immediately she felt blackness descend on her and slid to the floor in a heap.

She awoke to find Sebastien on his knees beside her, his powerful frame simmering with pulsing tension, his jaw clenched hard as he held her hand and tried to revive her.

As her eyes flickered open he released a juddering breath. '*When* are you going to stop doing this to me? I never knew the meaning of the word fear until I met you.'

She closed her eyes again, wishing that the feeling of sick-ness would pass. 'Sorry,' she mumbled weakly. 'I don't know what's wrong with me—'

'I do,' Sebastien contradicted her in a grim tone. 'You have been under severe strain. Starting with the wedding, then worry about your mother, followed by a traumatic ex-perience in my pool and then the stress of having the truth discovered. Then meeting your grandfather again.'

Alesia squeezed her eyes tightly shut, unable to look at him. 'Don't remind me. My grandfather tried to kill your family. You saved my life and my mother's life and I repay you by forcing you to marry me, even though I can't give you the children I know you want. I feel *so* guilty.' She covered her face with her hands and gave a soft groan, just tortured by the enormity of everything that had happened. 'Do other people have lives as complex as mine?'

'Possibly not,' he drawled, a hint of humour in his dark tone. 'But I'm sure their lives would be very boring by com-parison.'

She shook her head, utterly swamped by guilt and unable to raise a laugh. Her hands dropped to her sides and she forced herself to look at him. 'I never intended to marry anyone, you know. I decided that it wouldn't be fair.'

Sebastien inhaled sharply. 'Presumably that's why you were still a virgin on our wedding night?'

Alesia nodded. 'I never let men get close. I didn't want to risk becoming attached to any of them.'

'But marrying me was easy because you hated me so much,' Sebastien said wryly. 'You blamed me for everything.'

'It was the wrong thing to do,' she groaned in mortified tones. 'I see that now. But I was desperate for the money and I couldn't see any other way of getting it. And I didn't have all the facts—' The room started to swim again and she lay back against the cushions of the sofa, her face ashen.

'Neither of us had all the facts, *agape mou*,' Sebastien said quietly, his eyes clouded with worry as he looked at her, 'but now we do. Stop worrying. You're making yourself ill. The doctor will be here in a minute.'

'It's probably nothing,' Alesia mumbled, placing a hand on her churning stomach. 'I just picked up a bug when I swallowed all that water.'

'Well, whatever it is I want it sorted out,' Sebastien growled and Alesia almost smiled at that. The doctor had better have an instant diagnosis to hand; otherwise he was going to experience Sebastien's legendary lack of tolerance.

There was a knock on the door and one of the Fiorukis security team entered with a tall man who Alesia assumed to be the doctor. Under Sebastien's eagle eye he asked her all sorts of detailed questions, some of them more than a little embarrassing, but Sebastien didn't flicker an eyelid, his expression grim and expectant as he watched the doctor.

Finally the other man straightened and closed his bag. 'How long have you been married?'

'Six weeks.'

'Then I think congratulations are in order,' he said lightly. 'You're going to have a baby.'

There was a hideous silence and finally Alesia found her voice. 'But that isn't possible,' she croaked and the doctor gave a wry smile.

'After what you've told me about your medical history I can understand why you'd think that, but I can absolutely assure you that you are pregnant, Mrs Fiorukis.'

'But—'

'I've been a doctor for thirty years,' the doctor said calmly, 'and, although every doctor is occasionally in doubt about a diagnosis, this time I'm completely sure. The sickness you've been experiencing is a normal part of pregnancy. It should pass in a few weeks' time, as will the tiredness. Hopefully then you'll be able to enjoy the experience.'

Alesia didn't dare breathe. She was *pregnant*?

Sebastien raked long fingers through his dark hair, a stunned expression in his eyes. 'But how could the other doctors have got it so wrong?'

The doctor shrugged and walked towards the door. 'There is much that we understand about fertility and conception but equally there is much that we don't understand,' he admitted. 'Why else do desperate couples adopt, only to produce a child naturally? I have seen men with virtually no sperm count succeed in fathering a child. Although we doctors like to pretend that we have all the answers, the truth is that nature can sometimes produce miracles. You've just experienced that miracle, Mr Fiorukis. Be grateful.'

Sebastien closed the door behind the doctor and walked back to Alesia, who was still lying on the sofa.

'I'm afraid to move,' she whispered and he gave a wry smile of understanding.

'I don't think it will fall out,' he said huskily, scooping her up in his arms and carrying her into the bedroom.

'What are you doing?'

'Getting you the rest you badly need.'

She closed her eyes. There was still so much that needed to be said. 'Do you realize what this means?'

He tensed slightly as he lowered her gently into the middle of the bed. 'What does this mean?'

'We are now allowed to divorce.'

He stilled and then he stretched out a lean bronzed hand

to flick off the light. 'Go to sleep,' he said, strain thickening his deep drawl, 'and we'll talk in the morning.'

Alesia closed her eyes to hold back the tears that threatened to give her away. She was pregnant. She was having a baby. She ought to be filled with joy.

So why did her life suddenly seem so empty?

When Alesia awoke it was daylight and Sebastien was sprawled in a chair in the corner of the room, watching her through veiled eyes.

'Sebastien?' She struggled upright. 'What are you doing there?'

'I didn't trust you not to do one of your disappearing acts,' he said gruffly, running a hand over his roughened jaw, 'and you're not going anywhere until we've had a conversation. Stay there and don't move.'

He left the room and returned moments later carrying a plate of biscuits and a drink.

She sat up and looked at him quizzically. 'What's this?'

'The doctor suggested that dry biscuits before you move in the morning might help the sickness,' he said, the strain of the past few days visible in his face. He waited while she nibbled the biscuit. 'Is that better?'

She chewed and then nodded. 'Yes, actually, it is.'

'Good.' He inhaled deeply and then sat on the edge of the bed. 'Because we need to talk and I don't want you finding excuses to leave the room. And before you speak another word, there is one thing you should know. I am willing to agree to almost anything you ask, but I will not give you a divorce. So don't ever ask me again.'

Alesia put the half-eaten biscuit back on the plate. 'You're not responsible for what happened, Sebastien. I know that now. It was all my grandfather's fault. I wonder if that is part of the reason he couldn't bear to have my mother and me in his life? Perhaps it intensified his guilt, reminding him of what he'd done.'

'You assume that he is capable of guilt and remorse,'

Sebastien muttered, 'but frankly I'm not so sure. And the reason I don't want you to leave has nothing to do with my own feelings of responsibility and everything to do with the way I feel about *you*.'

Alesia gave a wobbly smile. He was Greek to the very backbone. He'd fathered a child and his traditional macho instincts wouldn't allow him to let her go, even though he didn't love her.

'This is just because you know I'm pregnant—'

'The way I feel about you has nothing to do with the fact that you're pregnant,' he groaned. 'Although I can't pretend I'm not delighted about that because it ties you to me. I cannot believe that a woman as loyal and giving as you would willingly deprive her child of a father.'

She closed her eyes. 'Sebastien, this is ridiculous. You made it perfectly clear what you thought of me right from the beginning. You thought I was the very worst type of gold-digger, and in a way I *was*—'

'That was before I knew you,' he breathed, the skin stretched taut over his hard bone structure. 'And I feel *very* guilty about the way I treated you.'

'I don't blame you for any of that—'

'Then you should,' he said roughly, removing the tray from her lap and putting it on a nearby table. 'You seem to have forgotten that I'm not exactly blameless. 'You were forced to marry me for money but I just assumed you were like all the other women I'd ever known and I treated you abominably.'

'Sebastien—'

'But you have to understand that I'd never met a woman like you before,' he groaned as he came down beside her on the bed. 'All the women I've met in the past have only ever been interested in material things. I assumed that was why you wanted the money.'

She opened her eyes and gave a faint smile at that. 'I can't pretend I don't enjoy being able to wear nice things and eat delicious food—'

'Then stay with me and I will teach you how your sex is supposed to behave,' he said with a sardonic smile that wasn't quite steady. 'I'll teach you how to spend, spend, spend and party, party, party. You deserve it.'

It was so tempting just to say yes. 'It isn't enough, Sebastien,' she said shakily, lifting a hand to her throbbing head. 'You'll get bored.'

'Never—you constantly surprise me—'

'You've never stayed with one woman for more than five minutes—'

'And with you I can't be away from you even for that long,' he pointed out in husky tones. 'Or has that fact escaped you?'

She blushed. 'That's just sex.'

'*Not* just sex,' he contradicted her, inhaling deeply as if he were bracing himself to say something. 'I love you and I know that you don't feel the same way about me, but I still can't let you go.'

She stilled. 'You don't love me—you just said that for the benefit of my mother and grandfather.'

'I said it because it is true,' he said quietly, stroking a hand over her tumbled hair and giving her a strangely uncertain smile. 'I never thought love existed before I met you and now I've found it I can't let it go, even though I know it isn't reciprocated. I still think I can make you happy.'

Alesia was in a daze. He *loved* her? 'You can't possibly love me—after our wedding night you just walked out. You didn't even spend the night with me.'

'Don't remind me what a total louse I was,' he groaned, sliding his hands around her face and forcing her to look at him. 'I was so cruel to you.'

'Because you hated me—'

'Because I didn't trust myself in the bed with you,' he corrected her, bringing his mouth down on her softy parted lips and stealing a drugging kiss. 'It took a monumental effort on my part not to climb back into bed with you and make love until you couldn't move.'

'Then why didn't you?'

'Because what I felt for you scared me and I didn't like feeling that way,' he confessed with unusual candour. 'You made me feel out of control and I just hated that. Particularly given the sort of woman I believed you to be.'

'So you vanished for two weeks without any contact—'

He gave a rueful smile. 'I wasn't used to being faced with powerful emotions because it had never happened to me before. I decided to keep my distance and on top of that I was working twenty-four hours a day trying to unravel the mess your grandfather had made of the company.'

She stared at him. It hadn't occurred to her that he'd been under pressure at work but of course he must have been. 'We were so close on the island but after I told you that I was infertile you didn't come near me. I thought you *hated* me.'

'At first I was angry,' he conceded, sliding an arm round her and tucking her against him, 'but when I calmed down I realized that you'd had no choice but to marry me. Because of the person that you are and because of your circumstances, you made the only decision open to you. Once I recognized that, I didn't want you to be forced to endure my company.'

'But you announced that you were going to continue to support me because you felt responsible for the explosion even though you weren't even there.'

He sighed. 'I'd sensed trouble all along. I'd advised my father not to have the meeting because I didn't trust your grandfather not to intervene. But he thought it was time to mend fences and I was only nineteen—why should he listen to me? I was arrogant—thought I knew everything—'

Alesia looked up at him. 'But you were *right*.'

He shrugged. 'As it turns out, yes. I decided to go to the meeting anyway but, as I reached the bay, the boat exploded. In the chaos afterwards I never knew who was on board.'

Her gaze softened. 'I still can't believe it was you who saved me—'

'It was fate,' he growled possessively, tightening his grip on her. 'You were meant to be mine all along.'

'That's guilt, Sebastien,' she whispered, 'not love, and you have no reason to feel responsible for what happened.'

'It's *not* guilt,' he said fiercely, 'and one day I will make you love me the way I love you.'

The breath jammed in her throat. 'Do you mean it?'

'I am devoting every waking hour to finding ways of making you love me,' he vowed and she shook her head, her gaze suddenly shy as she stared up at him.

'No, I mean do you really love me?'

'You need more convincing?' He gave a wry smile. 'I have made myself vulnerable for the first time in my life, *agape mou*, and for a very proud Greek man, that should say it all. The fact that I'm prepared to confess my love, knowing that it isn't returned—'

'It is returned. I do love you, Sebastien,' she whispered softly, her blue eyes reflecting everything she felt. 'I've loved you from the moment I realized what sort of man you really are. Strong, dependable, responsible. Everything that my grandfather isn't.'

His powerful body tensed and he stared at her intently. 'You don't have to lie to me to make me feel better—'

She shook her head. 'No more lies, ever. From now on, only the truth and the truth is that I love you.'

He caught the words in his mouth and kissed her. 'Tell me again,' he groaned against her mouth, 'and again—'

'I love you.' Alesia gave a womanly smile and then gasped as his mouth found a sensitive spot at the base of her neck. 'Oh, Sebastien—'

'No other man is ever going to discover just how hot you are,' he vowed, pulling her down next to him and curving her trembling body into his.

'I forgot to add that as well as strong, dependable and responsible, you're also macho, overbearing and impossibly possessive,' she teased, and he gave a smug smile.

'I'm Greek, *agape mou*. What do you expect?'

'I like the fact that you want to protect me. No one has ever done that for me before.'

He tightened his hold on her. 'From now on, *nothing* will hurt you. And we need never go to the island again,' he promised her in thickened tones. 'We can live in cities if that is where you feel more comfortable.'

'I don't mind where we live as long as you're there,' she confessed breathlessly, snuggling against him like a contented kitten. 'You make me feel safe. I don't think swimming in the sea will ever be my speciality but I can learn to fly over it as long as you're holding my hand. I love the island, Sebastien. It's the place where I fell in love with you.'

He gave a groan and dropped a kiss on the top of her head. 'We will find the very best counsellors to cure you of your fear of water and I'm never letting you out of my sight again, *agape mou*,' he vowed huskily. 'From now on you're mine and I *always* protect what is mine. Anything you want, you have only to ask.'

'Anything?' Her eyes twinkled and he gave an appreciative laugh.

'Now you're making me nervous.' His wickedly sexy eyes gleamed. 'What is it you want? At this point perhaps I ought to warn you that I won't permit the mother of my child to walk around dressed in a miniskirt and three-inch heels.'

'Possessive again,' she teased, but her arms slid round the strong column of his neck and she pressed a kiss into the corner of his mouth. 'Did you mean what you said about my mother living in Greece?'

'Of course. The doctors feel she will recuperate much faster in the sunshine,' he told her. 'As soon as she is well enough to travel we will have her transferred to a private hospital in Athens.'

Alesia sighed. 'What it is to have money—'

'You still have to ask me for something for yourself,' he reminded her, a trace of amusement lighting his dark gaze.

'What are you, the genie of the lamp?'

He gave a groan of submission. 'I just want to give you everything,' he confessed and she smiled the smile of a woman who knew she was truly loved.

'In that case, can we go back to Greece as soon as possible? I'm in love with Greek food and Greek sunshine.'

'And Greek men?' He dropped a kiss on her parted lips. 'Are you in love with them also?'

'Just the one Greek man, Mr Fiorukis,' she replied with a laugh in her eyes. 'Just the one.'

* * * *

Look for more passion in Sarah Morgan's
Powerful Greek, Unworldly Wife,
available September 2009, in Mills & Boon®
Modern™ romance

The Sons of Avrom